Meanwhile, in the [sur]real world…

Tracey Valentine

Chapter 1

Greville looked at the note from his boss that he held in his hand, a note that had mysteriously appeared on his door mat. He had no idea how it had arrived - he hadn't heard the letter box rattle, and Satan certainly hadn't barked. He glanced up doubtfully at the fast food restaurant, then back at the note. Written in Mr Valentine's exquisite copperplate, it said 'Ecstatic Murder-Disk, eleven thousand hours, day of the Sixth Planet'. Or at least, that was what it had said once Greville had realised that he needed to hold it up to a mirror to turn it the right way round.

He was slowly getting better at translating Mr Valentine's peculiar turns of phrase. The man (or, he conceded, because Greville was a scrupulously fair and precise man, the man-shaped entity or, to be even more fair and precise, the entity that could take on more or less the shape of a man if it were so inclined) believed that all synonyms were absolutely interchangeable. This had led to some interesting conundrums, and Greville had learned to be especially cautious if his boss used words such as 'terminate' or 'execute' as their parent company had a somewhat cavalier attitude towards the disposal of staff. But knowing that his boss had a somewhat literal mind, as well as a tenuous grasp on Earth chronology, Greville had decided that 'Happy Burger at eleven o'clock on Saturday' was the most likely translation.

There was no sign of his boss yet. Greville had never seen him beyond the vicinity of the office, and it was going to be odd to see this strange personage in an everyday setting. Perhaps he would be less terrifying out of the office, when his behaviour would be constrained by having to appear fully human. Greville definitely hoped so.

The second conceivable venue for the meeting was, of course, the 'Jolly Tea-room'. It was owned by a diminutive, stout, sour-faced, flame-haired woman of such unfriendly demeanour that Greville, on his first visit and having intended to order a selection of cupcakes for an occasion, had instead scuttled out with just the one. He had never been back since. On April Fools' Day, someone had amended the sign with an addition so that it read 'The Jolly Miserable Tearoom'. While Greville disapproved of the desecration of property, he disapproved even more of inaccurate descriptions (the shop's owner pretending to be jolly when she was nothing of the sort), and when a picture of the vandalised sign had appeared on social media, he had come exceedingly close to 'liking' it. Reluctantly, he decided that if his boss didn't materialise soon, he'd have to try there next.

Greville's problem was that a fast food restaurant seemed such an unlikely venue for a work-related meeting. Then again, the work to which the meeting related was pretty unlikely, too. He had never met anyone else who worked in a place where the rules of time and space weren't so much rules... more suggestions, and suggestions that weren't given overmuch heed, either. He would much rather have met his boss in the office which, in Greville's view, was where proper work-orientated meetings should occur. On the other hand, because his contract said that he didn't officially start work there until Monday morning, it was more than possible that the office building wouldn't even let him in before then.

He had a surreptitious glance to left and right. He was looking for anything abnormal...a tremble in the air that could indicate a hidden doorway; an odd quality to the light meaning that if he walked in that direction, he might be stepping out of the car park and into...somewhere else; a *blurring* that might...

'Are you going to stand here all day or are you going to go in?' said a voice at his elbow, making him jump so much that he let go of his bit of paper. He grabbed for it, but the breeze caught it and sent it drifting across the car park, flip-flapping in a way that, had he yet come across an air-fish, would have reminded him of one which had accidentally found its way into water and was attempting to catapult its way back out.

Greville had been brought up not to litter and had never knowingly done so in his entire life. He therefore felt obliged to chase after the note. His embarrassment made him even clumsier than usual, and he had to snatch for it three or four times before he caught it, and no sooner had he done that than he tripped over the kerb. He could feel his face flushing a deep, hot red, and when he finally managed to right himself, he saw that Magnolia was watching him with detached amusement.

He had read that the eyes were usually the windows of the soul, but hers, rendered enormous by her thick, heavy-framed glasses, were more like mirrors, reflecting rather than giving anything away. And whenever he was near her, what they most reflected was awkward stupidity.

'You got the note, too?" he said, and immediately wished that he hadn't. He tried to recover by adding, decisively, 'We'll go in, then?' He spoilt it, though, by allowing a questioning note to creep into his voice as if he knew that it was really she who had done the deciding. He tried to assert his masculinity by boldly pulling the door open for her. The gesture backfired when it turned out to be the sort of door that needed to be pushed but it made such an impressive rattle that several people inside looked round to gawp at the idiot who was trying to open a door the wrong way around. His face flushed redder still.

Magnolia, appearing mercifully oblivious to his ineptitude, ordered a vegetable burger with cola and chips, and Greville ordered the same, having long ago eschewed murder-disks. He was grateful that he managed not to drop his change, or drop his food, or upset his drink on his way to the table. Magnolia smelt her burger.

'Not bad,' she pronounced, and took a hearty bite. Greville's previous experience of female behaviour in fast food restaurants was limited to his ex-fiancée. Poppy would have ordered a black coffee or maybe a diet cola and then nibbled abstemiously on one or two of his chips. This lack of female self-denial was new to him. He picked up his own burger and started to eat, grateful for something to do that precluded talking. He wasn't very good at small talk, he was worse in front of women in general, and he was even worse still in front of this particular woman.

They sat in fairly companionable silence until Magnolia had finished two thirds of her burger and most of her chips, and had drunk as much of her cola as she was inclined to. She looked around the restaurant and then towards the door, trying to spot their boss.

A fat child in the next booth caught her eye. He was eating chips as if there was no tomorrow. Which, indeed, there sometimes wasn't in Greville's recently adopted environment. Sometimes, there was no yesterday, either, although you could usually get it back through judicious use of a Room that Time Forgot. Not always, though, and all it would take was one wrong click when someone was using The Calendar and there might not just no yesterday anywhere, there might be no tomorrows at all. Sometimes The Calendar skipped straight to the day after tomorrow, or it entangled itself so that while tomorrow might never come, yesterday did, again. This had begun to alter Greville's perspective on life such that he could feel himself edging towards the temptation, like the chip-eating child, to enjoy the present, rather than perpetually deny himself in preparation for a future that might already have happened.

Magnolia was growing bored of marvelling at the child's single-minded gluttony. 'Where *is* he? I've got other stuff to do and can't sit in here all day.'

'So have I,' said Greville importantly. Until recently, his weekends had involved a predictable schedule of chores around the house and tiny patch of lawned garden, and perhaps a visit to his formerly prospective in-laws. It had all been the stuff of duty, though, not the stuff of fun, except for maybe the very mild fun of being able to tick activities off on a mental jobs list and feeling gently satisfied with himself, albeit in a rather restless way. These days he was busy cultivating vegetables, learning about weight training and looking after his new dog. Admittedly, it wasn't quite the sort of fun that would lead to the appearance of a frenzied mob of joiners-in if publicised on a social media site, but at least it was heading in the right direction.

'How are you getting on with Satan?' she asked.

No-one had bothered to teach the dog even the most basic commands, so Greville was filling in the gaps in his education, as well as making sure that he was thoroughly exercised. In many ways, he felt that dogs were easier than people. You told them what to do, and they did it, and were happy to do so. It was as simple as that. They didn't ask you why you couldn't do it yourself, or point out the errors in your proposed course of action, or inform you that if you were going to be *that* jolly bossy, they would be heading off to their mum's to have a good moan about you. And of course, there were never any awkward silences.

'He can catch a ball now,' Greville said.

To start with, Satan had been uncertain what to do with a ball, and the first few times that Greville had thrown it for him, he'd simply allowed it to bounce off his nose. But then he'd made a tentative snap at it, and after that had cottoned onto the idea pretty quickly. Greville wondered who on earth had managed to have a dog until it was three years old without ever having played ball with him. Surely the first thing that you did when you acquired a dog (after having taken out an appropriate insurance policy – there was no excuse for being reckless) was to buy him a ball, as indeed Greville had done on their way home from the animal shelter. He was about to tell her that Satan would now sit when told, and would stay on command for thirty seconds, when her attention was diverted by a portly figure crashing out of the gents' toilet.

'There he is,' she said.

It took a long second for Greville to realise that she was right as Mr Valentine was wearing a very smart, grey, pin-striped suit instead of the somewhat grubby black one that he'd always previously worn, which had been shiny from over-use. In fact, it had been more than somewhat grubby. It had looked and smelt as if its owner had worn it continuously for years, keeping it away from washing machines or dry cleaners and frequently getting it damp and then not drying it properly. To Greville's inexpert eye, this suit looked expertly tailored rather than off the peg, and it was cut extremely well, disguising his boss's bulk rather than accentuating it and straining at the seams. Mr Valentine unhurriedly took his place at the serving counter and perused the menu. When he joined them, his tray held two large vegetable burgers, four chocolate doughnuts and a strawberry milkshake.

'Oh it's you two,' he said. 'I thought it would be the other two. But I suppose you'll do. Unless you're flammable. You're not flammable, are you?'

'Not particularly,' said Greville, having become inured to being asked rather strange questions.

It was a little odd that their boss never recognised them, but in his natural state, Mr Valentine resembled a sack of glitter thrown into a cyclone, and Greville supposed that if he were to see two glitter cyclones side by side, then he'd be hard pressed to tell them apart, too.

His boss opened one of the polystyrene burger boxes and held it up, examining it critically. He shut it again, pushed it to his mouth and his jaws with their jagged sharks' teeth began to work ferociously. Burger and box were thoroughly munched, to the accompaniment of 'nyum nyum nyum' noises. He picked up the other burger and munched that too, without even troubling to open its box. Two and a half doughnuts were subjected to the same treatment but then he seemed to tire midway through the third, setting down the half-shredded clear plastic box containing the half-shredded doughnut.

'Not enough salt,' he pronounced. 'Now, you know what you've got to do.' He regarded them comfortably, hands folded over his considerable stomach.

'No,' we don't, said Magnolia. 'You haven't told us yet.'

He peered very hard at her face as if trying to determine whether she was telling the truth, and she stared impassively back, her grey eyes magnified by her huge-framed glasses.

'All right then,' he conceded. 'A client has a job for you. They can't keep hold of their staff.'

'Why not?' Magnolia asked. 'Don't they pay them enough? Or do they make them work for idiot managers?'

The midnight eyes were back on her face, twin black holes which sucked in all light, and she returned the gaze in her cool, unruffled manner.

'They just disappear. One minute they're there, and the next… gone. So you need to go there and see what's going on. You'll have to pretend that you're compliance auditors.' He wagged a pudgy finger at them. 'And you'll have to do a better job of it than you usually do.'

His nails were still over-long and yellow, and today they appeared to have dried blood under them.

'We *are* compliance auditors,' said Greville. 'In fact, we're…'

'Are you?' said Mr Valentine. He scratched his head, which made a rasping, sandpapery noise. 'Are you sure? I thought that you were... were…' He pulled a crumpled piece of paper out of his pocket and consulted it, lips moving as he read. 'Well, never mind. You'll do. So you need to go there and find out what's what. And don't disappear yourselves, either. Because if you do, you won't get paid.'

'We need a bit more to go on than that,' Magnolia said.

'No you don't,' he said. 'You're paid to work things out. Where would be the point in me giving you something to do if I'd already got to the bottom of it myself, eh?'

She tried to glean a sliver more information. 'So these people just disappear?' she asked. 'And are never seen again? Aren't the authorities looking into it?'

'No!' said Mr Valentine. 'No, no, no, no, no! They don't go in for that sort of thing! Most places don't, you know. In fact, *this* is the only planet for a good long way where you can't do anything without authorities and procedures and forms.'

Greville drew in his breath. A world where one's degree of flammability was pertinent sounded dangerous, but one bereft of authorities, procedures and forms sounded positively alarming.

'Might I ask whether…'

'No, absolutely not. No asking. That's the trouble with your sort. Far too much asking and not enough doing. No good ever came of too much asking. All you have to do is find where they've gone and get them back. That's all.'

He went to look at his watch, and Greville noted that his boss was in fact wearing two watches. Neither was telling the right time, and one of them was upside down. However, Mr Valentine seemed mollified by whatever it was that he divined from them as he then opened several salt sachets, spread the contents carefully on top of the remaining doughnut boxes and then shredded his way through them. He eyed the milkshake and Greville prepared to step back out of range, shredded milkshake cups not being likely to retain their semi-liquid contents. Luckily it appeared that that particular misadventure was going to occur elsewhere as Mr Valentine rose to his feet and picked up the cup.

'So we'll see you after the weekend,' he said. '21 Bridge Street. Don't be late.'

And with that, he disappeared back into the gents'. Magnolia frowned at his departing back, then turned to Greville.

'Have you got some transform glasses and a translator?' she asked.

Greville shook his head.

'Well, you'll probably going to need them. I'll get you some from the off-world galactic surplus store. Come on – give me your phone. If I try to explain how to do it, we'll be here all year.'

She virtually snatched his phone from him and began to download some sort of application, only handing the phone back to him for him to input his payment details.

'There. They should be with you before you get home.'

'But…'

'They'll be in your virtual locker. And you can claim them back on expenses.'

She stood up, and hoisted on her rucksack.

'What's a virtual locker?' he asked.

'It's like a *real* locker, but virtual,' she said. 'It will appear…I mean, it *won't* appear outside your front door because I set you up an account. If it *doesn't* not appear, let me know and I'll reset it. It doesn't always work first time.'

He thought about asking her how would he know if it didn't appear but he was fed up with sounding like an idiot. 'Oh, okay,' he said. 'See you on Monday?'

She regarded him gravely. 'Yes. Yes, I suppose that you will. Unless one of us is out of phase, or in a time loop, or in a thousand room, or…' She shrugged, as if all these possibilities were too boring to list, her t-shirt riding up just enough for a tiny strip of taut waist to register on the rogue part of Greville's peripheral vision that wouldn't quite behave itself.

She strode out, and Greville watched her go. He'd half-hoped that she might suggest that they do something together over the weekend, and had even entertained the faintest idea that *he* might dare to ask *her* if she wanted to do something. But then he thought the scenario through in more detail, imagining several hours of sitting in a café or walking around a fairly local semi-ruined castle or the gardens of a not too distant stately home (the three potential activities that had struck him as being the most suitable). Several hours of trying to make conversation. Several hours of awkward silences. Several hours of wondering for how long the encounter would have to limp onwards before they could decently abandon it. On reflection, it would be altogether less terrifying to spend the weekend alone. And with that decided, Greville got up and went home to his dog.

Chapter 2

Satan was extremely pleased to see Greville when he came into the kitchen through the back door. His previous method of showing this had been to jump up repeatedly, which wasn't really acceptable in a dog of this size; he was easily big enough to put his paws on Greville's shoulders, and his claws were a lot sharper than they looked. Greville had consulted his dog behaviour text book and consistently followed its advice so that Satan would now (if reminded) greet him by sitting in front of him, with his quarters held just shy of the floor so as not to impede the furious beating of his tail.

'Shall we play with the ball?' Greville asked. He had acquired a plastic device which allowed him to throw the ball a lot further than he could by hand, meaning that Satan could get a good workout in a short space of time. The post had arrived while he'd been out, and he went to pick it up. There was a compliance magazine, a letter that looked to be from the company that insured his car which was probably confirming his change of address, a catalogue from a running shop and a parcel delivery postcard.

Greville turned the postcard over, expecting the usual instructions about rearranging delivery. There *were* instructions, but they were far from usual. They said to click on the link in his confirmation email to activate his virtual locker. Greville did so. Nothing happened. He wasn't sure exactly what he had expected to happen, but even so, the utter lack of action was disappointing.

It occurred to him that perhaps, as Magnolia had suggested, the 'nothing' (that might or might not have happened) might have done its happening (or not) outside. He went out of the front door, looking around and feeling rather foolish. To start with, he couldn't see anything out of the ordinary, then out of the corner of his eye, he caught a shimmer to his right, like the heat given off on a hot summer's day. It also reminded him of a force field's warning wobble. The instructions said for him to enter the pin code into the link on his phone, and then the shimmering solidified very slightly into the translucent outline of a locker. It had a curved door with a handle. Greville pulled it open and retrieved the parcel, and as soon as he'd let go of the door, it clanged shut with a very solid bang considering that it was barely even there; indeed, a fraction of a second later, it *wasn't* there, having disappeared as if it had never existed.

Greville regarded the empty space. He didn't trust anything that looked like a force field, having encountered more than one face first, but he needed to know if anything tangible remained as there would be Consequences if he allowed any non-employees to blunder across a strange phenomenon. Exactly what those Consequences would be had not been made clear, but it *was* clear that those who were rumoured to have suffered them were no longer around.

It was also uncanny how many times various audit failings were attributed to colleagues that had suffered Consequences and who were therefore conveniently not able to answer for them. At that point, the audit trail went unsalvageably cold as once a person had suffered Consequences, their name was obliterated as if (like the virtual locker) they had never been there at all.

There were several categories of people that Greville thought thoroughly deserved to be obliterated from history. In no particular order, these included (and were not limited to) people who didn't file telephone notes, people who were heedless of version control protocol, people who failed to keep adequate records of what was in archive boxes and people who were incapable of filing things in date order. However, before they suffered Consequences for not keeping their secret lives and the accompanying secret technology strictly secret, Greville would at least have liked to have imposed some Consequences of his own, involving training sessions, checklists and sternly worded emails.

He steeled himself to pass his hand through the space recently occupied by the locker, and it met with neither resistance nor a jolting shock. Satan had been watching with interest, growling when the locker had appeared, and now he tentatively sniffed where it had been. Finding nothing there, he promptly started bounding around, reminding Greville that they were supposed to be playing with the ball.

Greville wanted to investigate the parcel further, but he had promised Satan that they would go out. A promise was a promise, so he put the package on the sofa for later, picked up the ball and the plastic throwing device and headed for the huge expanse of lawn.

His cottage sat in the grounds of a much bigger house, and had been converted from a barn in order to accommodate an elderly relative. However, the relative had died before taking up residence, and the owners, the Deans, had decided to rent out the cottage. Even if they weren't quite elderly themselves, they were on the stairlift in that direction, (and rather above the second landing), and had readily accepted Greville's offer to help with the maintenance of the enormous garden. He quite enjoyed driving the ride-on mower, and had been allowed to take over a section of the vegetable garden for himself. And when one had a big secret to keep, it was easier to keep it from those whose hearing and eyesight were not of the first order, and who were separated from his residence by a deterring length of lawn.

Mr and Mrs Dean were even happy to let Satan out for him during the day. To start with, they had been scared by his sheer size – as had Greville, if truth be told. The acquisition of the dog was a prime example of what happened if Greville let his heart (a freewheeling, wayward creature which paid no regard to reason or common sense) rule his head (a sort of live-in book keeper equipped with cabinet after cabinet of principles and procedures, and methodologies for carefully weighing one course of action against another). Usually the heart only triumphed over the head if Greville had been drinking as the book keeper's tolerance for alcohol was very low, but on this occasion the book keeper had been overwhelmed by an unexpected and unstoppable charge down the blindside from the heart.

Greville, in accordance with the laudable principles for the rotation of stock (which dictated that items which had been acquired first must be used first) said to the animal shelter that he would have the dog which had been there the longest, but once confronted with the black and tan creature who weighed probably two thirds as much as he did himself, he had had second thoughts. In fact, it had been a thought, singular, of large dimensions: NO. NO I CAN'T HAVE HIM. HE'S TOO BIG.

He had started to say that maybe he'd have the dog which had been there the *second* longest. But then he'd wondered who else would take on this vast dog, whose tail-wagging had flagged to a forlorn going through of the motions, perhaps picking up on Greville's lack of enthusiasm. Greville imagined what it must feel like to spend day after day after day in the shelter, with no idea whether anyone would ever come for you. And in a surge of compassion over sense, he decided to have the dog.

Greville threw the ball until Satan flopped down on the grass, his tongue lolling, and then they walked back to the cottage together, Satan carrying his ball.

It was almost a surprise that the parcel was still waiting for him as sometimes things that mysteriously appeared were wont to mysteriously *dis*appear again. He turned it over. The return address on the back was: The Off-World Galactic Surplus Store, 1,846,487a High Street, Very New Town, Red Country, Eighth World, Fourth Galaxy, Second Solar System, The Universe (not the one next to the one which exploded).

He opened the parcel, which contained a headset of the sort that might be worn in a call centre, and some transform glasses. The glasses came in a case which had hieroglyphic-looking writing on it, and the instructions were also in hieroglyphics. He put the glasses on, in front of the pair that he was already wearing, and looked at the case again. Now he could see that it said 'Transform glasses'. He turned his attention to the instructions. They were the usual exhortations to only clean them with the cloth provided, to keep them in their case when not in use and not to sit on them. And some interesting health and safety recommendations.

Apparently, the glasses shouldn't be used for more than half an hour at a time, because extended wear could lead to headache, eye strain and brain explosion. Greville assumed that the latter was a mis-translation. But then he became less sure, as when he read on, the suggested remedy for brain explosion was to submerge the affected bodypart in a bucket of cold water for an hour.

The trouble with a universal marketplace was that instructions had to be universally applicable, so as not to exclude any species, but with the proliferation of species across the abundance of universes, the lowest common denominator had devolved and devolved until it had arrived at the level of the single-celled organism. So health and safety diagrams depicted amoebae going about their business either healthily and safely or unhealthily and unsafely, depending on the point being illustrated.

Even this didn't cover everything, as some beings were formed of atoms or energy or light. Although beings formed of light presumably didn't have much need for transform spectacles, or for instructions telling them what they should do and avoid doing with them, because they didn't have a nose to perch them on or eyes to see through them.

The diagram about the remedy for brain explosion was a case in point. It appeared to depict a corpulent woodlouse sitting in a bath, illustrators having interesting ideas regarding what a single celled organism should look like. He raised the glasses, and the text swam back into hieroglyphs, although the woodlouse illustration remained unchanged. There was a time when he would have mentally added this to a list of things that didn't make sense and which warranted further investigation, Greville being of a type who liked to pursue all anomalies to the bitter end, but he had recently learnt that it was often expedient to mentally shrug his shoulders and move on instead. Even mentally chalking these things up to experience would use up an awful lot of mental chalk.

He went into the spare bedroom, Satan at his heels. Lately, he'd been acquiring odds and ends of weight lifting equipment. He'd bought a barbell, some weights for it and a bench via a postcard on the village shop's notice board, and had since added an inflatable exercise ball, then a replacement ball because Satan had accidentally burst the first one, some dumb bells and some heavier weights for the bar. Greville had never really got into weight training before because the only place to do it was at a gym, into which he had only ever made the odd infrequent foray as he was embarrassed about his lean physique. However, now that he had a spare room which was big enough to train in, and no-one to deride his efforts or remind him that there were windows waiting to be cleaned and bins awaiting their weekly thorough disinfection, he was free to see whether it was something he wished to pursue.

So far, he was cautiously optimistic. He could lift appreciably more week after week, and he thought he was starting to add muscle, albeit very, very slowly. The biggest difference was to how he felt. He noticed that instead of walking with a slight stoop, which he had always done as he was self-conscious about his stringy height, he held himself straighter and strode out with more purpose. Even if he was still a long way from being the sort of person who was not to be messed with, perhaps he was becoming the sort who was only to be slightly untidied.

He finished his training, took a shower and then completed his outstanding chores. For the first few weeks after he had separated from Poppy, he had deliberately left dishes in the sink and newspapers on the coffee table and the vacuuming undone, but it hadn't taken long to realise that he preferred his surrounding to be clean and tidy. It wasn't the actual process of leaving chores undone that he found pleasing; it was the knowledge that he could do so if he wanted without any Consequences whatsoever.

Now Greville found himself short of things to do. His gaze stole towards his phone. He could call Magnolia. There was nothing stopping him. Except somehow the *idea* of calling her was more beguiling than actually doing it. In his imagination, they could have a perfectly pleasant conversation, whereas in reality that was unlikely to happen.

Instead, he picked up his ereader and ploughed on with a novel. It concerned the adventures of a police detective who was trying to solve a series of murders while simultaneously battling alcoholism and a soured relationship. Greville had started the novel (recommended by Poppy's book group) in the aftermath of their split, and had initially felt sorry for the protagonist, empathising with his lovelorn state, if not his inability to stop at one or two drinks. But now, from the vantage point of having survived a break-up, he was growing less sympathetic. In fact, the man was exasperating him. In Greville's opinion, there were few adversities (temporal anomalies aside) that couldn't be overcome by a resolutely positive mental attitude, and few that weren't made worse by excesses of alcohol and self-pity.

He set the ereader aside and looked at his watch. It was too early to go to bed, and in any case, he didn't feel tired. He didn't fancy watching television. He had already done all the puzzles in this month's Compliance Monthly, including the Mathematical Fun Super Teaser, which hadn't really been all that much of a tease, let alone a Super one. It had only involved some relatively easy logarithms, and he preferred it when they needed calculus. He went to his fail-safe solution for being at a loose end, which was his giant book of puzzles, and turned to the next undone puzzle. Puzzle number 46 was a giant cryptic crossword. Greville would have preferred to skip to number 47, which was a giant logic puzzle, but if he did so, he wouldn't enjoy it, knowing that number 46 still awaited his attentions. He clicked his pen open and got started on the crossword.

The next morning was bright and clear, and he and Satan went to play with the ball when the grass was still saturated with dew. At the far end of the lawn, Greville saw Mr Dean pull into the big house's driveway, returning from the newsagents with the Sunday papers. He saw Greville and Satan and raised a hand in greeting, and Greville did the same in return. Satan brought the ball back, skidding wetly to a halt at Greville's feet. If they carried on playing, then that would be the dog's exercise requirements taken care of in no time at all. And then Greville would have to think of enough other chores to fill the rest of the day.

'Shall we go for a walk instead?' he asked. Satan picked up on the word 'walk' and began to wag his tail furiously, so Greville went back to the cottage and got his lead, and they set off down the lane.

By the time they got back, it still wasn't quite ten o'clock. Satan went to lie on the patio in the shade of the house. Greville sat near him on one of the patio chairs and put his phone on the metal table. All this free time was an unanticipated side effect of splitting up with Poppy. He deliberated, as he'd done so many times before, whether to call her. If he was penitent enough, perhaps their relationship could be repaired? He could claim that he'd just panicked at the thought of the wedding. Poppy had a sufficiently low opinion of men in general to accept that this was how they behaved under pressure.

He wondered what he'd done with himself before Poppy. Mostly revising for exams, and as Greville was a very thorough reviser, this had taken up quite a lot of time. Pre-Poppy, he hadn't had a car because parking had been prohibitively difficult at his old flat, and just the bare rudiments of everyday life such as grocery shopping had eaten up time as it took forever to do anything if you had to go on the bus, particularly at weekends. He had also visited his parents with judicious frequency, but he couldn't do that now as they kept trying to persuade him into sorting things out with Poppy. He wasn't in the mood for their well-meant pressure, especially as he wasn't totally sure that he wanted to resist it. He picked up his phone and dialled before he could change his mind.

'What do you want?' Magnolia demanded, answering on the first ring, which threw him off guard.

'I wondered if you wanted to do anything today?' he managed, rather awed at his daring.

There was a pause, just long enough for him to repent of the whole endeavour. He imagined her frowning at the unwanted intrusion.

'Well, you've left it rather late, so you'll have to do something that I'm already doing,' she said.

Not quite a 'yes', but not a flat 'no', which was more than Greville had expected.

'Okay?' he ventured.

'I'm going to the supermarket now, then I'm going swimming, then I'm visiting my aunt,' she said. 'Then later on, I'm shopping for clothes online and painting my nails. What do you fancy?'

Greville thought fast. He didn't need anything from the supermarket, and it seemed rather creepy to follow her about, watching what she bought. He would feel awkward joining in with the online shopping and nail painting. And he certainly didn't fancy letting her see him in an advanced state of undress at the swimming pool. On the other hand, he was quite happy to visit elderly relatives.

'Aunt,' he said.

'All right, I'll pick you up at four,' she said, and rung off before he could say anything else. Which was probably just as well as it was likely that he'd have said 'thank you', which would have been rather pathetic. Feeling less at sea now he had an activity planned, Greville went to get his gardening things, in order to spend the day weeding.

At five past four, a clattering, spitting roar heralded Magnolia's arrival. She had the Mustang's top down, and was wearing sunglasses. He locked the cottage and got in next to her, and she headed the car's long nose up the lane. They drove in silence for several minutes.

'What's your aunt like?' Greville asked.

Magnolia shrugged, her shoulders bony in the pink vest top.

'Like everyone's aunts. Smells of lavender. Has a cat. Drinks lots of tea. Has flowery sofas.' She paused a beat. 'Obsessed with people getting married.'

Her mouth seemed to purse after this last point, but it could have been because she was concentrating on the road. The silence began to lengthen again, although once the Mustang picked up speed, conversation was impossible anyway over the sound of the air rushing past, and the car's spluttering burble. Magnolia appeared oblivious to the attention the car attracted from onlookers, or maybe she was simply inured to the turning heads by now.

The aunt's house was a large, red brick, detached old house – the sort of place which might hold afternoon tea on the lawn, at which someone might be murdered, said murder being solved in a genteel way by either an elderly female detective or one of foreign extraction. Magnolia parked on the circular drive, designed so that carriages could sweep in, deposit their occupants and then sweep out again, and they went to knock. The front door was flanked with columns and the door itself was really *two* doors, of heavy oak, filling a stone archway. One of the doors swung inwards and he was face to face with Magnolia's aunt.

Margaret was tall, with Magnolia's angular leanness, the same raven's wing hair, only streaked with grey and drawn back into a severe bun and the same sharp, grey-eyed gaze that made one feel that one was an insect under observation. She was wearing a beige trouser suit with lots of pockets and a belt, as if about to set out on safari seventy years ago, and peered keenly at Greville.

'You've brought a friend,' she said to Magnolia, with a brisk smile. 'Jolly good. Let's go.'

They followed her through the house, which was stone floored with oak panelling, and was reminiscent of a vicarage. Greville looked at the framed pictures on the walls. There were school photos of Magnolia at various ages, instantly recognisable by the large glasses and long straight blue-black hair, including some portraits of her wearing a mortar board and a succession of gowns with different coloured edgings and hoods. There was also Margaret's cluster of accountancy exam certificates, dated not long into the decimal era.

A tea tray was waiting, laid with beautifully painted bone china, with a plate of perfectly cut triangular sandwiches with the crusts removed. Margaret poured boiling water into the teapot and carried the tray outside.

They sat outside on floral garden chairs, and made polite conversation for a while about work, as far as it was humanly (or even inhumanly), possible to do so without trampling over the borders marked 'Keep Out – or there will be Consequences'. Fortunately for Greville, Margaret turned out to be more interested in ISO9000 than anyone he had ever met outside of his dreams, and was as fond of accounting as he was of compliance – that is to say, very fond indeed. This didn't stop her from switching topics smoothly but firmly while Greville was raising the question of whether the American single audit system should be imported.

'Talking of single entities,' she said, with all the subtlety of a SAS70 Type 2 auditor, 'Are *you* one?'

'Err…I…err…that is to say…' Greville began, temporarily flummoxed firstly because he was not used to being asked personal questions in such a blunt manner (and few people probably were used to this style of interrogation, outside Margaret's sphere of acquaintances and the Special Forces) and secondly because his demotion from fiancé to nobody hadn't really bedded in to the point that it tripped off his tongue. 'Err…well…yes.'

'Are you and Magnolia…?' she began. If allowed to end, then the ending would probably have been something in the order of 'stepping out', 'courting' or similar archaism.

'Oh, no!' said Greville with an unexpected hint of regret.

'Oh, no!' said Magnolia with disappointing vehemence.

And not just disappointing to Grev's ears but also, it appeared, to Margaret's, who said, 'That's a shame. So, work colleagues, eh? Work colleagues,' she repeated.

Greville looked at Magnolia out of the furthermost corner of his eye. She had coloured though he could not tell whether it was from anger or embarrassment.

'You could do with a husband, my girl,' added Margaret. 'You're not getting any younger, you know.'

Greville considered what Margaret had just said. While it was probably true that people doing something straightforward like sitting in a garden might not be getting any younger, it might be less true if a Room That Time Forgot was involved. He wasn't totally sure of how the ageing process worked there. Say you went back six hours. Once you re-reached the time it had been when you left, would you be the same age as you had been then when you had left, or would you in fact be six hours older because you'd lived through the same six hours twice? Taking that further, suppose you went back twenty-four hours the day before your thirtieth birthday – would this mean that when you celebrated your birthday, you'd actually be thirty years and one day old? He was getting quite absorbed about the ramifications of this when he realised that Margaret was talking to him.

'I'm sorry,' he said, 'what did you say?'

She gave him a smile as if she had divined his thoughts and said, "I've been keeping a space on my wall for Magnolia's wedding photo since I first moved here. No-one's good enough for her, you know.'

Flicking through his mental Rolodex of social cues that was his only worthwhile legacy of Poppy, he realised that he was now supposed to side with Margaret in lamenting her niece's fussiness. However, the Rolodex hit a snag, and he found he couldn't bring himself to do it.

'You're right,' he said before he could stop himself, feeling his face begin to glow red. 'No-one probably is good enough for her.'

He was very aware of Margaret's sharp eyes on his face, and as she was a blood relative of Magnolia's, she would have a sharp mind too. He pushed the Rolodex to one side and hurried onwards before wrong conclusions could be drawn. He raced towards a much safer area that only a compliance auditor could spot.

'What I mean is,' he said slowly, his auditor's brain whirring like a coffee machine awaiting the final delivery of essence of Arabica, 'that no-one should marry the wrong person just for the sake of it. It's…it's…' He could feel an idea forming deep in the recesses of his brain and, with a final effort, dragged the half-formed thought into existence. 'It's *fiscally irresponsible*,' he managed. 'Imagine what Magnolia could lose if she had to agree to a pension sharing order as part of a divorce.'

He held his breath as he waited to find out if he had managed to assuage Margaret and deflect further curiosity regarding his personal interest in the matter.

He had. It was the right thing to say since Margaret had strong views regarding pension sharing, and was more than happy to expound upon them. He patted himself mentally on the back and, because he really was a well brought-up boy, forced a look of interest on to his face as Margaret's exposition took them through tea, all of the sandwiches, and half of the home-made Victoria sponge.

Luckily Greville knew more than most about the topic, having made himself spectacularly unpopular not long ago when he'd discovered that a department had been carrying out the calculations incorrectly for the last eight years.

They'd had to re-do them all, and pay everyone compensation, and had also got into quite a lot of trouble with the regulator. A director or two had also had to give back their bonus. The administrators had hated him; the heads of department had hated him; the professional indemnity insurers had hated him; the people who were now going to lose even more of their pension would probably have hated him, if they'd known who he was. The only people who possibly *didn't* hate him were those who would now be paid a little bit more, and they didn't know who he was either.

'And I see that you're still driving that…thing?' Margaret enquired of Magnolia when the topic had finally been exhausted. 'It's not very practical, is it? I expect that it simply *drinks* petrol.'

Magnolia's face pinched, and she seemed to be struggling not to say something sharp.

'It's fun though,' Greville put in quickly. 'And it takes an adventurous person to drive it, as it's not easy to manage. I expect that Magnolia gets her adventurousness from you, doesn't she?'

Margaret looked down at her tea cup, pleased. 'Well, I suppose she does,' she said. 'I've had some adventures in my time, I can tell you.' It turned out that Margaret had travelled extensively, in the days when it was harder to do so, and once she got started, she really was quite entertaining.

Time passed quickly, and soon they were taking their leave.

'Don't leave it so long next time,' Margaret admonished. 'Anyone would think that you'd got lost in a Room that Time Forgot.'

Greville froze, looking from aunt to colleague in open-mouthed horror. Magnolia must have divulged their unusual occupation to her, which meant that her personal integrity was towards the bottom of the scale when he'd believed that it was closer to the top. She noticed his expression.

'It's okay; Margaret used to work there. She still does the odd bit of consultancy. In fact, she lost Uncle Herbert in a Thousand Room.'

'*I* didn't lose him; he lost himself,' Margaret corrected tartly. She addressed herself to Greville. 'He had a theory about the Thousand Rooms. An algorithm. It turned out not to be right.'

A shiver ran down his back. Greville had come across several Thousand Rooms and a couple of Hundreds, and he hadn't enjoyed them at all. All those doors, leading to other rooms, which in turn led to *other* rooms, which in turn led to yet more rooms…only none of the doors led back again. He couldn't think of a worse place to be lost.

'Yes, we'll come back in a few weeks,' Magnolia said carelessly. Greville's ears seized on the 'we' with imprudent alacrity, and he tried to forget it again before it could take root. 'Have a good week.'

She fired up the burbling monster and they headed home.

'Thanks for that,' she said. 'I hope you weren't too bored.'

'No,' said Greville honestly. 'She was fun.'

'You always know what to say to people.'

Greville stole a glance at her to see if she was making fun of him. He could never tell what she was thinking, and it was even more impossible when she was wearing sunglasses. He didn't consider that he knew what to say to people at all. At social gatherings of any kind, he inevitably found himself drink in hand, standing up against a wall, and if anyone ever spoke to him, it was usually to ask if he knew where the toilets were.

And now he wasn't sure what to say to Magnolia. If he told her that he wasn't that good really, he would be refusing the compliment, which seemed rather rude, and if he agreed with her, then he'd sound arrogant - and he'd also be lying. He was spared from saying anything as she continued.

'*I* never know what to say to anyone. I'm hopeless at that sort of thing.'

Greville wanted to say that she wasn't, and that she always said exactly what *he'd* want to say, if only he were braver, but he was still trying to decide if it was an appropriate opinion to voice when she spoke again.

'Do you want to drive?'

'Pardon?' he asked, surprised by the change of topic.

'Do you want to drive?' she enunciated. 'This car. Do you want to drive it?'

'I…errr…I…' said Greville, his default response. To tell the truth, he was a little afraid of the car, with the steering wheel and gear stick on the wrong side, and always sounding as if it were just about to stall. But it was too late as she was already indicating and slowing down. She pulled into a layby and got out, and Greville found himself bunching into the driver's seat. He located the lever to push the seat back, put his seat belt on and adjusted the mirrors while the car idled in its uneven splutter.

'Come on,' she prompted. 'We haven't got all year.'

Even with this spur to action, he still took a moment to familiarise himself with the controls. It was nothing short of reckless to undertake to drive an unfamiliar car without at least knowing the indicators from the windscreen wipers. He moved off when he was ready, and went steadily at first to get used to the strange driving position and the vast amount of power, edging gradually upwards until he reached his customary prudent velocity. His passenger remained mute, and as usual, seemed almost bored. He began to push the car a little harder, and a little harder still, and suddenly he was enjoying himself. The car ate up the miles, and he was sorry when he pulled into the cottage's drive. Magnolia raised her sunglasses and examined his expression.

'You liked it,' she said, a statement, not a question. 'Muscle cars suit you. You should get one.'

She got out and he did the same. There was a long moment when anything could have been said, but it wasn't, and the moment passed.

'See you on Monday,' she said, and got into the car and roared away.

Chapter 3

After a restless evening of ball throwing, assorted household chores and puzzle-solving, Greville waited for Magnolia at 21 Bridge Street. The building still looked totally deserted, nestled between an Indian takeaway and a bookmakers, exactly as it had been the first time he'd seen it. The blue door's paint was peeling slightly, its brass effect letter box and lock pitted and dull as if it had been there for a long time. Greville kept a wary eye on it because he knew by now that the door could disappear on a whim, as if it had never existed at all.

No-one was in reception and the lights weren't on and when he tried the door, it was locked. He heard the sound of quick, light footsteps, and when he turned around, Magnolia was coming towards him. Today she was wearing a very tailored grey suit, nipped in at the waist, and the inky hair had been pulled into a rather severe bun, reminiscent of her aunt's. He was almost disappointed that she was wearing ordinary, perfectly sensible black shoes instead of something more surprising. Then he reminded himself that he had no business being interested in her footwear, and turned his mind sharply to the matter at hand.

'The door won't open,' he said.

She tried it herself, as if she didn't wholly trust his door opening capabilities, then tried it again for good measure. This wasn't a pointless exercise as in the circles in which they sometimes operated, trying the same thing twice didn't always yield the same results.

'The instructions said ten o'clock,' she observed, holding up her too-large watch so that she could observe the seconds rolling past. 'It's not ten yet, which is probably why it won't open.'

When she thought that it was ten o'clock exactly, she tried the door again and it opened. Greville went to follow her but paused in the threshold, looking back at the sunny street. Normal people were going about their normal business, during the course of which it was likely that only normal things would happen. He looked into the dusty building, where it was likely that nothing that was going to happen would be entirely normal. With one last glance outside, he went after her into the building's musty gloom.

The lift was still tiny, old and creaky, with the back fitted with tarnished mirrors. The joining instructions had said to go to floor five, so Magnolia pressed the appropriate button and the lift dropped like a stone, down and down, so fast that Greville's stomach was left behind. He glanced at Magnolia in alarm, and found her expression impassive. If anything, she looked slightly bored. To avoid appearing to be staring at her, he directed his gaze to the floor, and his attention returned unbidden to the conundrum of the sensible shoes. In the sort time that he'd known her, she'd never been shod in a way that could be described as utilitarian. In fact…

'Why are you staring at my feet?' she demanded, startling him from his thought process so thoroughly that his head jerked up and he banged it on the wall. He immediately felt his face flush with guilt.

'I'm not,' he said. 'I just… I mean, I…'

He was spared from answering as the lift was slowing down almost as quickly as it had accelerated, then the door sprang open.

'Disembark,' encouraged a distorted voice which emanated from the lift's speakers. 'Disembark. You have reached your destination. Disembark.'

When neither of them moved, the floor began to vibrate. '*Disembark*,' the voice repeated. '*Disembark*'. The floor shook with increasing vigour.

It seemed wise to do as the voice directed, and they stepped out into a gloomy concrete corridor. It was lit by fluorescent tubes, which were dim because the casings were so dirty, and full of flies.

The corridor had doors on each side – the sort with a small panel of glass set with a crosshatch of wire – and they bore utilitarian labels, such as 'Boiler Room' and 'Cleaning Cupboard', except for when they got a bit further along, when they said things like 'Execution Room', 'Nasty Surprise Room' and 'Danger! Beetles!'

Greville hesitated in front of the 'beetles' room. He had a fondness for creepy crawlies of all descriptions, and was tempted to have just a tiny look. Unlike the others, this room had a window just a few inches square at nose height, glazed with very thick glass and reinforced with thicker wire. Greville peered carefully through it, hoping for a glimpse of the vivaria…and something very heavy and angry hurled itself at the door, making it clatter in its frame. He stepped back hastily as the thing crashed into the door again. Magnolia was contemplating a door labelled, 'Only Enter if the Tide is Out', and after Greville's experience with the beetles, thought better of investigating further.

They reached the end of the corridor and were faced with a solid brick wall with peeling grey paint.

'It's definitely this way,' Magnolia said. Indeed, a large arrow had been painted on the wall with 'It's definitely this way' written along it, although the effect was rather spoiled by the question mark at the end.

'I bet it's a force field,' said Greville. 'There's a box there.'

He pointed at a square grey metal box on the wall, the sort of everyday fixture that everyone assumes has a reason for being affixed to a basement wall even if they wouldn't like to say exactly what that reason was.

'I'll try it,' she said. She held her pass to the box. Nothing much happened, although somehow the cast of light on the wall seemed to change, and when she stepped forward, she went beyond as easily as passing through a bead curtain. Greville knew by now that force fields usually only shut down for a second or two, springing back just in time to zap the next person, and so he used his own pass to follow her.

They arrived in an office exactly like the compliance department. There was the same glass walled corner room, the same arrangement of desks facing towards the middle of the office, even the same name plaques on the desks. The one on the desk that would have been Magnolia's read 'Gordon', as it had before.

'That's lazy,' Magnolia commented. 'They've just copied the other room.'

Greville wandered around, peering at the fixtures and fittings. Arabella/Rose's desk had a few cat claw marks on the legs, and some knitting sat in the in-tray. Myhill's in-tray contained empty crisp packets, opened the wrong way up, and a wrinkled, stained tie. If the room was a copy, then it was a very faithful one. The only change was that an extra desk had been inserted between the Cuthberts', which also bore the name 'Cuthbert'.

There was a rush of air in the glass walled room which set all the papers fluttering. It turned into a spinning eddy and solidified into Mr Valentine.

'It's you two,' he said in surprise. 'I wasn't expecting you.'

'You recruited us,' Magnolia reminded him. 'You told us to come.'

'Yes, but I was expecting the *other* two.' He brought his face close to hers and scrutinised it as if looking for blemishes, then subjected Greville to the same treatment. It was hard not to back away. But at least the wet washing smell had disappeared along with his old black suit.

'Oh well, I suppose you'll do,' he conceded, sounding somewhat disappointed.

The door opened and Myhill came in, carrying a paper bag from the sandwich shop and the biggest size of cardboard coffee cup. He stopped when he saw them.

'What are you lot doing here?' he demanded. 'You two don't work here any more, and *you...* ' (gesticulating angrily at Mr Valentine with his coffee cup) ... *You* NEVER worked here. You just came waltzing in here under false pretences and poached my staff. So you can just waltz back out again before I call Security.'

Mr Valentine didn't budge.

'We're allowed to be here. It's all agreed. Here's the agreement.' He produced a brown envelope from nowhere and dropped it on Myhill's desk next to the pile of straightened out paperclips that he used as toothpicks. 'We're hot rooming.'

'Hot rooming?' Myhill repeated, scowling.

'Yes. You know – when you can use a space if no-one else is using it. Like hot desking, but bigger.'

Myhill put his bag and cup down, opened the agreement and began to read it in his habitual slow, thorough way, his scowl deepening as he read.

'All right,' he said. 'It says that you're allowed to share our room. But it doesn't say I have to be happy about it.'

'Yes it does,' put in Magnolia. 'On page two.'

Myhill turned the page over, then checked the envelope again.

'There *isn't* a page two.'

'Oh. Well, there *was* one. I'll make sure you get a copy, but in the meantime you'd better act in accordance with it, otherwise we'll have to issue a retrospective rectification order and you'll then have to be *twice* as happy for a bit to make up for it.'

Myhill opened his mouth to argue, and something in her bearing made him think better of it.

'Well, okay then,' he said gruffly. 'I suppose you can stay. But you'd better not steal any of our stationery. Or eat it,' he added, with a pointed look at Mr Valentine. 'It all has to come out of our budget.'

'Turn that frown upside down,' Magnolia reminded him, and he levered a grim smile into place before sitting down at his desk.

Mr Valentine glanced at his watches. 'We need to wait for Dylan. He's been checking the Displacers.'

He stood where he was, hands behind his back, rocking himself forwards and backwards and emitting a humming noise.

'Why?' Magnolia demanded. 'What's wrong with them?'

'Nothing,' he said, a little too quickly.

Before she could question him further, the door opened and a Cuthbert came in. He made no attempt to hold the door for the person behind him, so it slammed in their face. The second person was the other Cuthbert, who also let the door slam. A third person came in, as neatly turned out and as fair-haired as the Cuthberts, only the newcomer was wearing a smart skirt suit instead of trousers and their hair was in an impossibly neat plait instead of a foppish quiff. A female Cuthbert. Suddenly the nature of the Displacer's affliction was apparent.

'Are they replicating people again?' Greville asked.

'No, no, not at all,' Mr Valentine said. 'That is to say, I suppose they might be, a bit. Or at least, one of them is, but you can just use one of the others. They're probably not *all* doing it, or at least, we haven't had any complaints yet.'

It was hardly a ringing endorsement.

'Yes, it's doing it again,' said one of the Cuthberts. 'But this time, worse. Look what it's done. It's corrupted the file and made a woman.'

The woman in question had the same willowy height as the others, and her icy beauty was a feminisation of their sculpted visages.

'It certainly *has* done it again,' she said, her voice mirroring the Cuthberts' cultured tones. 'And it's made another one of *them*.'

'*You're* the one it's made,' said the second Cuthbert. 'There were two men before and now there's two and a woman, so *you're* the new one.'

'Not at all. *I've* got the original CPU, just in a new shell. One of *you two* has got a copied CPU.'

Before the argument could escalate, Dylan crashed in with the post trolley. He languidly distributed post without needing to read to whom it was addressed, dropping a bundle of envelopes and two magazines encased in plastic sleeves on Greville's desk. Greville hurried over. The current edition of Compliance Matters (a publication close to Greville's heart as even the title encapsulated how he felt about his profession) had promised that the next one would contain a new exciting perspective on the art of drawing up a risk assessment matrix, and he'd been looking forward to it.

He looked through his post, and was startled to see that there were a few personal items, addressed to a house where he hadn't lived for a good ten years. The first was a birthday card from his grandmother, containing a book token, and the second was an old phone bill. He vaguely remembered the missing birthday card. His grandmother had called him to see if he'd liked the book token, and he hadn't had the heart to tell her that it had never arrived, so he'd pretended that he'd put it towards the new edition of Tolley's Tax Guide. His grandmother approved of people having a thorough knowledge of the taxation system. And he distinctly remembered the missing phone bill as it had left a hiatus in his filing system between May and July.

He became aware that Dylan was watching him carefully, waiting for a reaction, so he neutralised his expression. There was no point in trying to work out how they had wended their way to him. Sometimes it was better to simply accept that the logic of the universe was anomalous – even capricious – and move on.

'How are the Displacers?' Mr Valentine asked.

'They're working,' said Dylan. He was smiling in a way that Greville didn't trust.

'Are they doing what they're supposed to do?' Mr Valentine persisted.

'More or less. The main one is okay. The one in conference room five is working, but it's making everything five percent bigger. The one in six is making everything five percent smaller. The one in seven is disassembling all solid articles into atoms. The one in eight is working properly, but it will only transmit living matter, so you can use it but you'll come out with nothing on at the other end.'

Mr Valentine considered. 'You'd better use the main one,' he concluded. 'Now, off you go. This is where you're going. Everything you need to know is on here.'

He handed Greville a clipboard which was a quarter of the size of a normal-sized clipboard, with a quarter-sized pen tucked into the pocket at the side. It was oddly heavy and when he turned it over, Greville saw that there was another pocket in the back which held a truly enormous eraser. Mr Valentine noticed the direction of his gaze.

'That's for rubbing things out that you wish hadn't happened,' he explained.

Greville examined this statement for reasonability, verifiability and sarcasm, but he had insufficient frames of reference even to hazard a guess. He filed the information away in the somewhat overcrowded mental cabinet specifically for snippets which might equally be helpful, life-saving or just plain wrong. He had better have a clear-out of the mental filing cabinet in the not too distant future, because if people kept supplying him with questionable information that he couldn't help but file, he wasn't going to be able to get the mental drawers closed. Or maybe it would be safer to acquire a second mental cabinet.

He looked at the ruled pad secured to the clipboard, which held a single arrow, scrawled in biro, and the words, 'this way' in an untidy hand. Greville tilted it to face the other direction and the arrow re-drew itself, and the words, 'no, THIS way' appeared in the same hand. The word 'this' was underlined as well as being in capitals. When he hesitated, the invisible pen got to work again, writing, 'HURRY UP – WE HAVNT GOT ALL DAY', the writer evidently being in too much of a rush to pay much heed to the conventions of spelling and punctuation.

'We need to go this way,' he said to Magnolia, and headed towards the door. They met Arabella/Rose in the doorway. She didn't seem at all surprised to see them.

'Make sure you take a handkerchief,' she said. 'You'll need one.' And with this ominous piece of advice dispensed, she waved a heavily ringed hand in valediction.

'This way!' encouraged the arrow, 'this way!'

Greville held the pad where Magnolia could see it, and with every few seconds of immobility, the unseen writer added another exhortation, and began underlining words with increasing ferocity.

'We might as well do what it says,' said Magnolia, and they headed up the corridor together. Greville wondered how long it would be today as there were never any guarantees with this building that things would be where they had been the day before, or even the hour before. It was almost as if the edifice was no more than a drawing on a designer's computer, with the project still in its embryonic stage, and components being moved about by no more than the click of a mouse.

Unimpeded by too-large high-heeled footwear, Magnolia easily kept up with him, and it was strange to see her without her usual clumping gait. Again, Greville's gaze was drawn inexorably to her shoes. The sensible black lace-ups ground to a halt and lined themselves up side by side.

'Why do you *keep* looking at my feet?' she demanded. 'And don't say that you're not because you jolly well are.'

There was no possibility of avoiding the question.

'You're wearing…different shoes,' he said. 'Usually you're wearing heels. Bigger heels. Heels that…don't fit.'

'Well, there's nothing I can do about that,' she said, briskly. 'They came with the house.'

The pad, having no truck with conversations about shoes, had started under-lining again. Greville ignored it. There were some strangenesses that were doubtless better left unplumbed, but where he came across a strangeness that looked relatively plumbable, like the shoes anomaly, he felt that he really ought to plumb it for fear that he might otherwise lose his bearings altogether, not to mention his auditor's instinct to investigate.

'So…your house came with shoes…and you have to wear them?' he asked. It sounded a somewhat unusual rider to a house purchase.

'No – of course not. Are you mad? No – the last owner left a cupboardful of shoes. I can't return them because I don't know where she's gone and they're too beautiful to waste, so I feel I ought to wear them.'

Capital letters were appearing on the pad, so they began to follow the angry arrow again.

'Couldn't you buy some more that fit?'

'No! I can't buy *those* sort of shoes! There are always too many in the shop and I can't work out which ones I want. It's safer to stick with the ones I've got.'

'Could you run them through the Displacer so they come out 5% smaller?'

She looked at him appraisingly. 'You know, that's not a bad idea.'

If Poppy had said this to him, her tone and diction would have conveyed ex-aggerated surprise that he'd managed to say something that wasn't wholly idiotic. However, Magnolia said it like it was. If she thought you were an idiot, she would say so. If she thought you *weren't* an idiot (a verdict reserved for very, very few members of the human race) she would also say so. It was as simple as that. Greville had the odd sensation of having prepared himself for a hen-peck that never came.

The arrow was pointing at a door on their right. Magnolia took a look.

'We're not going in there,' she said, addressing herself equally to Greville and the pad. 'It's a Thousand Room.'

Greville was whole-heartedly behind her, but the pad just redrew its arrow, ever more insistently.

'Do they work in there?' he asked her. Magnolia had been employed in this environment for six months longer than him, and sometimes knew things that he didn't.

'I don't know. These things are new. Didn't you see the notice on the notice board? It said that until the testing phase was complete, staff should take directional advice from the Global Orientation Devices with a big pinch of salt.'

He *had* seen the notice and had also read the smallprint. Greville always read smallprint, and the level of scrutiny to which he subjected it was in inverse proportion, so that the smaller the print, the more attention it merited. In fact, he didn't really even think of it as 'smallprint' any more; he regarded everything that *wasn't* smallprint as bigprint. The notice's smallprint had declared that the reference to salt shouldn't be held as dietary advice and that employees ingesting more than the recommended daily amount of salt and developing a consequential health problem would be sacked. A relatively mild consequence; for leaving unwashed mugs in the sink, the consequence was being beheaded. Twice.

'We're NOT going in there,' Magnolia insisted to the pad, and when it started writing something in capitals, she snatched it from his hand, grabbed the miniature pen and stabbed it into the paper several times. The pad wiped itself blank.

'Stupid thing,' she said, and set off up the corridor again in her new, lithe gait.

'You've broken it!' said Greville, more anxious than censorious.[1]

'We'll see,' she said. She looked into several offices before selecting one to burst into. It was Marketing, an enormous space populated with lots of bright young things who were all walking about very fast while holding clipboards (full sized ones) – presumably to make people think that they were busy rather than because they were incapable of finding their own desks. 'If it's broken, then we'll just have to shred it.'

---

1. The nearest he'd got to the wilful destruction of company property was in his old job when he'd once tried to use his ordinary stapler to staple a document which really needed the services of its bigger brother in the legal department (legal services having been granted custodianship of the heavy duty stapler as they produced a significantly higher volume of waffle than any other department). His stapler had jammed somewhat terminally, and Greville had guiltily put it in the bin and gone off to legal services, which is what he should have done in the first place. Then later he'd retrieved the stapler from the bin, taken it home and managed to persuade it back into service with the careful use of several screwdrivers and his soldering iron.

Marketing had a whole bank of shredders as they produced a significantly higher volume of waffle that was also completely wrong than any other department, and Magnolia marched up to the nearest one. No-one appeared to be paying them any attention, but they'd definitely been spotted; they were being shot sidelong glances and the pace of the fast walking had noticeably increased. People tended to ignore Compliance personnel with grim determination, in the misguided hope that this would prompt the Compliance personnel to extend them the same courtesy and not investigate them after all. And of course, if they walked very fast indeed, this would demonstrate that they were far too busy to be interrupted.

'It's broken; it hasn't got a paper slot,' said Greville, going on to the adjacent shredder. This didn't have a paper slot either, just an open top, as if someone had removed the shredding part in order to change the sack and had then found out that there were no more sacks and had subsequently lost enthusiasm for the whole endeavour. And had then thought better of replacing the shredding part in case they were spotted, not wanting to be tarred with the 'deliberately left the shredder emptying to the next person because they couldn't be bothered to find some more sacks' brush. Which was nearly as bad as the 'leaving mugs in the sink' brush or the 'jammed the printer then resent the job to the other printer rather than unjamming the first one' brush.

'That's because you might want to shred something that isn't paper,' she said. 'Like a stupid GOD device that's got an attitude problem.'

She held the pad over the shredder which, sensing prey, sprang into life. The gaping maw sprouted a circle of turquoise light and Greville could hear a gnashing sound, although he couldn't see what was generating it.

Magnolia moved her hand lower and lower, until finally the pad drew a very small arrow and a begrudging 'this way', and they were on their way again. The pace of the fast walking all around them dropped back from agitated to normal.

There was something on Greville's mind.

'None of those shredders had plastic sacks. Perhaps we ought to...'

'They don't need them,' Magnolia said. 'They don't really shred; they atomise, so there isn't anything left to collect. But we can't call them 'atomisers' as that means 'transporters' in a couple of the clients' stupid languages. Unfortunately, the smaller clients, who were the perfect size to climb up on a footstool and just jump in.'

'So they...?'

'Yup. You'd think it would have made a mess, but it didn't. They were just... atomised.'

They walked along in silence, Magnolia frowning at the pad and Greville wondering at the sort of service level agreement that could accommodate the loss of personnel with barely a ripple.

'It was all right in the end,' she assured him. 'It turned out that no-one really liked them. In fact, their company wanted to send us a few more to get rid of as it was cheaper than sacking them, but the ethics committee wouldn't sign it off.'

'Oh,' said Greville, glad that at least someone in the entire company was possessed of some ethics.

'Joking, Greville,' she said, rolling her eyes. 'It *was* okay in the end, but only just. They have one of those restorative justice systems – an eye for an eye and all that. They were happy to let it rest, but only if they got to atomise a few of *our* people. We persuaded them to accept instead a 20% discount on the next year's contract and some free places at the annual conference.'

He looked at her face to see if she was telling the truth this time; a pointless endeavour as her expression was usually either inscrutable or scowling, then he looked away again quickly before he could be caught looking.

'If the shredders atomise, why are there so many of them?'

'They're for different things. Black is confidential waste; blue is non confidential waste, red is atomic waste, green is recycling, brown is biological waste…it's all written down somewhere. You have to use the right one for the right sort of waste.'

'But if they all atomise, then what difference does it make?'

'There have to be rules, Greville,' she said sternly. 'If we all did exactly what we wanted and took no notice of the rules, then where would we be?'

Greville was admittedly a great fan of The Rule, although he was an even greater fan of the Auditable Rule.

'But if we're doing an audit on waste disposal, how do we tell if someone's been putting the wrong sort of waste in the wrong bin, if it's all been atomised?'

'We check for evidence of improper use. And if we can't find any, then we conclude that improper use has not occurred. It's all perfectly logical.'

He thought it through, adopting a frown of his own. The logic was irrefutable. One of the most unshakeable principles of compliance was – if you have no evidence, it didn't happen. Greville had quoted this countless times to people who insisted that they *had* carried out spot checks, reviewed objectives and filled in paperwork relating to money laundering, despite there being no evidence of this whatsoever. It sat awkwardly that this most noble principle could be subverted to work against them.

It would be interesting to see if there was a peak of shredder use when departments got wind that they were about to be audited. In fact, it would probably be depressing rather than interesting. If it was up to him, he would ban shredders altogether and insist that everything had to be archived (properly archived, with a verified list of contents so that 'archiving can't find the box' could be removed as a reason for not being able to supply evidence), and kept indefinitely. There were already 11 mathematically proven dimensions, and there were probably several times that in this building, tucked away somewhere. It was inconceivable that a dimension or two couldn't be set aside for a really good archiving system, and…

'Greville! Stop thinking about audit trails!' she said, with uncanny accuracy. He parked the thought, adding it to the list of things that he would do if he were in charge, underneath 'making everyone use the guide when utilising a hole punch so that all the pages lined up properly'.

The pad had led them to a Displacer, and a smirk appeared next to the arrow. If Greville was currently thinking his last thought, then at least it was a tidy one.

Chapter 4

The Displacer resembled a common or garden photo booth, the consequences of using which, instead of being shrunk, replicated or rendered bigger, smaller or naked, were limited to a picture that made you look like a homicidal maniac, with your eyes shut or in the throes of a terminal disease. Only with a door instead of a curtain.

'Shall we?' Greville said, and opened the door. He had watched enough science fiction to understand how this was supposed to work, inasmuchas the inside would inevitably be much larger than the outside. So as not to appear to be an inexperienced traveller through time and space, he prepared to adopt an air of nonchalance instead of surprise on discovering this phenomenon, and then was surprised after all when the inside was exactly the same size as the outside, or maybe even smaller. There was a bench seat instead of the plastic adjustable stool with which photo booths were usually equipped, and it looked as if it would be a very tight fit for both of them. In fact, the booth itself, let alone the seat, was a very tight fit, especially with the door closed.

A light had automatically come on when Magnolia had shut the door. Where the coin insertion area ought to be, there was a row of toothed, rubber wheels which reminded Greville of an enormous date-stamp - that distinctly under-employed staple of the paper audit trail. As they watched, the wheels began to turn, until they had aligned themselves as they thought fit. The pad scrawled an explanation.

'It knows where you want to go.'

'It can't do,' Magnolia contended. '*We* don't even know where we want to go. And what if we *need* to go and look at a job, but we actually *want* to go home? How does it tell the difference?'

'The Displacer knows everything.'

She looked inclined to argue the point, but it was hard to argue with a biro scrawl on a scaled-down pad. Even as they watched, the letters erased themselves and were replaced with the instruction 'press the big red button'.

There *was* a big red button, exactly where one would expect it to be if one were under the misapprehension that one was fully prepared to start the photographic process, but Greville remembered the instructions which Myhill had given him on his induction.

'But we're *not* to press the big red button,' he said to the pad. 'It's in the Seven and a Half Commandments, before x and after y. It's quite specific.'

'Thats not this red button; it's the other one.'

Greville wanted to explore the red button issue in more detail; he also wanted to grab the quarter-sized pen and add a quarter-sized apostrophe; however, it didn't seem wise to anger an entity on which their lives possibly depended. He looked at Magnolia for guidance and she made a face.

'We've got two choices. We can do it or we can bottle it.'

This was the sort of decision that merited a proper think-through, preferably with the aid of a spreadsheet, a flowchart or at the very least a force field diagram. In this odd place, there were so many unknowns that it would be impossible to list them, let alone quantify them, even less map them onto a decision-making matrix. Against his better judgement, Greville pressed the button.

There came the humming noise of a photocopier warming up, and with no further warning, flashes of light emitted from the front panel. He sat down hastily, managing not to sit on Magnolia who had pressed herself into one corner of the bench seat. The booth began to rock from side to side, although no more violently than a bus driven by a boy racer in a bad mood through an area with lots of round-abouts, and a thumping clatter began, like an overloaded washing machine trying to spin. Just as Greville was beginning to hope that the journey would not be a long one, everything stabilised and returned to normal.

He looked cautiously about. All was exactly as it had been before he'd pressed the button. He tried to think what to say without actually uttering the immortal words, 'Are we there yet?'

'Do you think we've arrived?' he asked.

'ᴪ۞ᑫ☼ʘ' opined the pad.

'It looks as if it's switched to the native language, so we must have done,' Magnolia said. Again, the utter lack of hen-peck. She wasn't trying to make him feel stupid for not knowing as she didn't know either.

'I wonder if we can switch it back.' He took the pad from her and looked all round it, including under the pad, and found that it was utterly devoid of controls. There was nothing for it but to put on his transform glasses, perching them awkwardly in front of the spectacles that he was already wearing, and the letters swam into the more familiar forms.

'Yes.'

'Okay, then. Here goes.'

He put a gauging hand on the door handle. A long time ago when starting a new job, he'd seen the obligatory health and safety video on Fire in the Workplace, and it had imprinted on him the necessity of assessing the heat in door handles lest there be a raging inferno in the room you were attempting to enter. This had stayed with him throughout his career, and he always felt a touch reckless if he just entered a room without giving proper consideration to the possibility that it might be on fire.[2]

The door handle was warm; *very* warm, in fact. Greville didn't remember enough of the video to be confident about what he ought to do next. It probably involved raising the alarm, but the Displacer was not equipped with fire alarms. Instead, he decided to open the door a crack and peek through, hoping that he would be able to shut it again before the fire was alerted to their presence.

They had arrived in an atrium area, with a flagstoned floor and high stone walls, reminiscent of a castle. Nothing appeared to be on fire, although it was extremely warm.

'What's the hold-up?' Magnolia demanded, and without waiting for an answer, barged past him into the atrium. He followed her. It was like stepping out of an air conditioned plane onto the tarmac of a destination that was somewhere on the equator.

People were coming and going. Disappointingly ordinary people. Greville had been hoping for something like the insect people which he had seen attend a meeting, all shiny brown carapaces and quivering antennae. These people were clad in dungarees and T—shirts, and heavy duty work boots. It was as if they had arrived at a plumbers' convention.

One of them was sitting on a bench reading a newspaper. He looked up when he saw them, folded up his paper and tucked it into a long pocket evidently designed for this purpose, then made his way over.

'Ⱳⴼⵏⴶ ⵝⵔ ⴹⴱⳐⵕⱳ ⸗ ᴂⴄ⴫⥅Жⴑ,' he said.

'Greville – translator,' Magnolia prompted, and he donned his headset.'

'You must be the strange ones,' the man repeated, having not received an answer to his first utterance. 'The ones that are supposed to be coming.' He seemed to be looking at them rather disdainfully; although perhaps it was too early to ascribe

---

2   Although it had to be said that the nearest thing to a fire that he'd so far discovered was a very heated debate on whether the failure to have a process in place to conduct random sampling of administrators' work was an amber on the RAG scale (red-amber-green) or whether there was a case to be made for using the newly minted category of amber*. One side felt that this was a clear case of a procedural breach that was more momentous than could be conveyed by a mere amber rating; the other felt that the first side just wanted to experience the heady rush of using their new category.

meaning to expressions. Perhaps this kind of haughty aloofness was the default expression here, much as nervy hyperexuberance was the default expression in marketing in Greville's home company, while truculent bemusement was the default in the facilities department.

'That's right,' Magnolia said. 'We're here to find the missing people.'

Greville heard the words that came out of her mouth; they were also translated into the alien language a fraction later, almost like a feedback echo.

The man cocked his head and gazed at her quizzically for several seconds, as if he was taking some time to process the translation. Then he held out his hand to Greville in a reassuringly traditional fashion, and when Greville went to take it, withdrew the hand and thumbed his nose instead, in the traditional fashion of the playground, the gesture at odds with his supercilious bearing.[3]

The man was still looking at Greville, as if awaiting some sort of response, but the only one that came to mind (pretending that he thought the 'joke' was funny by forcing a laugh) didn't seem appropriate. While he was deliberating, the man turned instead to Magnolia and repeated the whole performance. She too was non-plussed by the nose-thumbing, but then uncertainly tried thumbing her own nose. It was evidently the right thing to do as the man gave her a grudging nod of approval, then managed to dredge up another nod when Greville joined in – although it was at the back of Greville's mind that this might be a trick that they played on visitors and then laughed about afterwards. If people here even laughed. Perhaps they were like the actuarial department in that they restricted themselves to dry, acerbic comments.

'Let's get started,' said the man, 'I haven't got all day,' and he headed through the stifling heat towards one of the heavy oak doors. On their way, they met some other people, equally ordinary-looking, coming in the other direction, and he noted that their guide nose-thumbed all of them, who in turn nose-thumbed him back. It was either their accepted form of greeting or a more elaborate charade than he had first thought.

As they stepped through the door, the heat ramped up again, as if they were going from Hell's reception area into Hell itself. The air was almost too hot to breathe, and it was filled with the clang of metal against metal. It seemed inconceivable to spend

---

3   If the exchange played out to its inevitable conclusion, next he would ask, 'What's up, gravelly Greville', and then would stuff a handful of gravel down his collar if there was a conveniently placed supply, or imaginatively substitute it for a handful of earth or a handful of torn-up grass if there wasn't. However, Greville's playground tribulations had not extended to having his lunch money stolen: he had nullified that threat at an early stage in exchange for being a reliable source of correctly completed maths homework. In fact, he'd quite enjoyed doing the homework of the lower orders, where dividing was still called 'sharing' and the things to be divided were items of fruit rather than algebraic functions.

more than a few seconds in here, yet their guide pressed on without appearing even to notice the suffocating temperature.

All around them, vast cauldrons of molten metal were being stirred, carried, poured, and once poured, hammered, ministered to by overall-clad men and women who seemed utterly oblivious of the heat.

'This is it,' said the man, making a curt gesture to encompass the whole smouldering environs. 'I'll take my leave,' and he went to move off.

'Hang on,' said Magnolia. 'You haven't shown us round.'

He stopped, irritated. 'The people that have gone went missing from here,' he told them. 'They must be here *somewhere*.' He looked up into the steamy fog, as if they might be dissolved in the hot mist. 'So this is where you need to start looking.'

'Can you show us around?' Magnolia asked, either oblivious to the man's affronted expression or choosing to ignore it. 'So we know where everything is?'

He put his hands on his hips and looked critically and searchingly from one to the other.

'You must be Fives,' he said at last. 'I've come across the odd Six before, but never a Five. I thought that Fives were all extinct, hundreds of years ago.' A modicum of respect crept into his expression. 'Got to give you credit, really, for surviving this long if you're only Fives. You must be cunning, and I suppose that's what's needed for this sort of work. Cunning Fives. But Sevens would be better.'

It was odd to watch him speak, with his mouth utterly out of synch with the words from the translator, like a poorly dubbed film.

'What's a Five?' Greville asked, hearing his words echoed in the strange language.

The man regarded him pityingly. 'Five senses. That must be all you've got. I don't know how you manage with only five. It must be like being blind, or deaf, or…'

'What's the sixth?' interrupted Magnolia, having grown bored of being patronised.

'Don't you even know? But I expect it's better not to know what you're missing. Six is Knowing Things; seven is magic; eight is telepathy, nine is telekinesis; ten is…no, no, I don't think I should tell you any more. It might be bad for you, with your limited brains.'

The man made for a set of stairs fabricated from metal lattice and tramped up them in his heavy boots. When Greville and Magnolia joined him on the platform at the top, they were looking into an enormous cauldron of white hot metal. There was nothing preventing them from stepping straight off the edge and into bubbling oblivion.

'There's no guard rail,' managed Greville, recoiling from the heat.

'Why would there be?'

'So that people can't accidentally fall in.'

'Fall in? Fall *in*? What sort of idiot might fall in...? I ask you. Would *you* want to fall in there? There's no place here for the careless.'

He looked thoughtfully at Greville.

'You're not from the Idiots in the Workplace department, are you?' he asked, with an air of disappointed resignation. Their expressions must have conveyed their lack of comprehension. Even with the alien language feedback loop, it was obvious that he'd slowed down his speech to take into account their evident lack of mental capacity.

'IIW. Idiots in the Workplace. You lot come round once or twice a year and try to make us put 'danger – hot' on everything in here that's hot...which is pretty much everything, as it goes...and then you want us to put up railings everywhere, and fire extinguishers in case there's a fire, and what have you.'

A colleague who appeared to be rubbing surplus glitter off her hands and into the cauldron stopped what she was doing.

'Not more Idiots in the Workplace,' she said, rolling her eyes. 'The one thing we *don't* want is any more Idiots. I know that we're all supposed to be equal and that, but if we have to put up all these railings to stop them going over the edge, then that's *not* equal treatment, is it? They should have the same chance of falling in as everybody else. Now *that's* equality. There's no room for idiots in a place like this. They're a danger to everyone else and to themselves. The place for idiots is in a nice, safe office away from the heat.'

She turned back to the cauldron, rubbing her hands briskly into the steam. Glitter floated downwards, sparkling as it went, and sending up multi-coloured, effervescent steam as it hit the surface.

'What are you doing?' Magnolia asked.

'Adding the magic,' the woman said, surprised. No matter how much she rubbed her hands, the amount of glitter coming off them never seemed to decrease. 'Metal's not much good without magic, is it?'

'Our metal doesn't have any magic,' Greville put in.

The woman looked him up and down, as if she didn't much like what she saw. 'No, I don't suppose it does. And I expect your metal objects just obey the laws of universal dynamics and don't think for themselves? Well, you can only get out what you put in.'

There was simply no way even to begin to break this statement down and make sense of it. Greville wanted to file it away to revisit later, but had the feeling that it would be a wasted effort as it was likely to be superseded by a deluge of other statements that made even less sense. Perhaps there were some things that you should let sail over your head without making any attempt to catch them, like a fast-moving, finger-breakingly hard cricket ball if you had a piano exam the next day.

'So, this is where we make metal objects,' said the man, and led them back down the steps. It turned out that the rest of the floor was also dedicated to making metal objects, and after they'd observed the first few stations, the man pulled up.

'They're all the same. I've got work to do.'

He made a side-to-side hand-tilting gesture – the sort that Greville might make if asked whether a department had passed their re-audit when they had yet to provide a satisfactory account of their business continuity plan in the event of a power outage.[4]

The gesture was evidently valedictory in nature, the reverse of the thumb-nose, as he departed, leaving them standing in the middle of the hotter incarnation of hell.

'It's too hot to think,' Magnolia said. She wasn't wrong. Greville could feel his shirt sticking to him, and rivulets of sweat were running down his face. Maybe the missing people had simply melted into puddles. He tried to think of a course of action, but it was impossible to form any thought that extended beyond how hot it was.

A woman carrying a glowing steel rod in only a gloved hand paused on her way past.

'If you can't handle the warmth, go to the habitat cube,' she said briskly, pointing somewhat animatedly with the rod and nearly singeing Magnolia's dampening hair. 'We've got it all set up for you.'

They went off in the direction that she had indicated and found a glass-walled cube like the habitat ones back at the office that were set up to accommodate the requirements of incoming aliens. Greville pushed open the door, and they stepped into deliciously frigid air. The flagstoned floor was beautifully cool and there was the whirr of an air conditioning unit. The room was also equipped with a litter tray, bucket and scoop, a small pond and some bowls of foodstuffs. The contents of some of the bowls were moving, while others, resembling cabbage leaves, were rotting gently and pungently.

Greville pulled out a chair for Magnolia and another for himself, and they sat at the glass table.

'Right then,' said Magnolia, as if it was just another day in the office. 'Where do we start?'

---

4   Their earlier efforts were probably on the lines of 'Go home', 'check with Compliance and then go home' and 'get written authorisation from Compliance and then go home'. Experience dictated that they would next try a neat hyphen indicating that the department wasn't even prepared to try if Compliance was going to reject so unreasonably their earlier efforts, which was probably closer to the truth. Greville couldn't think of anything that better represented the activities of a department devoid of power than a hyphen. Not until a symbol was invented that represented playing games on a mobile phone.

Chapter 5

The exquisite cool of the room made a perfect vantage point from which to observe the activity in the factory. Magnolia sat and observed the hammering and pouring. A bead of sweat that had not yet been chilled by the air conditioning dripped off the end of her nose and landed on the toe of one of her sensible black shoes. Greville watched another droplet begin the same journey. Being sweaty suited her. It didn't suit Poppy at all; she'd had a horror of getting dishevelled, whereas Magnolia didn't appear to notice, let alone mind. The droplet joined the pathfinder on her shoe, expanding the salty wetness.

'You're looking at my feet again,' she said, without looking round or even moving one iota.

'It's odd to see you wearing sensible shoes,' he said, surprised into honesty. He was beginning to get the hang of saying what he thought, as soon as he thought it, rather than running it through a filter first to check for anything that could be misconstrued. The Poppy-induced pause was becoming a thing of the past as his confidence began to grow.

'So usually, my shoes are…silly?' she asked.

'No, no, not at all…I just meant…' It occurred to him that she was teasing him, and he regrouped. 'I just wondered why you decided to wear something different today.'

'I got this,' she said, passing him a piece of paper that had been folded inside her notebook. She passed him a handbag mirror too, and Greville understood why – the note was written in Mr Valentine's immaculate copperplate handwriting, only backwards. Once reflected, it read, 'Do not wear the foot encumbrances tomorrow. You may need to run for your life.'

'Someone put it through my door yesterday,' she said. 'I didn't see who did it. It was a bit odd really.'

Greville had other concerns than the invisibility of the note-deliverer. 'It says we may need to run for our lives.'

'Yeah, well,' she said, waving a dismissive hand. 'You're good at running. I'm good at running. And it says 'may', so it might not even happen. We'll be fine.' She replaced the note. 'Now, we need to decide what to do next. Those people have disappeared, so we need to find out who exactly disappeared, when and where they usually work. Then we can see if there's a pattern.'

At the end of the day, it was basic audit work, and it was oddly reassuring that the principles of auditing held firm even in this strangest of environments, far, far from home.

'We need to find HR,' Greville decided. People were coming and going from the inferno of the factory floor, so there were evidently other visitable areas. He picked up the pad.

'Show me where HR is,' he said.

It remained obdurately blank.

'Please?' he added. He felt a little foolish to be entreating a pad, but at the end of the day they had a job to do, and if this was the quickest way to set about it, then it is what he would do.

The pad drew a slow and grudging arrow in the direction of the door, and they stepped out again into the wall of heat. No-one took much notice of them as the arrow on the pad led them deeper into the factory and then to a door in the wall, which opened onto a stone-flagged corridor. It was like being in a castle, with stone walls, the sort of narrow, stone-mullioned windows designed for the firing of arrows and lit by torches hanging from wall mounted holders.

Magnolia eyed the torches. 'You'd think that they'd have enough heat here without generating any more.' She moved closer to examine the torch, to check whether it was real or an electrically powered copy, and held up a cautious hand to it.

'It's cold,' she said.

Greville had a look as well. The flames were crackling, flickering and generating soot, but they were giving off cold, not heat. He had been a fair chemist at school, and had never heard of anything like this. A geyser of sudden joy swelled up inside him. Here he was, admiring a cold flame in the middle of a castle, instead of (for example) wading through a stack of spreadsheets from the sales team which purported to prove by excel sleight of hand[5] that their excessive bonuses didn't breach the ethical commission's guidelines on performance and reward, even though they did. He was having fun at work. Proper fun, and not the sly and vaguely shameful

---

5   There was only so much that could be blamed on 'rounding errors'. And the magnitude of the errors was not so much rounded as positively obese.

sort of finding a serious error in the records of someone that he didn't much like.

Magnolia was peering through one of the window slits.

'They're *all* castles,' she said.

Greville took a look through the next window along as they were only wide enough to admit a single archer. She was right. It was exactly the same view that would be afforded over their own business park, if all the buildings had been replaced with castles. Even as they watched, someone rode up to an adjoining castle on an approximation of a horse, but was prevented from going any further as there was a moat and the drawbridge was up. The person on the horse had some sort of exchange with someone on the other side, which involved a lot of pointing at a sun dial. It appeared that the rider had conceded defeat as he rode angrily away, only to wheel around again and charge his horse-like steed at the moat. It seemed for a long second that the horse was going to try to jump it, but at the last moment the strange creature changed its mind, sliding to a stop and propelling its rider headlong into the murky water.

Magnolia turned reluctantly away. 'I suppose we'd better get going.'

Greville kept watching. The moat appeared to be only neck-deep, as the man surfaced and began to wade laboriously to the far side, where he was repelled with some vigour by the other man, who had armed himself with a pitchfork. He felt a tug on his sleeve.

'Come *on*. I want to get back by lunchtime so I can go for a run.'

It seemed utterly incongruous to be thinking about doing something so mundane in the midst of so much strangeness. Greville himself was still somewhat overawed by the whole interplanetary travel thing, whereas Magnolia already seemed to have accepted it as no more peculiar than a bus journey[6]. He wanted to say that perhaps they should worry about getting back across time and space before they concerned

---

6   Although, of course, some bus journeys were more peculiar than others. For example, there was the shuttle bus that was supposed to convey employees from the train station to the business park. No-one ever took this bus as the combination of rush hour and the lengthy one-way system meant that it was quicker to walk, or indeed to hop, crawl or teeter. Greville had once taken this bus to test the prudent use of resources and had found that instead of running from the train station to work, it ran from the train station to sheltered housing complex, to the supermarket, to the farm shop that sold better veg than the supermarket, back to the supermarket for things that had been forgotten, onto the doctors (where it was parked for a considerable length of time) and then the scenic way back via the woods. The bus driver having reasoned that if no-one wanted to go on the bus, the bus might as well go where someone wanted it to go. Strictly speaking, Greville should have reported it, got the driver arrested for fraud and launched a thorough investigation. He'd disembarked at the supermarket (so as not to arouse suspicion) and had somehow ended up being conscripted into basket carrying, reading out labels and reaching things off high shelves, and he'd gone home with a great deal of food for thought. He had written a report on corporate responsibility, and the company had ended up sponsoring the extra bus route and had achieved a community in action award for it. So the old people had kept their bus, the driver had kept his job and Greville had kept the ability to face his own reflection in the mirror.

themselves with the particulars of how they were going to spend their lunch breaks, but she was looking brisk and determined, and Greville was bored with being the one who always applied the dampener of common sense, so they began to follow the arrow.

The HR department was through an oak door further up the corridor, and while Greville was pondering whether they ought to knock, Magnolia opened the door. There were two neat rows of people sitting behind perfectly ordinary desks, but there the ordinariness stopped as the people were doing absolutely nothing, as if they were frozen in time and space.

'Hello…?' Greville said, and eight blank faces swivelled to look at him. There was something very eerie about the sea of expressionlessness; the hairs on the back of his neck stood on end, and he wondered whether it was time to start running.

'What do you want?' said the nearest face, as if an animating switch had been pressed.

'We're here to find the missing people,' Greville began.

'Are you real?' Magnolia asked. She grabbed the person's arm and felt for a pulse, and was limply shaken off.

'Of course we're real!' said a rather bovine woman.

'Why are you just sitting there then?'

'Because we've got nothing to do! If we've got nothing to do, then we do nothing. What else would we do?' [7]

Magnolia opened her mouth to make some suggestions, never being short of recommendations for things that other people could usefully do.

'Well, you could…' She pulled herself up, deciding for the sake of expedience to treat the question as rhetorical, gave a brisk shake of her head, setting her glossy blue-black bun bouncing, and changed tack. 'Have you got any files on the people who have gone missing?' She said. 'Please?'

'Yes,' the woman replied, making no effort to be any more helpful. Was she being insolent or not? It was hard to be certain. As a general rule, no-one ever told auditors more than they absolutely had to, and very often, not even that.

'Could you give them to me, please?'

'Yes, I could.' It was impossible to tell if the woman was being literal or deliberately obtuse, a behaviour that seemed to be engendered by the very presence of

---

7 Greville had observed this phenomenon in a variety of departments over the span of his career where, if there was nothing to do, nothing was indeed done. And administration departments everywhere (staffed [in the loosest sense of the word] with school leavers)were so attached to this frugal methodology that sometimes nothing was done even if there was in fact quite a lot that required doing.

auditors. Magnolia tried a command instead of a request.

'Give them to me, please.'

Eventually they managed to obtain the personnel files of the missing people which were filed in an order which could be called whimsical or perhaps arbitrary (although of course, there were really only two principal ways in which things could be filed – the right way and the wrong way) and headed back to their glass cube. The burst of activity which they had caused settled unnervingly back to stillness, as if they were enchanted dolls whose animation had worn off. Greville learned that Magnolia gritted her teeth more tightly as she got more annoyed.

'We need to start a spreadsheet,' Greville said. Already it was forming in his mind; the left-most column containing the names of the missing, with successive columns recording other items of data such as which department they worked for, at what time they had disappeared and where they had last been seen. A good spreadsheet could tease order out of chaos, and…

He became aware that Magnolia was no longer at his side, and looking back, he found her gazing reflectively at the top file.

'Give me that,' she said, holding out a thin hand for the pad. She took it from him and spoke into it. 'Where is…' she squinted at the name on the file '…Dddo-giar Vessssetxxxx?'

The pad drew a lazy question mark, and she repeated her request, this time spelling it out. The question mark was replaced by a pulsating arrow, leading them back towards the foundry. Greville paused to glance out of the window as they passed. The man in armour had given up with trying to cross the moat and was now trying to catch his horse-creature. A space ship no bigger than a four wheel drive vehicle had been parked on the vast expanse of concrete, and it was being used by man and beast as an impromptu roundabout, with the horse managing to keep itself diametrically opposed to its dripping, limping owner.

The arrow jabbed sideways, indicating a heavy oak door with a brass plaque depicting a mop and bucket. The door opened easily and they looked inside, it already being nature not to go blundering about. It wasn't a Thousand Room; more like a thousandth of a room, big enough to contain only the promised bucket and mop, plus Magnolia's spare frame when she forced herself in. She frowned at the pad.

'Now it's saying *that* way,' she complained, pointing back outside. She rotated the pad through three hundred and sixty degrees and the arrow remained obdurately in the same direction, like the needle of a compass.

'I wonder…' she said, almost to herself, and inched the pad slowly forwards. At a certain point, the arrow pinged sideways, then almost immediately spun to face back into the cupboard.

'Ha! Did you see that?' She moved the pad until the arrow flickered again, holding it steady so that it pointed sideways. 'There! Did you see? They're in the wall!'

'They can't be,' said Greville, his head swimming with magnetics and forcefields and other rules of nature. 'It must just be that…'

'Perhaps they're mice…or ants…or real people, only the same size as mice or ants, or…' She was already on her hands and knees, examining the skirting by the threshold. 'My house had mice in the walls once. I could hear them scratching about.'

'Did you get them exterminated?' Greville asked, more for the sake of saying something as he felt as if he was contributing very little.

'No!' she said, with a vehemence that caused her head to bang against the metal bucket. 'I got a piper to entice them away.' Sarcasm or eccentricity? There was no clear way to tell, especially when her nose was pressed virtually to the floor.

'Little people? Can you hear me, little people?'

'Magnolia, I really don't think…' Greville began, the quelling voice of reason naturally bubbling forth.

'Shhh!' she said, raising her head just far enough to be able to glare at him satisfactorily. She tried again, her lips nearly touching the door lining.

'Little people? Are you in there?'

She looked up, excited. 'I can hear them!' There was a vertical mortar seam between two stones, and right at the bottom, someone had squished in a lump of discarded chewing gum. She prized it out, revealing a minute gap and a few seconds later a stream of very tiny people appeared, each no higher than half a pin. The one in the lead was waving a minute fist, and she angled her head to pick up what they were saying through her earpiece.

'What the something is going on?' she relayed to Greville. 'We've been in there five something days. Some something something shut us in the something something break room.'

'We're auditors,' she explained, trying not to speak too loudly in case she deafened the overall-clad diminutive people. 'We…' She switched to relaying again. 'I don't care who you something are. Some something something's going to pay for this! This is a something mammoth's idea of a joke! Well, this time, they're going to be sorry.'

And the cluster of microscopic people set off in a bad-tempered crowd through the open door. Greville watched them, open-mouthed, until they disappeared from sight, which didn't really take that long.

'Come and look at this,' Magnolia said. He knelt and put his eye to the gap where the chewing gum had been. A mortar-free channel led the width of the stone lintel, and behind it, a block of stone was missing from the solid wall. The empty space had been fitted out like a dolls' house, only the scale was more in line with that of a dolls' house belonging to a dolls' house. There was a tiny table with tiny chairs, a tiny kitchen, a tiny bathroom equipped with tiny toilet rolls, tiny newspapers and a tiny stack of empty beer cans. She used her nail on the tiny light switch located just past where the chewing gum had been to turn off the tiny lights and they set off for the foundry, keeping a careful eye on the floor lest they crushed the newly liberated workers.

They were ignored in their journey through the suffocating, searing heat, and found the transporter exactly where they had left it, which was a relief as Greville had rather feared that it might have done. They squeezed inside and shut the door.

'So…' Greville said, eyeing the rubber date stamp dials and the red button.

'So…we think about where we want to go and then we press *that*,' she said. She closed her eyes, clenched her fists and *thought*, the very embodiment of fierce concentration, then whacked the button before he could even think of stopping her.

The journey back was no more or less jarring than the journey there, and when the flinging around and flashing had stilled, he felt the door for heat and then opened it. They were in a toilet. A women's toilet. But at least it looked like an Earth toilet, and the colour and style of the tiling gave a strong indication that they were in the right building.

'We're in a toilet,' he said to Magnolia. 'A…'

'Well, of course we are,' she said. 'Because that's where I wanted to go. Now, go away! You're not going to stand here and listen, are you? And you shouldn't even be in here really.'

Greville bolted for the door, face burning, although he wasn't exactly sure how he had turned from bold interplanetary traveller and solver of conundra into some sort of accidental Peeping Tom in the course of a few seconds. It felt equally wrong to wait for her outside, so he moved along the corridor to what he felt was an appropriate distance, and waited for her there.

Chapter 6

She seemed surprised to see that he'd waited, greeting him with a wordless frown and pushing her enormous glasses back up her nose, and they walked back to the office together, Magnolia still unnaturally lithe in her ordinary shoes. When they got there, everyone was working quietly at their desks, except for Mr Valentine, who was pacing around and appeared to be dictating a letter both loudly and without the benefit of any sort of recording device.

'…no less than forty thousand pounds,' he was saying, 'in weight, not money. And in return, I expect…'

He noted their arrival, and stopped pacing.

'What are you…you…' he paused to look from one to the other and then back again. 'You *two* doing back already? Did you forget what I sent you to do? That's the trouble with Your Sort – you don't have chips fitted as standard. And when I suggested it…grrr…'

His pallid face began to recolour itself in raspberry at the memory of the conversation which had resulted in him being denied permission to insert chips into people; this produced an interesting marbled effect, like pouring raspberry cordial into a glass of slightly soured milk. Greville took advantage of the lull in his speech and cleared his throat.

'We've finished. We've found them.'

Mr Valentine regarded him with deep suspicion.

'Found them, eh? Are you sure you haven't just been having a kipper somewhere? If you reckon you *found them*, then what did they look like, pray tell?'

'They're very small,' Greville said. 'And you might have *told* us they were very small, because then we'd have had more idea of what we were looking for.'

'I can't tell you everything,' he said breezily. 'We'd be here all epoch. It's simply ridiculous. I didn't tell you lots of things, like their age, or their hair colour or their atomic weight. Or their gender, or educational achievements or what they smell like. Once you start with all that stuff, where do you stop? Anyway, I gave you an easy one to start with. A simple exercise in forward thinking.'

'*Lateral* thinking,' Greville suggested.

Mr Valentine stared at him as if he'd said something very stupid indeed, the bottomless black eyes boring into his soul.

'No, *forward* thinking. Lateral's sideways, isn't it, and if you move sideways, then you're further away from where you're going, because you're on the diagonal to it. It's a simple matter of Pythagoras' Suggestion. I thought *everyone* knew that. Forwards is the way to go. Onwards and upwards and *forwards*.'

'Isn't it Pythagoras' Theorem?' Greville ventured. When all else failed, surely at least his steadfast friends the laws of mathematics could be relied upon to stay faithful.

'No, no, no, I wouldn't go so far as to call it a theorem,' Mr Valentine told him. 'It hardly ever works. I mean, it more or less works *here*, but it doesn't really work anywhere else. It's a suggestion at best, and not a very good one.'

'Well, we've found them,' said Magnolia, getting back to the matter at hand. 'What do those little tiny people do, anyway?' It was hard to imagine an occupation for people who were only as big as half a pin.

'What do you *think* they do? They do all the tiny jobs that the others are too big for, of course. They probably wonder what *you* do, seeing as you're so enormous.'

She scowled, unsatisfied with the answer. 'Right, I'm going to lunch.' She picked up her capacious flowery bag from its position by the coat stand.

'Remember not to use the main entrance,' Myhill reminded her. 'You don't work here any more. You've got to use the Bridge Street one.'

'But the main one's nearer the park,' Magnolia protested. 'And the Bridge Street door doesn't always open.'

'It will open if it wants to let you in,' Mr Valentine intoned. 'And if it doesn't – you're simply not good enough to be let in. Don't blame the door for your own failings.'

'I want to use the changing rooms downstairs,' she said.

'No-one's changing any rooms,' he told her. 'It's not allowed. They change quite enough all by themselves without anyone interfering with them.'

She rolled her eyes. 'No, *I* want to get changed,' she said.

'What into? I'm not sure we've got any rooms that can shapeshift. Although I suppose it would be more efficient if you turned into a…'

'I want to get changed into my running things.'

'You don't need a special room for that…well, not unless you want to go for a run yesterday, in which case you might need a Room That Time Forgot. I don't see what difference the room makes. They're all the same. You could 'get changed' right here.'

Myhill abruptly stopped poring over the crossword and looked up, wearing an eager and expectant expression. Magnolia's colour rose, angry pink spots intensifying on each cheek. She snatched out the wooden pin that held her bun together and gave her head an irate shake, and the thick, luscious hair swung loose. Suddenly, Greville couldn't breathe, winded as if he'd been hit in the mid-section by a fast-moving football[8], but luckily she flounced off in the direction of the ladies' without noticing his reaction.

'You know, we could make that a rule,' Myhill offered. 'That people who want to get changed have to do it right here in the office. Because otherwise it's a waste of company time, with all the walking to and fro. And we could have a shower put in over there, by the printer, and…' He retreated into the cesspit of his imagination.

Mr Valentine had grown bored of the topic, and began to address Greville.

'You've finished too soon,' he complained. 'I haven't got anything else for you to do yet.'

Greville felt a wave of mischief crashing over him. Up until recently, he had conducted his personal and professional life strictly by the book, but now he was seeing the book in a whole new light – as guidance rather than legislation – and once seen thus, it was proving impossible to un-see.

'That's okay,' he said, with the strongest sense of straying onto thin ice. 'If we've got nothing to do, then we'll do nothing. It's the most efficient use of time, really. Otherwise we'd just be wasting energy, and we ought to be saving it.'

His manager regarded him quizzically.

'It says it right here,' Greville told him, pointing to a poster on energy saving that explained the benefits of turning lights off and of not using the Displacers to get from one end of the corridor to the other because you were too lazy to walk.

'All right,' he said. 'That sounds reasonable. You can do nothing, but you've got to write up what happened this morning first. I've got a template somewhere.'

Greville set to work. As it was really Magnolia who had solved the mystery, it seemed only fair that he should take on the task of writing up. The template invited him to record how many people were missing in action as a result of the exercise, how many were confirmed dead (the deaths had to be broken down by root cause into categories such as Eaten, Shot/stabbed/beheaded, Temporal Misadventure, Act of Deity and Own Stupid Fault), whether any civil wars had been started and there was also a section to reclaim expenses, in which the mileage was to be expressed to the nearest light year.

---

8   A fate which quite often befell young footballers of Greville's mental inclinations, who were often daydreaming when they should have been paying attention.

He was just spell-checking what he'd written (not a straightforward endeavour as the word processing program contained 1,500 languages and was insistently fond of its default) when Magnolia came back in, her face now flushed all over from her exertions and her hair hanging damply down her back because the shower in the ladies' did not have a hair dryer. She glared at the room in general, daring anyone to say anything about her bedraggled appearance, then sat down at her desk.

'Did you remember to take a handkerchief this morning?' said Arabella/Rose. 'It's never nice to be dripping with sweat and not be able to do anything about it.'

'H'mm,' said Magnolia, her default if she was feeling too cross to answer properly and not quite cross enough to do the speaker the rudeness of ignoring them completely. Arabella/Rose (or indeed, Rose/Arabella) might have the appearance of a harmless old lady or of a cat, but if you looked more carefully, you could see the ruthless, steely core which lay not too far below the surface, and you would be aware that there was a certain line which only the unwise would cross.

Magnolia started logging on. Now that the computers had been upgraded, workers could log on by doing nothing more than clicking the mouse, which recognised the user's fingerprints. It not only logged one on, but also immediately opened up whatever the system thought that one ought to be working on, regardless of whether one wanted to work on that particular thing, or whether one would much prefer to email one's friends or enjoy oneself on social media before bowing to the unwelcome necessity of doing whatever it was that one was being paid to do. Magnolia let out an exasperated sigh.

'What's up?' Arabella/Rose asked, neither impressed nor intimidated by Magnolia's various moods.

'It wants me to update my personal statement,' she said, clicking away angrily to try to bypass it.

'You *have* to do it,' Mr Valentine informed her. 'You're in a new job, so we have to check that your personal aims and objectives are aligned with our corporate mission statement.'

'Well, tell me what the corporate mission statement is and I'll put that down as my aim.'

'More,' encouraged Mr Valentine. Magnolia sighed.

'Please?' she added.

'More! More, more, more, more, MORE!'

'*Please* could you tell me what the mission statement is, please? Please, please, please, PLEASE?'

'MORE! MORE, MORE, MORE…'

'This mission statement's "more"', interjected Arabella/Rose, who disapproved of raised voices in the office.

'What sort of a mission statement is that?' Magnolia demanded.

'A better one than last year's. Last year's was 'cheese', and the year before's was, 'If we can put a man on the moon, then we can holistically align our synergies towards a new paradigm'.

'There's a competition each year,' put in Myhill. 'We have to put all our suggestions in the suggestion box, and the best one wins.'

'Fair enough,' said Magnolia. 'My aim is "more".'

'Perhaps it will be "less" next year?' Myhill wondered. He was always up for doing less of something, provided that the 'something' wasn't eating or having a surreptitious nap.

Mr Valentine wandered over.

'Are you any good at accounts?' he asked, hovering at Greville's elbow.

'Ye-es, sort of,' said Greville, trying to offset the truth with his desire not to get involved in anything that would turn out to be dangerous or burdensome. He had dabbled in the subject at A level and could find his way around a simple balance sheet, and he'd picked up odds and ends from Poppy as their conversation had chiefly revolved around topics such as profit and loss accounts, trial balance and general accounts ledgers. It was almost as if they had nothing much else to say to each other.

'Good. What can you do with this, then?'

He made a gesture as if flinging a handful of sand into the air; the twinkling particles rose and swirled, then coalesced into spreadsheets. Greville began to lean forward for a closer look, but the spreadsheets started to rearrange themselves, folding into each other in bizarre and complex ways, and once they had stopped moving, the end result was a chequered piece of modern art, a hybrid comprised of spreadsheets, chessboards, skewering shards and a flashing cursor.

'There's your string,' he added, putting a metal tin on Greville's desk which had a strand of the sort of string that might be useful for tying up parcels emerging from a hole in the top. Mr Valentine picked the tin up again and read the label (which said 'string') running a finger from right to left under the word.

'No, sorry, wrong sort – you need *super*-string,' he said, replacing the tin with a similar one labelled 'super-string' and which had hemp garden twine in it. Greville couldn't determine where the first tin had gone to, or from where the second had emerged.

Greville sat back and looked at the faintly glowing sculpture hovering over his desk and the tin of string.

'I need you to find the accounting anomalies,' Mr Valentine told him. 'As quick as you like. The client needs this done the day before yesterday, as they've got a meeting with their auditors the day before.'

He frowned at Greville's lack of action.

'It's only a five-dimensional spreadsheet, and I've given you the super-string. What more do you need?'

That was a question with a lot of corners, and it was eventually established that while Greville could manage normal spreadsheets in normal space, he was a novice at any involving string theory. Having made a failed attempt to persuade him to have a bash anyway, Mr Valentine screwed up the spreadsheet sculpture and threw it in the bin, from where it continued to pulse and glow.

'You're about as much use as a teapot,' he said, his face darkly purpling.

'What do you mean?' Greville asked, rather boldly for him. 'Teapots are *very* useful.'

'No they're not. You put water in the top and then you tip it out again through that nozzle thing at the front. Where's the point in that? If you want to moisturise yourself, you should just absorb water from the air.'

He spread his arms and pushed his face forward, as if basking in an invisible sun.

'You see? That's much more efficient. No point in all that filling up and tipping.'

It was easier to accept the criticism than to embark on an explanation of tea and teapots, so Greville kept quiet. Mr Valentine began to pace again, starting his letter dictating and repeating the last sentence verbatim, with exactly the same intonation and gesticulation as he'd used the first time.

'...in weight, not money. And in return, I expect...' He paced all the way into the corner office and shut the door behind him, and silence was restored.

It was a pleasant afternoon. Arabella/Rose alternated between knitting something that could have been a jersey for an octopus and making tea for everyone; the Cuthberts all wrote in furious synchronicity, key strokes in perfect time, Myhill wrote a report very slowly and with much sighing, Magnolia did her nails and Greville settled down with Compliance Matters for a good read. There was even time to pore over the quiz.

Mr Valentine emerged on the dot of five, carrying a copy of 'The People-Centric Manager' (which had a neat bite out of the top right hand corner) his finger inside to mark his place. He glanced back to the page as if to refresh his memory, then addressed Greville.

'Are you doing any hobbies or interests, tonight, Gravel?'

'It's Greville.'

'No it isn't.' He turned to Magnolia. 'Are you doing any hobbies or interests tonight, Norman? Very good.' He checked the book again, and was evidently satisfied that he'd fulfilled the exhortation to make his team feel nurtured by asking them about their private lives as he began to spin around, dispersing into a whirlwind of glittering particles and disappearing.

'Don't use *that* vent,' Myhill called. 'That's *ours*. You don't work here any more, so you have to use the other one.'

Greville tried to shut his computer down, which turned into something of a battle of wits as it had decided that he ought to do some work on the audit plan for the year. He was also pondering the wisdom and appropriateness of asking Magnolia if she wanted to do something that evening, but by the time that he had circumnavigated the computer's various trickeries, she had already gone.

Chapter 7

Greville arrived home to a rapturous welcome from Satan, who barely managed to contain his excitement long enough to sit for the required ten seconds before he was allowed to greet him properly. As soon as Greville said 'okay', the dog exploded into a whirlwind of tail-wagging and bouncing which was the chief reason why anything breakable had already been broken, with surviving articles having been placed securely in a high cupboard. Satan couldn't decide whether to bound about, bring Greville a ball or chase his own tail, and flitted between the three activities, which necessitated a lot of crashing into things, one of the things being Greville.

A collection of Greville's shoes had been made into a pile on Satan's bed, together with a glove which had been missing since the spring, and an empty blackcurrant squash bottle. The latter had been put on the shelf by the back door, which served as a halfway house to the recycling bin; high shelves were no obstacle to a dog of his size. Satan never actually chewed anything; he seemed to find it comforting to collect an assortment of Greville's things and lie on them, and always did this if Greville forgot to close the door to the hall.

Greville really wanted a sit down and a cup of tea to allow his brain time to decompress from the day, but the combination of bounding and tea had often resulted in the less desirable combination of dustpan and mop, so it seemed easier to bow to the inevitable.

'Shall we play with the ball?' he enquired, and the wagging and bouncing increased geometrically.

He took the ball thrower, and they played on the long lawn until Satan was panting hard, and lay down with the ball instead of bringing it back. Mr Dean arrived home from wherever he'd been, which was likely to be the bowling green, some committee or other at the church or perhaps the garden centre, and he and Greville waved to each other.

Greville checked his watch. It was too early to start dinner really, and it seemed a shame to waste a lovely evening. Now that he was actually outside, he'd gone off the idea of sitting about indoors with tea. He decided to get changed and take Satan for a long walk instead.

They went Satan's favourite way, which was partly through the woods where there were lots of things to smell, and which involved crossing a stream (Greville balancing from rock to rock; Satan splashing around and plunging his head in to look at things that had caught his eye), then back along the bridleway which was quiet at that time of night. Satan could now be trusted to stay a sensible distance in front or behind without being called, which gave Greville the space to stroll along and think.

He had assumed that he would want to think about all the strange things that had happened in the course of the day – his first taste of interplanetary travel, the heat and drama of the forge, the cold flames, the business park full of castles – but now that his subconscious was free to wend where it would, he found that his brain seemed to have accepted that Strange Things Now Happen At Work. Perhaps it was just as well; after all, if he were to be awed into astonishment by every single oddity he encountered, he would probably be stupefied to a complete halt.

His thoughts turned instead to Poppy, or if not exactly to *her*, then to the space she had left. Greville was trying to maintain his belief in the maxim that it was better to have loved and lost than never to have loved at all. He had never expected to love; before Poppy, he'd only been involved in a few tentative romances, and he'd imagined that he was destined for a life of bachelordom and that at some stage he would have to pick an interest to sustain him such as bird watching or rambling. The whole Poppy thing had been a surprise and a revelation.

They had progressed from the initial date to a series of dates, and had then become regular partners and after that, had moved in together, with all the stages following on from each other in the appropriate order and at appropriate intervals. Greville had privately maintained his sense of awe of it all, and he had also continued to feel the bizarre sensation of being a spectator on his own life. It had been almost like being in a play and following a script; during conversations, Poppy said something, and then he gave one of a possible selection of responses and then she did the same. There had been no awkward silences (although there were angry ones if Greville's behaviour had not been within acceptable parameters), yet somehow the conversation hadn't been real. Questions were asked and answered, which was pretty much the definition of a conversation, but even so, it had been like conversing with a very sophisticated computer that was programmed to do so.

Greville mulled the situation over. Sometimes he thought that the difference between what he had with Poppy and what other people had with their significant others was all in his mind; he was over-thinking it and imagining difficulties where in fact there weren't any. He ought to have just accepted that their relationship was as good as it got, so he should have apologised to her, smoothed things over and carried on as before. And sometimes he thought that there was probably something amiss with him; he should have tried harder to be a better boyfriend. If he'd just tried a bit harder, he could have been engaged by now instead of being on track for membership of the rambling club. And no matter how much he thought about it, he couldn't put his finger on the difference between what he'd had and what he wanted; he only had the vaguest idea of something else being Out There. Perhaps he'd fallen to the 'grass is greener' problem that he'd heard about?

But then Satan bundled past him, nearly knocking him over in his pursuit of a rabbit and temporarily deaf to all entreaties to stop, so Greville had to abandon his train of thought and race after his dog. The sudden burst of energy together with increased vigilance for the rest of the walk in case Satan saw another rabbit served to dispel his pensive mood, and he arrived home feeling upbeat about having been relegated to the single life. After all, at least there would now not be any more break-ups to endure.

He cooked himself a supper of pasta with a tomato sauce, which really didn't take all that long when using a microwaveable sauce from the supermarket, and fed Satan as well, then he had a large slice of black forest gateau for dessert. Poppy had been censorious towards desserts of any kind; in fact, this suspicion extended to cakes and biscuits as well. If she ever decided to allow herself a biscuit, it would be a reduced-sugar, reduced-fat, reduced-salt (it had been news to Greville that biscuits contained salt) flavour-free, fun-free sort of biscuit. Greville himself would rather have a calorie-dense double chocolate cookie that was a fraction gooey in the middle, and enjoy every last crumb of it. Where was the harm if you ran it off afterwards, or had already run it off beforehand? Life was too short to be marred with disappointing, tasteless biscuits.

Having spent the afternoon reading Compliance Matters, Greville wasn't in the mood for any more sitting about. The joy of living in the middle of nowhere was that he was free to do whatever he wanted, whenever he wanted, so once he had let his dinner go down by watching the news, he ran the vacuum cleaner all over the cottage, 'helped' by Satan who liked to growl at the head with the spinning brushes before launching an attack. He just had time to squeeze in a bit of weight lifting before it was time to get ready for bed.

The next day was bright and having exercised Satan, Greville arrived at the blue door just before nine. He tried the handle, and was relieved when it turned easily. As he stepped through, he was jostled hard once, and then again, yet when he turned to have a stern word with the culprits (or more realistically, to give them a stern look and perhaps a tut), there was no-one to be seen. He picked up on a thread of conversation:

'…so I said to Simon, there's no way that we can countenance the continuation of the funding stream, unless we get some assurance relating to…'

He could see the carpet being depressed by two sets of footprints and frowned. Compliance departments everywhere were very hot on building security, and in particular on imprinting on all personnel the importance of not holding the door open for strangers in case those strangers were 'fraudsters' intent on stealing industrial secrets and causing havoc. But if he ran after them and demanded that they showed him their passes, then even if he could see the passes (which he probably wouldn't be able to) he would have no idea of whether they ought to be in the building or not. It seemed expedient (if a little cowardly) to walk very slowly until he'd heard the lift arrive and depart again, carrying away its invisible cargo.

Today the lift accelerated upwards instead of downwards, opening onto the same basement corridor with the same doors bearing the same warnings, except that there was an extra door saying, 'You May Enter, But You May Not Leave'. In no time at all, he was walking into the office, and then stopped. Something was different. It was as if someone had fitted a huge mirror along the left hand wall of the office as there was a perfect reflection of it to the left. He paused on the threshold, reflexively grabbing hold of the handle in case he was in the process of blundering into a Thousand Room. This is what happened when one became so inured to strange surroundings that one stopped treating with them with the respect that they deserved.

'It's all right,' called a Cuthbert. 'They've just been doing some remodelling.'

Greville stepped further into the room…as far as he could manage without actually letting go of the handle. There were no other doors leading in or out, except for the one leading to Mr Valentine's corner office, and that had glass walls which were definitely not reflecting any other rooms.

'It's all right,' said the other male Cuthbert. 'It's not a Thousand.'

There was nothing for it except to let go and walk in. Greville looked in wonder at the duplicate room. It really was a perfect reflection, down to the signs on the desks, which were all spelled backwards. This mirror-world was intriguing, and he went over the have a closer look; just as he reached the point where the wall would have been, he banged head first into something very invisible and very hard.

'They haven't finished yet,' said the first Cuthbert. 'They've left the divider there for the time being to prevent…accidents.'

Greville suspected that the Cuthbert had left his warning so late on purpose, but there was no point in remonstrating with him. Except, maybe there was. A small part of Greville was beginning to grow impatient with being perpetually disrespected.

'Why didn't you tell me that there was a force field?' he demanded.

The Cuthbert gave him a cool stare, one eyebrow arched in the sort of detached amusement that Greville found particularly vexing.

'That was really unkind,' Greville continued. 'And dangerous.'

He turned back to the invisible barrier. It really was a very curious phenomenon; when he approached it, it was completely unreflective. There was no mark where his head had come into contact with it, and when he touched it, no fingerprints were left behind.

Myhill bustled in, bearing his bucket of coffee and his paper sack of lunch, and glanced at the extension to the room.

'They did it, then,' he said, waddling over to his desk. He opened his bottom drawer. 'They replicate *everything*, you know, so I made sure this was nice and full, just in case.'

The drawer was fuller than usual of crisps, boxes of jaffa cakes and other assorted snacks, and even a bottle or two of maximum sugar fizzy drinks.

'They can't do it while we're here because otherwise it replicates all the staff, and the whole point is to get more space so that we can fit in more people, so if they replicate all the people as well, then there wouldn't be any more room, really, would there?'

'Are you getting more staff, then?' Greville asked. Myhill pulled a face.

'*We're* not; *you* are. I'm not allowed any more staff because they say that I've already got enough, even though I've lost you two. But *him* (he jerked his head in the direction of Mr Valentine's office) *he's* allowed whatever he wants. All he has to do is…'

'Remember that you're supposed to be happy that we're here,' intoned Magnolia, who had entered without her customary clumping. 'Otherwise we'll have to sanction you.'

Myhill shoehorned on a rictus of a smile, which did little to improve the neatness of his eating when he started on his lunch.

'We're getting some more staff,' Greville told her, as she took in the empty reflection-room. 'But don't try to go in there because there's a force field.'

He wasn't sure how he felt about there being more staff. Having more people might act as a kind of anchor against the weirdness; with just the two of them and Mr Valentine, who, it had to be said, added to the weirdness rather than acted as a barrier against it, it was sometimes like being adrift in a very strange sea. But if there was another person, there was the possibility that Magnolia might prefer them to him. In Greville's experience of friendships, as soon as two became three, Greville became one and the other pair trundled on happily without him.

Mr Valentine spun into existence and was hugely pleased by the new room. He rubbed his chubby hands together gleefully.

'There!' he said, 'my new wing for all my new staff.'

Myhill seemed about to say something unpleasant, and changed his mind when he caught Magnolia's eye.

'You know, I wouldn't have had to get anyone else, only *you* and *you* are so jolly useless,' Mr Valentine informed them, not at all shy about attributing blame where he thought it belonged.

'Can't get the staff,' Myhill commented, the barb directed towards Greville and Magnolia. Mr Valentine gave him a quizzical look.

'Well, *you* might not be able to get the staff, but *I* can, because I've got these ones, and I've got another one as well. A better one. A *proper* one, not a clone. One that can do all sorts of things, not like yours, who can only seem to replicate themselves or turn into cats.'

The door was opened very tentatively and a person peered around it. A tall person with a lick of very ginger hair and extremely thick glasses.

'Errr…I've come about…errr…' he said.

'Come in, come in,' said Mr Valentine, and the man – although he was really more of a boy – edged his way into the room and looked around him, Adam's apple bobbing nervously. Greville experienced the curious sensation of viewing a distillation of himself. The boy was taller than he was, thinner, more angular, definitely more ginger, more anxious, more awkward-looking (or at least, Greville sincerely hoped that he himself didn't look that awkward) and had a higher lens prescription.

'This is Leers,' said Mr Valentine. '*Leers* understands spreadsheets.'

'It's Piers,' said the boy, looking even more anxious.

'Peers, Leers, it's all the same thing. Exactly the same, and both equally likely to get you into trouble with HR. It's not the done thing, you know. One sort isn't allowed to peer at the other sort, or something like that. Or maybe no-one is allowed to peer at *anyone*. Or perhaps…' Mr Valentine realised that he was travelling into tricky waters and decided to give up before he got any further in. 'Well, it will have to be Leers now because that's what I put on the form.'

He waved an expansive hand towards Greville's desk.

'You can sit here, Leers.'

'Urrrr…the lift went down when it should have gone up?' said Piers, staying where he was. 'And it went really fast?'

Mr Valentine made a tutting noise.

'Nonsense! It went completely the right way, because if it had gone the *wrong* way, then you wouldn't be here, would you? Now, sit down.'

This time, Piers did as he was told, sitting very tentatively as if he didn't trust the chair. Mr Valentine went over to the bin, retrieved the screwed-up spreadsheet and the string and put both on Greville's desk. The spreadsheet didn't like to do anything as pedestrian as remaining on a desk and bobbed gently a few inches above it.

'Now, show me what you can do with this,' Mr Valentine encouraged. He pressed his hands together in the manner of one expecting to be impressed, and waited.

'What is it?' the boy enquired.

'It's a spreadsheet. A five-dimensional spreadsheet.'

'But I…but…I…'

'You said that you were good at spreadsheets. Accounts and spreadsheets. I asked you quite specifically.'

'But I've never seen anything like this before!'

Piers reached toward the glowing multi-dimensional structure and received a shock for his trouble.

'I got a shock!' he exclaimed.

'Well, of course you did. It's password protected and you didn't unlock it first.'

He performed a practised gesture and the quality of the glow changed perceptibly.

'There. Now it's unlocked, so you can get on with it.'

The boy continued to protest that he didn't know what to do until at length Mr Valentine produced a very futuristic gun, pointed it at Piers' gabbling head and pulled the trigger. The boy collapsed over Greville's desk, sending the crumpled spreadsheet bundle jouncing across the office. Only Greville and Magnolia seemed alarmed; everyone else carried on with whatever they were doing, and didn't even take much notice when Dylan turned up with an empty post trolley, folded in the limp body with laconic strength and wheeled it out again. Greville realised that he'd just witnessed the 'zap in the head' with which he'd been frequently threatened. It appeared that it wasn't an empty threat after all.

'Oh well,' said Mr Valentine. 'I didn't think he'd be much good, but it was worth a try. Now then, I've got something else for you and you to do today. It's a simple case of something being up. That's all. Arabella/Rose will tell you about it.'

There wasn't really much to tell. Arabella/Rose had had the strongest feeling that something was going on in the offices of one of the clients, and that was as far as it went. She wandered in just as Mr Valentine finished speaking, the cat not far behind.

'Someone's up to something,' she said, without needing anyone to get her up to speed with the conversation. 'I *know* it.'

She kept a watchful eye on the bobbing spreadsheet sculpture as she spoke. Rose/Arabella stretched out lazily, then walked across the carpet and began to bat languidly at the screwed up mass.

Mr Valentine clapped his hands, making a disproportionately thunderous noise.

'Off you go,' he said. 'We need some results on this one. If it's big enough for Arabella to know about, then it needs sorting.'

And armed with no more than some vague directions to use with the Displacer and a pad, they were sent on their way.

Chapter 8

They walked along in a silence that from Greville's point of view was placed midway between companionable and awkward, and the longer it lasted, the closer it edged to the awkwardness end of the spectrum. If only he was one of those people who could effortlessly say something both insightful and interesting, which would spark a rich conversational vein. Emboldened by his decision to remonstrate with one of the Cuthberts, he decided to plunge in, like a person teetering on the edge of an outdoor pool which is likely to be cold.

'Do I look like Piers?' he asked, very aware that this probably wasn't the received way to start a conversation. Magnolia looked up, her forehead wrinkling in puzzlement, which made the enormous glasses slip down her nose.

'Do you look like *Piers*?' she repeated. 'What, Piers just now?' She stopped and subjected Greville to her full scrutiny, looking him critically up and down as if he were a horse that she was thinking of buying and that she rather suspected was harbouring a few conformation faults. It was rather disconcerting being the subject of such a minute inspection. She started walking again.

'Not really. I suppose that you're both tall and have got red hair, but apart from that, you're not much like each other.'

'But what about…manner?' Greville persisted. 'Do I look that self-conscious?'

'No!' she said, and now she was laughing. 'Honestly, Greville, you're much more normal than that! You always look…I don't know…quietly competent. As if you've got a plan, and as if you've got it all under control.'

He flushed, surprised and pleased, and they walked along a bit further. He noticed that she was wearing some very beautiful shoes. They were a deep, rich purple, overlaid with lace, and had a large two toned bow on each toe, made of the same sort of net as ballet dancers' skirts, only finer and in iridescent black and purple.

'I like your shoes,' he said. 'They're stunning.'

'They fit, too,' she said. 'I ran them through the Displacer, like you suggested.'

They were also very, very high, and he wondered how she managed to walk in them so easily. Most women in heels seemed to turn their toes out like ducks to keep them on, or walked with the heel at an awkward angle.

'I went to a deportment school,' she said, in answer to his unspoken question. 'Not the whole thing; I just did a course on walking in heels. If you're going to do something, you might as well do it properly.'

'How do you *do* that?'

'Well, you have to imagine that you're trying to balance a book on your head, and then you take smaller steps than usual, and you…'

'No, not *that*. I meant, how do you know what I'm going to say before I say it?'

'Oh. Okay. Well, it's quite simple, really. I've got slight chronnitus. I tried to use a Room That Time Forgot when it was down for maintenance, only the sign wasn't up because the room was malfunctioning, so it was in a time stream before it went wrong, and before the sign had been put up, only it *was* wrong because it had *already* gone wrong…'

She shrugged, impatient with the vagaries of time travel and the impossibility of explaining it coherently.

'Anyway, I ended up slightly out of phase. It's wearing off gradually, but I still get a couple of seconds' deja vu quite often.'

'Is it ever useful?' Greville asked, thinking how much easier his life would have been if he could have gauged people's reactions to what he'd said before he'd said it, so he could then have said something different. Or maybe it wouldn't work like that, because if he said something different, then they wouldn't have reacted how they had, which would mean… It all got very confusing, very quickly.

'Not really – it only works when I'm not really thinking about it. I can't do it on purpose.'

They reached a Displacer after a considerably shorter walk than the day before. Greville examined it distrustfully. They all looked the same to him.

'Is this the one we used yesterday, or is that still in the…er…ladies'?'

'No – it's not there any more. In fact, it had gone by the end of lunchtime,' she said. 'They're kind of like homing pigeons, or like slightly psychic homing pigeons. They seem to know when they're wanted, and where. I reckon that if we went back into the ladies' and waited long enough, one would turn up.'

'Let's just use this one?' Greville suggested hastily, having no wish whatsoever to venture back into the ladies' toilets, let alone hang about in there. 'Unless it's the one that makes everything five percent smaller?'

'This one's all right,' she said. 'In any case, we can test it.'

She poked her head in through the Displacer's door.

'Are you working properly today?' she asked. The machine whirred and hummed, making a noise like a big photocopier running through its warming-up sequence.

'Yes, I am!' said a mechanical voice, and it was either Greville's imagination or the voice sounded somewhat indignant.

'Are you sure?'

'Yes!'

She turned back to Greville.

'This one's okay.'

'How do you know that it's telling the truth?'

'They all do, except for a rogue one that mostly lives in the meeting rooms.'

Greville scratched his head.

'How come you know all this stuff and I don't?'

'I found the building's handbook yesterday when we weren't really doing much. It was in a folder labelled, "Danger! Danger! Do not open!" Come on, let's get going.' [9][10]

Magnolia wedged herself into the corner of the bench seat, shoving over as much as possible to make room for Greville, who was vaguely wondering how someone had managed to name a file using exclamation marks. Did none of the rules which formed a reliable bedrock apply here, if even non alphanumeric characters could be used in file names? Or perhaps he'd implied the exclamation marks from her tone. Magnolia's tone often implied exclamation marks, and equally often implied a full stop that was stronger than a normal full stop, in the way that a double yellow line was stronger than a single one. A *full* full stop, which brooked no argument, or maybe a double full stop, although the latter could possibly be mistaken for an incomplete ellipsis, which was *weaker* than a full stop...

'Take us where we need to go!' she said, cutting off his musings, and unusually for her, decided that perhaps a little less peremptoriness might not go amiss. 'Please.'

'All right,' said the Displacer. 'Hold on!'

The ride this time was more of a glide, and when they emerged, they were in an ordinary office foyer. People just like them were walking about doing ordinary office things. They put their earpieces on and ventured out.

Those coming and going were dressed in uniforms – not the brightly coloured jerseys and black trousers of science fiction but the epauletted jackets with shiny buttons of contemporary Earth dress uniforms. There was a sharpness of tailoring and an attention to neatness which pointed strongly in a military direction. Everyone was walking briskly, too, and presumably they weren't all doing so to give the impression of industry to the compliance incomers. The effect on the whole was one of brusque efficiency.

---

9   Of course, it would have made a lot more sense to have this information freely available; but in this strange world, important information seemed to be secreted away, whereas trivial information was provided in relentless detail. For example, there were leather-bound, gold-tooled manuals on how to make a cup of tea on the shelf by the kettle, evidently (from Greville's brief perusal of them) written in a time before the kettle, or indeed, the tea bag, had been invented. At first, Greville had thought that there were two copies of the same book, but on closer inspection, it had transpired that they were volumes I and II.

10   And in fact, calling a folder 'Danger! Danger! Do not open!' was of course precisely the way to encourage Magnolia to investigate further, not being the type of person who appreciated being told what to do, and being exactly the type of person who liked flouting seemingly pointless edicts.

A woman with her hair in a severe bun came stalking over, looking irate.

'Name? Designation?' she asked, the earpieces perfectly translating the irritation in her tone.

'X, Magnolia and Y, Greville,' said Magnolia promptly. 'AS3749A and AS3753F.'

Greville looked at her, wondering how she always knew what to say. He didn't have time to take the thought any further before the woman with the bun asked another question.

'Issue number?'

This time, Greville's stomach turned over. He was fairly sure that he was the only one of himself which had ever been issued, but then the whole point of clones was that they were identical to the original. He was reminded of the Cuthberts, all of whom were utterly convinced that they had been the first in the series.

'11,371.55,' Magnolia said.

Greville's stomach reversed its somersault and settled back down. And he was on home territory now that he could see that it was *that* kind of an issue number – the kind that appeared on root cause analysis spreadsheets in compliance departments throughout the known and unknown universes, provided that said compliance departments were being properly run.

'We've detected that there is an issue with one of your departments,' Magnolia added, remaining resolute despite the froideur in the air. 'It's a serious one. We've come to track it down.'

'We don't acknowledge that issue number,' said the woman. 'And even if we did, there still isn't a problem.'

'*We* don't acknowledge your refusal to acknowledge,' Magnolia countered. 'Therefore the issue stands.'

The woman didn't look convinced.

'It's a Code Pink,' Magnolia added. [11]

'If you don't co-operate, we will be forced to cancel your professional indemnity

---

11 Not all species saw colours in the same way, and thus the generally accepted audit codes of red-amber-green often meant little to those on other planets. It was therefore necessary to refer to the Received Colour Chart before every expedition. Magnolia had evidently done this, and Greville had forgotten. It was disconcerting to be so permanently on the back foot. In previous roles, he'd always been the one who had remembered everything in the most relentless detail; in fact, a previous colleague had even nicknamed him 'Dumbo' for his elephant-like ability not to forget to do anything. *

*In any department other than Compliance, there would of course be an element of doubt regarding whether 'Dumbo' was a compliment or whether it was in fact an insult – and rather a barefaced one at that. But in Compliance, the ability to remember was esteemed, those who remembered were valued, and if anyone wanted to insult anyone else, it would involve such words as 'superficial', 'unsupported' or 'unprofessional'. No-one would stoop to citing Disney characters to score a point.

assurance and you will have to cease trading with immediate effect,' she continued.

The woman now added a scowl to her range of expressions, although it was a scowl was making a slow transition from truculence to resignation.

'Well, I suppose we have no choice but to go along with this for now,' she said, 'but you can be sure that I will be taking this further. What do you need in order to get this ridiculous business finished?'

'Can we speak to your compliance department?'

It was the kind of question that usually only has one answer, or two if you counted the wrong one, and both she and Greville were taken aback when the woman came up with a third.

'Our *what?*'

The woman hadn't appeared to be deaf thus far, so Magnolia assumed that perhaps the translator wasn't doing a good enough job with the technical term.

'Your compliance department,' she repeated. 'The department that ensures that your internal controls are sufficient to comply with externally imposed rules and identify and adequately manage the degree of risk that is present.'

The woman's face assumed a similar expression to Satan's when he'd stolen and joyously bitten into half a lemon left over from making a vegetarian paella – surprised and disgusted in equal measure.

'We have no need of that sort of thing here. Everyone knows their duty and everyone does it. Every last person here is honourable. There is no need for a checking-up department.'

Up until this point, Greville hadn't said anything as it had been easier to let his formidable colleague take the lead, but now he was so surprised that he couldn't have made a sound even if there was anything he'd wanted to say. An office without a compliance department? It was like a car without a steering wheel, or an orchestra without a conductor, or even worse, a school without teachers. With no-one in charge, chaos must quickly and inevitably ensue. He was trying (and failing) to imagine the irresponsible and reckless heights of fiction that his employer's marketing[12] communications would reach without the steadying hand of Compliance when Magnolia spoke again.

'In that case, we just need to go to the admin department that deals with personal nest-eggs,' Magnolia said, in tones that did not invite a refusal. 'One of our trouble-shooters thinks that that's where the problem is.'

The woman (she still hadn't volunteered her name) seemed to recognise that

---

12 Marketing being the first department that inevitably sprang to mind when words such as 'irresponsible' and 'reckless' were already on the table.

she'd met her match as she made a military type of turn on her heel and strode off, and Magnolia followed her with Greville tucked in behind, assuming that she was taking them to where they wanted to go and that she wasn't just returning to whatever she had been doing previously.

When they reached the nest-egg office, it was like all Earth offices everywhere – no castles, no foundries, no cold flaming torches – and the nest-egg department could have been located anywhere on Earth, with ordinary-looking desks topped with ordinary-looking computers and ordinary-looking in-trays. In a world with no compliance department, Greville had been anticipating some sort of civil unrest at the very least, but it was all very ordinary. People in uniforms were doing their work, and doing it rather industriously. No-one was setting fire to files. No-one was standing precariously on their chair to make unauthorised adjustments to the air conditioning. No-one had even stacked archive boxes more than three high. It was rather disconcerting that the lack of compliance was having no visible effect.

'Commander on the floor!' said a man at the front, and the whole department rose to its feet as one, standing to attention until the woman with the bun ordered them to sit. The man who had spoken did a double take when he saw Magnolia, and Greville noticed that his gaze lingered. A few seconds later, the man noticed Greville watching him, and before he knew it, Greville had accidentally become involved in a staring contest.

Ordinarily he would have looked away as quickly as possible, before his opponent could ask him what he was looking at.[13] But Greville couldn't break eye contact, and the flush he could feel warming his cheeks wasn't fear…it was something else… something he couldn't quite place. And all of a sudden, the other man dropped his gaze and looked away.

The woman with the bun spoke again.

'We weren't given any notice that you were coming, so we haven't prepared anything for you,' she said. 'You can use that empty room over there, but I don't know what you're going to use it for. There is nothing to see here.'

They went into the tiny office and shut the door, and Greville wondered whether it usually belonged to someone as he rather thought that he could smell a lingering scent of aftershave.

'How come you always know what's going on and I never do?' Greville asked. Code pinks, issue numbers, cancelled professional indemnity insurance – it was all

---

13 The honest answer being, 'a big scarey man'; the easiest answer being, 'nothing…sorry…nothing' before scuttling away, and the answer which Greville would never dare to utter being, 'an ugly, lecherous so and so who's about to get a punch in the face'.

news to him.

'How come you *never* know what's going on and I *always* do?' Magnolia responded, with some asperity. 'Don't you read your skymails?'

'I read all my emails,' Greville protested. It wasn't an easy job, either – the company did not appear to have any filters regarding which group emails were sent to which groups. While the transform glasses rendered the emails legible, many of them referred to matters of questionable relevance such as telling people off for parking their shuttles in the disabled bays of the interdimensional shuttle park, a collection and card-signing for someone who had reached their 1,000th birthday and a reminder that personnel in a galaxy far away should acquaint themselves with the updated disaster recovery plan for a meteor strike, a demagnetisation of the planet's core and a coming of the fourth ice age.[14]

'Not emails…*sky*mails,' she said. 'Honestly, hasn't anyone told you about your skymail account?'

She judged from his expression that no-one had, and continued less abrasively.

'Okay, you've got a skymail account, and because it's in the singularity, you can access it from anywhere.'

'Because it's in the…?'

'The singularity. There's no point in it being in the cloud, is there, because that would make it Earth-centric, and an Earth-centric account's no good to you if you're not on Earth, is it? So the accounts are all hosted in the singularity because that can be everywhere at once. So all you do to access it is this…'

She made a gesture like opening both doors of a bathroom cabinet at the same time, reached inside and brought out a piece of paper that appeared to have been torn from a notepad and written on in careful cursive script. She glanced through it and threw it back in.

'The fridge in the break room is being cleaned on Friday so we have to take all our stuff out.'

It was news to Greville that there was even a break room, let alone a fridge, but this was something to be pursued at a later date.

'Have a go,' she encouraged. 'Just open your account like this.'

She did it again, and Greville could clearly see the note lying there. He pretended to open two little doors, not really expecting anything to happen. However, there

---

14   Sometimes, Greville was tempted to delve deeper as the disaster recovery plan for the demagnetisation of a planet's core sounded a lot more interesting than the usual plans for 'disasters' such as the phone system going down (which in truth would be more of a relief than a disaster), the electricity supply being interrupted or the computer system playing up. But if he investigated every single thing that caught his interest, he would never get anything done that he was supposed to be doing.

was definitely something underneath his fingers, and a second later, a deluge of handwritten notepaper pages poured onto the floor.

'That's what happens when you don't check your skymail,' she observed, but she helped him scoop up all the notes and demonstrated how he could delete the ones he didn't want to keep by screwing them up before he threw them back in. Apparently, any skymails that weren't screwed up would file themselves in date order. She had him shut the doors and open them again, and indeed the skymails were now in a neat stack inside an A5 cardboard folder.

'So this is where all the briefs appear,' she said, 'but we really don't have much to go on this time. Rose/Arabella said that there is something going on…something *bad*…but that's all she could give us.'

'Right then,' said Greville. 'I wonder if they keep any performance metrics?'

It turned out that they *did* keep exhaustive performance metrics, and the little room was soon full to overflowing with red binders. This was a tried and tested technique by administration departments across time and space – to swamp compliance with information in the hope that they would have a cursory glance and not have the appetite to look too closely through the whole lot. However, it was interesting that this department had instinctively gone for the 'swamp' method, despite having had no previous experience of compliance departments, or indeed of compliance. And of course, if they really knew anything about compliance departments and those who worked in them, they would understand that compliance hearts were swelled by data, not dismayed by it.

'Okay,' said Magnolia. It's the nest egg department, so they accept contributions, they invest them and then they pay the money out when people retire or die. So we need to find out what exactly they get up to in a typical year.'

Greville sat back and looked at the red binders in the manner of someone contemplating a good meal. *Here* was something that he knew how to do. There was no trickery here; no technological intricacies; no tangled timelines – just pure data. He took a deep breath, enjoying the slightly dusty, slightly papery aroma, and plunged in.

A picture began to emerge. Over the past few weeks, the amount of treachery had increased steeply, 'treachery' being the nearest the transform glasses could get to the term which the department used for the transfer of funds to a rival firm. The numbers of address changes had gone up as well. The numbers of new policies taken out had dropped a little, as had the number of fund transfers.

'It all looks pretty normal,' said Magnolia. 'I wonder what Rose/Arabella saw?'

'Can't we ask her?'

'Well, we *can*, but we'd only get what she's already told us. She thinks that something bad is going on…something that could affect their professional indemnity insurance, which we underwrite.'

'Fraud?' wondered Greville. 'Either fraud or incompetence.'

He preferred incompetence over fraud as then you could just insist that an auditable training program was rolled out, whereas with fraud, ugly scenes would be played out, people would be sacked & there would be general unpleasantness.

Magnolia was standing behind him and reading the file over his shoulder, standing very close. So close, in fact, that he could smell her clean, soapy aroma. As she leaned in to look at something, a long skein of blue-black hair fell forward, brushing his neck. It felt like silk against his skin. Suddenly, it seemed to Greville that the temperature of the room had increased by ten degrees.

'What are you thinking?' she demanded, almost directly into his ear due to her position.

He started guiltily, flushing very red.

'I…errr…I…' He had been so enthralled in the realm of silky hair and soapy scent that it was impossible to rustle up a convincing sentence.

'I was thinking that we ought to trace a few transactions from start to finish,' she said, oblivious to his discomfort. 'Just to get a feel for the weaknesses in the process.'

'Yes, that's exactly what I was thinking,' he lied hastily. 'We ought to look at a few member files.'

'All right,' she said. 'Let's see if we can find the archives. Come on – we'll go and ask.'

Chapter 9

They made enquiries, and woman-with-a-bun opened a door.

'It's in there,' she said.

Greville peered in, doubtfully. His previous house had had a similarly sized cupboard, designed to contain an ironing board and not much else. This cupboard contained nothing at all. Perhaps the woman was trying to make the point that their archiving department was non-existent, having no more need for one here than they did for a compliance department.

'Do you want to go to Archiving or not?' she prompted.

Greville wondered if this was a trick, to see if unwanted visitors could be made to stand in a cupboard[15]. He checked to see whether the door had a lock. It was one thing to be made to look silly in front of a roomful of people, but quite another to be locked inside an ironing board sized space. He stepped into the cupboard, and straight through into an enormous, chilly, dark warehouse packed as far as the eye could see with shelves and shelves of cardboard boxes. The lights far overhead flickered on, triggered by the movement, illuminating only a tight cylinder where they were standing.

Magnolia joined him, stumbling as she did so, seeming to trip over something. Maybe she had been taken by surprise that the wall hadn't really been a wall at all. Greville felt a draught from behind, just for a second, and was sure that he could smell the same cologne, but when he looked around, there was nothing there.

---

15   This was a favourite tried-and-tested trick that the operations department of his previous employer played on the fresh-faced Pierses of the compliance department, should they venture to ask where anything was, from Mr so-and-so's office to the records store. The steadily increasing supply of fictitious laminated signs for cupboard doors had only been stemmed when Greville's boss had begun an inquiry into the rate at which the lamination machine was gobbling up cartridges, simultaneously reducing the amount of time that compliance auditors spent in cupboards (some of them were too embarrassed to come back out and face the jeering mob) and cementing the department's reputation of Ultimate Fun Stamper.

'Wow,' she said, looking upwards. The roof was so far above them that it was impossible to see, with the shelves stretching up, and up and up. It occurred to Greville that light should never form a perfect cylinder. It should start from a focal point and then diverge outwards, and if he remembered his physics correctly (and he probably did), the angle of divergence would be the arctan of...

He shut down the train of thought as there was simply no point in pursuing it. Up until recently, the constants that applied in maths and physics had been exactly that – constants. More than that – constant *friends*, that could always be relied upon, no matter what the circumstances. With them subverted to 'unreliables' or even 'bizarres', it was best just to accept the status quo and bumble onwards. This is what it must feel like to be the sort of person who could happily hand in (without any qualms whatsoever) productivity sheets which showed on one month that the department had billed more hours than could have been achieved if four times as many staff had worked twenty four hours a day, the next month that they had possibly all been hibernating and the month afterwards, a significant negative balance of hours billed. And when the inconsistencies had been brought to their attention, could say, 'Really? That's odd. Oh well, it will all come out in the wash,' without the slightest compunction to get to the bottom of it. This mindset of incurious complacency was dangerously beguiling. Greville must remember to be extra vigilant about other things, lest he should start being tempted to write audit reports that said things like 'revisit next year' if the issue seemed to be one that was particularly thorny and which might go away, given a judicious amount of time and a blind eye.

Magnolia walked over to the nearest bank of shelves and reached out to touch a box, to see if it was real. Her hand passed through it, although the shelves seemed to be solid enough.

'Virtual', she pronounced. 'We need some reality gloves.' She hunted up and down the shelves, the corresponding lighting flickering on and off, until she found some orange knitted gloves – the sort designed for builders with squiggles of an orange glue-like substance across the palms and fingers for grip.

'This is how the gloves work,' Magnolia told him. She used the gloves in the way that one might use a tea towel to get something out of the oven, nudging a box from its shelf. It eased out gently, like a helium balloon that was old enough not to want to head upwards to the ceiling and not quite old enough to sink of its own volition. She pressed the box to the ground, then in a quick motion, put on a glove and suddenly the box and its contents were solid under her touch.

'See? They have no substance without the gloves; you can move them *using* the gloves, and they're solid *wearing* the gloves.' She picked the box up with evident effort. 'And if they're using virtual storage, it's probably voice activated. But there's something we need to do first, before we summon the boxes.'

'Oh?' Greville didn't even want to guess at what mad rituals might be required.

'We need to run about and screech.'

This was no more mad than he'd expected, to be fair.

'Why?'

'Because it's fun! The sound quality is interesting in here, and there's so much space. Come on – let's go!'

She took off the elegant heels, placing them neatly side by side, and disappeared up an aisle, shrieking as she went, her voice oddly flat in the vast space. The lighting far, far above was activated by her movement, allowing him to track her progress. Her voice floated back to him. 'Come on, Greville! Run!'

He looked down one or two aisles and then looked upwards. If anyone else was in here – the type of 'anyone' who might report them for behaviour unbecoming to an audit senior – then the light would give them away. This vast space surely must be empty. Feeling very foolish, he began to jog.

As he reached the end of the aisle, Magnolia crossed his path at some speed, zipping along the row that was perpendicular to his, lights flickering on in front of her and darkness settling again in her wake.

'You've got to screech,' she encouraged. 'Like this!' She released some wild whoops as she went, which were distorted by the strange acoustics.

It wasn't that Greville didn't want to join in (although if he had to swear on a compliance manual, he'd have to admit that the larger part of him didn't); it was more that he *couldn't*. If he was given something to shout (such as, 'What do we want? An audit procedure that is flexible enough to incorporate relevant audit objectives. When do we want it? By the beginning of the next fiscal year, or the one after if a carry back facility will be provided', he could probably manage it, but he was no good at generating random, senseless sounds.

'Oy?' he ventured, making the sound of an irate park keeper coming across a very young Greville who had accidentally dropped his ball on the forbidden grass and who had been pondering whether he ought to dash and grab it or find a stick to retrieve it to avoid setting foot where the sign said he shouldn't. 'Oy!' he said more firmly, and began to pick up some speed. 'Oy, oy, oy.' He experimented with a different prohibitory exclamation. 'Hey! Hey! HEY!'

He fell automatically into his normal running rhythm, a smooth pace that ate up kilometres at the rate of one to every four minutes with very little effort.

'Whee,' he tried. 'Whee. Wheeeeeeeeeee.'

Magnolia was triggering lights in a zig zag pattern far ahead, and he found himself accelerating in roughly that direction. 'WHHHHHHEEEEEEEEEEEE…!!!!!'

He wondered what the lights would do if he stopped altogether. Would they stay on or, unable to detect movement, would they turn off after a set period of time, leaving him in darkness?[16] He slid to a halt on the smooth concrete and the pool of light halted with him, then he stood very still. A minute passed, and then another one. He could still hear Magnolia shrieking and whooping, a long way away now, the lights flickering in the distance. Suddenly the lit column that he was standing in snapped off and he was left in utter blackness.

Except it *wasn't* utter blackness. No further than a few aisles away, a light was still on. It moved a few metres more, then stopped. There was someone else in the warehouse with them. Greville's heart sank. They were probably going to get into trouble for all the running around and screeching.

He listened. The other person was making no noise at all. He couldn't even hear them breathing, although they were two aisles further over, so perhaps the distance was too great. He couldn't hear them rifling through papers, either. Did virtual paper rustle? Presumably it did, when rendered solid by the gloves? He tried to still his breathing to listen better – he wasn't properly out of breath as he hadn't really run fast enough, or for long enough – but he was breathing slightly more heavily than normal, making it harder to hear. He was straining his ears to their fullest extent when their light too switched off. Now the darkness was complete.

What he'd expected to happen next was for the person who had come to peruse the archives to move and reactivate the light, so that they could carry on with what they were doing, which they had presumably interrupted in their astonishment at finding the usual calm of the archive storage facility being violated by intruders. Instead, what happened was…nothing. Greville waited, torn between going to apologise to the person and explain himself (an acceptable explanation not immediately springing to mind) and carrying on as if nothing had happened.[17] As he waited, the

---

16 A previous employer, ostensibly seized by a fit of enthusiasm for protecting the environment, had installed movement activated lighting in all the managers' offices which turned itself off after a set period. Thus those who were sitting quietly at their desks, getting on with whatever it was that they ought to be doing, were suddenly plunged into darkness unless they succumbed to the indignity of waving at the ceiling at appropriate intervals. And of course, those who were having a quiet doze would be found out when they failed to reactivate their lights. Not long afterwards, the facilities manager had been deluged with requests for oscillating fans which activated the motion detectors, but necessitated the heating being set at a higher level to offset the cooling action of the fan, and really the environment would have been a lot better off if the whole thing had been left alone.

17 This was the preferred methodology for the executive committee for whom the phrase, 'never apologise; never explain' might have been invented. In fact, they probably invented it. And if pressed on a point (usually a point connected with the gifts register and either things not being entered on it at all, things being entered on it that weren't allowed or, their habitual defence was, 'oh, we won't worry about that now…it's all in the past', which of course it was.

smell of aftershave drifted towards him, very faint but definitely there. Then their light column reactivated, and moved another few feet. Greville had been beginning to feel uneasy, but now they were back in the realms of normality. Whoever it was had obviously been startled into stillness by the shrieking, and now they were getting on with their work again. Except that there was still no noise. It was almost as if *they* were listening to *him*. And no sooner had he finished the thought than their light flickered off again.

They were following him. The realisation came suddenly. Whoever it was wanted to reach him clandestinely and was being foiled by the automatic lights, which illuminated their every step. Greville's heart began to beat a lot harder and louder than it had when he was running.

If he stayed still, then the other person wouldn't be able to reach him undetected. Unless the motion detectors only picked up on speedy movements? Greville moved very, very slowly, stooping to peer over a row of boxes to try to catch a glimpse of his stalker. The lights didn't activate, and he couldn't see anything at all either. Next, he tried a very slow, deliberate step, and then another one and the utter darkness remained.

What was waiting for him in the blackness? His short time in his new employment had already taught him that anything was possible. After all Death himself ran his own employer's archives. Perhaps all archiving storage units were run by versions of Death, and perhaps the Deaths didn't like employees from other organisations poking about, let alone taking liberties with the facilities? Or perhaps…

Greville became aware that he could now hear breathing – harsh, ragged breathing – and the smell of aftershave was stronger. While he'd been standing there, someone…some*thing*…had been creeping up on him. He could still see nothing at all; his eyes were incapable of adjusting to this level of darkness.

The door into the cupboard wasn't far away, and he hadn't run a great enough distance to lose his bearings (and of course Greville naturally preferred careful straight lines to Magnolia's joyful zig zags) so he could reach safety in seconds. But then a faint whoop reached his ears and without a second thought, he ran in that direction, far, far faster than he'd been running before. Behind him, another set of lights snapped on, and he heard heavy footsteps in pursuit, but he didn't look back. He ran towards Magnolia – towards the flickering source of light in front of him.

The ragged breathing trailed him, becoming rougher still. It was now almost a snarl…a jagged roar which came on every inhalation.

'Magnolia!' Greville shouted, trying to go faster, but hampered by the fact that he was trying to accelerate on polished concrete in smooth-soled shoes. He had to get to her before the…the *thing* did. And suddenly one of his shoes felt funny…

it was coming loose… He barely had a chance to register this thought before he trod on his shoelace and crashed down, hard. It was the sort of fall that really hurt, kneecaps on very hard floor, elbows as well, and his shoe had come off. Still, he tried to scramble up, while the flailing footsteps grew closer. He slipped over twice more in his haste to get to his feet, and behind him, he could hear that his pursuer was slowing down, then drawing to a stop. Perhaps it was an assailant who enjoyed the *prospect* of a kill as much as the kill itself.

'Wait up!' called a voice. A voice that was panting heavily. 'Just wait, can't you?'

Greville, half-steeled for painful death, stopped scrambling and turned round, surprised. The aisle behind him was illuminated by a cylinder of light with absolutely nothing in it.

'Wait!' the voice repeated, and there was no doubt that it was coming from the light. 'I can't run any more.'

Magnolia's light was making its way steadily towards him, and she appeared in the aisle, some distance away. He'd rather it had been further so at least she'd have more chance of being safe, but at least Greville was between her and the entity. He got to his feet, one shoe still off, and faced the illuminated cylinder, which advanced one light fitting at a time, the preceding ones switching off.

There was probably a received procedure for addressing hostile, invisible aliens, but Greville didn't know what it was, so he said the first thing that came to mind.

'Hello? Who are you and what…' he paused for a fraction of a second, as he had been going to say "what do you want", which would sound rather rude considering that *they* and not *it* were the visitors. 'What can we…errr…*I* do for you?'

'You can stop running, for starters,' the voice said, still wheezing, and its patch of light drew closer. Greville took advantage of its slow progress to replace his shoe. If he had to run for his life, then it would be better to do it with both shoes on.

'Who are you talking to?' Magnolia asked, approaching from behind him.

'I'm from the professional indemnity reinsurers,' said the voice. 'I'm supposed to be stress-testing the robustness of your procedures, but thanks to you two, I'm done here already and I was hoping to be here for weeks. Months, even.'

The voice sounded aggrieved, but it was more like Myhill's kind of whingeing aggrievement than anything likely to evolve imminently into violence. And the harsh, chesty wheeze was that of an asthmatic or a chronically unfit and possibly overweight person, rather than the snarl of an animal, so the unseen person would easily be outrun. Unless they were armed, of course.

'What do you mean?' Magnolia demanded, now at Greville's shoulder.

'We visit your clients now and then – tamper with a few records, that sort of thing – to see how long it takes for it to be picked up. The longer it takes, the more we put your premiums up. But you've spotted it right away. You've realised that something was up, you've come down to investigate and you were about to find out what I've been up to.'

Magnolia picked up a pair of orange gloves from a pile on the shelf, eased out an archive box and blew dust into the pool of light. A ghostly, dumpy shape could just be made out before the dust dissipated. A ghostly, dumpy shape that was now flailing its arms and coughing.

'What did you want to do *that* for? Isn't it bad enough that you've spoiled my audit? What am I going to put in my report now? This was supposed to take *weeks*.'

Magnolia didn't apologise, presumably because she wasn't sorry. It turned out that the man had been sent to perpetrate a fraud. Using his powers of invisibility, he had accessed computers and tried to transfer funds from dormant accounts, and done various other things that had set Arabella's/Rose's alarm bells ringing.

Greville had a number of questions, but Magnolia beat him to it with one of her own.

'Are you wearing any clothes?' she demanded. The fleeting outline provided by the dust hadn't really been sufficient to give certainty one way or the other.

'Yes I am! What do you take me for?'

'I'm not sure,' she said. 'I can't see you. At the moment, you're just a strange man who follows people about and gets too close to them without them realising. You were in the office, weren't you, and you tripped me up in the cupboard.'

'I had to follow close behind, otherwise the forcefield wouldn't have let me through!' he protested.

She pursed her lips and made an unconvinced noise.

'Are there many invisible auditors?' Greville asked. The concept was fascinating. One of the biggest problems of being a *visible* auditor was that people tended to stop whatever it was that they shouldn't be doing as soon as they saw him. He would love to spend an invisible day in the post room, observing them climbing on chairs to get things from the top shelf, using the franking machine without its protective guard and pouring vodka into one of the compartments in the drinks machine so that every coffee was a white or black Russian.

'A whole planet of us,' he responded. 'But of course, we can see each other; it's only the rest of you that can't. And we're not all auditors; those who stay planetside have normal jobs. It's only those who go offworld who are mostly auditors, detectives or poltergeists.'

There came a rustling noise, and a second later a business card flipped through the air, becoming visible at the exact point that it must have left his hand. Magnolia picked it up gingerly using a tissue, as if she still strongly suspected he was naked and that the card might have been secreted somewhere it shouldn't have been. It bore the legend, 'A1 Auditors. For *in*visible results', only there was an 'in' in front of 'visible', italicised and in a different colour.

'Okay, here's what we usually do. I'll go back to base and write up my report; I'll give this lot a copy of everything I've changed so that they can put it back to how it was, then that's that. Done and dusted. Job's a good 'un.'

'All right,' said Magnolia. She dexterously managed to enshroud the card in the tissue without touching it at all, and tucked it into her organiser. There followed a long silence, during which she gazed quizzically into the middle of the cylinder of light, hands on hips, as if she'd like to probe its mysterious contents in more detail, if only a suitable implement were to hand.

'Well, I'll be off then,' said the invisible auditor, the first to reach his tolerance for the awkward silence. Magnolia had infinite capacity to ride out such silences, never really appearing to notice then, let alone be discomfited by them, whereas Greville felt them acutely, only his inability to think of something to say to break them increased in direct proportion to the length of the silence.

'Yes, run along,' she said. 'Greville and I have things to discuss.'

The light cylinder seemed to bristle, then the invisible auditor must have weighed up all possible retorts and found them pointless because he began to retreat towards the door. Magnolia waited til he was probably out of earshot.

'What do you want to do now?' she asked. 'Do you want to stay here a bit longer or do you want to go back? I was wrong about this place being a voice-activated facility – look at those things on the floor. I reckon it's a zero G. You just switch off the gravity and you float to where the box is stored.'

Greville looked up again. The ceiling was very, very high.

'What happens if someone switches it back on again while we're up there?'

Magnolia shrugged her bony shrug. 'I guess we come down a bit quicker than we went up.' She sighed. 'I suppose we'd better leave it for another time.'

They began to walk towards the exit.

'You could have run away, back through the cupboard,' she observed. 'But instead you came towards me.'

'Mmm,' said Greville. Now that he had time to think things through, he'd been mad to lead what he'd thought was a monster straight towards her. He should have distracted it. He should have tried to incapacitate it. He should have…

'You were trying to protect me,' she said.

Greville looked at the floor, heat beginning to spread across his cheeks. If she'd been a heroine in a film, it was at this point that she'd tell him tartly that she was perfectly capable of looking after herself. And that in future he wasn't to entice any compliance auditor eating monsters in her direction.

'Thank you,' she said simply. '*I'll* protect *you* next time. Or you can protect me, if you're nearer.'

They reached the cupboard exit and found the auditor's cylinder standing there waiting for them.

'Can I follow you through?' he asked. 'I can't get out by myself.'

This time, it was Greville's turn to be tripped as they returned to the brightness of the office.

Chapter 10

The journey back to the office was uneventful, and they returned to find the office empty, apart from Mr Valentine, who was contemplating the ceiling, and Arabella/Rose. The cat, Rose, was asleep in the in-tray, and Arabella was counting stitches. At their entrance, the cat opened one eye, then the other, and something seemed to pass between Rose and Arabella. Suddenly, the old lady seemed less benevolent, while the cat seemed more contented, snuggling itself comfortably on the folded-up scarf and beginning to purr.

'You sorted it out,' said Rose, who was now the old lady. It was a statement, not a question. 'I realised it was a PI stress-test about five minutes after you'd left, but I couldn't call you because of the time difference. They're too far behind there.'

She turned back to her knitting, beginning to count again exactly where she'd left off, only this time more briskly and two stitches at a time.

'You're back,' said Mr Valentine, still looking upwards. 'Go and do lunch, then when you get back, we're going to go orienteering. Not the sort with maps – the other sort.' He licked his lips with a reptilian flick. 'You have to work out where you're going, without using a map – although of course there *is* a map. But it doesn't always work.'

Greville hesitated, waiting to see if any further elucidation would be forthcoming.

'Well, hurry up, then,' Mr Valentine urged. 'Do lunch! Time abates for no man, you know.'

Magnolia made the most expressive snort that she thought she could get away with, treading on the very edge of insubordination.

'Well, *I'm* going running,' she said, and went to collect her vast flowery bag.

'Can I come?' Greville squeaked hastily. It wasn't at all what he'd meant to say; he'd brought his running things with him that morning, and had practised utterances for this very occasion, hoping that it might arise. He had intended to say something casual, such as, 'mind if I join you?' delivered with mild indifference, but her pace was a notch up from purposeful, and if he'd waited to sort out his words, he might have missed the opportunity completely.

'It's a free country,' she said, and continued on her way.

This was an encouraging improvement on 'Do what you want'.

'I'll see you in the corridor in five,' she added, just before the door swung shut behind her.

They found their way out into the sunshine, and Greville was going to remark on how much brighter it was out here than in the dustiness of the disused reception area, but when he turned back to look at the blue door, it had gone.

'I expect it will come back when we need it,' Magnolia said, following the line of his gaze. 'Do you want to go around the park? We've probably got time to do the loop past the factories.'

Without waiting for agreement, she sprang off, darting across the pelican crossing which had just turned to green. Greville sighed and made to go after her. He seemed to spend a lot of time one way or another chasing after her receding back.

He made it safely over the pelican crossing while the green man was still flashing. She was well ahead, about to swing through the gates into the park. Greville wondered whether he could keep up with her. He usually liked to trundle along at a comfortable speed, but experience had shown that he could be quite speedy if pursued by little dogs or similar. He sped up a notch and then another notch. His stride was a lot longer than hers due to his greater height; even so, he had to push himself to catch her, and it was an effort to pull alongside and then stay there.

'Why…do you always…run off…without….waiting?' he managed, only having enough breath either to speak or to keep up, but not both.

She gave him a quizzical look, no less penetrating for being delivered at speed.

'To avoid awkward conversation?' she said. 'But I can't be going fast enough because it isn't working.'

They ran along in silence for a while, on her side from choice and on his from compulsion because he was trying to muster enough breath to attempt further speech.

'But…how do you…know…that…it would…'

'It would be,' she told him. 'It always is with me. I'm not very good at conversation for the sake of it.'

Greville digested this. It was actually convenient being out of breath as it gave him time to think.

'It always…is with…me too,' he admitted.

This was absolutely true. If Greville came across someone who had an interest – any interest – then he could quite happily chat away, for hours if necessary, learning about the intricacies of repairing old clocks or the fun which could be had

Morris dancing or, indeed, the main tenets of the Sarbanes Oxley audit act. But if he was sitting with a group of people in a pub, who were talking about nothing in particular, he simply couldn't work out to join in. The conversation ebbed and flowed, yet didn't seem to be *about* anything.

'Well, why don't you run by yourself, then?' she asked.

He was growing more familiar with the nuances in her tone, and judged that she was asking a genuine question rather than requesting that he left her alone.

I get…fed up…with being…by myself,' he managed. 'Don't you?'

'I'm used to it. It's just how things are. No-one ever wants to talk to me, so I don't want to talk to them.'

Greville felt the inevitable sickness which came from over-exertion beginning to steal over him, and he had no choice but to drop to a walk, which was probably propitious because he was feeling over-stretched with the conversation as well. Predictably, she carried on ahead, her wiry limbs tireless and her heavy plait bouncing. As he watched, she pulled up, and he thought for a moment that she was injured, then she turned and jogged back towards him.

'We'll walk for a bit,' she directed, 'just until you get your breath back. But if you want to run with me, you'll have to learn to go a bit faster.'

She gave him a sharp, appraising look. 'Have you been working out?'

'Well, yes, a bit, that is to say…'

'It suits you,' she said, cutting across his embarrassment. 'Keep it up.'

They carried on walking up the path. Greville had a slight stitch, and was trying to pretend that he didn't.

'So, how *are* you?' she asked. 'The whole Poppy thing. Are you okay? I've been meaning to ask, but I wasn't sure whether to.'

He stole a glance at her. She was keeping her gaze fixed ahead, and there was a spot of pink colour high on her check that somehow didn't seem to have come from running.

'I'm all right,' he said, honestly. 'It's almost a relief. No more walking around on eggshells trying not to say the wrong thing, no more being criticised all the time. And I can't really be lonely with Satan around.'

The house certainly didn't feel quiet or empty as the enormous black and tan creature seemed to fill every inch of it with his galumphing, tail wagging and insistence on following Greville about wherever he went. Even if Greville was doing something mundane, like filling the dishwasher, Satan would follow him from counter to dishwasher and back. If they'd had a particularly long walk or ball-throwing session, the dog might retire to his bed, but he would still follow Greville's every move with his eyes, like a tennis spectator.

'Do you think…I mean, would you…are you planning on…'

She was still very determinedly not looking at him.

'Are you planning on staying single, or do you think…'

'Well, I'll be single,' Greville said, surprised. 'I don't think that relationships suit me. There's too much to get wrong.'

'But the right person wouldn't get hung up on stupid stuff,' she persisted. 'The right person ought to appreciate you for what you are.'

'Do you think so?' Greville said, doubtfully. It seemed to him that the market for red-haired compliance auditors who thought that maths problems were fun and who enjoyed pottering about with housework and DIY was a very limited one.

'Well, I think…' she began, then her tone change abruptly. 'I think we ought to start running again,' she said, and set off with a jerky start. For the rest of their run, she kept the pace slow enough that he could keep up, and fast enough to make it unwise to try to converse, and when they arrived back at the blue door (which had reappeared), he was drenched with sweat and his lungs hurt, whereas she looked as fresh as when they'd first set out. She regarded him dispassionately.

'Same time tomorrow,' she suggested, and although she was unsmiling, there was an inquisitive arch to her eyebrow. 'Work permitting.'

****

'Aha, it's you two!' Mr Valentine exclaimed as soon as he saw them. 'Come on – hurry up! We need to do the orienteering. We should have done it yesterday, but the days weren't running the right way. We'll do it in there.'

He pointed to the new mirror image part of the office.

'Then we can check that the room's working properly. Get a move on – the sooner we get finished, the sooner we start.'

Greville regarded the division between the original and new parts of the room, which fell on the seam of the carpet. It was impossible to tell whether the invisible barrier was still there, and so he took the safer option of balling a tissue and throwing it in. The tissue passed unimpeded, and so Greville stepped through as well. Five of the eight desks in the new half of the room, which had appeared empty from the far side of the barrier, were inhabited – one by a man who looked well over a hundred years old, one by a lady with two heads, one by a cyclone of glitter much like Mr Valentine in his natural form, one by a man who could have been an accountant and who kept sighing and checking his watch and one by a sphere of fire like a gym ball-sized sun, which bobbed and rotated over the desk. Greville went to sit in one of the empty seats.

'Oy! Find your own desk! *I'm* sitting here,' said an angry voice. 'Am I invisible or something?'

Greville cautiously tried another empty desk and sat down without being challenged, and Magnolia took the last empty place.

'Right then, we're all here,' said Mr Valentine. 'The Human Rejects department says (and he glared in the direction of the glitter cyclone) that we have to do a session to make sure that everyone knows who they are and what they're doing and who everyone else is, and what *they're* doing, and *where* they are, and *where* everyone else is, and where they *ought* to be, which isn't always the same thing as where they *are*, and what they *ought* to be doing, which isn't always the same as what they *are* doing, and…and…'

He consulted one of his pieces of paper, which always looked as if they'd been in his pockets for rather a long time, his mouth moving as he read.

'No…no…that's about it. They specifically said that we're not to do *why*, because that can get rather involved. It's best to avoid the whys if you can, as a general principle, otherwise you can get so bogged down that you don't have time for the wheres and the oughts, which are really more important.'

He pulled up an imaginary projector screen which solidified into existence, and at a gesture from a laser pointer, a three dimensional map appeared of a solar system - only there were too many planets, the dotted lines representing their orbits were very strange shapes and none of the planetary bodies had familiar sizes and dimensions.

'This first bit's easy enough – where we all are,' he continued. 'You're here,' he said, addressing himself to the gently bobbing sun and pointing to the sun on the diagram. A gesture from the laser pointer replaced the solar system with another equally strange one. He peered at the fourth planet and enlarged it, then pointed south of the equator.

'You're here,' he told the old man, 'And you're here,' he informed the two-headed lady, indicating the seventh planet. Another unfamiliar galaxy replaced the last one. 'You two are here,' he said to Greville and Magnolia, pointing to a large planet with rings around it, 'And you're…'

'No we're not,' Magnolia said. 'That's not Earth. It's not even the third planet.'

'Yes it is. It's just a matter of perspective – viewpoint if you will. You're looking at it from your own viewpoint, which isn't necessarily the right one. All your sort are very centred around your own point of view, which I can't say is a good thing. Anyway, you're…'

'None of them are where you're saying they are, because all of them are *here*,' she continued. 'Look! They're all in this room.'

'Of course they're not!' he said, his face beginning to flush purple. 'They're *there*, but they just look as if they're here. Because if they really *were* here, then that would pretty much use up the expenses budget for the year, wouldn't it? Now then, *you're* here, and...'

It was pointless to argue, so she didn't, and soon he had explained where everyone was.

'There,' he said, clasping his plump hands together in satisfaction. 'So now we all know where we are.'

The cyclone of glitter seemed to sparkle more brightly, and he frowned at it, his complexion darkening.

'Well, apparently that's not good enough. I need to be more precise.' He went around the room again in the same order. 'You're in payroll, you're in the assassination department, you're in marketing, you two are in the office police, you're in the training department, you're in the augury department and you're in Human Remains.'

The glitter flared up again.

'All right, non-denominational and non-discriminatory remains.'

Magnolia raised her hand and spoke without waiting to be asked.

'How can a sun work in payroll?'

'Because we're an equal opportunities employer,' Mr Valentine said smartly. 'And you want to be careful what you say, or you'll find yourself on the wrong side of a diversity education course.'

He glowered at her, and she glowered back, but she didn't say anything else as no-one wants to find themselves on a diversity education course, or, indeed, any of the HR-run courses such as Life and Death Coaching, Stress Development or Business Anger Skills for Personal Growth.

Deciding that she had been suitably quelled, he waved his laser pointer, and an image of a Displacer appeared on the screen.

'These are the Displacers,' he said. 'You can use them to get from A to E.'

'A to B?' suggested Greville, trying to be helpful.

'No, no, no, no, no, not to B! You must *never* take a Displacer to B because that's not far enough for it to be economically viable. You mustn't use them unless you're at least going as far as E, and preferably further.'

A wave of the pointer, and the image shifted to the inside of the Displacer.

To use them, you ask them if they're working correctly, and if they are, you think about where you want to go and they'll take you there. Probably.'

There was an accompanying list of things that were not to be attempted while using a Displacer, which included eating, drinking, reproducing by binary fission, exploding, going nova or making personal calls using company equipment.

'Is that clear?' he asked, looking round at the group. 'Right. Good. Very well.

As you were.' And he turned to go.

'Hang on,' said Greville. 'We need to know more than that.'

'Not all at once, you don't,' he said. 'Some of you have very small brains, you know. I'm supposed to dribble feed all this sort of stuff.'

'Well, can't you tell us something we don't already know?'

It seemed desperately unfair that Mr Valentine had decided to expound upon the one thing that he and Magnolia had already worked out, given that the choice of unknowns was virtually limitless – although to be fair, they hadn't known about the prohibition on binary fission or going nova.

'I could….' said Mr Valentine, 'but then you'd have to tell me everything you *do* know first, and I'm not interested in hearing all of that. Class dismissed.' And he wandered back to the familiar side of the office.

The sun winked out, the glitter being span itself into invisibility and the other participants simply vanished (although it was impossible to tell what the invisible man had done; he might have lingered on so that he could sit undisturbed for a while and then lie to his manager that it had been a *really* long course), leaving Greville and Magnolia to go back to their desks.

Chapter 11

Mr Valentine was consulting one of his pieces of paper, which he was holding upside down.

'You two,' he said. 'You need to go and do some pitching at new clients. The forks are in the cupboard.'

He smelt the paper very thoroughly in a dog-like manner, then ate it.

'The forks are in the cupboard?' Greville repeated. He'd meant to ask an insightful question, the answer to which might shed some light on the whole matter, only the part of his brain that dealt with the abstract seemed to be napping. Either that or it was exhausted by the constant flow of random and semi-sensible information.

'The forks for the *pitching*,' Mr Valentine said, more slowly and loudly. 'You *have* to use forks. Not knives though; all sorts of things can go wrong if you use knives.' And he shook his head solemnly as if in recollection of a new-client-related bloodbath.

'No, the pitch forks aren't for that,' one of the Cuthberts said. 'They're only for use if the animals come back. Pitchforks are nothing to do with pitching.'

Etymologically speaking, Greville wasn't at all sure that this was correct; from his point of view, the lexicological link was quite clear.

'You need to tell the new clients what we do,' Mr Valentine elaborated, displeased that he was having to explain himself further.

'But *we* don't know what we do,' Magnolia pointed out.

'Well, you jolly well should do,' he told her, beginning to tower. The purpling face and growth in stature and width were an indication that the rage was beginning to build.

Myhill tore himself away from a file that he had been auditing, a process which had involved a lot of huffing and sighing and the application of many colour-coded page markers.

'They don't need to *pitch*,' he said, applying another page marker and drawing a careful asterix on it. 'They just need to go and watch, to learn what to do. And I shouldn't even be telling you that. They're not our employees any more. None of you are.'

'But what about the forks?' Mr Valentine persisted. 'How is any pitching going to get done without the forks?'

'We don't pitch physical things *at* clients, only ideas and concepts,' Arabella/Rose put in. 'Not unless they pitch things at us first. Remember all that business with the dimension clash that the PI insurers wouldn't cover, with the tangled timeline so it happened *before* the insurance was renewed? We wouldn't have got out of that one alive without a bit of pitching.'

'It put the fire insurance premium up a bit,' Myhill recalled. 'And we had to do a stationery cupboard audit of flammable and incendiary materials.'

Mr Valentine was properly towering now, his eyes bottomless black holes that seemed as if they could suck in souls, his teeth beginning to sharpen and his nails growing longer and more yellow.

'GO NEXT DOOR…NOW!' he commanded, and although his voice wasn't particularly loud, the bass rumble resonated throughout the whole room and vibrated within Greville's body, as if he was standing on an unsafe bridge while a heavy lorry crossed. It felt as if an increased volume could shatter every cell in his being. He fled, and was grateful when the closing of the door cut off the dreadful, core splitting tremors.

'Who rattled *his* cage?' Magnolia said, close behind him. Greville knew that she was accustomed to standing her ground and arguing her case, and it sat ill with her to give way to someone employing a tactic as crude as shouting. Usually shouting had no effect on her whatsoever – she didn't get flustered or red in the face and she certainly didn't get angry herself. Once her adversary had vented their spleen, she would simply carry on from exactly the point that she'd reached before they'd started bellowing. But of course, the noise made by Mr Valentine hadn't been ordinary shouting; it had been a visceral, powerful threat, the aftershocks of which still thrummed deep inside him.

Technically, it had been she who had provoked him, but rather than saying as much, Greville went to peer into the room next door. If it turned out to be a Thousand Room or a toilet block, he wasn't sure he would dare to face Mr Valentine again to ask for further directions. Happily, today, it was one of the gym-sized rooms, set up in a conventional fashion with a projector hanging from the ceiling and some chairs arranged in a semicircle. Two suited individuals were doing something with packs of papers that were probably sales brochures judging from their size and colour. Even the sight of a sales brochure triggered a Pavlovian desire in Greville for a red pen.

They went in, and the man and the woman looked up.

'Oh, you're the newbies,' said the woman. 'Sit over there. Don't move. Don't talk. Don't breathe. We don't want you messing this up.'

The man thrust brochure packs at them.

'You might as well have these,' he said, not sounding particularly pleased about it. 'But I want them back afterwards, so don't scribble on them or eat them.'

'What's this meeting about?' Magnolia asked. The woman gave her a look as if Magnolia was something she'd trodden in, and Magnolia returned the look in full measure. Greville thought that there wasn't the slightest difference between the two looks, only Magnolia's had the advantage of being magnified by her enormous glasses. The woman gave way first.

'Why don't you know?' she snapped.

'Because you haven't told us yet,' Magnolia returned, and Greville was awed and at the same time oddly thrilled by her cold, calm confidence.

It seemed that the staring match would resume, but the man stepped in.

'The company that owns this building is called Interplant Outsourcing,' he said. 'They want to appoint independent auditors to guide one of their administration areas through the ZZ402/118 accreditation process. Valentine & Accomplices is pitching for the business, as are several other companies. Now, go and sit down. They will be here at any minute.'

They went to sit towards the back, and Greville opened the brochure pack, on the one hand eager to learn more about what Valentine & Accomplices actually did and on the other, rather afraid of the compliance transgressions that would doubtless have been committed. Although perhaps in this strange environment, barefaced lies were perfectly acceptable – even expected – and after all, Greville had not been asked to review the material, so its degree of mendacity and the lack of regulation-compliant wording was therefore not his problem.

The door opened again, and some ordinary-looking people in suits came in, arranging themselves in the front few rows. They had the air of condescending impatience that people seemed to magically absorb as they made their way upwards through the rank and file.

'Shall we get on with it?' said one of them, and the man and the woman went into action. It was fascinating stuff. Greville discovered that there were actually several thousand 'Accomplices', spread throughout multiple universes and dimensions, who carried out independent audits and certifications in all sorts of areas. Accounting audits, investigations into financial crime, process accreditation…if it was an audit or compliance activity, Valentine & Accomplices had it covered, and if the presenters were to be believed, they had it covered competently and in a manner which complied with all sorts of standards which Greville had never heard of.

The suits asked a few questions to do with timescales and pricing structure, and had a more searching discussion relating to the track record of the personnel who would be carrying out the task, then the most senior suits shook hands with the presenters, who gathered up their things and left.

'Should we go too?' Greville wondered aloud. He had already got more from the meeting than he'd been hoping for; it was very grounding to learn a little more about his employer.

'No,' said Magnolia. 'I feel like sitting here for a bit. If we go back to the office, we'll only be given something else to, and I've done enough for today. Let's stay.'

They waited, and just as the suits were becoming impatient, a chattering bunch of insect people came scuttling in, antennae waving angrily and front legs flailing. Greville put his earpiece in.

'...*told* you that we should have left earlier. And who's brought the slides?'

'Not me! Don't look at me like that! No-one said I had to bring the slides. That's *your* job.'

'So no-one's brought the slides?'

'*I've* brought them, but it wasn't my job, because...'

Eventually the insect people managed to organise themselves coherently and gave their presentation, the gist of which was that they would be all over the department like ants[18] and would get the accreditation in no time at all by dint of teamwork. At this point, the effect was rather spoiled when one insect person said something that another disagreed with, they divided into opposing sides and a furious fight ensued, multi-jointed legs raining ineffective blows onto shiny brown carapaces. The fight made its way into the corridor and the door shut behind them.

Magnolia caught Greville's eye, hand over her mouth to suppress a smile. She looked completely different when she was smiling, even with her mouth hidden... younger and less fierce.

'Did you see the one with the laser pointer trying to bite the other one with the clipboard?' she said. 'I thought they were going to...'

The door opened again, and Greville expected that the beetle people were going to make a precipitous reappearance. Instead, it was the next round of presentees – a red haired woman in an unflatteringly tight navy suit and another woman with mousy hair who was wearing a beige trouser suit and carrying a briefcase.

'Greville?' Magnolia repeated, aware that she had lost his attention. 'I said that I thought they were going to...'

---

18   Not the bad sort of ants who bit people and spent all day getting high on sugar water, they were at pains to point out; they were like the good sort who did useful things like cutting up leaves and carrying them about.

As she spoke, she was following the line of his gaze to see what he was looking at. The mousy haired woman looked up at the same time, and she too tailed off whatever she had been saying to her companion as her eyes locked with Greville's. Her expression was first surprise, then disbelief, and she said something else to the other woman, who looked up at Greville too.

'That's Poppy,' Greville said, suddenly winded. It was so strange to see her in front of him, *here* of all places. After so many weeks apart, it was like looking at a stranger instead of an ex-nearly-fiancée.

Magnolia's mouth pursed tightly.

'I don't know why you wasted so much time on her,' she said. 'She's not even pretty.'

Greville wanted to say something sharp back; it was disappointing to hear her speak like that when usually Magnolia would be the first person to champion the unlovely or unloved and the last to be scathing on the basis of appearance. He didn't know whether she had any pets of her own, but when he'd idly contemplated it (there was a lot of time for idle contemplation on long runs) he had decided that she too would probably choose the dog who had been in the rescue centre for the longest, or the elderly black cat who was otherwise destined to spend the rest of his days there. However, the words lodged around his heart and could get no further.

Poppy was *here*…a bona fide member of this strange and wonderful environment. Poppy knew about Displacers, and Rooms that Time Forgot, and insect people and virtual paper. Had she just started here? Had she been here for years, before they'd even met? It was hard to reconcile her orderly, meticulous personality with this flamboyant, dangerous world where only the fleet and the flexible-minded survived. *Poppy* looking for tiny people in the midst of a foundry? *Poppy* having a manager whose natural form was an eddy of glitter, or Death himself, or indeed a sun? *Poppy* accepting colleagues who had been replicated or who shared a body with a cat?

If she was able to thrive here, then perhaps she had changed, become more open, become more *fun*…

A hard pinch on his arm brought him out of his reverie.

'You were staring,' said Magnolia.

She was right, of course, and even as he stared, Poppy made a remark to her companion, who looked up at Greville and said something in reply.

'Ouch – that hurt,' he complained, somewhat belatedly. Magnolia muttered something that could have been, 'So did that', but he barely heard her.

The pitch started, and its essence was that their company, PBS Limited (Professional Business Services) could do everything that Valentine & Accomplices could do, but more efficiently and with fewer entries in the accident register and a guarantee that there would be no new rifts in the space-time continuum. There were lots of slick statistics and graphs and bullet points, all disseminated with brisk efficiency. Hands were shaken all round, Poppy gave Greville a lingering glance which he struggled to interpret, and then she and the other woman departed.

Greville's tidy mind had been thrown into a disorder; Poppy's unexpected appearance had pulled out and upended all his mental drawers. He'd more or less succeeded in filing her away in a folder marked 'exes', and even if the drawer hadn't altogether been slammed shut, it would only have taken a small nudge to finish the job. Now the file was open on his mental desk again, like a pended insurance claim where the claimant has finally decided to send in the required documentation after a protracted pause while they have been weighing up the bother of looking for them against the lure of potentially getting some cash.

He turned to Magnolia, hoping to make use of her recent camaraderie to talk through the situation, but her face was unexpectedly tight and closed and he had the feeling that anything he said would provoke a scathing remark. Before he could decide whether he dared to proceed regardless, the next presenters entered, or rather, they were trying to enter as either they were too large or the doorway was too small.

Greville found that he was staring again, but this time for different reasons. It looked as if a green, translucent inflatable sofa, or maybe an inflatable slug, only sectioned like a worm, was trying to squeeze itself into the room. One of the panel (unused to having to lift a finger himself) got up reluctantly and unlatched the other of the double doors, which sped up ingress. In fact, it sped up ingress a bit too much as deprived of its impediments, the thing oozed forward, and somehow its rescuer ended up inside it. The man's mouth was open and he was trying to scream, but the thing's gelatinous body mass captured all sound.

'Come on; we're leaving,' Magnolia commanded, getting up.

'But I want to see this!' Greville said. The man was flailing as if in slow motion to free himself; the thing's consistency evidently being closer to that of translucent jelly rather than air. Another member of the panel was looking on, wondering whether to put in an arm and seeming to decide against it, and a second creature was trying to get through the doorway.

'Well, *I'm* going,' she said. 'You do what you want.'

'Thanks; I will,' he said automatically, his mind on the scene that was playing out in front of him.

It was fascinating; the creature's eyes appeared to be scattered throughout its body like football-sized cherries in a room-sized cake, looking in different directions and swivelling slowly and independently; and in a captivating and rather revolting way, everything that it had consumed was visible in various states of digestion. He switched his earpiece on.

'…I think I've trodden in something,' said the lead creature, its eyes looking around rather aimlessly. 'Something squishy. Poo…I can smell it.'

'Is there any food?' said the second creature. 'I missed lunch.'

'Hey! Get out of my way!' said a third creature, as yet unseen. 'Don't eat all the lunch! *I* want some lunch!'

'So, I'm going,' said Magnolia, making him jump as she was still close behind him when he'd thought that she'd gone.

'Okay,' he said. 'I'll see you later.'

Even so, she lingered another second or two before making a huffy noise and stalking off. There was another door at the back of the room, the one at the front currently having its hands full dealing with two battling creatures trying to enter at the same time, and she left via that one. Logically the door at the back should open into the office, but there was no corresponding doorway there, so it would probably release her into the corridor.

Someone had evidently pressed some sort of panic button as help had arrived in the form a janitorial team, although what good a mop and bucket and a 'caution: wet floor' sign would be to the trapped and possibly soon to be digested man was unclear. As the crisis was outside the compliance team's jurisdiction, Greville felt entitled to settle down and prepare to watch.

Chapter 12

When Greville got back to the office, Myhill was still reviewing the same file, all three Cuthberts were also doing file reviews, only at less of a glacial speed, Arabella/Rose was knitting and Rose/Arabella was playing very idly with the wool. Mr Valentine was in his office bellowing down the phone at someone, only he was wielding it in front of him with both hands. The thick glass deadened the sound very effectively, but it couldn't deaden the purple face or the yawning, sharp toothed mouth. As soon as he saw Greville, he put the phone down mid-sentence upside down on its cradle, and came out.

'You!' he said, pointing at him. 'Come here! Now!'

Greville edged over. Myhill looked up, happily anticipating trouble, marking his place in the file with a pudgy finger.

'They've decided to do a competition,' Mr Valentine continued. 'Between us and some of the others. They're going to give us a small task to do, and whoever wins, gets the contract.'

'Should have gone to sealed bids,' Myhill said. 'That's the most important thing. Otherwise you might try really hard with the task just to *win* the contract, but then not work very hard once you've *got* the contract.' He spoke with the authority born of being something of an expert in not working very hard.

'It was you lot who insisted on this,' Mr Valentine said, glowering. His glower did actually glow…even though his face was a normal face, it somehow had the black and red cracked appearance of cooling lava where the black outer crust did not quite conceal the roiling red fury beneath.

'Yes, because *you* lot aren't to be trusted,' Myhill continued, oblivious to the danger. 'You steal staff. You mess about with people's office space. You don't put people's hole punches back when you've borrowed them. So I wouldn't put it past you to cut corners as well.'

Steam was gently rising from Mr Valentine's head and where it hit the ceiling, it left an oily mark. Greville took a step back because it was like standing face-scorchingly close to a bonfire, then another step.

'THE TEST STARTS TOMORROW,' he bellowed in Greville's direction, his voice a bubbling roar of hot air. 'DON'T BE LATE.'

Greville hesitated, unsure whether he had only been given information or whether he was being dismissed.

'GOOOOOOOOOOOOO....!' Mr Valentine added, and so Greville went to his desk, shut down his computer, grabbed his bag and hurried away.

It was barely three o'clock, and it felt deliciously naughty to be driving home so early in the day. It occurred to him that he hadn't said goodbye to Magnolia, but she hadn't appeared to be in a very good mood and maybe it was for the best that he'd been spared any more awkward encounters.

He stopped at the village shop on his way home. It was a curious place, built in the days before spirit levels and building regulations, the overhanging wooden-beamed first floor and gravity defying angles giving the impression that it was held up by magic and belonged in a fairy tale. When Greville had first moved to this location and needed to buy supplies to top up his weekly shop, he'd assumed that it would only be good for the basics such as tea and toilet cleaner. However, he had yet to require anything that the shop didn't stock – he had successfully sourced a new red pen, some semolina flour and a tin of lychees, and he had come to trust it to meet his needs.

Today, he bought some interesting-looking marmalade (the brands found in the shop never seemed to be sold elsewhere), a magazine on weight training and a new ball for Satan. The dog didn't exactly require a new ball because the existing one was proving durable, but every new toy was met with such raptures of delight that it was fun to indulge him.

'You're early today, Greville,' said Mrs Drew, who ran the shop. She had the disquieting air of *knowing* everything; one would have expected her to be a gossip, but if she ever passed on information, Greville never heard her do so.

'My boss said I could go early,' he said. Somehow she always made him feel as if he ought to explain himself.

She eyed his purchases.

'No eggs or furniture polish, then?'

Greville thought back. He *hadn't* wanted any eggs, until this morning, when he'd made an omelette for breakfast and had foolishly left it unattended while looking for his shoes, so had had to make another one. Still, at least Satan was big enough to jump up and eat the omelette directly from the plate rather than pulling it onto the floor, so it had saved him clearing up a broken plate. And only the night before, he'd noticed that his can of furniture polish was getting rather light.

Once upon a time, he would have classified Mrs Drew's omniscience as a Very Strange Thing, but now it was just a pleasant convenience that prevented extra return visits to the shop. She took his lack of protest as consent and went to fetch the extra items.

Satan was beside himself with joy to see Greville home so early, and even more pleased (if that was possible) with the ball. Today, Greville had remembered to shut the door to the hall, so the dog had continued his egg-themed mischief streak by fetching the empty egg box from the recycling shelf and shredding it very finely before lying on top of the pieces.

'What shall we do?' Greville asked him, intent on getting the eggs safely to the cupboard before they were wagged or frolicked out of his hand. 'Do you think it's too hot to…?'

It was best not to say the word 'walk' unless he had definite plans to go on one. Even this half-finished sentence was enough for Satan to freeze mid-bounce and mid-wag, fixing his gaze hopefully on Greville's face. It was still warm, but there was a slight breeze, and just enough cloud to stop the sun's heat from being too intense.

Greville thought it through. If they went on a walk now, it would give him a very long evening in which to entertain himself. But on the other hand, if he just pottered about until their usual walk time, it seemed a criminal waste of some un-expected free hours. He didn't really have a lot with which to occupy himself. The house was already clean and tidy. He had planned to put some washing on so that he could get it on the line before he left for work the next day, which would give him some ironing to do on the following evening. It wasn't a weight training night – the magazines that he had read on the subject were of the opinion that three days' training a week was plenty, or he would risk 'over-training'. Apparently muscles grew best when they were rested on alternate days. He supposed that he could always use up the last of the old can of furniture polish, but…

A spitting, burbling noise interrupted his thoughts, so unexpected that it took him a few seconds to place it. The noise cut off abruptly, and soon afterwards, a heavy car door slammed. Satan took off through the open back door. If he was excited over Greville's homecoming and ecstatic over a new ball, there wasn't even a word for the extent of the dog's delight over visitors. Greville hurried out after Satan, and found him bounding around Magnolia, although he noted that the dog seemed to realise that it would be wise to maintain a distance of about two feet.

'Sit!' she said, and Satan did his quivering sit-hover, which was the best that could be expected under the circumstances. She held out a solemn hand, and the dog equally solemnly put an enormous paw into her palm, which she shook.

'Pleased to meet you. Good boy. Off you go,' she said, and Satan erupted into an ecstasy of leaps before running circles on the lawn at top speed.

'He gets a bit excited over visitors,' Greville said, somewhat unnecessarily.

'H'mm,' she said, watching as the dog ran. For such a big, heavy creature, he was surprisingly fleet of foot.

He assumed that she had come to impart some information about the following morning's assignment, although he noticed that she'd been home to change and was now wearing well-worn, soft looking three quarter length jeans that hung slightly loose on her slender frame, a fuchsia t-shirt and grey trainers with fuchsia trim.

'I just came to see what you were doing,' she told him, continuing to look at the dog and not at him. Satan had executed a complicated skipping movement and was now circling the other way.

'I was going to take Satan out for a walk,' Greville said. He paused expectantly, still waiting for her to tell him whatever it was that he needed to know about work.

'Can I come?' she asked.

'If you want,' he said, surprised. 'But didn't you want to tell me something about tomorrow?'

'No,' she said. 'Because if I'd wanted to tell you something, I'd have done it by now, wouldn't I?'

She was right. She'd have delivered her message and would already be roaring back the way she'd come.

'Okay, let's go on a walk,' he said hastily, not wanting to seem unwelcoming. 'I'll get his lead.'

Satan's lead was part chain and part leather, and the dog could discern the clank of the chain no matter where he was or what he was doing, and by the time Greville had fetched it, the dog was already at the back door. He put the lead on so that they could make their way safely down the lane.

'We'll go through the woods,' he decided. This would be shadier and cooler for Satan than some of the other routes. Magnolia fell into step beside him.

'What are you doing later, then?' she asked.

Greville hesitated to tell her anything that involved furniture polish, laundry or puzzles in compliance magazines, but he couldn't actually think of a more interesting sounding lie. What *did* people do all evening if it wasn't an exercise night and there were no pressing chores?

'Nothing much,' he said, flushing.

'Do you want to get a pizza?'

He shot her a puzzled glance.

'A pizza?' she repeated. 'You phone up the shop and tell them what sort of pizza you want, then they bring it for you? And sometimes it's even similar to the pizza you asked for?'

She misinterpreted his astonished silence as concern over the pragmatics of the situation.

'Do they deliver out this far?'

'I don't know,' he admitted, lamely. 'I've never tried… I mean…'

'*How* long have you lived here, Grev? It must be a few months now. You've lived here a few months and you've never tried to order a pizza? What's *wrong* with you?'

Her tone was amused rather than unkind, and when he stole a glance at her, her impassivity had twitched towards the mischievous.

'I usually cook from scratch,' he said, aware that he was sounding starchy and superior, although he didn't mean to. 'That is to say, I…errr….I…' It would sound even worse to admit that he sometimes ate a ready meal for one if he didn't feel like cooking. 'I think that a pizza restaurant sent a menu a few weeks ago,' he said instead, 'so perhaps they deliver?'

'Well, we'll find out when we get back,' she suggested. 'That is, if you want to?'

'Yes, yes, let's get a pizza.'

'Unless you'd rather make us a Timbal de tártare de aguacate from scratch?'

She was looking mischievous again.

'No, no, pizza's fine.' If he thought about the implications of spending the evening with her – all that empty space to fill with conversation – he would simply freeze, so he forced himself to stop thinking about it and instead concentrate only on the moment at hand.

'Are you any good at cooking?' he asked, before he could over-think it and snarl up his vocal cords.

She shrugged. 'I get by,' she said. 'I can do the basic stuff.'

And as easily as that, they fell into conversation. It was a lot more fun walking with her than alone. She invented all sorts of things to do – balancing along fallen logs, climbing a big rock outcrop, looking for mushrooms. The walk took longer and was less of a route march than usual, and Greville learned a lot more about her and her family, such as that both her parents were scientists, and that her younger sister was a dentist. The further they walked, the more her dry sense of humour came to the fore and her brusqueness diminished, and she was laughing and joking by the time they arrived back at the cottage.

'Let's get that pizza,' she said, and Greville went to find the menu. While he did so, Satan licked his water bowl dry and Magnolia refilled it for him unasked, then the dog went to find a shady bit of the patio to lie on. It had been purely on a whim that Greville had tucked the menu into a drawer rather than putting it straight into the recycling. At the time, keeping it felt as if he was somehow bracketing himself with the sort of people who had lots of friends and who ordered pizzas with gay abandon, rather than the sort of people who ate ready meals for one.

She took the menu and scanned through it.

'What about the vegetarian supreme?' she asked. 'Do you fancy sharing a large one? Do you want some coke? And what about dessert? Do you want to order or shall I?'

In the end, Greville ordered, taking curious pleasure from doing something so out of the ordinary. Magnolia asked if he had any beer and he got them a bottle each, and they went to sit neat Satan on the patio. She had declined a glass, drinking straight from the bottle and grimacing at the coldness and the dry taste.

'Nothing tastes better after a long walk,' she said, leaning back in her chair and taking in the view. She seemed content to gaze out across the countryside, and Greville took the opportunity to enjoy looking at her. Her bone structure really was exquisite – delicate and angular, and he guessed that even when she grew old, far older than her aunt Margaret, she would still be beautiful. She turned to say something to him, and he quickly reined in his stare.

The pizza arrived, and they ate it out of the box on the patio, washing it down with cola and feeding the crusts to Satan. They had ordered two desserts so that they could try half each of two different ones, and Magnolia took charge of dividing them, making sure that they were split very scrupulously in half. All too soon, the food was gone and she was looking at her outsize divers' watch which was far too big for her thin wrist, but which somehow looked right on it. It was nearly half past seven.

'Do you want to watch a film?' she asked, which wasn't at all what he was expecting; in fact, he only just stopped himself from replying 'Yes, see you tomorrow' in response to the wrongly anticipated valediction.

'A film?' he repeated, stupidly. 'But we've got work tomorrow.'

She rolled her eyes at him.

'I said, watch a film, not go clubbing til six in the morning,' she said. 'What's the matter? Does it say in your contract that you're not allowed to have any fun in the week, on pain of death?'

It wouldn't surprise Greville if his contract *did* say something like that – after all, it was several inches thick, and the ink turned invisible outside of the office environment, so for the first and hopefully the last time in his life, he'd signed something without reading it. But for now he would hope that it didn't.

'Okay then,' he said. 'Let's watch a film.'

They went into the cottage, and he fed Satan, who then trailed them into the living room and arranged himself across Greville's feet. They found a film to watch that involved a renegade cop, time travel and lots of wild action. The sofa was a two-seater meaning that they were on separate cushions, and there was no elegant way of nudging closer, and in any case Greville's feet were securely pinned by Satan's solid weight. There was nothing to do but enjoy the film.

It was dark when he walked her to her car after the film had finished. She turned to face him, and suddenly it was another moment where anything could happen yet nothing would…only this time she stepped forward and hugged him firmly, her cheek pressed flat against his chest.

'Thank you for a great evening,' she said into his shirt. 'I'll see you tomorrow.'

She released him quickly, got into her car before he had recovered the power of speech, gunned the mighty engine and drove away. He watched until her tail lights disappeared and then wandered back into the house, the big dog at his heels. What had just happened? He could still feel her strong, bony arms around him, and her cheek on his chest.

He pottered about tidying up. He hadn't done anything that he'd planned on doing that evening, yet it felt as if he'd accomplished a great deal. Even as he showered and got ready for bed, her hug lingered on. Head spinning as if he'd had much more to drink than a single beer, he went to bed and tried to sleep.

Chapter 13

The journey to work was uneventful, except that the corridor in the basement had acquired another door. This one bore the legend, 'NEVER enter. Never, never, never, never under any circumstances. Never.' Then a second very tiny sign said, 'Oh all right then, just this once'.

He found that he was humming cheerily as he went, and had to stop himself three times. He didn't want anyone to ask him what he was so happy about; in fact, he wasn't completely sure himself. The night before already seemed to have been a dream – a very lovely dream.

When he reached the office, Mr Valentine was already there, and was examining a stack of post. He held up each envelope in turn, peering at it as if he could divine the contents by some sort of super-sight, then smelling at it with the inquisitive snuffling of a dog before either throwing it in the direction of his desk or biting off a corner and then hurling it into the bin. He looked up when Greville came in, fixing him with the bottomless stare that seemed to see to the very bottom of his soul. Today the dreadful examination seemed to last for longer than usual, and Mr Valentine's countenance seemed to colour itself a shade darker, and it was a relief when the man eventually looked away and ate another envelope.

Greville sat down at his desk and logged on, only realising that he was humming again when it registered that Myhill was watching him curiously, breakfast pastry poised half way to his mouth. Greville stopped humming, and the pastry continued its journey.

Today, the computer would not allow him to get any further until he'd filled in a questionnaire regarding how he would like his assets to be distributed in the event of his demise. This was entirely usual; there was normally a life assurance benefit of a multiple of salary to be shared out amongst one's dependents. What was less usual was to be required to specify this depending on how exactly he had come to meet his maker. He was pondering why on Earth he would want to settle his affairs differently if he'd been "decapitated (accidentally)" as opposed to having "exhausted" his "life essence" when Magnolia came in.

This morning, she was wearing an ankle length black cotton dress, cut to fit but with the habitual looseness that suited her, a matching black jacket and racing green low-heeled shoes with a bow. She had coiled the magnificent, heavy hair into a bun, which held in place with a piece of matching dark green fabric. The whole effect was breath-taking, yet she seemed utterly heedless, sitting down and logging on without so much as a glance in his direction. Mr Valentine paused in his gnawing of a fat brown envelope to subject her to the same suspicious scrutiny, and she ignored him absolutely.

'Right, you two,' he said, marching to a point that was equidistant between their two desks and looking from one to the other. '"The client" has decided that they want to go to a full ordeal, so we'll be kicking off this morning.'

He put energetic finger quotations around 'the client', envelope contents in danger of spilling out, and treated Myhill to a glare as he did so.

'Well, it's going to be a long-term thing,' Myhill said, comfortably. 'So we've got to make sure that we select the right people and don't just employ any old idiots.'

Mr Valentine scowled, sensing that there was an insult in there somewhere but not quite certain of what it was.

'Anyway, it's you two, the beetles, the jelly people, and…'

'Gelapegos,' Myhill interrupted rather crumb-sprayingly, around his pastry. 'They're called Gelapegos because they're from Gelapagos.'

'Are they? Okay then, it's between you two, the beetles, the jelly-pagos and the other lot that look like you but aren't.'

Poppy's firm. They were up against Poppy's firm. Greville felt a tightness in his chest that he really didn't want to be there. He became aware of Mr Valentine's disquieting, coal-black eyes boring into him as if he was looking inside his head, and not liking what he saw there.

'There's a link between them,' Mr Valentine pronounced. 'This one and one from the other lot. I can *see* it. I can *smell* it.' He sniffed the air. 'Yes, a definite link.' He pointed two fingers at Greville, a sharp-nailed gun which somehow seemed to be more than a childish gesture. 'Don't let the other lot win! I'll *know* if you do, and…' He shook his head very slowly from side to side, chin tucked in, which made his stare all the more intense, and he made a rumbling, jagged teeth-baring growl like Satan's only deeper. Indeed, it was like looking into the face of a fierce dog that was just about to attack, and Greville couldn't help but back away.

'Not for much longer,' said Myhill easily, and Greville was too unsettled by the enraged countenance glowering into his even to wonder what he meant.

'So you have to report to the Great Hall today for the first challenge,' Mr Valentine continued, snapping back to his normal (or if not quite normal, then usual) demeanour. The only remaining evidence of his threatening behaviour – except it had been more than a threat as threats often had the ring of emptiness whereas this had had been ominously foreboding - was a slight reddening above the collar.

'Why us?' asked Magnolia, unmoved by the display of aggression. 'We didn't do the pitch. Why can't the business development team do it?'

'Because they're busy doing something else' he said. 'And you're virtually the same as them, anyway.' He pursed his lips and sighed up at the ceiling. 'Except you're all unique individuals who bring something different and exclusive to the table', he added, in the tones of someone who had been coached to say something that he didn't really understand, let alone mean.

Myhill finished his pastry and wiped his fingers on his trousers.

'It's a ten thousand year contract,' he said. 'So we're probably going to want you to do something really hard, like a year-long quest or a duel or something.'

'But if you award the contract on the basis of our performance, how do you know that the people who are going to be carrying out the other nine thousand, nine hundred and ninety-odd years are going to be as good as us?' Magnolia asked.

'Because you're all the same! Apart from being unique and different,' Mr Valentine said. 'You haven't evolved *that* much in the last ten thousand years, have you? I mean, you've still got two arms and two legs. You haven't evolved to have an extra head, have you? Although goodness knows that most of you could do with one. You're still essentially human beans, aren't you?'

'Beings,' Magnolia corrected. Mr Valentine frowned at her enquiringly.

'Human *beings*,' she repeated. 'Not beans.'

'No, no, no, no, that's not right. You're *beans*. There are all sorts of beans, aren't there? Baked beans, green beans, blue beans, kidney beans, and *human* beans.'

'Beans are edible seeds, often kidney shaped, which grow in long pods,' supplied a Cuthbert without looking up.

'There!' said Mr Valentine, in triumph. '*You've* got kidneys! *You're* edible. Kidney pie, yumyumyum.'

'You two are runner beans,' Myhill said slyly. 'You go running about at lunch times, don't you?'

'The term is "human *beings*",' Magnolia insisted, coldly unamused.

'They're more human *fruit*', observed the other male Cuthbert. 'Because they contain seeds, if you peel them and pull them open.'

'Human fruit….human fruit…human fruit full of seeds. Yes, I think that will do,' Mr Valentine decided. 'Because you grow if you're planted, don't you, or is that the other sort?'

'We're human *beings*,' Magnolia repeated. 'We're…'

'What's this "being" then?' he asked, beginning to become belligerent. 'It doesn't make sense.'

It wasn't easy to think of how to start such a definition, and the female Cuthbert got there first.

'It's the present participle of the verb "to be",' she supplied, a typical Cuthbert answer inasmuch as it was both perfectly correct and at the same time utterly unhelpful. Oddly, Mr Valentine latched onto her reply with no difficulty at all.

'Present participle…h'mm. I suppose you only really participate in the present as your lives are over in a flash. Beforehand, you're inside *another* human fruit, and afterwards, you're…dust, or mush, or gas. Now, what are you still doing here? You should be participating in the present in the Great Hall! Run along, human fruit!'

Magnolia's face was pinched with disapproval, her mouth pressed into a thin line, but instead of arguing, she picked up her notepad, pens and the quarter-sized clipboard and headed out. Greville gave up on deciding who he wanted to get his life assurance if he was "dissolved (acid)" or "dissolved (alkaline)" and followed her.

'Where's the Great Hall today, please?' she said to the pad.

The untidy handwriting began to scrawl across the page, and they read it as it unfolded.

'Where do you WANT it to be?'

She drew in a breath, intending to huff it impatiently out again to make her feelings about riddling pads quite clear, but then she changed her mind.

'Right opposite, please,' she said.

A spidery arrow appeared, pointing to the opposite door. Greville peered through the glass. If it wasn't *the* Great Hall, it was definitely *a* Great Hall, and it wasn't a Thousand Room, either, which was most important.

'Thank you,' she said, and the pad drew what would have been a cheery smiley face if it hadn't had such long, sharp teeth, and a certain evilness about the eyes, and which instead looked distinctly ominous. Or perhaps it was just that the pad's drawing was no better than its handwriting.

The Great Hall was not misnamed; it was very similar to the room in which Greville had done his very first interview, proportioned like a school gym with a row of wide but shallow windows very high up and wooden climbing bars on the walls. Only it was as if someone had grabbed the corners of the room and stretched them outwards, until it was very, very big indeed. It was raining very hard outside the hall, torrents of water lashing down, and the slice of sky that was visible was purple.

In the middle of the room sat a metal box - a living room sized, smooth cornered object made of something chrome-like. An ordinary desk had been placed near the box, at which sat a neat little man, who was probably in his late thirties and who was wearing a grey suit and matching tie.

'Hello,' said Greville. 'We're here for the… the…' He didn't quite want to use Mr Valentine's word of 'ordeal', yet was struggling to think of a better one. His previous business vocabulary often seemed too straitened for this environment. 'Tender process', he managed.

'You mean "the ordeal",' said the man. He volunteered nothing further, regarding them both expectantly as if that should be more than enough information.

'What do we have to do?' Magnolia asked.

'I can't tell you *that*!' the man said. 'The rules of the ordeal are quite clear.'

A few months ago, Greville would have felt completely at a loss if deprived of a properly scoped project plan, with the objectives, key stages and sub-stages carefully laid out, and properly approved and authorised by the appropriate person or persons. Now he merely turned his attention to the problem at hand.

They walked all the way around the object; it was a rectangle with smooth, round corners and no door. As they walked, the man watched them impassively.

'We must need to get inside it,' Magnolia said. 'There's nothing else we can do with it.'

Greville threw a balled-up tissue at the metal box and it bounced off as it would with any ordinary object. There was no force field flare and no odd deflections, so he reached cautiously towards it, tensed for a shock, but his fingers met only cold, smooth metal. Encouraged, he began to feel all over the box, inch by inch, and she did the same on the other side. They didn't find any concealed openings.

'Perhaps there's a door on the top?' she suggested. She helped him pull the gym bars over, fastening them to the floor as remembered from long ago PE lessons, then looked crossly down at her shoes and long skirt.

'I'll go,' said Greville, and climbed the bars. They seemed closer together than he remembered from school, and he kept trying to put his foot on bars that weren't where he'd thought. He looked down on the top, which was as smooth and shiny as the rest of the box.

'Nothing,' he said. 'Unless it's hidden?'

He scrambled on top of the box, the metal cold and hard and slippery under his knees and hands, and inched his way along cautiously and methodically until he'd covered the whole area. From his vantage point, he could see that the man in the grey suit was making notes. When Greville stopped moving, he stopped writing, watching with motionless detachment, and when Greville began moving again, he began to write. Greville stopped and started a few times, just for the amusement of watching the man do the same. He climbed back down.

'Nothing there.'

It occurred to him to check his skymail account, and he was rewarded with a neat stack of notes. The top one was from Mr Valentine, and said, 'Do Not Mess This Up,' with the word 'mess' heavily underlined, which threw rather an unsettling cast on the whole message. The one underneath was something completely incomprehensible about pay dates being realigned in accordance with some trick of the space-time continuum, the upshot being that they would still be paid on the same day, except for existential purposes it would now effectively be a completely different day, and a reminder that he hadn't completed his life assurance form. Finding nothing useful, he stuffed all the messages back in.

He glanced towards the door, wondering when the others in the tender process would be putting in an appearance, or more specifically, when one person in particular might show up. Magnolia caught the direction of his gaze and correctly interpreted its purpose.

'She won't be coming,' she told him, a distinct dash of tartness in her tone. 'They'll have their own metal box things in their own Great Halls. Otherwise they might copy us, mightn't they?'

The man in the grey suit was scribbling down their exchange, and looked up expectantly when he'd finished. He really was a very fast writer. She said something in French, too fast for Greville to catch more than the odd word, and the man transcribed it with no effort at all.

'H'mmph,' she said, annoyed. 'Come on – let's go.'

She stalked towards the door, Greville following on, and the man trailed after them, giving Greville a sense of how irritating it was to have someone perpetually at one's heels. He sped up until he was beside Magnolia instead of behind her.

'Where are we going?' he asked.

'The Archives,' she said. 'I think we'll have to dice with Death.'

Dr Death ran the company's archive storage. Greville had met him once before and wasn't over-keen on repeating the experience.

'Why? Do we need to look something up?' The library was so vast that it was entirely possible that somewhere it would contain instructions on how to get into impenetrable metal boxes. Greville would rather not come face to face, or was it face to skull, with Dr Death, but he quite liked looking things up, and perhaps they wouldn't run into him at all.

'Not exactly.'

'What, then?'

'I just think he might be able to help us.'

'How?'

'It's the quickest way,' she said. 'Or do you *want* this to turn into a year-long quest?'

He was at a loss to explain her sudden frostiness, and was sorely tempted to explore further, but he didn't like to do so with their companion poised to write down every word. They went into the corridor and waited in silence for the lift. The man's pen began to scratch again. Greville craned his neck. 'This silence is awkward,' the man wrote, recording Greville's thoughts precisely. Even as Greville watched, he wrote, 'Oh no, that man's writing down my thoughts!' followed by,' Oh no, I'd better not think about anything embarrassing, like…'

The image that was about to enter Greville's head was the most fleeting glance of the bottom centimetre of white cotton bra when Magnolia had carelessly pulled up her T-shirt weeks ago to show him a martial arts injury.

'Do you want to go running at lunchtime?' he asked Magnolia suddenly, anxious for the man to switch to writing down what he said rather than what he thought. To Greville's relief, the man did just that.

'Not today,' she said. 'I'm going to Arabella's after work and we're going to practise martial arts. You can come if you like.'

Not martial arts. *Anything* but martial arts, which summoned again the very image that he was trying to suppress.

The man's pen was poised expectantly, and now it twitched dangerously.

'I haven't done martial arts before,' he blurted, trying to camouflage his thoughts with speech.

'Well, that's the whole point of practising. To get better. No-one's *born* good.'

Greville hesitated. If the man with the pencil hadn't been there, he'd have made an excuse as there was nothing appealing about embarrassing himself in front of two colleagues – or indeed, three, depending on whether one counted Arabella/Rose as separate individuals. But somehow, it seemed that a white lie would be worse if recorded for posterity by the little man. And of course he had the compulsion to *say* something to avoid his inappropriate thoughts being written down. There was something deeply dishonourable about that particular thought, even though he was desperately trying not to think it.

All right,' he said, and the man raised a sardonic eyebrow before scribbling down the words.

'Okay – I'll pick you up at seven.'

The lift came to a halt and the doors opened onto the bricked up car park. The green door was in the opposite wall, and even as they watched, it began to move from left to right. They chased after it, their companion falling behind as he was trying to write as he ran, and they dived through the door into the perpetual night of the archives. Magnolia slammed the door shut behind them, and it continued to slide along the wall, disappearing around the corner and then winking out altogether when it moved behind a shelf. A shadowy, hooded figure was sitting at the desk, pen in hand, carrying out paperwork, although when they drew closer, they could see that it was in fact filling in a Sudoku puzzle.

'What quest brings you to my umbrous realm, from which the unwary never return?' intoned Dr Death in his most ominous voice, his diamond teeth sparking in the gloom. 'Are you prepared for trials, the likes of which…'

He broke off when he recognised Magnolia, pushing back his hood and revealing the skull underneath.

'What brings you to my shady kingdom, fair princess?' he enquired. 'Have you come to join me as my consort in everlasting darkness?'

'No,' she said. 'I've come to ask a favour. Do you still have the Key to Everything?'

Dr Death laid a flesh-stripped hand across his ribcage, splaying the bony fingers wide.

'It's the key to everything except your heart,' he lamented. 'It will open everything but that, which is a tragedy, because that's the one thing that I would *die* to open.'

'Can I borrow it?' she asked, appearing unmoved, except that there was a certain tightness in her voice.

Dr Death's face assumed a calculating expression, if that was even possible for a bare skull with empty sockets where the eyes had once been. He scraped dry fingertips against his bony chin while he considered her request.

'What's it worth?' he asked. 'What will you do for it? One favour deserves another, after all. A kiss? Would the lady give a kiss?'

Greville didn't know whether to intervene. It wasn't lost on him that Magnolia was upset, and probably more upset than she was letting on. But he was reluctant to plunge in, in case she preferred to fight her own battles especially as he didn't understand the history between the two of them.

'*I'll* give you a kiss,' he said, the words coming out in an odd, forceful voice before he even knew he was going to say them. He strode forward, seized Dr Death's hard, bony shoulders and planted a kiss on an arid, cold cheekbone.

'There. Now can we have the key, please?'

Dr Death angrily scrubbed the kiss away, the noise of bone on bone an unpleasant scraping, while Magnolia looked on, astonished.

'How dare you,' he said. 'How DARE you? HOW…'

'How dare *you* infringe the 'Dignity at Work' policy," said Greville equably. Anyone who had come face to face with Mr Valentine's volcanic rages would hardly be impressed with the rantings of a mere skeleton. 'Perhaps you'd like to go on a 'Dignity Awareness course?'

Dr Death began to splutter, but subsided, as did most people when threatened with a course.

'All right, then, you can borrow the key. But only this once. And you have to bring it straight back.'

He turned to a safe that sat under his desk, and after much clacking of bones and dials, produced they key. Considering that it was the Key to Everything, it wasn't very impressive. It was small and rusty, and reminded Greville of the key to his first bike lock, back in the day when a token padlock was thought adequate to deter bike thieves.

Greville took the key from him.

'Thank you,' he said.

After all, good manners cost nothing. He noticed that the green door was still doing lazy laps of the building, and that the man in the grey suit - their invigilator - had not yet managed to catch up with them. Every fibre of his being was screaming at him to terminate the encounter with Dr Death, quitting while they were ahead, but his sudden and unexpected boldness seemed to have propelled him into a heady world where he was temporarily immune from the fear of rubbing people up the wrong way. Even people who were already quite annoyed. Even people who were already quite annoyed and who literally had the power of death at their fingertips.

'Is there a way to get back to the Great Hall without going through the car park?' he enquired, before he could think better of it.

'That depends,' Dr Death said. 'On whether you've got the nerve for it. I'd say you haven't.'

He regarded them craftily. Greville thought it through. On the one hand, he was familiar with reverse psychology, and suspected that he was being tricked into doing something dangerous. After the danger had happened, Death would simply be able to say that he and Magnolia had *chosen* to do it, and that it was their own stupid fault. On the other hand, he really did want to elude the invigilator as it was evident that once the man had run out of words to record, he moved smoothly onto thoughts, and who wants their thoughts recorded for posterity?

'We've got the nerve for it,' he said, speaking for both of them, reasoning that whatever his own level of nerve and determination not to look wet in front of Dr Death, Magnolia's own feelings on the matter would be even stronger.

Dr Death shrugged, a clatter that sounded like a stick being run along a set of railings.

'All right. On your own heads be it.' He gave Magnolia a look that was perhaps intended to be wanton but instead was somewhat chilling. 'Maybe you'll be the queen of my realm sooner than you think.' He set off through the shadows, his cloak swirling behind him, and Greville observed that if he himself ever wanted to stride along dramatically, then it would be best done cape-free because it rather spoiled the effect when one had to exercise a certain degree of caution not to step on one's own hem.

It was somehow inevitable that they would end up in the room which was used for the secure destruction of the boxes of files which had reached their expiry date as designated by the appropriate legislation. Greville had only been in the room once before. The 'Abandon Hope' notice was still on the door, and the hole in the foot-deep concrete floor was still there, surrounded by a safety rail. Far, far beneath roared a fire so hot that it could be a conduit straight to the molten core of the Earth or to the very depths of Hell.

'Here we are,' he said. 'I'll just set the co-ordinates and you can pop straight in.'

There was a desk in the corner with a computer terminal, and he grabbed the mouse, clicking about busily, and sounding even busier because the bony clacks which ensued made every single click a double one, and every double a quadruple.

'There. Just jump in. It will take you straight to where you need to go, and warm you up as well.'

Greville thought hard and fast. When Dr Death said, 'where you need to go', did he mean that they both needed to be sent straight to Hell, or could the utterance be taken at face value? Would he dare to kill them both? Greville knew for a fact that there was some sort of policy on not murdering colleagues (it was considered wasteful as it put up the life assurance premiums that the company paid for everyone else, and incurred unnecessary recruitment consultancy fees) and indeed there was a corrective course which 42 people had attended in the last quarter. He'd assumed that the course was preventative, rather than rehabilitative, and that people got sent on it if there had been a near miss rather than after the fact, but...

He hadn't finished thinking when Magnolia vaulted over the railings and disappeared into the bottomless chasm. Without hesitation, he flung himself after her, but lacking her easy grace, he caught his ankle on the railings and tumbled head first towards the devastating heat.

Chapter 14

It was like riding a flume built inside an oven. If he'd been asked five seconds ago to name the hottest place he'd ever been, Greville would have said the offworld foundry without any hesitation, but this scorching rollercoaster made the foundry seem positively cool and temperate. He thought that he could feel his skin blistering as he slid along, and every breath seemed to sear his lungs. It was simply impossible to survive another second without desiccating altogether, as vampires did when exposed to light. Surely this was the end…

…and then suddenly he was back in the Great Hall, landing on an invisible cushion of hot air which broke his fall very comfortably, and then deflated slowly, depositing him on the floor with barely a bump. Even the concrete beneath him had been warmed by the blast, and he moved away to a cooler patch and struggled to his feet.

'Wow,' he said.

Magnolia had removed her enormous spectacles and was using a corner of her jacket to polish off the steam and Greville paused to do the same. She was still looking rather out of sorts.

'What's the story with you and Dr Death, then?' Greville enquired. She looked away from him, colouring.

'I don't want to talk about it,' she told him.

Greville felt it incumbent on him to keep the conversation going, although he really wasn't very good at this type of thing.

'You might not *want* to talk about it, but maybe you *need* to?' he offered tentatively, remembering something that he'd read in one of Poppy's magazines. He had read her magazines religiously and surreptitiously, in the hope that he could learn how women's minds worked. Disappointingly, they tended to repeat the same three topics over and over again – How To Improve Your Man, How To Claw Your Way Up At Work and How To Lose That Stubborn Last Seven Pounds. He'd read them anyway, determined to learn how he could be A Hero (the best type of boyfriend) and not A Zero (the type of boyfriend who needed to be 'kicked to the kerb'), but never really becoming any better at it.

Magnolia's eyes honed in on his, her gaze hardly less ferocious than Mr Valentine's, and Greville had the uncomfortable feeling that she was looking right through him, and that she realised that he was just quoting from a magazine article. Or maybe she was only checking that he wasn't making fun of her as she looked away again, and continued.

'It was a few months before you joined,' she told him. 'A bad day. I'd been stuck in the stairwell for ages because it was slipping, so I had to climb four thousand stairs to go up one floor, then Mr Valentine yelled at me for being late, then the spreadsheet I was working on set on fire because I forgot to refresh the damper field.'

She glanced at his face to verify that he wasn't laughing.

'So was really late when I'd finished reconfiguring it, and I was pretty much the last person left in the building. All I wanted to do was go home, and then when I got out to the car park, I was so desperate to go that I accidentally locked my keys in the boot.'

Greville could imagine the scene. The Mustang was solid and old fashioned, and had no electronics that could be easily tricked. It would have been a job for the breakdown services.

'I didn't think there was anyone else about,' she said, 'so I was…I was…you know…crying. And then *he* came along and saw me.'

She looked at him defiantly.

'I wouldn't have done it if I'd known anyone was there. But I didn't know. I honestly didn't know. But he saw me, and he wanted to know what was wrong, and then he opened the boot with his magic key. And I was just so grateful.'

'So you…so he…' Greville began, feeling somehow irritated, and disappointed, although he couldn't have said precisely why, or with whom.

'So now he thinks he *knows* me,' Magnolia said. 'Because he saw me like that. He thinks he knows what I'm like. But that's *not* what I'm like…it's not what I'm like at all.'

Greville wanted to ask if she'd kissed him. He wanted to ask very badly indeed, not least because he didn't think he'd like the answer, but a deeper instinct was telling him to ask anything but that. She mistook the reason for his censure.

'I bet *you've* cried sometimes, when you didn't think anyone was looking,' she said, suddenly fierce. 'And I didn't mean to! It just happened!'

'Mmm,' said Greville, hedging his bets as he was not sure whether it was more appropriate to admit or deny having cried.

'And now every time he sees me, it's as if he's *laughing* at me. Or as if he's entitled to *flirt* with me.'

'I'll punch him for you if you want,' he said, surprising himself, and then even more surprised to discover that he actually meant it. Magnolia was looking equally astonished.

'Really?' she asked, and for a long second he wondered whether going Neanderthal had been the wrong thing to do, but then she smiled. 'Well, perhaps wait til tomorrow after Arabella/Rose and I have trained you up a bit, then you could make a better job of it. Now, what did you do with that key?'

Luckily, the trauma of the searing rollercoaster ride had caused Greville to grip the key so tightly that it was imprinted deeply into his palm rather than drop it, and he handed it over. She held it against the cool, polished surface of the metal box.

'Open! I command you, open!' she intoned, and a door-shaped seam appeared in the smooth chrome, and a section slid forward and then sideways, allowing them access to the interior. The inside was as smooth as the outside, and held a desk with several fat paper files, and they took half each, leaving the Great Hall to find somewhere to work undisturbed. Greville looked about for the invigilator.

'Where could we go where *he* wouldn't find us?' he wondered aloud. He didn't need to tell her which 'he' he was referring to.

'The library,' she said at once. 'You can't get in there unless you're authorised.'

Greville opened his mouth to ask a question, and was too slow.

'Of *course* we're authorised, Greville,' she told him. 'We're Compliance. We can access all areas. We just need to find the entrance.'

It sounded like the sort of thing that might be easier said than done, but she led him confidently to a door that was labelled as a fire exit and which contained nothing more interesting than a flight of grey, utilitarian stairs. There was a notice on the wall that said, 'No Running! No Ball Games! No Smoking! No Plotting!' They descended as far as the next landing down, and Magnolia tugged on the handrail, causing a section of wall to swing open. Inside lay a cross between a cathedral and a library, with shelf after shelf of leather-bound tomes reaching upwards towards an exquisitely painted, vaulted ceiling. The floor was an intricate and awesome tile mosaic; the roof was held up with stone pillars and touches of gilt were everywhere.

'There,' she said, pointing to an empty desk, made of oak darkened with age. 'We'll sit over there.'

The surroundings were intimidatingly grand.

'Are we allowed to?' he asked, his voice echoing in the vast space.

'We're Compliance. We can do what we want. The only rule is…'

Greville flinched. She was going to say, '…that there *are* no rules', and then he was going to spend the rest of the day pondering whether the fact that there was a rule that there *were* no rules meant that there *was* a rule, or whether it was the exception that proved the rule (he was uneasy with this; there were no exceptions to rules, ever, although sometimes there was a case for an exemption or a sub-clause), or whether it could be got around by careful drafting, for example by saying that there were no rules *except for this one*, or whether…

'…that you're not allowed to throw books,' she finished. 'There's a sign.'

She pointed, and there was indeed a sign depicting someone throwing a book, which had lodged rather bloodily (and somewhat improbably, Greville thought) in someone else's head. A censorious red circle and diagonal line had been superimposed to leave the reader in no doubt that this behaviour was prohibited.

'If you want to throw books, you have to go into the next section.'

He thought that she was joking, but he could just make out another sign in a similar vein, and went over for a closer look. This time there was no red circle or diagonal line, and both the thrower and the person with the book lodged in their head were smiling and giving a thumbs up.

There were some things that it simply wasn't worth trying to get to the bottom of, and even the most superficial consideration told Greville that this was one of them. Instead, he carried his half of the files over to the indicated desk and sat down.

'Do you want some lunch first?' she said.

Now that she'd mentioned it, Greville was quite hungry, but he wasn't sure that he wanted to run the risk of being found by the invigilator by venturing down to the canteen.

'We'll order some,' she decided. She went over to a dumb waiter built into a wall, scrawled the word 'menu' onto a page from her pad and lowered the rope, and when she pulled it up again a minute later, the note had been replaced by a menu from the canteen. It turned out that all they had to do was write on the menu how many they wanted of each item and send the order back down, and another minute later, they had their lunch.

Eventually, she put the empty plates and mugs back onto the dumb waiter and they turned their attention to the files. They were lovely fat files, and to Greville's trained eye, they were pension files, which were the very worst if you wanted to hold onto a rose-tinted view of administrators being paragons of virtue and the best if you wanted to compile an equally fat file of transgressions in no time at all. He contentedly went to open the battered orange cardboard cover of the first file. Here was something he knew how to do…something he could do well. Something safe. Something…

'DON'T OPEN THAT FILE!' Magnolia yelled, making him jump and reflexively yank the file fully open. A sooty cloud swirled out, forming the loose sem-blance of a man armed with a sword. Even as Greville watched, the man divided and regrew, so that there were two men, then four, all advancing with their curved swords hacking in front of them.

'Quickly!' she said, running into the 'book-throwing allowed' section, and Greville ran after her. Magnolia had seized some books and was hurling them at the men, who were following steadily but with a dreadful resolve. Greville picked up some books as well, and hesitated. There was something utterly *wrong* about throwing books, especially these beautiful, leather-bound, hand-tooled volumes.

'Throw them!' Magnolia exhorted, launching books fast and furiously, and after sending a brief but fervent apology for what he was about to do, he joined in. They retreated slowly, throwing as they went. The men's outlines were dark and hazy, but there was nothing hazy about their murderous intent, and their sword edges caught the light in a very real way. They reached a long shelf of encyclopaediae (Greville had time to note with approval that it was properly spelt; it pained him to see it spelled 'encyclopediae' or worse still, the wince-inducing 'encyclopedias') and had thrown around half of them when suddenly the men stopped coming for them, placing their swords point downwards and resting their hands on the pommel. The man in the lead was wagging a stern finger at Magnolia as they dissipated into the air and were gone.

'What just happened?' Greville managed to say. He looked around at the denuded shelves and the lifeless corpses of the books.

'The files were password protected,' she told him crossly. 'Didn't you smell it? I tried to warn you.'

She was already picking up books and he began to help her. To his relief, the books' metal corners had protected them from sustaining too much damage from the ignominious treatment to which they had been subjected.

'Why did they stop?'

The books had seemed to pass harmlessly through the men rather than doing them any injury.

'Because we hit on the password,' she said, loading encyclopaediae back onto the shelf. 'You know how you can set a computer to crack a password? Well, it works in the same way. If a book goes through them, their software compares all the words in the book with the password, and if there's a match, they stop.'

'What happens if you *don't* get a match?'

She straightened up.

'Well, you get hacked up, don't you? And you jolly well deserve it too, if you're the sort of idiot who goes around opening files without smelling them first.'

They finished putting books away and went back to the desk.

'Don't touch that file! *Smell* it!' she reminded. He did as she said, feeling extremely foolish.

'It smells of vanilla?' he ventured.

'That's right. So that means it's password-protected and if you open it when you don't have the password, those men will be back to defend it.'

'So…how do we get the password?'

She rolled her eyes.

'Well, the book that did the trick was the encyclopaedia index, L to Z, so why don't you have a flick though it and see if anything jumps out at you?'

Greville let her tone ride, assuming that it was the unexpected shock of being nearly hacked to death that had caused her abruptness. He thought about it. Presumably, obtaining the password was part of the challenge? He wandered towards the encyclopaediae again, for want of anything better to do, letting his mind idly tickle at the problem. It was a basic tool in the auditor's kit, approaching every problem with no fixed view on what you were going to find, only the confidence that you would know it when you saw it. When you came across something material, as Magnolia had said, it would indeed jump out at you, and…

'I think I know what the password is,' he said.

'You think, or you *know*?' she asked. 'Because given the choice, I'd rather *know* I wasn't going to get hacked to death.'

Greville retrieved Mr Valentine's note, with the word 'mess' underlined, and showed it to her.

'I reckon he's giving us a clue?' he suggested. 'Although I'm not sure that we ought to use it. It's cheating really, and he shouldn't have done it because it's contrary to the spirit of "fair competition".'

Magnolia was regarding him with a mixture of pity and impatience.

'Greville, have you actually *read* the staff manual? Do you even know what it says about 'fair competition'? It says that all is fair in love, war and competition, and that all possible ways of gaining an advantage are to be seized upon. In fact, it's an offence *not* to exploit advantages because it looks as if you're being a bit half-hearted about the whole thing. Now, go and get that encyclopaedia index as back-up and we'll give it another go.'

They readied themselves, Magnolia holding onto the orange cover but not yet peeling it back.

'Right then, as soon as they appear, I'll say the password and if that doesn't work, you throw the book.'

It didn't seem the time or the place to point out that they were standing in the non-book throwing section, so Greville didn't.

'Okay – on three.'

She opened the file, and the sooty smoke began to pour into the room.

'Mess!' said Magnolia. 'Mess, mess, mess!'

The three figures started to take shape again.

'MESS! MESS! MESS!'

It had no effect at all. The swords solidified, glinting through the smoke. Greville threw the book; it was a good throw and it passed straight through the nearest man; however, it made no difference to the advancing swordsmen.

'Run!' Magnolia advised, and once again they headed for the shelves. This time they didn't get very far; the men materialised in front of them, and when they changed direction, the smoky figures got there first, nearer and nearer every time. The swords caught the light as they were raised overhead, and Greville wasn't quite quick enough to step back from the nearest flashing blade, which grazed stingingly across his hand. The sword swung again, and he held up an arm to deflect the blow away from his neck. There was no time to think; only to parry as best he could, each impact jarringly bruising, and he could see in his peripheral vision that she was doing the same, with little more success. He was going to die right here in a cathedral-library, without getting to ask Poppy how she had made the transition to an other-world career. He wondered who would find them, and when. The building had a disused air, as if no-one ever came there. He ducked and felt a blade whirl so close to the top of his head that it must have cropped some hairs. Surely his luck would run out soon.

'Hey! Roland?' said Magnolia. 'Is that you?'

The hacking and slashing paused, as if an invisible freeze-frame button had been pressed.

'Marigold?' said one of the men, who seconds ago had been trying to run her through with his sword.

'Magnolia,' she corrected acerbically. 'What are you doing, trying to kill us?'

'We're only doing our job,' said Roland. 'These files are password protected, and protect them we shall. To the death.'

It seemed to Greville that an unhealthy number of employees at this company were obsessed with death.

'But we *said* the password,' she told him. '*I* said it. I said it six times.'

'What was it, then, if you know so much?'

'Mess.'

'No it isn't – it's "anopisthography".'

'That was last week's password,' said the man who had grazed Greville's hand

and nearly cut his head off.

Roland's nebulous face darkened, like a lowering storm cloud, or maybe like Mr Valentine transitioning to a bad mood.

'What's this week's, then?'

'Mess. Like she said.'

'So we shouldn't have…' Roland clapped a hand to his head, which made a noise like cotton wool meeting cotton wool. 'These wretched passwords! Why can't they just leave them the same instead of changing them all the while?'

'Because then everyone gets to know what they are, so they're not really passwords any more?' said the third man.

Roland sighed. 'So now we've got to file another incident report, and fill in the accident book again, and…'

'I'll tell you what,' said Magnolia. 'Why don't we do a deal? We won't report you; in return the next time this idiot here opens a file without the password, you whisper it to him before you try to kill him?'

Roland pondered. 'But we're the Guardians of the Files. We're supposed to defend them to our dying breath. This would compromise our honour.'

'I'll bring you some charcoal tomorrow,' she bargained. 'I'll put it down there, next to the card drawers.'

He hesitated just long enough to let her be in no doubt that he was calling the shots.

'All right, a five kilogram bag, and I want that proper oak lump stuff, not those supermarket briquettes.'

He held out a meaty hand, which she shook, then touched a valedictory finger to his forehead as the three dispersed into the air. Magnolia scowled at her hand, which looked as if she'd been grasping coal. Greville looked at his, which was bleeding lightly. Luckily, they had some paper napkins left over from lunch which they put to good use.

'I came across Roland on his first day,' said Magnolia, scrubbing away at her hand. She dipped the napkin in her water and tried again. 'He wasn't very good. I was in one of the Great Halls carrying out file reviews and he kept turning up every time I opened a file, whether they were password-protected or not. Then he had to keep ringing his supervisor a lot because he forgot what the password was, and then he couldn't remember how to get back, so flapped about for ages getting soot everywhere.'

'And the charcoal?' Greville asked, binding his hand with a napkin. The cut wasn't really very deep; he thought that it would probably stop bleeding fairly quickly.

'It's what he eats. He wore himself out with all the flapping, and I didn't want him sitting there watching me for the rest of the day, so I went and stole him a few lumps from the bag in Mr V's office.'

They turned to the files. It seemed rather an anticlimax to carry out an ordinary file review after having been involved in a sword fight with beings made out of soot clouds. The files contained the best efforts of a pensions department to tackle diverse member events such as transfers, divorce, death and retirement. It appeared that the species concerned was somewhat bellicose as most people's time in the pension scheme was ended by death, and surviving to retirement was such a rarity that no-one was really certain of how to do the maths. Hence the growth of the enormous files as everyone's interpretations of the calculations, good (and wrong), bad (and wrong) or mind-blowingly inventive (and spectacularly wrong) had been carefully filed for posterity.

There was the predictable litany of absent telephone notes, weak checking procedures, unexplained delays and things not being filed in date order, and before the end of the afternoon, they had put together the bones of a very comprehensive report.

'Right, we'll put these back,' said Magnolia, and they headed back towards the Great Hall. The man in the grey suit was sitting at his desk, utterly immobile, and he sprang to life when he saw them, poised to scribble. He wrote furiously as she unlocked the metal box and placed the files inside.

'How did you…how…how on Hades did you…'

She gave him a radiant smile and tapped the side of her nose, and he followed them as far as the door, writing as he went.

They did a detour via the post room, swiping in, and then Magnolia put the Key to Everything in an internal envelope, addressed it to Dr Death, and dropped it into a whirling vortex in a waste paper bin, from whence it disappeared. Then they went back to the office.

Chapter 15

The office was deserted except for Myhill, who was intent on fishing out every last crisp crumb from the very bottom of the packet, and Mr Valentine, who was typing away busily in his office, the very picture of normality…until he stopped, smelt his space bar and licked it very thoroughly.

Myhill paused, index finger keeping his place in the corner of the crisp bag.

'You two have decided to give up and call it a day, then?' he asked.

'No,' said Magnolia. 'We've solved your puzzle. All we have to do now is write up our findings.'

He scrutinised her face, trying to work out if she was lying.

'No you haven't! No you haven't! That was a really decent problem! I set it myself! You shouldn't even have found the first clue yet. And tracking down all the clues and solving them will take you at least a week! They're really hard clues. You'll never solve them, ever, so there's *no way* you've done it yet.'

Having convinced himself, he turned his attention back to his crisps. Mr Valentine emerged to see what all the noise was about.

'Can't you solve that silver box thing?' he asked. 'You've got to think *inside* it, you know. That's the thing. Think i*nside* the box.'

'It's "outside"', corrected Myhill, himself no stranger to the management book. 'Think *outside* the box.'

'Oh no,' said Mr Valentine. 'That's wrong. Because they're *already* outside the box, and they need to get *inside*. And wherever the mind goes, the carcase will follow, so if they *think* inside, then they'll *get* inside.'

'No,' said Myhill. 'Because in order to work out how to get *inside* the box, they need to think *outside* the box, because…'

'No, no, no, they can *do* their thinking outside the box because that's where they are already. They need to think *inside* the box, because otherwise they'll never get in there, will they? The time to think *outside* the box is when they're *inside*, and need to start thinking how to get back *outside*.'

'No,' said Myhill, 'That's completely wrong, because...because...'

There were simply too many layers to this philosophical onion, and he gave it up as a bad job.

'Well, you haven't solved it yet anyway – that's all there is to it,' he said, and dropped the very empty packet near his bin, fishing out a fresh one from his drawer.

'Yes, we have,' said Magnolia.

'No, you haven't,' he said.

She shrugged, bored with him and disinclined to waste any further effort on the conversation.

'Whatever. Come on, Greville – we need to get this written up.'

They used her computer as his was still insisting that he finished the life assurance form before he did anything else, and had got the basic structure of the report sketched out by the time five o'clock rolled around. Magnolia closed down the computer and picked up her gigantic floral bag.

'See you later,' she said briskly, and marched out.

When Greville got home, he submitted to Satan's customary exuberant greeting. After the initial 'sit', it was easier just to accept that five minutes of crashing about would ensue, and let the dog get it out of his system. There was only an hour and a half until Magnolia's arrival, so he had a quick shower and dressed in running things while Satan whined outside the bathroom door and tried to get his nose underneath.

'Shall we play with the ball?' he enquired, which set off another round of crashing about.

Greville threw the ball until Satan was hot and panting, then he went back into the cottage to get his paint chart and wallpaper samples, and they headed across the enormous lawn to see Mr and Mrs Dean. The cottage's main bedroom and the living room were wallpapered rather garishly, and Greville wanted to ask if he could redecorate. He had pored over several interior design magazines to get an idea of the style of décor that might suit the cottage and that Mr Dean might find inoffensive. The house that he'd shared with Poppy had been painted (at her insistence) a very beige shade of yellow throughout, and he was looking forward to trying something that was more fun.

To his relief, Mr Dean was very keen on the idea, and even insisted on giving him some money towards the materials.

'If you were thinking of getting started this weekend, we could have Satan for a bit?' he offered. 'The grandchildren are coming over on Saturday.'

There were three boys – twins and an older child - as well as two girls; robust children who were at exactly the right age that being galumphed into, knocked over and then solicitously licked was the source of great hilarity rather than tears. The dog was equally happy to join in with any sort of entertainment - games which involved the garden hose, any fun where balls were employed or even being dressed as a bride. Greville had witnessed a game whereby Satan stood still while a row of action men were arranged along his back, and on the command of 'go, boy!' he would leap about, scattering the dolls in all directions.

There were no circumstances under which the combination of joyful exuberance, flailing tail and open pots of paint would have a good outcome, and it seemed wise to remove the inevitable source of a lot of clearing up from the equation.

'That would be great,' Greville said, very sincerely, and he and Satan went back to the house together. He was just getting a glass of water (and feeling the butterflies building inside him) when he heard the noise of a car engine. Magnolia was early, and she was driving with more restraint than usual. Satan flew out to investigate, and Greville followed. However, it wasn't Magnolia at all – it was Poppy, standing backed up against the wing of her Nissan, hands held high out of biting range and a shocked expression on her face.

'Greville! Make it stop!' she ordered, trying to back up even further, but prevented from doing so by the car. Satan wasn't actually doing anything that required stopping – he was only bounding about making his curious sneezing sound. Nevertheless, Greville sighed inwardly and called the dog.

'Come here, boy.'

Satan did one or two more half-hearted bounces, then gave up, giving her a puzzled look before coming over to Greville, ducking his head down so that it rested under his hand.

'Is that thing yours?' she asked.

Greville nodded. Poppy managed a smile.

'It's…very big.'

There didn't seem to be anything else to say on the topic, so he nodded again, and they looked at each other across the driveway. It occurred to him that there was one thing he *did* want to know.

'How long have you been working offworld, then?' he asked.

'About five years,' she said.

'So you were doing it before…' he ran the dates in his head. She must have been doing it before they even met, so the whole time they'd been going out, she'd been…

'It's only been about three weeks in 'here' time,' she explained. 'I've mostly been working somewhere that has different time, so it's five years' worth of days, but only three weeks here.'

'How did they recruit you?'

'There was a poster. At work.'

This was a surprise. Poppy wasn't usually much of a one for puzzles, and had frequently expressed the opinion that they were a waste of time, effort and intelligence that could be better applied to a *real* problem and not a made-up one.

She looked as if she was building up to saying something, and Greville waited.

'About this tender process,' she said, in a tone carefully pitched to be conversational. 'How are you getting on with it?'

'So-so,' said Greville, crossing the fingers of the hand that did not contain Satan's head behind his back.

'You've solved clue three, then?'

'No,' he replied truthfully, although he still kept his fingers crossed for good measure. Technically, they *hadn't* solved clue three; from what he'd heard from Myhill, it seemed that there was a long and arduous clue trail which he and Magnolia had completely circumvented by going straight for the Key. In fact, they hadn't even got as far as locating the first clue. Poppy narrowed her eyes.

'But you've *found* clue three?' she persisted.

Suddenly, Greville lost patience with this game.

'I don't think we should discuss it. We're on opposing sides, after all. It wouldn't be right.'

She looked at him in astonishment.

'How can you *say* that, when…when…when we were nearly married?'

Abruptly, she crumpled and began to cry, great, wracking sobs that set Satan whining. The dog hated anyone being upset, and Greville had to grab his collar to stop him bounding over to her. To be fair, Greville himself hated people being upset, especially when he had probably caused it. Instead of comforting her, though, he stood and watched, feeling very ungallant but at the same time, irritated.

It took a minute or two for her to realise that the crying wasn't having the desired effect; in fact, it was having the very *un*desired effect of escalating the whining. She stopped and peered over at him, red-eyed and blotchy-faced.

'I keep going over and over it in my head, trying to work out what went wrong with us,' she said. 'Trying to think of what we…*I*…could have done differently. What I could do to get us back on track.'

Greville's heart sank. In a split second, he could see how this would play out. More tears, he would buckle, he'd move back to the tiny beige-yellow house with the tinier garden, he'd be 'allowed' to keep Satan for maybe a week or two before the hints about dirt and hair and 'not really practical' started piling up, he'd go back to the jeweller's and buy that wretched ring again, and…

'It was nothing *you* did; it was nothing *I* did – it had just run its course,' he said, dredging up something on which he'd read many variations in his years of magazine-perusing. 'We've grown apart, that's all.'

'What do you mean?'

'What I say. I've grown into the sort of person who likes dogs and lifting weights and martial arts.' The last was a bit of a stretch, but it served to illustrate his point. 'And you're the sort of person who…who…who *doesn't* like those things.'

'But…perhaps I could *learn* to like them?'

Even as she spoke, she was looking doubtfully at Satan.

'It would be easier if you just found someone who likes the same things as you,' he suggested. 'Someone who likes accounts, and being clean and sticking to a schedule.'

'But Greville…we're a team! We belong together!'

The silence lengthened, and he could think of nothing to say to fill it – or at least, nothing that was both true and gentle – and she started crying again.

'I just…miss you…so much.'

It tore his heart to see her like this, and he felt himself begin to waver.

'I'm sorry,' he said. 'I really am,' he said. 'But I don't think we belong together.' And feeling like the worst person in the world, he went back into the cottage, tugging his dog along with him. After a while, he heard a car door slam, and she drove away.

He picked up his glass of water and Satan followed, wagging his tail anxiously. Greville gave him his dinner and sat reflectively at the kitchen table while the dog ate, but he didn't have much time to ponder because the Mustang announced its presence a few minutes later, snarling onto the drive.

'No!' he said to the dog, forestalling the rush to greet the visitor. 'You've got to stay here. Good boy. Guard the house!'

Magnolia was waiting in the car, and appeared to be dressed in running kit, which was a relief as he'd wondered whether he was wearing completely the wrong thing. She was also looking out of sorts.

'What did *she* want?' she asked, forgoing the polite preliminaries.

'Nothing much,' said Greville, getting into what would have been the driver's seat if the car's steering wheel had been on the correct side. 'She wanted me to tell her how to solve the metal box. And she wanted us to go back out.'

Magnolia turned the car around, and headed down the lane.

'What did you say to her?'

'No to both.'

It sounded harsh to his own ears, and he thought that Magnolia too must have found his response somewhat unsympathetic as she shot him a surprised look.

'Really?'

'Yes,' he said, feeling more like a zero than he ever had before. 'And I made her cry.'

They drove along in silence for a minute, Magnolia concentrating on the road ahead while Greville unhappily raked over what he'd done.

'Did you *make* her cry, or did she just start crying when she wasn't getting her own way?' she asked suddenly, startling Greville out of his reverie.

'Well, I…errrr….I….that is to say…' Greville began.

'There you go, then. That wasn't proper crying; it was using tears as a weapon. People should *never* do that. The only justification for crying is if you simply can't hold it in any longer, and if you're *sure* no-one is watching.'

They drove further, the car spitting and spluttering along the winding road. Greville wanted to say something to shift the conversation away from crying, but he couldn't seem to form a coherent sentence.

'Or rather, *human fruits* should never use tears as a weapon,' she said. 'It's all right for the others.'

'Is it?' he said, puzzled.

'Oh yes. For example, those beetle people – the ones at the presentation. They cry acid and use it as a weapon, but they cry when they're angry, not sad. And the tall ones who eat nothing but toast. They cry hallucinogens, but again, only when they're angry, so you have to wear a breathing mask if you're planning a robust meeting. And the ones who hibernate for ages. When they cry, it makes a noise that shuts down your neural pathways. And…'

It turned out that there were quite a lot of species that Magnolia had come across and that he hadn't, who used various bodily secretions to their advantage, and she gave him an animated (if somewhat nauseating) run-down of some of them. The upshot was that there were certain clients with which one should not meet unless one was either made of rock, equipped with lead shielding or ambivalent about emerging with the same level of aliveness with which one went in.

His butterflies gradually subsided; usually he dreaded being alone with anyone for any length of time as he simply didn't possess the natural ease to converse appropriately and he was especially nervous about being alone with her; while he had had plenty of years to resign himself to being socially inept and had largely made his peace with it, demonstrating his ineptness in front of her was something altogether worse. But it didn't happen; he heard himself asking her questions and picking up on things she'd said as if he were someone else entirely – someone more confident – and he was sorry when they drew to a halt outside Arabella/Rose's house.

She lived in an industrial looking building on the edge of a business park (it popped into Greville's head that the surrounding wasteland looked as if it might afford rich pickings of rabbits and mice) and the cat was on the door step to greet them, tail twitching. Magnolia hoisted a sports bag out of the boot, the cat disappeared through the cat flap and they followed through the unlocked door into a neat, modern living room.

Greville was starting to regret his decision to come. He didn't really like to try new things unless he'd read up on them first, and also watched a few online videos, and he much preferred his early attempts at anything to take place in privacy. This evening's activity left all three boxes very conspicuously unticked. He felt gawky – all knees, elbows and lanky height – and his face was beginning to flush in anticipation of getting everything wrong.

Rose/Arabella emerged from the depths of the house, clad in lycra leggings and a t-shirt. Greville would have put her age at mid-60s, but her usual dowdy work apparel had been hiding the hard curves of an obsessive exerciser, and his heart sank even lower.

'Let's get started,' she said, and led the way. A large area of the ground floor had been converted into a proper gym, complete with hard, tiled floor, wall of mirrors and extensive array of equipment, some of which Greville now recognised. Beyond the weight training machines and the aerobic equipment, boxing bags hung from the ceiling, there was an area covered with matting and chillingly, a boxing ring. He tried to see if there was any blood spatter on the floor of the ring, and Magnolia noted his horrified expression.

'It's okay,' she said. 'We'll just be doing some basic stuff. You'll enjoy it.'

She put her bag down and unzipped it, pulling out two bottles of water in different flavours and offering them to him.

'Which one do you want?'

He chose, oddly touched that she'd troubled to think of him, and he also accepted a towel, hoping that its purpose wasn't the mopping up of blood. His misgivings increased further when Magnolia removed her sports watch and glasses, placing them on a tray that was expressly for that purpose. It somehow seemed to underline that this would be a serious session. She turned to him, and without the outsize glasses, she looked younger, and he could see that her eyes were a curious dove grey.

'You've got to take off all your stuff as it's safer,' she explained.

He removed his watch and glasses, feeling as if he was preparing for his own execution, and everything went slightly out of focus.

'We'll warm up by doing some skipping,' Rose/Arabella said, handing out some very professional, hard-wearing ropes. 'Now, watch me Greville.'

After a little too much skipping, they moved onto bag work (he was presented with some very musty-smelling gloves from a basket of spares), and Magnolia and Rose/Arabella took it in turns to explain to him how to hit the bag, leaving him to practise while they either hit their own bags or held the pads for each other to hit. They kept an eye on him, coming over to correct his technique, or calling out reminders such as 'elbows down' or 'swing from the hips', and it wasn't long before he graduated to joining in with the padwork.

One of them wore the pads, one hit the pads and the third watched and called out instructions or corrections – except that Rose/Arabella did Greville's coaching when it was his turn to stand and watch. The emphasis was on technique rather than raw power, and soon Greville found that he was actually having fun. He had rather expected that both women would mercilessly attack him, fully exploiting their superior skills, but instead they were relentlessly encouraging, Magnolia with humour and Rose/Arabella with a little more acerbity. He noted that when the cat was in charge, Rose/Arabella's movements were faster and more agile, and when it wasn't, there was more power and intent.

He was beginning to tire when they paused for a water break. Magnolia took her gloves off, mopped her face and drank from her bottle.

'Do you want to try some stick?' she asked.

'Errr…' he said.

To start with, he wasn't sure what 'stick' was. Was it a type of hardcore sports snack? Or was it something that they might want to hit him with? And he felt that he really didn't want to try anything else this evening, but was struggling to think of how to explain this without looking wet.

'Come on – it will be fun.'

Before he could demur, she picked up some broom handles which had been wrapped in foam and duct tape and handed one to him.

'This is easy. It's the same as the stuff you've already done, but with a stick. I'll show you.'

He regarded the stick uneasily. He'd done a bit of fencing at university, although he'd had to give up after less than a term because the maths club had moved its meetings to the same day. He'd never got more proficient than pretty hopeless, and he'd only persisted as long as he had because a girl he liked from his course had said something about finding fencers rather dashing. The activity had chiefly seemed to consist of getting poked in the eye with the blunt practise spoils, and apologising to people for causing accidental injury.

Magnolia demonstrated a few moves, letting him try them haltingly one at a time while Arabella/Rose nudged his limbs into a more correct position using the back of a boxing gloved hand. Then she showed him how to block the same moves.

'Right then, I'll attack like this…' and she moved her stick very slowly and deliberately, '…and you try to block.'

They worked like that for a few minutes, her attacking with slow precision and him blocking and feeling stupid, awkward and self-conscious, then they swapped roles. When she swung for him (and her swings were exaggeratedly careful) Greville had to get his stick into the right place to fend her off. There was something primeval about swinging the stick…about knowing how to attack and defend, and suddenly he was beaming, not caring how he looked, putting his heart into the movements instead of feeling embarrassed. This…this was something that he was meant to do.

Rose/Arabella glanced up at the clock.

'Right, we'll have to stop there. I've got a class coming at eight thirty.'

Magnolia relieved him of his stick and put them both back with the others.

'Are you sure you don't want to stay for the class, Mags?'

She pulled a face.

'No. Maybe another time. See you tomorrow.'

They gathered up their things and left, just as a batch of students started filing in. Greville was extremely glad that she was driving because from the second that he sat down, he felt every last atom of energy had evaporated from his body.

'You could have stayed for the class if you'd wanted,' he said. 'I wouldn't have minded waiting.'

This wasn't quite a lie; although he was exhausted, there was something compelling about the idea of watching her in action, and working at a more advanced level.

'They're a bit testosterone-fuelled,' she told him. 'And you never know who you're going to get as a partner. I prefer to go there by myself – just me and Arabella/Rose, without all the others. But you were really getting into it, weren't you?'

'Yes,' he said. 'It was fun.'

Even that basic introduction to martial arts had made him feel different about himself, transforming him from someone who couldn't to someone who *could*.

'We'll go again when you're ready. I expect you'll be a bit sore for a few days.'

Greville expected as much as well, and it was already a real effort to get out of the low-slung car when they arrived at the cottage. They had reached the awkward point of trying to conclude the evening. Magnolia showed no inclination to turn the engine off and get out, yet neither did she start to turn the Mustang around, and the mighty car sat and burbled while neither of them said anything. Greville knew that for every second that he dithered, it became more and more likely that she would drive away, leaving him annoyed at himself.

'Do you want to come and say hello to Satan?' he blurted, before he could overthink it. 'He'd love to see you.'

She turned the engine off and got out, and before Greville had even unlocked the cottage door, they could hear the rapid beating of a heavy tail against the kitchen cupboard. Satan exploded out of the kitchen and capered about, and Magnolia wisely allowed him to let off steam before attempting to make a fuss of him.

'You're a good boy,' she said, rubbing his head. 'Good boy.'

Satan sat weightily on her feet and leant against her, leaving a damp patch of drool on her t-shirt, which she either didn't notice or didn't mind.

'Do you know what,' she said suddenly. 'I don't feel like going home and cooking for myself. Why don't I make us both some poached eggs on toast?'

'If you're sure,' he said, feeling as if all his birthdays and Christmasses had come at once. He fetched the full box of eggs and found a saucepan, and they set to work together. Even something as mundane as cooking eggs was so much more enjoyable when done with another person, and the simple meal, accompanied with glasses of squash, was the perfect end to the day.

She stacked the plates in the dishwasher.

'Right then. I'll see you in work tomorrow,' she said. She stepped forward quickly, kissed him firmly on the cheek and was gone, and even with Satan's larger than life presence, the house seemed empty without her.

Chapter 16

Greville arrived at the office the next morning feeling distinctly bruised and battered, which was odd considering that both women had been very careful not to injure him. His arms hurt; his legs hurt; his chest hurt; even his neck was feeling stiff and sore. Still, at least it was Friday.

He glanced into the other half of the office – the extension created in a mirror image – and for a second it seemed as if it *was* an odd sort of mirror because there at the mirror-image of Greville's desk sat a mirror-image Greville. He wondered what contortions of the space-time continuum were occurring in order for a mirror to be reflecting something that hadn't happened yet, but then the mirror-image Greville looked up, and he saw that it was Piers, and the strange optical illusion fell away.

Mr Valentine was sitting at his desk reading a big file, upside-down and very, very fast, and stopped when he saw Greville.

'That's your mitigation,' he said, pointing at Piers with a yellow nailed forefinger, then beginning to read again.

Greville looked at Piers and Piers looked back at him earnestly. Greville had the feeling that many fathoms would have to be plumbed to get to the bottom of this new development, whereas if he simply accepted it, anything salient would probably emerge in due course.

'Good morning,' he said to Piers, who bobbed his head nervously in reply. He sat down at his computer, swept through the life assurance form in a wave of enthusiasm and started to flesh out the report that had been started the day before.

The Cuthberts filed in and sat down in perfect synchronicity, and Magnolia wasn't far behind.

'That's your mitigation', Mr Valentine informed her, pointing into the mirror-image office. She looked in the indicated direction.

'That's Piers,' she corrected, putting her bag on the rack and sitting down at her desk.

He stopped reading again, marking his place with a mug of coffee in a way that made Greville wince, and then came out of his office.

'No, no, no, not at all. It's…'

He looked into the mirror office himself, and seemed annoyed at what he saw.

'Well, really! After I specifically *said* not to be late. I specifically *said*, you know. It deserves to get zapped in the head and sent back, but I can't zap it because it isn't here yet. But if it was, I would.'

Even as he was beginning to billow into a purple rage, the door crashed open and an angry young woman came in. A very tall angry woman – possibly as tall as Greville, which was quite an unusual height for a lady.

'There was an enormous beetle,' she said, glaring at Mr Valentine. 'No-one said anything about beetles.'

She had Magnolia's blue-black hair, enormous glasses and very slender frame, although somehow none of the elements came together to make a cohesive whole.

'I should really send this back,' Mr Valentine grumbled, almost to himself. 'It won't do at all. Not on the very first day. But then, it's taken petaseconds to find one that ticks all the circles. And at least this one's alive.'

'There was a beetle?' the young woman repeated. 'In the corridor? A really big beetle? I couldn't get past it.'

'Well, you *could*,' he said, 'because you *did*. The trouble is that you didn't try hard enough to start with.'

She drew herself up to her full height.

'Right, that does it. I'm off.'

'Fair enough.' His hand shot out at an impossible speed and clamped around one of her bony wrists. 'But first I'll have to zap you in the head.'

Greville found it interesting that Piers reflexively flinched when the zapper appeared in Mr Valentine's other hand, even though the very act of having been zapped in the head would have removed his memory of the procedure.

'Let go of me!' the woman demanded, tugging strenuously, which did not cause Mr Valentine to move one iota. It was as if he was suddenly forged from steel.

'And your salary will be put back to its previous rate,' he continued implacably.

It was the right thing to say as she stopped struggling and glared at him instead.

'All right,' she said, unsmiling. 'But next time, you've got to *warn* me if there's going to be beetles.'

Mr Valentine released his machine-like grip.

'Go and sit at that desk there, Irina,' he told her, indicating the mirror-desk to Magnolia's. 'Read your new joiners' pack. And don't cause any more trouble.'

It looked as if the young woman had quite a lot more that she'd like to say, but instead she went and sat at the desk, face pinched in disapproval.

'They're your mitigation,' he said to Greville and Magnolia. 'In case you're killed.'

'How do you mean?' Magnolia asked.

'In case you're *killed*,' he repeated, with slightly disconcerting aplomb. 'It's on the risk register as an amber risk, which means you're 'quite to moderately' likely to be killed, and that it will be 'quite to moderately' inconvenient to the company if you are. So therefore we need to mitigate that risk, and we've recruited back-ups, so that if and when you *are* killed, it won't really matter.'

'It will matter to us,' Greville said.

Mr Valentine treated him to his most excoriating 'you're an idiot' look.

'No it won't. You'll be *dead*. You won't care one way or the other.'

'That's not how the risk register works,' Magnolia said. 'You're supposed to mitigate the *risk* of us being killed, by putting safeguards in place so that we're *not* killed.'

'No, no, no, we couldn't *possibly* do that. There are *far* too many risks; it's more or less inevitable that one of them will eventually get you. So we've got replacements instead. They can follow you about and learn what you do, and then if you're killed…it won't matter at all. They can just pick up where you left off, and you'll get a posthumous warning for not taking proper care of company property by allowing yourselves to be killed.'

It was on the tip of Greville's tongue to point out that they *weren't* company property, but then he remembered the employment contract which he'd signed in blood, and was no longer quite so sure.

'But what if the *mitigations* get killed?' Magnolia asked, the utter impassiveness of her expression highlighting to Greville that she was being mischievous. 'What's the mitigation for that?'

'Well…I…err…well, of course…that is to say…' Mr Valentine began, glaring at her. 'I mean…' He thought fast and furiously, and his brow cleared as he hit on a solution. 'Well, that risk isn't in the risk register, is it, so we don't have to mitigate it.'

Greville found it saddening that the owner of a compliance auditing company should take the same superficial attitude towards risk registers as the common herd. Mr Valentine should be leading by example, not electing to observe the letter of the risk register while trampling on its spirit.

'Perhaps we should add it?' She suggested innocently. 'And while we're at it, we could add the risk that the *mitigations*' mitigations could be killed, and that *their* mitigations could be killed?'

'No!' he said briskly. '*I'm* in charge of the risk register. And anyway, you can't interfere with it because you don't know where it's saved.'

He treated her to a superior smirk.

'Get back to work,' he added, before Magnolia could decide to probe any further. 'I don't pay you to stand about spouting nonsense.'

He returned to his office and Greville logged onto his computer, and given the tenor of the previous conversation, felt it incumbent on him to complete his life assurance form. It was sobering that at his age, he was still leaving the proceeds of the death benefits to his parents, but whether his demise was because he 'burst', 'became irretrievably scrambled' or simply 'winked out of existence', his parents would be getting everything.

Magnolia meanwhile finished their joint report on the file review, and sent it over to him for his input, and in no time at all, it was emailed to Myhill.

'He prefers a hard copy,' she said. 'But in order to print anything, you have to… to…' She made an irritated gesture. 'Well, it hardly ever works.'

She called to Mr Valentine, who was still reading very, very fast.

'Can you tell the printer to print my report, please?'

There followed an irritated growl, but then he also shouted, 'Printer! Do as you're told! Right this second!' and it could be heard whirring into life. Magnolia collected the report and put it on Myhill's desk. He arrived not long afterwards, carrying two large cardboard cups of hot chocolate precariously balanced on top of each other, and a bag of croissants. The smell of chocolate and buttery pastry pervaded the office, and for a moment, Greville wondered if he had bought breakfast for all his colleagues. Greville's habitual breakfast revolved around various incarnations of eggs, grapefruit or the more earnest types of cereal, but he was sure that he could squeeze in a croissant in order to show that he appreciated the gesture. However, as soon as Myhill sat down, he opened the bag and started tucking in, and Greville realised that it was just a Myhill-sized single portion.

'What's this?' Myhill demanded, applying buttery fingers to the report. 'Is this some sort of joke?' He began turning pages, leaving greasy paw prints on them. 'How the…how the…you've *cheated*! Hey, Mr Valentine, they've *cheated*. They're disqualified! There's no way they've solved it already! They shouldn't even be on the third clue yet.'

Mr Valentine came out again, displeased by the interruption, and held out his hand for the report. He smelt it, then read it from back to front, upside down.

'It looks valid to me. We win the contract.'

'No!' Myhill protested. 'No, no, no! They *cheated*! They're *disqualified*! You're disqualified too! You can't just cheat your way through the tender process!'

'We win,' Mr Valentine insisted. 'We win. We get the contract.'

'No!' said Myhill. 'No! Because…because…'

Mr Valentine turned his back on him.

'You two. You can't just sit there all day not doing anything. Go and check whether the installations team has completed their audit actions.'

He thrust a file at Magnolia which hadn't been in his hands a second earlier, and they collected their equipment and headed out, trailed by Irina and Piers. The door swung shut, cutting off the argument between Myhill and Mr Valentine which had picked up again.

Magnolia flicked through the file. According to the map at the front, the installations team was located to the left of their office, whereas usually they went to the right. Just in case, she brought out the clipboard and addressed it.

'Where's the installations department, please?'

The spidery scrawl began to work its way across the page.

'You don't want to go there today,' it spelled out.

'Yes, we do,' said Magnolia. 'We've got to check whether they've done their audit actions.'

'Not today,' it insisted. 'It's bad karma.'

'But we've *got* to. We've…'

The pad began writing again.

'They've done items one to 10. They've done most of 13. They've had a go at 41. If you send them a stern email, they'll have done the rest by the end of next week.'

She held the clipboard so that Greville could see.

'What do you think? Shall we go and do something else instead?'

Greville was going to agree that they should do something else instead (after the appropriate amount of prevarication to demonstrate that he wasn't the sort of feckless person who bunked off on a whim), but he was too slow.

'What? We're not going to go there in person and do it properly?' Irina demanded. 'We're going to take that thing's word for it?'

'We'll email them,' Magnolia said. 'And we'll go back next week.'

'But we're supposed to do it now,' she persisted. 'And make sure that they're taking it seriously. What does 'bad karma' even mean? It's rubbish.'

'Why don't *you* go with Piers, if you're sure you can manage?' Magnolia suggested, with exactly the right amount of studied scepticism to inflame Irina further.

'Of *course* we can manage,' she said, and snatched the file from Magnolia's unresisting grasp. She held out her hand for the clipboard, which was scrawling furiously.

'Well, *I'm* not going,' it stated, and wiped itself clean, before drawing an 'out of order' sign.

Irina gave an irritated huff, unused to being cheeked by stationery, and stalked off, her back rigid. Piers gave them such an imploring look that Greville nearly relented and said that he could come with them, but something stayed his tongue, and after the longest moment, the boy scuttled glumly after Irina.

'Let's go to the canteen,' Magnolia said. 'But let's go the long way.'[19]

They walked back towards the lift, she somewhat pensively.

'She's my mitigation,' she mused. 'My replacement. So does that mean that *I'm* like *her*?'

Greville pressed the button for the lift and got his key ready.

'Of course not. You're no more like her than I'm like Piers.'

She took time to digest this, and Greville hoped that the point he'd made was that neither of them were anything like their mitigations, because the alternative was the opposite - that he was closer to Piers than he wanted to admit. Certainly on the inside he was timid, over-anxious to do the right thing and easily cowed as Piers appeared to be, and on the outside…it was impossible for him to be certain because, after all, he couldn't see himself as other people did.

'Why not? Aren't I…cold and abrasive and obnoxious?'

She looked at the floor instead of meeting his gaze, and Greville reflected that that was exactly how he'd have described her on the first day he'd met her, but of course, that had been months ago, and since then he'd seen past her natural reserve.

'No! Not at all! You're warm and funny and…and…uncompromising,' he told her.

She didn't say anything, and he wondered if he'd accidentally insulted her. Was it an insult to call a lady uncompromising?

'You're brave and you don't back down,' he explained, hastily. 'You don't give in if you don't think you should. You…'

'I know what 'uncompromising' means, Greville,' she said smartly, but she sounded pleased underneath.

The lift arrived, and today the canteen seemed to be four hundred floors up, rather than four floors down. It was already busy with clusters of little meetings, and they sat down at an empty table with some tea, but it was barely cool enough to drink before Mr Valentine came bundling in. Greville flushed guiltily, a few not-very-convincing excuses circulating in his head, and they got to their feet as if they'd been just about to go and get industriously on with something after an energising cup of tea.

'You two!' Mr Valentine said. 'There you are! You haven't had an accident at all!'

He turned to go, got halfway to the door and then stopped as if he'd forgotten something. He walked over again, looking back and forth between them with a

---

19 The short way involved going into the cupboard in the chapel, which led directly to a cubicle in the gents' right opposite the entrance to the canteen.

rather unnatural grin locked in place. The silence lengthened until it was incumbent on them to say something.

'No, we haven't had an accident,' Magnolia said carefully. It didn't seem as if he was being sarcastic, nor did he seem annoyed, so it seemed wise not to say too much until the lie of the land could be determined.

While continuing to grin, he pulled out his management book from under his jacket and turned to a marked page.

'You're valued members of my team,' he read. 'Good job.'

He read onwards to himself, lips moving, his fixed grin steadily being replaced by a frown.

'You matter?' he said. 'That's what it says here. It's wrong, though, wrong, wrong, wrong. It should say that you *are* matter. That's right, isn't it? You occupy space and have physical substance, don't you? But why is it motivating to tell you what you're made of? You should know already. And why is being made of matter better than *not* being made of matter? It doesn't make any sense.'

He put the book away, and sighed.

'You are made of matter. Good job,' he said, and treated them to another rictus grin before heading off again.

'Hang on,' said Magnolia. 'You said there was an accident?'

He waved an airy hand.

'But it didn't happen to you, because you're still here occupying physical space, aren't you? So therefore it's no concern of yours.'

'What happened?' she persisted.

'There was an accident with a Thousand. Two idiots wandered into one. Two of your sort.'

Greville's blood ran cold. Two people…two people who wouldn't recognise a Thousand Room or know that they should be avoided at all costs. Two people that he'd only been speaking to minutes earlier, whose safety had been entrusted to him, and who were now dead. Perhaps they weren't dead right at this second, but they would be before long, blundering from room to room to room. How long would it take for them to realise that there was no way out? It had been Greville's responsibility to make sure that they learned everything that they needed to know, and he'd failed them utterly.

'Irina and Piers,' Greville began. 'They've…gone?'

'Is that what they were called? I suppose so. But if they can't say out of trouble, then they're no loss really.'

'The mitigations?' Magnolia said.

She'd gone very pale, and when Greville met her gaze, he saw a mirror of his own guilt in her face. They were murderers; there was no way around it. He heartily wished that they could wind back time. Maybe if they used a Room That Time Forgot, they could go back and try to undo this tragedy? Suddenly, Irina's imperiousness and Piers' feebleness seemed endearing rather than irritating. If only they could go back and save them.

'What? Oh no, no, no, not them. *Another* two. They look like you but they're *not* you, which is good because otherwise I'd have to go out and get some more, which would be very inconvenient.'

'Are you sure?' Greville said.

'Quite sure. Because it was either you or the other two, and it's not you, so it must have been them,' he said.

This wasn't really a convincing endorsement.

'But…' Magnolia began, prompting him to hold up a quelling hand.

'You are matter!' he said firmly, and spun himself into a tornado of glitter before dissipating into the air.

'What do you think?' Greville said, hardly daring to hope.

'I think we'd better get to Installations,' she said.

They took the short cut this time, too afraid to speak further. Greville wondered if it made him a bad person, that he was so keen for the stricken pair to be some random unknowns rather than Irina and Piers. Shouldn't it be equally tragic that *anyone* had been irretrievably lost? They passed the door to their office and continued up the corridor, and with every step, Greville became surer and surer that his new colleagues were no more. He was more convinced than ever when they passed two Thousands, located on opposite sides of the corridor. A door opened further up, and out came their colleagues.

'You're all right!' Greville said, feeling sick with relief.

'Of course we're all right,' Irina told him. 'We were only checking up on audit actions. It's not rocket science, is it?'

Her words were still aggressive, but it was noticeable that some of the fight had gone out of her tone.

'You need to learn about Thousand Rooms,' Magnolia told her, not wasting any time. 'This is one. They're dangerous. Once you get into one and let go of the knob, all the doors move about and you will never get back out.'

Irina peered in.

'What's so dangerous about a room with lots of other rooms leading off it?' she demanded.

'I just told you. They move about. Every time you go into the next room, the doors move. Even if you let go of the knob for a second, that door won't open onto the corridor again. It will open onto another room. People blunder into them now and then, and no-one has ever got back out.'

Irina's face arranged itself into its customary haughty expression.

'That's rubbish. I'm sure *I* could get back out. People probably get disorientated. It must be something to do with mirrors.'

She put a hand on the door knob and Greville stood in her way.

'This is serious. Two people have gone missing just now, lost in one of these. Magnolia's uncle was lost a few years ago. You mustn't go in. Not ever. Not to try them out. Not for any reason.'

Before Irina could say anything, Greville carried on.

'Promise me. Promise me that you won't ever go into one? Never, for as long as you work here?'

Greville was not habitually a vehement person; in fact he'd never been vehement about anything before, but those few minutes of not knowing whether he had been jointly responsible for two deaths cut straight through his usual tactful and oblique approach. This was not the time to make a polite suggestion about perhaps avoiding the Thousands if it would be convenient to do so.

Irina arched an eyebrow, surprised rather than argumentative, and a few feet away, Magnolia did exactly the same, regarding Greville in thoughtful wonder.

'Okay. I promise.'

'Right then, we'll give you the tour and tell you everything you need to know.'

'I promise too,' said Piers, not wanting to be forgotten about, and perhaps quietly hurt that no-one was concerned that *he* might be lost forever.

Greville's sudden burst of intensity wasn't so overwhelming that it blinded him to other people's sensitivities.

'I expect you're quite a careful person, aren't you, Piers?' he said kindly. 'I expect that if you saw something you couldn't quite work out, you'd come and find us and ask, wouldn't you? You could be trusted not to rush in and get into a scrape.'

Piers bobbed his head and hunched his shoulders.

'Well, that's a good thing. You'll get on well here if you're not too hasty.'

It seemed incredible to Greville that he was in the position of acting as a guide when he still didn't feel that he knew even a tenth of one per cent of the building's mysteries. Still, he knew more than they did, and was able to point out the basics such as how to recognise a force field before you walked nose first into it, what the Displacers were for and where the canteen could usually be found. Irina grew more and more bewildered.

'But none of this makes any sense,' she protested, on hearing how the big printer/copier in the mail room could disgorge hard copies of correspondence that the writer hadn't written yet, how the corridor was seldom the same length going out as it was coming back and how the Room that Time Forgot worked.

'It doesn't need to make sense,' Magnolia said. 'You just have to remember the rules, that's all. It's quite fun when you get used to it.'

Irina was unconvinced.

'But…but…'

There was simply an overwhelming number of buts; far too many to settle on a single one.

'How did you get on with the installations department?' Magnolia asked, recognising the signs of a flooded brain and wanting to help her to latch onto something concrete. It was a mistake.

'I'm…not telling you,' she said, in haughty tones. 'It's *our* job, not yours. I report to Mr Valentine, not you.'

She marched off, Piers scrambling apologetically in her wake, and the effect was rather spoiled as she had to stop to peer in every door in her quest to find the office, with the result that Magnolia, who naturally walked very briskly (and who was still feeling mischievous), and Greville, who didn't want to be left behind, were constantly at her heels.

Magnolia went out on an errand at lunchtime and Greville went for a run by himself, and the afternoon passed pleasantly enough. Irina and Piers got sent to the HR department, which was a significant test of initiative and resolve in itself, Greville was given a 400-page document to summarise and Magnolia worked on another gigantic spreadsheet which covered the entire floor of the office and the mirror-office and which was still folded up at the edges.

Greville kept an eye on the clock as it inched towards five. He wanted to ask Magnolia if she was doing anything at the weekend, hoping that she would choose to understand that he was in fact asking whether she wanted to do anything *with him*. He was running out of time, and also the Cuthberts were all in attendance, typing in bad-tempered rhythm, and Myhill was dozing over his audit planner, so there would be too many witnesses if the conversation went humiliatingly badly. But if he tried to catch her in the corridor, it would mean an undignified contrivance to 'co-incidentally' leave at the same time. And even if he *did* catch her, she could still say no, which would throw a dampener over the entire weekend before it had even started.

She began to follow a snaking line on the vast expanse of paper which led her nearly to Greville's desk.

'Are you doing anything at the weekend?' she asked, tapping industriously at her calculator.

'Err…I…not really…I mean, yes, but…' Greville managed, taken unawares and flushing bright red. 'I mean…'

'I was just wondering if you were going to do anything interesting,' she informed him, still coolly doing calculations and scribbling down the results. 'Because if you are, I could join in, and if you're not…' she gave her bony shrug. 'I'll just do what I was going to do anyway.'

'I'm going to redecorate my living room…' Greville began, his mouth a few seconds ahead of his brain. Instantly, he began to berate himself. Why had he said that? Why hadn't he invented something more interesting, like going for a walk and calling in at a pub along the way, or going to the theatre, or going on a bike ride? All activities that could be arranged easily enough. Whereas instead he'd come up with the only thing that was a certain deterrent to any right thinking female…

'Okay, I'll come and help with that, then,' she said. 'But I hope that you've already stripped off the old paper because I don't like stripping paper.'

She peered more closely at her calculator, wrote down some figures and then shuffled off on her hands and knees again, following a different coloured line. Greville's stomach began to turn gentle somersaults of elation and trepidation. Getting so exactly what he wanted was somehow more terrifying than simply yearning for it, and when he went home at five o'clock, there was a spring in his step.

Chapter 17

Greville called into the village shop on his way home, to pick up a few odds and ends. Mrs Drew rang up his purchases, packing them neatly into his hemp shopping bag. She wordlessly added a box of his usual brand of tea bags, gave him a speculative look, then went to fetch some rather expensive biscuits and a large carton of coconut water. She added another item, wrapped in thin, transparent plastic – a very large bone. Greville definitely needed the tea bags, but he wasn't at all sure about the biscuits and was even less convinced by the coconut water. He wondered whether the idea all along had been to lull him into the habit of buying whatever ordinary goods she suggested before starting to slip in some more expensive items. And of course, she knew that he was a soft touch where his dog was concerned. He was still buoyed up from the unexpected end to the day, and in a fit of self-assurance he very nearly told her that he would only take the tea bags… but it simply went too strongly against the grain, and he paid for them meekly, thanking her as he left the shop.

He kicked himself all the way home. What sort of person lets themselves be talked into buying things they don't want or need – and not even 'talked into', strictly speaking, because Mrs Drew hadn't said a word? What if she'd produced an enormous bottle of the finest deli-quality olive oil, or a magnum of champagne? Where would Greville draw the line? It was disappointing that his new confidence had ebbed so quickly, and that he was back to being just his ordinary self, a pawn to other people's whims.

Satan's joyful welcome cheered him up, as it never failed to do, and by the time they'd got back from a longish, leisurely walk, his good humour was restored. Even if he wasn't any good at standing up for himself in shops, his dog still loved him.

After dinner, he contemplated the wallpaper. It wasn't going to strip itself and he didn't relish the thought of facing Magnolia in the morning if it wasn't done. He got himself a bucket of water, a sponge and a scraper and set to work. Satan watched the paper being peeled off with puzzled fascination, seeming to be aware that something was going on that was usually forbidden. He drew nearer and nearer, tail wagging slowly, then grabbed at the paper and tore off a long strip. Greville had feared that the dog might get a taste for pulling wallpaper off, and that he might amuse himself by doing just that if left unattended. But if he shut the dog out so that he couldn't watch, he would just whimper very quietly, which made the sound all the more piteous, and he'd end up letting him back in.

An idea dawned very slowly, and he walked into the kitchen trailed by Satan, and got the enormous bone out of the cupboard. He put it in Satan's bed, and for several seconds the dog stood where he was and wagged his tail at it, unable to believe his luck, then settled down for a good chew. He hardly even seemed to notice when Greville went back to the living room and carried on with the wallpaper.

Greville was up early the next day, and Mr Dean and the grandchildren came to collect Satan soon after eight. The house seemed too quiet and empty without him, and this was one morning above all mornings when he could have done with some company. He was worried in case the day was awkward. They had fallen into an easy rhythm at work, where it didn't really matter if they spoke or not, but here at home without the distractions of work, it was another thing altogether. At half past eight, he heard the Mustang growling up the drive and he took a deep breath and went out to meet her.

She was already getting a plastic trough full of decorating materials out of the passenger seat, and she was dressed for labour in light, threequarter length jeans, a grey striped t-shirt and old baseball boots that were already paint splattered. Her hair had been pulled back into a French plait that was distractingly elegant.

'Morning,' she said. 'I've brought some stuff because I didn't know what you've got already.' She followed him into the kitchen, taking in the empty dog bed and the abandoned bone. 'Where's Satan?'

Greville explained and put the kettle on, while she put down her plastic trough and wandered down the hall. He was pleased to see her, but at the same time, plagued with something that felt very much like exam nerves. He felt at his most tongue-tied and awkward.

'You've started in here?' she called. 'I thought you were going to do the bedroom?'

He had indeed chosen to start with the living room instead; it had seemed inappropriately rakish to be working all day in somewhere as private as his bedroom. And even the very presence of the bed would act as an unspoken, indelicate and inappropriate connotation.

'Did you wash the walls down with sugar soap?' He could hear her stroking the walls assessingly. She came back into the kitchen. 'That's okay – I brought some.'

She reached into her trough and took out a bottle of yellow liquid.

'It doesn't taste of sugar, though.'

'You've *tasted* it?'

'Yes,' she said, filling his washing up bowl with warm water and a splash of the yellow stuff, and finding a sponge from her trough.

'What for?'

'Well, to see what it tasted like. It *says* it's sugar, and it *looks* quite nice…but it isn't. I wouldn't recommend it.'

'It hasn't got any sugar in it. It's called 'sugar soap' because the dry ingredients look like sugar before they're dissolved,' Greville said, before he could stop himself. He sounded like his dad, or worse, one of his schoolfriends who had got beaten up a lot. When would he manage not to sound like an idiot in front of her?

'Strawberry soap doesn't taste of strawberries, either,' she continued, appearing oblivious to his acute embarrassment. 'Which is a shame because I love strawberries.'

She dropped the sponge into the bowl and carried it into the living room, mercifully leaving him alone to make the tea, which meant that he managed to accomplish it with less fumbling and spoon-dropping than if she'd been watching him.

'That would explain why it's not sticky, if it hasn't got any sugar in it,' she said, washing away energetically. 'I've always wondered that. And questioned the wisdom of washing walls down with something sticky-sounding.'

She turned to look at him.

'Have you got a radio?'

'Err, I…err…*yes*,' he said.

There had been an offer at the garden centre several months ago whereby if you bought a certain number of plants, you could buy a radio at a reduced price. Greville had never owned a radio before, and in the bemusing post-Poppy whirl when he had been trying to make sense of his life, he had wondered if he might be the sort of person who had one. The sort of person who 'had people round' in a spontaneous sort of way. The sort of person who did jaunty things around the house that required musical accompaniment. It had turned out that he *wasn't* that sort of person. He'd had the radio on once or twice when he'd been gardening, but he'd been worried about disturbing the Deans. He'd tried having it on in the house, only it had been irritating rather than companionable, and the frequent time-checks heightened the feeling that his life was slipping through his fingers.

He went and fetched it, and she plugged it in and found a station which played songs that Greville remembered not dancing to at school discos.

He and his friends had attended these with grim determination, and no matter how earnestly they had agreed beforehand that *this time* they would *definitely* dance, they never had. It seemed easier to be made fun of for not joining in at all than for joining in badly. The best ever disco had been when he and his friends had found an unlocked classroom and had had an impromptu tournament of speed chess. Only one of them had been confident of the rules for chess, so it had become a speed draughts tournament but using chess pieces and reckless on-the-fly rule amendments. Someone had smuggled in an unauthorised two litre bottle of something fizzy and full of e-numbers, and it had been the first (and last) time that he'd truthfully been able to say to his parents that he'd had a great time at a school disco.

'Right then, I'll wash down these two walls, you do those two, then we'll do the painting,' she said. 'You're wallpapering that one, aren't you, so we won't have to paint it.'

She set to work again and Greville did likewise. He found it vaguely embarrassing to have the radio playing because it made him feel uncomfortable when the DJ talked utter rubbish, which this one tended to do. But the first time the DJ tried to contrive a joke with his guest that wasn't remotely funny, Magnolia laughed and put on a voice and said something just as ridiculous, and had something else to say to his next utterance as well. Greville felt the tension inside him evaporate and his embarrassment eased as if it had never been. After a few minutes of listening to her, he even felt brave enough to join in.

It didn't take long to finish washing the walls, and while they dried, she drank her tea and walked back down the hall. The door to the second bedroom was ajar and she pushed it fully open, looking in on his gym equipment.

'You've got some good stuff,' she said. 'You might have room for a heavy bag if you want one later on? You can get freestanding ones if you don't want to hang one up.'

He noted that she didn't even try to open any doors that weren't already partly open; instead she went into the kitchen and inspected his choice of paper and paint.

'This will look a lot better. I think you're supposed to paint first, then wallpaper afterwards, because if you do it the other way around, you might get paint splattered on the paper.'

She went to her trough again and showed him a curious brush with angled bristles.

'I brought my edge brush. I can do edges with a normal brush, but it's much quicker with this. Why spend ages doing something when you can do it a lot quicker with the proper brush?'

Greville had misgivings about this. *He* always did the edges, if there were any to be done. To be fair, he did the middles too…it had been Poppy's job to choose the colour, tell him if he'd needed to do another coat and complain if he'd got specks of paint anywhere. But edges required a steady hand, relentless concentration and a determination not to get slap-dash in an unwise haste to finish as the job wore on.

Magnolia went over to his kitchen paper dispenser, helped herself to a sheet, folded it and then tucked it into her pocket so that it was ready to whisk away any mistakes before they set, and his reservations eased a little. At least she was approaching the task with the right mind-set.

It turned out that she was very good at edges; she was scrupulous at getting them absolutely straight, and she also knew exactly the right width to paint to make it easy for the roller to do the rest. There was something oddly compelling about her expression when she was concentrating, her magnified grey eyes peering closely at what she was doing, her mouth pressed thin in absorption. He had caught himself staring once or twice, watching her instead of looking at what he was doing, with the result that he'd rollered the same bit over and over again. He'd been relieved that she hadn't noticed; however on the third time, without looking up, she said, 'I think you've done that bit, now, Greville,' making him start so much that he'd nearly stepped in his paint tray.

They were finished at a convenient time to break for lunch, giving the paint some time to dry before they started on the wallpaper. Magnolia looked in his fridge.

'Coconut water!' she exclaimed. 'My favourite! Can I have some?'

When he assented, she lifted out the carton, noticing that the seal was intact.

'Are you sure? It's a new carton?'

He said that it was fine, so she poured a glass and had a long drink.

'Do you know the two best things about coconut water?' she asked.

Greville didn't because it hadn't really been a product that he had thought about before yesterday evening, but luckily she continued without waiting for him to answer.

'Firstly, it tastes fantastic, and secondly, it hasn't got many calories in it, so you've got plenty of calories left to eat. What's the point in life if you drink all your calories so you can't eat what you want?'

She opened cupboards, scouring the contents.

'You've got my favourite biscuits too!' she exclaimed, taking them out and looking at them. 'Have you been stalking me or something?'

He flushed guiltily. While he couldn't exactly explain what it was that went on at the shop, neither could he rule out the word 'stalking' with a clear conscience. It was true that he hadn't been physically following her about, but he must have done *something*, consciously or unconsciously, for Mrs Drew to have...

'Joking, Greville,' she said, putting the biscuits back. 'Now then, what shall we have for lunch?'

They had pasta with tomato sauce, then wandered up the garden to see how

Satan was getting on. The grandchildren had acquired an inflatable pool, and both dog and children were soaked. One of the boys showed Magnolia Satan's trick with the action figures; as well as throwing them in all directions, the dog would now bring them back, one at a time, dropping them in an untidy heap.

It seemed almost a shame to go back inside after being out in the sun, and just as they got indoors, Magnolia's phone gave an unearthly shriek. She looked at the message.

'Technology upgrade,' she said. 'We've got to put our phones in our lockers.'

'Have we? But why? I haven't heard…' He tailed off. There had probably been a message in his skymail account, which he still didn't always remember to check. He got his phone and obediently put it in his virtual locker, hoping that it wasn't the last time that he'd see it.

They'd hung the first few lengths of paper and were mid-way through another length when the house phone rang. It wasn't an opportune time to stop, so Greville let the machine pick it up. It was his uncle from the lavender farm, wanting to know if he fancied coming over the following day for a picnic.

'You should go,' Magnolia advised. 'This will wait. It's always better to do something outdoors than indoors if you get the chance.'

Greville thought about it. He liked seeing his uncle and aunt, but his parents would doubtless be there as well, and all of them would gang up on him about the Poppy issue. On the face of it, there were no convincing arguments for breaking up with a not totally unattractive accountant of child-bearing years, with a steady (as far as they knew) job and entirely sensible opinions on things like politics, the economy and the importance of always having an umbrella in the car.

'It would be better if *you* came,' he said.

He'd only meant to think it, but primed by a morning of making facetious comments to the radio presenter, the remark slipped out. It was an audacious idea to have an overlap between his work life and his family. Magnolia belonged in one sphere and his family in an entirely different one.

'Okay, then,' she said, matching pattern with thin, deft fingers. 'Who's driving? Is Satan coming? We can't have the top down in the Mustang in case he jumps out.'

Suddenly, Greville very badly wanted to turn up at the lavender farm in the formidable, snarling Mustang instead of his sensible, economical maroon family car.

'Have you got seat belts in the back?' he asked. 'He's got a harness for the car.'

It was agreed, and he wiped his hands, rang his uncle back and accepted his invitation, and no sooner had he started brushing out air bubbles than the phone rang again. It would doubtless be his uncle asking if he could bring a dessert or a blanket to sit on, or to change the time slightly, so Greville let the machine pick up again, but the voice coming over the speakers wasn't his uncle's.

'Greville?' said the voice. 'Greville? Pick up. I *know* you're there. Greville? I need to talk to you.' The voice assumed a wheedling tone. 'Please, Greville…? It's important.'

There was nothing that Poppy could say that he wanted to hear; even so, he froze where he was, as if she might hear him if he moved.

'I don't know why you're being like this,' she continued. 'I think we should… start again. Do things differently. Go out more. Greville…? I can't live without you.'

She made a noise that could have been a sob, and after a long pause (Greville counted to twenty), she put the phone down. He didn't know what to say, so he carried on brushing, until the phone rang again. The second message was largely the same as the first, only with more sobbing. The third message consisted of an anguished sigh, and after a similar fourth message, Greville got down from the stepladder and wordlessly unplugged the phone. Magnolia said nothing, giving no indication that she'd even heard any of the messages, so Greville followed her lead. The silence between them lengthened until the radio presenter said something stupid, Magnolia made a riposte and things were back to normal.

It didn't take long to paper one wall of a small living room, and all too soon, she was repacking her trough and heading off again. The Mustang's growl faded into the distance, and all that was left to show she'd even been there were several used tea mugs, an empty glass and a partly devoured packet of biscuits. Mr Dean brought Satan back, and although the dog was mercifully non longer wet, his fur had dried with a slight wave. Greville asked Mr Dean in to show him the finished living room, feeling that he ought to demonstrate that he was taking his responsibilities towards the cottage seriously. His landlord looked approvingly at their work and seemed happy with the transformation, but wasn't quite as effusive as Greville had anticipated and after he'd left, Greville was faintly puzzled. Then he noticed that Satan had picked up half a tin of paint by the handle (the lid was on, but this was a flimsy barrier to disaster) and he forgot all about Mr Dean's reaction.

Satan had a nap while Greville tidied up and removed all items to a safe place if they were the sort of things that would not survive an enthusiastic game, such as the paint, the wallpaper or the various brushes, then they went for a walk more because Greville felt like some air than because the dog needed exercise. His evening of catching up with his compliance reading was interrupted by a sudden, loud 'ping' of a microwave which had finished cooking something. He checked the microwave; he checked the batteries in the various smoke alarms; he checked the carbon monoxide monitor, while the ping continued to sound at regular intervals. It occurred to him that wherever he was, the ping was always the same distance away, and this prompted him to try his virtual locker. There inside was his phone, together with some work-related missives that floated gently around his feet.

The phone appeared to be undamaged; his text messages, photos and emails were still there. The only change was that its battery was very low – lower than Greville had ever seen it - as if its afternoon had been extremely gruelling, and it had also acquired a few extra apps. He also had an awful lot of missed calls, voicemails and texts, all of which he deleted, and slowly and thoughtfully, he blocked her number.

Greville flicked through the work papers, stuffing them back (they were the usual confusing mix of random nonsense about remembering to switch off the particle accelerator after use, that people should shuttle-share if they were going to the reverse-compliance conference because parking was short and that a certain department head had spontaneously reincarnated and would be on garden leave for twenty-one years until he had re-graduated), put his phone on to charge and went back to his compliance magazine.

The next morning rolled around all too soon. The decorating had been more strenuous than he'd expected, and he was still a little sore from the unusual move-ments required by the martial arts lesson. If truth be told, he could have done with another hour in bed, and then another hour pottering gently, so that's what he did. Of course, he had to get up to feed Satan and let him out, but while the dog was doing his morning patrol of his patch, he made himself a cup of tea, and when Satan had come back in, Greville picked up one of his interior design magazines and went back to bed. He had only read the magazines to the mid-way point to glean ideas on redecorating; the back halves were dedicated to 'radical transformations' and new bathrooms. He wasn't planning either, but it was still fun to look.

The novelty of being able to eat biscuits in bed (and not just any biscuits this morning – delicious, expensive ones) still hadn't worn off. Poppy was right that it made crumbs, but the pleasure of doing it outweighed the minor inconvenience. Then he got up and did some chores, Satan at his heels. It was strange how trundling about doing housework didn't feel so lonely, empty or somehow pointless when he was secure in the knowledge that he wasn't going to be alone for the entire day. Sure enough, Magnolia rolled up at the appointed hour, and it didn't take long to strap Satan securely in the back. She was wearing an ankle length, floral skirt which draped well on her spare frame and a neat white sleeveless cotton top, tailored to fit, and he abundant hair was in a long, relaxed plait.

'You can drive if you want,' she told him, 'as long as you promise not to thrash it.'

With the top down, it was too noisy to speak easily, and they were about half way when an imperious voice spoke up.

'Turn left here.'

Of course, the car was far too old to have sat nav installed, and there was no sign of a clip-on version.

'Turn left *here*,' insisted the voice, and even though Greville knew the way to the lavender farm, and turning left wasn't correct, he indicated and did it anyway.

'Have you got a sat nav in the glove box?' he asked her.

'No – it's your phone. They've upgraded it. We've got all the stuff we need on our phones now. That clipboard thing – it's on your phone.'

'Take the second right,' the voice instructed.

Greville had had enough interaction with the clipboard to be confident that the voice matched the tone of the device's writing. He wasn't at all sure that he wanted the clipboard to know exactly where he was at all times, but it seemed a bit late to do anything about it. Somewhere buried in the small print of his employment contract, he'd probably signed away his rights to privacy. And if the firm was interested in how many times he went to the supermarket a week, how many times he visited his parents (not very many of late) or what garden centre he went to, he supposed that they were welcome to the information.

He took the second right, and not long afterwards, was told to turn left so that they were back on the original road. There was an enormous stationary queue on the opposite carriageway, and in his mirror he could see blue flashing lights in the distance behind them.

'As you were,' said the pad, and subsided into silence.

It was a silent sort of journey, all in all, because Magnolia didn't seem disposed towards conversation, or it might have been just that she was disinclined to shout over the noise of the engine and the air rushing past. For his part, Greville preferred the silence so that he could concentrate on his driving. The car was still unfamiliar, and it was so very powerful; the slightest pressure on the accelerator sent it surging forward. She must have had the factory-fitted worm and sector steering replaced with a rack and pinion system because the steering was more responsive than he'd expected. As a boy, Greville had loved the old muscle cars, and had been thrilled to sit in a selection when his dad had taken him to a motor show. One man had kindly taken the trouble to talk him through an immaculate engine, explaining the processes that took place in all the different sections. He was as excited as his six year old self would have been to be behind the wheel of this beautiful car.

They made good time to the lavender farm and his uncle, hearing their approach, came around from the back of the house, his automatic smile of welcome fading to puzzlement as he took in the unfamiliar car. Magnolia got out, and Greville released Satan, trying to channel him through the open door rather than letting him jump for freedom in case he scratched the paintwork. He introduced Magnolia to his uncle.

'This is Magnolia,' he said. He was going to add, 'From work', but he didn't. He preferred the ambiguity of not labelling her as a colleague. He could tell that his parents were already there as he'd parked next to their car, and they weren't far behind his uncle. They did the same double take when they saw Magnolia, and he made the same introduction. Everyone shook hands very cordially, and they were all waiting for him to explain further, but he didn't.

They went around to the back garden where assorted family members were scattered on the patio and lawn, drinks in hands. It was a lot more people than Greville had been expecting, and he felt Magnolia stiffen at his side. Greville's great aunt was seated at a table, under the shade of an umbrella. He hadn't seen her for several years – probably not since a cousin's wedding. She exclaimed with pleasure when she saw Greville, then turned to Magnolia.

'You must be Poppy,' she said. 'I've heard so much about you.'

A hush descended as the family members who were more au fait with the latest state of play stopped talking, conversation suspended in collective horror. All eyes turned to Greville to see what he was going to say, which was unfortunate as he hated being the centre of attention. His colour rose as he tried to think of what he could say without embarrassing his great aunt or going into detail.

'No, Poppy was last year's model,' Magnolia said. 'I'm Magnolia. Pleased to meet you.'

She held out her hand to the great aunt, and around them everyone started talking again. Greville noted that Magnolia hadn't gone so far as to assert that *she* was *this* year's model. He had half wanted her to…or rather, to be accurate (and Greville was a stickler for accuracy) he had 49% wanted her to. 51% of him (a slim majority, but an important one) was pleased that she wasn't the sort of person to make public declarations of this nature. Whatever it was that they had (and for all his magazine-reading, he couldn't put a name to it) was a tiny seedling, the first leaves barely poking through the soil, and to hoik it out now before it was ready, and insist on transplanting it to a larger pot could kill it, even if the intentions behind such a transplantation were well-meaning. Far better to leave the little seedling to find its own way until its roots were better developed.

It was decided to eat by the lake, and Magnolia helped to carry the baskets, content to walk along very slowly with the great aunt and talk about knitting. One couldn't sit next to Arabella/Rose for as long as Magnolia had without picking up enough about knitting to make conversation. Greville pulled a garden trolley holding rubber ice buckets filled with wine and beer. The picnic benches and blankets had already been laid out, and it didn't take long to spread out all the food.

'Beer?' Greville's uncle offered. Greville automatically went to refuse.

'Have one if you want?' Magnolia said at his elbow. 'I don't mind driving. I've got to drive back from yours to mine anyway.'

He searched her inscrutable face for signs that she *truly* didn't mind. He'd played this game before with Poppy who often *said* that she didn't mind, but when he took her at her word and had a beer, he had inexplicably had to endure a lot of moaning and sighing, and had had to drive for their next few months' worth of excursions.

'You can drive next time,' she told him, and rummaged in the ice bucket to get a sophisticated soft drink in a glass bottle.

Next time! It was in her head that there was going to be a next time! Greville took a beer, clinked the bottle against hers and took a long, refreshing drink.

Chapter 18

The meal went well. Magnolia praised the food, eating her share, and neither complained about being too hot, nor about having to sit on a blanket so that the older people could have the benches nor about the sandwiches having crusts on them. She either ate her crusts without comment (Poppy had exclaimed loudly, 'Oh! You forgot to cut the crusts off!'), or fed the odd one to Satan to stop him feeling left out. And she was perfectly happy to trot back and forth to the kitchen to get the forgotten coleslaw or fetch more bottles for the ice bucket or to get the desserts out of the fridge. In between, she carefully fielded questions about the nature of their relationship. Greville's mother, a particular fan of Poppy's, sat stiffly on the edge of the blanket.

'So,' she began. 'How long have you two…errr…known each other?'

'We work together,' Magnolia said, not answering the question. 'Did you make the jam tarts? They're really lovely. I never can get the right amount of jam in them.' (At a previous gathering, Greville remembered that Poppy, pressed to take one, had done so with obvious reluctance and had left it on her plate.)

Greville's mother explained rather coldly the correct way to calculate jam volume and then had another go.

'Do you see much of each other?'

'We're in the same office, and sometimes we work on the same audit projects.'

To his dismay, his mother changed tack and tried a more direct approach.

'You do know that Greville's having a traumatic time at the moment?'

'Less of a traumatic time than if he'd married someone joyless who made him miserable,' Magnolia returned, utterly unruffled.

Whereas Poppy would have flounced off, Magnolia held her ground, and held his mother's gaze as well, steady grey eyes impassive and unafraid, waiting to see what would come next. She didn't have long to wait – his mother pursed her mouth, got up heavily and went to find someone else to talk to. Magnolia turned to a cousin and started a conversation about the cousin's children. Greville's dad, also fond of Poppy but amenable to the pretty faces and good figures belonging to viable alternatives, sidled over when Greville was getting another beer.

'Is she…serious?' he asked, nodding in Magnolia's direction.

'Sometimes she's serious,' Greville said, pretending to misunderstand. 'And sometimes she's good fun.'

'But what about Poppy? Are you really sure you know what you're doing?'

'I'm happy. A lot happier than I've been for a while. Life's too short to feel fed up,' he said, and smartly asked after his dad's allotment, which was always a rich and safe conversational seam.

Once everyone had had their fill of desserts, Greville's uncle suggested a wander around the lavender fields to walk off the meal. His land had deliberately been cultivated to incorporate areas to encourage wildlife, including several nature lakes, and it was very pleasant to have a gentle stroll in the fresh air.

'I'll go and change my shoes,' said Magnolia, and returned wearing some canvas plimsolls that went very well with the long skirt, with discreet sport socks underneath to prevent blisters. Greville had once thought that flat shoes and sensible shoes were the same thing. However, on one visit to the lavender farm, Poppy had been wearing strappy flat sandals which he'd assumed would be suitable for walking, but the flat soles were hard and slippery, and the abundance of straps were the sort that would cut your feet after walking only a modest distance, and they'd barely got as far as the first pond before she'd insisted on hobbling back again.

He understood that sometimes ladies liked to wear beautiful yet impractical constructions on their feet if they only needed to totter from car park to restaurant or bar, but he didn't understand why anyone would wear shoes that looked sensible and in fact were as torturous in their own way as high heels, but without the visual appeal.

Magnolia's self-contained, detached manner seemed to be a magnet for the younger members of the party, who plied her with questions about all kinds of things, but when they arrived at the lake, they ran off with Satan bounding along in their midst, and Greville could get closer to her.

'It's beautiful here,' she said, watching the dragonflies dance.

Greville looked out across the lake, where ducks were swimming serenely, bobbing now and then for food. He felt slender, wiry fingers making their way gently and insistently into his, and he didn't dare to look at her, or even to breathe, in case he fractured the magic of the moment. Then there came an almighty splash as Satan followed a ball into the lake, Magnolia withdrew her hand and the world began to turn again.

All too soon, they were back in the car and heading home, Magnolia at the wheel. He was ungallantly pleased that she was driving as he was feeling replete and sleepy, and not at all in the mood for concentrating on the road.

'Thank you for coming,' he said.

'Thank you for inviting me,' she returned, then gave a fractious sigh. 'I was rude to your mum.'

It was a statement rather than an apology.

'I was trying to be nice by asking about the jam,' she continued. 'I mean, any old idiot can get the jam right. It isn't rocket science. You read the recipe and do what it says. I just wanted to make conversation so that she'd like me, and I ended up being rude.'

'She was rude first,' Greville pointed out.

'Yes, but I should have…should have… I don't know. I always say the wrong thing, and now she'll *never* like me.'

'She'll get used to you,' Greville said. 'She needs a bit more time, that's all. She was quite fond of Poppy.'

'That's another thing I don't understand. Why is everyone so keen on Poppy? Why were *you* so keen on Poppy? Everyone likes her, and she didn't even *try* to be nice as far as I can tell, and no-one *ever* likes me, even when I *try*.'

She drove on steadily, mouth pinched into a hurt line, and Greville watched her.

'I never thought I'd get a girlfriend,' he said, in a drink-lubricated burst of honesty. 'Not a proper one. Friends started pairing up, and I never thought it would happen for me, so when she showed an interest, I was so grateful, and so surprised.'

This was the point at which he knew that he ought to stop with the honesty, because the more he said, the more he'd reveal himself as someone that no-one else wanted, which might make her reconsider whether *she* wanted him. He couldn't seem to stop though.

'So we started going out, and we carried *on* going out because there was no reason not to, then friends started moving in together, so we moved in together, and then friends started getting engaged so…'

It was the first time he'd ever said it out loud to another person.

'But I enjoyed it…I really enjoyed it, being able to do all the things I never dreamed I'd do. Buying flowers for someone, going home to someone, making a life with someone. It was amazing.'

'Did you love her?'

This was the million-dollar question, and it deserved a considered answer.

'I thought I did. I really thought I did. We were doing all the right things. But one day it started feeling empty, and once I started feeling it, I couldn't pretend I didn't. Maybe it wasn't love. Maybe it was just gratitude, that she was giving me the chance to play at being normal. And how could I tell what love's supposed to feel like? I thought that what we had was as good as it got.'

'If you've never seen a mountain, then a hill will seem like a mountain?' She suggested. 'Then when you actually come across a mountain, you realise that what you saw before was just a hill.'

They drove along in silence for a while as he digested what she'd said, and realised that she was right.

'Is your dad a bit hen-pecked?' she asked, surprising him. He was even more surprised by his answer.

'A bit, I suppose.'

He'd never really thought about it before, and now that he did, he realised that his mum habitually put his dad down, criticising what he did either directly or indirectly, and continued this pattern even in front of other people.

'That's probably why she liked Poppy, then. Did she moan about your dad to Poppy, and did Poppy complaint to her about you?'

'Well…yes. But I thought that was normal. Women bonding by complaining about their useless men. I thought that was how it was supposed to be.'

'So your mum's not going to like someone who breaks up the cosy pattern, is she? Because then she'll have to think about how she behaves to your dad. She would prefer to be friends with someone who also likes to complain about their partner. That's what she knows how to do.'

A lot of things were starting to make sense to Greville, sliding into focus when previously they'd been foggy.

'The pashmina thing,' she said, warming to her theme. 'She sent your dad all the way back to the car to get her pashmina, and then when he brought it, made a great song and dance about how he'd brought the wrong one.'

This was true, although it hadn't even registered with Greville at the time.

'Firstly, she didn't even *need* a pashmina because it was too hot. Secondly, if she wanted the blue one and not the red one, why didn't she say so? Thirdly, why didn't she accept it with a smile and make a mental note that the next time she makes an unreasonable request, she ought to make it a more *specific* unreasonable request? And fourthly, why didn't she go and get the wretched thing herself if she wanted it that badly? Did you notice, she didn't even *wear* it once he'd brought it?'

Greville hadn't really noticed; he'd been talking to his other uncle about the importance of having a proper maintenance regime for garden tools while simultaneously admiring Magnolia's profile. Now she'd pointed it out, the whole incident sat awkwardly with him.

'That's not how it should be,' she continued. 'One person always having a go at the other, because where's the point in that? You should *support* each other, no matter what. You need to know that the other person's always in your corner. *Always.*'

She had gradually caught up with a lorry.

'Do you think I've got time to overtake before the roundabout?' she asked.

'No,' said the pad. 'There's a lorry coming the other way.'

Greville waited until she'd negotiated the roundabout and overtaken the lorry in a heady rush of burbling power before continuing the conversation.

'Have you ever been in love before?'

Ordinarily, this was the sort of thing that he would not have dared to ask, but this was not an ordinary day as the unaccustomed three bottles of beer were playing havoc with his normal careful reserve.

She pushed her glasses up her nose.

'No. I've wanted to be. I've nearly convinced myself once or twice.'

He hadn't really expected her to answer; in fact he'd anticipated a smart rejoinder, but his own honesty seemed to have prompted her to reciprocate.

'It's never been the real thing. They just *say* all sorts of things, but never *mean* them. One guy told me that he went running all the time and was training for a marathon, and then he *never* went running, not once. It was too hot, or too cold, or he didn't feel like it, or his knee hurt... It's not important whether people like running or not, but why *say* things that aren't true? And someone else...he *pretended* to like me, but really he didn't like me at all; he just liked the car. Can you believe it?'

Greville could; he remembered rather guiltily that he'd been excited to arrive in the Mustang. But then, he'd been equally excited to arrive with *her*, and given the choice, he'd sooner have arrived in his own car, or a milk float, or the most beaten up, oldest van imaginable but with *her*, than in the Mustang by himself.

'Why do people tell such fibs?' she asked. 'I don't understand it.'

'Because you're a prize,' he told her. 'And they know that you're out of their league, so they have to make things up to get your attention.'

She shot him a quick, puzzled glance, then turned her attention back to the road.

'You're beautiful,' he said. 'Astonishingly beautiful. And brave. And clever.'

He would never have been bold enough to say such things if he was sober; yet now the words were out, he was pleased rather than apprehensive. He should have been worrying about overstepping the mark and spoiling it all, but in his slightly tipsy state, the consequences seemed far removed.

'The man who liked the car didn't like clever,' she said. 'He told me that I was too clever by half.'

She didn't conceal that the words still stung.

'*I* like clever. And people that don't…well, they're idiots, so who cares about them.'

He noted that she had let the 'beautiful' slide past without remarking on it. He had meant every word but perhaps it had been too soon for that; his current judgement was impaired. But she didn't seem offended, which was good, and maybe he'd get a chance to say it again when he was confident that it was the right thing to do.

The Mustang ate up another few miles, and now she was wearing her alluring and enigmatic almost-smile, and Greville was pleased that he'd put it there. It seemed a shame that tomorrow, they would be returning to the usual routine of work, and once thoughts of work had rooted in his head, he couldn't get them out.

'Your uncle who was lost in the Thousand,' he said. 'Did they try to find him?'

'Oh yes. The Internal Investigations department did everything they could. But you know how it is with the Thousands. *Everyone* knows. No-one ever gets back out.'

'Could you use a Room that Time Forgot and stop him from going in?'

'Nope. That's not how they work. You've used one, haven't you? Did you see any other people while you were in the alternative time? That's because it doesn't work with people – only things. So you can go back and have more time to do an audit, or you can go forward and check whether someone's done their audit actions, and if not, go back and alter your report to recommend weekly catch-ups rather than fortnightly, but you can't make contact with anyone else. They can't see you or hear you; you can't hear or see them. Otherwise…well, it would cause the most almighty muddle.'

It seemed indelicate to pursue the subject any further, and after a comfortable pause, she asked him what he'd made of the martial arts lesson, and in no time at all, they were pulling up in Greville's driveway. Greville looked cautiously about for Poppy's car; he'd been half-expecting to see it.

'You thought *she'd* be here, didn't you?' she said, watching him.

'Maybe,' he admitted. 'But I didn't want her to be. I'm hoping that Satan's scared her off.'

Magnolia was already aware that Poppy had visited on the night of the martial arts lesson, so there didn't seem any harm in telling her that Satan had accidentally pinned her to her car.

'I don't see why she's so keen on me now we're not going out,' he said. 'She did nothing but complain about me when we *were* going out.'

Magnolia sat in thoughtful silence, chewing it over. Most people would have said something non-committal, but she liked conundra to have answers.

'Perhaps *she* was surprised and flattered?' she suggested. 'Perhaps *she* never thought she'd get to play relationships? And you're quite a catch, you know.'

Greville ignored her last remark, assuming he'd misheard.

'So why was she so horrible?'

Magnolia sighed.

'We've been through this already. It was probably a pattern she learned from her parents, like you did from yours. One picking on the other all the time. She was playing her role and she wanted you to do the same – which you did for a bit. And now you've gone, she's realising what she's lost. But that's enough about her. Give me a kiss.'

She leant over and planted a firm kiss on his startled mouth.

'I've been dying to do that all day. In fact, I might do it again.'

She repeated the manoeuvre, and he managed to have the presence of mind to kiss her back.

'There!' she said. 'Not bad. Right then, I'll see you in work tomorrow.'

He obediently got out and unstrapped Satan – the dog had been hosed down once he'd finished playing in the lakes, and his coat had dried curly again – and went back to her door.

'Thank you for a great day,' he said.

The words seemed pitifully inadequate, but he didn't want to sound pathetically gushing either.

'Thank *you* for a great day,' she replied, giving him such an impish smile that his breath stuck painfully in his chest. She drove smoothly away before he could recover himself, which at least prevented him from ruining the moment by saying something idiotic. He watched until the car had completely disappeared from view, then went in to make some dinner for himself and his dog.

Chapter 19

Greville awoke early the next morning, and started smiling straight away. It was simply impossible to feel anything less than beatific given the events of the day before. He got up and began to get ready, caught sight of himself in the mirror, and stepped in for a closer look. It was still unmistakeably him; he still had the same tall, awkward frame (although he was definitely making headway along the path from gangly to athletic) and the same ginger hair, but there was something different about his bearing. His face looked different too…less anxious and more assured. He smiled, and the confident Greville in the mirror smiled back, and he kept on smiling all the way to work.

He made it to his desk without incident. Arabella/Rose was there already, rubbing her chin and staring thoughtfully into the middle distance, and occasionally consulting a very, very old and dusty book that was bound in crumbling gilded leather. The cat was in its customary place in the in-tray, and gave Greville a single mew in greeting. Mr Valentine was in his corner office, shouting into the phone, and when he noticed Greville, it seemed that he was watching him very closely indeed, and not altogether approving of what he saw. Greville sat down and logged on, and began completing an employee satisfaction survey, which his computer had decided was the most pressing priority for the week.

It turned out that the survey was on employees' satisfaction with stationery, and he was trying to think of a way to describe his stapler's performance in more than 20 words but less than 100 without sounding flippant (the penalty for flippancy was apparently exile, although to where or for how long was not specified) when Magnolia came in. On this occasion, she was wearing a very sharply tailored grey suit with a nipped-in waist, matching heels, and she carried an enormous matching bag. The suit's skirt was gratifyingly short. Her hair was in a loose plait which hung down her back, with tendrils escaping around her face.

She turned in Greville's direction, and now he could see that she wasn't wearing her glasses. Without them, she looked younger and formidably intellectual, when Greville had always assumed that spectacles lent the wearer an air of intelligence. Bare-faced, it was as if a safety barrier had been removed between her analytical gaze and the object of her attention, which was currently him. She gave him a steady, challenging look, with a certain playfulness around the mouth, then sat down as if she was oblivious to the cataclysmic effect she'd had on him, when surely she must have done it on purpose.

Greville tried to keep breathing, although his diaphragm felt as if it would never unstick, and it was completely impossible to continue with the survey with his senses in such disarray. Then Mr Valentine slammed down his phone receiver, picked it up again, peered into it very keenly, slammed it back down again and strode into the main office, which burst the balloon of enchantment.

'Right then, you and you and you have got a job to do,' he said, pointing at Magnolia, then Greville, then Magnolia again. 'There's a machine in the office at the end, and you need to find out what it does.'

'Where exactly?' Magnolia asked, stopping him from marching back into his corner office.

'Right at the end. *That* way,' he said, pointing to the right. 'At the very end. There's a machine in there and you need to find out what it does.'

'We're compliance auditors,' Greville said. 'We audit processes. We don't…'

'So *audit* its processes,' Mr Valentine returned. 'Find out what they are and see if it's doing them. That's all there is to it. And then write a report. In fact, write *two* reports in case I don't like the first one.'

'Where are the mitigations?' Magnolia asked. The mirror office was empty that morning.

'They've gone on a course. An introductory pre-course course. They can't go on the preliminary introductory course until they've done it, because you can't go on a preliminary course until you've done the pre-course introductory course, can you?'

He went into his office, picked up his phone and examined the underside very carefully, then shook it experimentally close to his ear before setting it down again. He still seemed perplexed, staring at it with his hands on his hips as if seeking answers that were not forthcoming – a feeling that Greville could entirely relate to.

'Let's get going,' Magnolia suggested. She unearthed her phone from the depths of her bag.

'Where's…' she began.

'A looong way. A very very loooooooonnng way,' said the pad app before she'd even finished asking about the location of the room at the end of the corridor. 'You won't get there today unless you hurry. Walk the first five miles and then we'll get a Displacer.'

'It would probably be quicker if we ran,' Greville said, pleased that he'd brought his kit. 'We could...'

'Not today,' the pad interrupted. 'Today, the quicker you go, the longer it will take.'

They collected notebooks and pens, and Magnolia kicked off her shoes, electing to walk in bare feet, and they were nearly at the door when Rose/Arabella nearly tripped Greville by winding around his ankles.

'You'll have to be fast,' Arabella said, and it was hard to tell whether she was speaking to him or to Magnolia as she was still looking into the middle distance. 'Your life may depend on it.'

She bent her head to the book again, and a musty-smelling dust was released as she turned the page. Greville wanted to question her further, but Magnolia tugged at his arm.

'She's busy, and she can only say what she sees,' she said. 'You won't get anything else out of her.'

They headed up the corridor at a purposeful speed, and Magnolia peered onwards, trying to see where it ended.

'The pad's right,' she said. 'It's going to be a long one today. You know, sometimes...usually around the winter solstice...the corridor can be so short that you can see the end from here.'

Greville thought about all the various departments located on each side of the corridor as it stretched into the distance.

'How is there room for everyone?'

'Well, sometimes the rooms go inside each other, like Russian dolls. So there are two doors, and one goes into one room and the other goes into the other, but they're occupying the same space. The people in the other room look like wraiths, and it's a bit like sitting on other people's laps. But luckily Compliance hardly ever have to share because we've got special exemption.'

This did actually sound vaguely familiar.

'I think Myhill explained it to me once before, with lunch boxes,' he said. 'Stacking one inside another.'

She snorted.

'He had a phase of bringing in his own lunch when he was on some sort of a health kick,' she said. 'But it didn't really work. If he brought in a normal lunch, like sandwiches and crisps and whatever, he'd have eaten the lot by ten and would have to go out and get some more, and if he brought in something healthy like salad, he'd open it, stir it around a bit, then go and get something from the canteen, and then go out again at lunchtime and get something else.'

She turned to look back the way they'd come.

'Everything looks sharper with contact lenses,' she said, covering up first one eye and then the other to see if she could still read the sign that pointed to the lift.

'Perhaps your glasses need updating?' he suggested, despite really preferring that she'd give up wearing them. They swamped her finely boned face, although it had to be said that there was also something compelling about the contrast between the heavy, over-sized frames and the dainty features underneath.

'It's too much effort. They kick up such a fuss about getting the right sized glass. Everything's gone metric and the frames are imperial or something. You can't get frames like that any more.'

Dylan emerged from the post room with his trolley as they were going past, and Greville's heart sank a little. He had yet to emerge unbruised from an encounter with Dylan, and he really wasn't in the mood for being made fun of in front of Magnolia. However, Dylan's perpetual insouciant smirk was missing, and if anything, he looked as dismayed to see them as Greville was to see *him*.

'Where are you two off to?' Dylan enquired, making an awkward attempt at conversation. He had his hands thrust into his pockets and his gaze flickered around the floor.

'That's none of your business,' said Magnolia, her cold manner descending like a metal roller blind.

Had Greville been bold enough to have dispensed some rudeness of his own, he would then have walked away swiftly so as not to allow Dylan the opportunity to continue the conversation. Magnolia, however, held her ground. Oddly, instead of coming up with a belittling witticism, Dylan flushed and looked more intently at the floor.

'Only, if you're going up *that* way,' he continued and jerked a grey-shirted shoulder in the direction in which they were headed, 'you might want to be careful because some of the force fields keep rebooting themselves and won't stay switched off. And the Displacer up there is stuck in a loop, so it will send you back to the other one, at *that* end.' He pointed over their shoulders, back towards the office.

Greville searched his face for signs that he was having a joke at their expense, and was surprised not to find any. There was not even the slightest suspicion of the habitual knowing grin. Magnolia was puzzled too, regarding Dylan analytically, and he blushed a deeper red under her scrutiny.

'Are you…all right?' she asked, not exactly kindly, but with her edge slightly sheathed.

Dylan shuffled his feet and wouldn't look at her, and she waited him out.

'I didn't *mean* it,' he said eventually. 'Those two who were lost last week. I didn't *mean* it to happen.'

'What happened then, Dylan? What did you do?'

It was obvious that he didn't want to answer her, but he'd gone too far to shrug the question off.

'They were trying to find their department,' he said reluctantly, 'and they thought it was four doors down from the post room because that's where it had been the day before, but a Thousand had moved there instead.'

'And?'

Dylan sighed, a sound that seemed to emanate from the very depths of his being.

'They asked me if the R&D department was in there, and I told them not to set foot through that door unless they wanted to get lost. And they did. I couldn't stop them.'

Greville could picture the scene all too well... Dylan might have spoken those exact words, and he would have couched them in mocking tones, making his questioners doubt what he was saying and draw the conclusion that the opposite of what he said was true.

'I couldn't stop them,' Dylan repeated, glancing at Magnolia's set expression and reading exactly what she was thinking. 'I did try. I really did, but they were too quick.'

She pursed her lips.

'Well...' she said, and Greville guessed from her tone that she was going to say something sharply censorious, but then she seemed to change her mind. 'Well...these things happen. *Accidents*...accidents happen, and accidents aren't anybody's fault.'

She patted his shoulder, and left her hand there.

'Don't worry. You didn't mean for them to go in there. It's the D&D department's fault really, for not doing anything about the Thousands. People are lost every year, and D&D just seem to...accept it.'

'Could you find them?' Greville asked. 'You can find your way through them, can't you?'

He shook his head dolefully.

'I can find my *own* way, but I can't find other people. Once they're gone... they're gone.'

'Come on, now, you didn't mean it to happen,' she said. 'It was an accident, that's all. A very sad accident. And I expect you've saved lots of people over the years from doing something worse, haven't you? Try not to blame yourself.'

She gave him a final pat and took a few steps up the corridor.

'We'll pop in on our way back and see if you're all right, okay?'

He nodded, eyes still downcast, as dejected a figure as Greville had ever seen.

He was no fan of Dylan's teasing manner, but Greville realised that he would far rather endure his 'jokes' than see him so defeated. As he watched, Dylan pushed aside some internal envelopes on the trolley's second tier, chose a chocolate bar from his hidden stash and held it out to Magnolia.

'Here. For the journey.'

Magnolia accepted it gracefully.

'Thanks. We'll see you later. Chin up.'

They carried on their way, with a lot of the shine taken off the morning, thinking their own thoughts. Greville stayed silent, wondering if she was mulling over her uncle's disappearance and not liking to interrupt. He also kept an eye out for force fields. They were completely invisible until one walked into them, but they were created by square, grey plastic boxes on each side of the corridor. Every time they reached a set, he threw his red pen ahead to see if it would be repelled. She opened the chocolate bar absent-mindedly, snapped it in half and offered one half to him, and Greville took this as an indication that she was ready to start talking again.

'You okay?' he asked.

'Yeah. It's hard when the bad stuff happens, but that's why we get paid three times the going rate. And I kind of *like* the danger. How about you? Could *you* go back to working somewhere where the rooms are in the same place every day, and there aren't any shortcuts or secret chambers?'

'No,' he said. A few months ago, he'd have been scared and horrified by their environment, but now he'd miss it very badly indeed. And it was still true that if you stuck to the rules (even though you had to puzzle out a lot of them for yourself) then you were relatively safe.

The pad piped up from Magnolia's phone.

'If you walk a bit slower, you'll get there quicker.'

Where once Greville would have compared the pad's statement to his A level knowledge of physics and made a fruitless attempt to reconcile the two, now he was perfectly content to accept the pad's suggestion and slow down. Even as he did so, the doors on each side started passing by more quickly, as if they had stepped onto an airport travellator. He looked down at his feet, and suddenly felt very queasy indeed.

'Eyes front,' the pad recommended, and he did as it said, stumbling along for a few strides until he regained his equilibrium.

'We're in a slipstream,' Magnolia told him, her own gaze focussed forward like a ballet dancer about to spin. 'You know the slipstream you get if you're in a racing car and you get close behind another racing car? It's a bit like that, except there's time involved as well, and we're not following a racing car. I don't know what we *are* following, mind you. Possibly something we don't want to meet, but it's in a different dimension, or out of phase or whatever, so it's probably okay.'

They walked on for another minute or two before Greville was confident that he wasn't going to throw up. It was quite a challenge to keep up with the force field generators, but it was worth it because, sure enough, they came across one that was on. His pen was repelled, and where it had touched, just for a fleeting second there was a dinner plate sized aura which resembled a porthole to a stormy sea. Greville tried to stop, but was going too fast and bumped into the force field anyway, although he managed to get his arms up in time not to bang his head. They used their passes to swipe through and were on their way.

They came across another two more switched on force fields before the end of the corridor came into sight, and each time he successfully identified one, Greville was aware that what *should* have happened was that he should have blundered nose first into it, exactly as Dylan materialised out of nowhere, complete with trolley, to witness him embarrassing himself and to offer an unhelpful remark. With him not only absent but also having crossed the line from tormentor to helper, something was severely out of balance in their little pocket of the world.

Greville had never been this far along the corridor before. The slipstream slowed and they arrived at the end. Magnolia regarded the blank wall with interest.

'I didn't think this corridor even *had* an end,' she said, and reached out tentatively to touch the wall.

It was solid enough, and she felt briskly all over it, then stepped back to look for anything to press on or swipe at that might let them through.

'It's as if we're on the edge of the universe, but what happens if you stand on the universe's edge and then throw a spear? Where does it go?' she mused, convinced that there was a way forward.

'It goes beyond,' said the pad, assuming that the question required an answer. 'But those who cross over can never come back.'

This was becoming a common theme, and she had no appetite for unnecessarily testing the building's architecture, so instead she peered through the last door before the end of the corridor. Greville had a look as well. It was just an ordinary, square room, the size of Mr Valentine's corner office, and it contained only a desk and a machine sitting on top of the desk, about the size and shape of a multi-function home-office printer. They went in to examine it more closely.

The machine appeared to be able to copy, fax, scan and print in colour. It was plugged into a wall socket, and an LED on the front glowed green, showing that it was ready to do something. All they had to do was determine what that 'something' was.

They successfully copied a page from Greville's notebook, then scanned it, and used the Bluetooth function to send a page to print, but they couldn't find what else it did.

'It's got a duplex function,' Greville said doubtfully, but really the machine ought to be able to do something like fax a person or print a thousand pages in a millisecond or be able to do MRI scans to be worthy of a special fact-finding mission.

'I wonder what this does?' said Magnolia, looking at a portal next to the USB port.

The portal was finger-sized, and it seemed that it was indeed for fingers as there was an illustration of a finger print above it.

'Perhaps it's for secure printing? Maybe certain things need a finger print to unlock them?' she wondered. 'I'll try it out.'

She put her index finger into the machine, up to the second knuckle, which was more than Greville would have done as he wouldn't entrust his digits to any of the machinery in this strange and dangerous building. A second later, his fears were realised when all expression dropped out of her face and it became a vacant mask. He stepped forward to catch her as she wilted forward, but in the next instant, she was fully aware again, and the machine whirred into action. It took a few seconds to warm up, then churned out page after page, neatly stapling them together when it had finished. Magnolia picked up the document.

'It's a Reporter!' she exclaimed. 'Fantastic! I'd heard a rumour about these, but I didn't think they were real!'

'It's a…*what*?'

Greville wasn't exactly bewildered as this was no longer a state which he entered easily, but he was definitely mystified, and also worried about her.

'A Reporter! If you're supposed to be writing a report and you can't be bothered, you just put your finger in here and *think* about what you're supposed to be writing a report on, and it sucks it all out of your brain and does it for you! Look!'

She handed over the report and Greville flicked through it. It presented an accurate and grammatically correct account of their quest to the end of the corridor and their examination of the printer, neatly separated out by well-chosen headings. There was a header page, an index and all the paragraphs were numbered.

'It's a good job that I happened to be thinking about the right thing because I wasn't expecting this,' she said. '*You* have a go! It's brilliant!'

'Isn't it dangerous?' he asked. He hadn't liked the way that all animation had simply been wiped from her face.

'Probably. Possibly. Well, I'm not sure as I don't really know much about them. I suppose they're probably dangerous in the same way that being on your mobile phone for too long is meant to fry your brain? But anyway, you've *got* to because Mr Valentine wanted *two* reports, and so far we've only got *one*.'

Greville looked at his finger and then at the portal, unconvinced.

'Fair enough,' she said. 'We'll go back, and then you can write your report the slow way.'

'All right. Hang on.'

He took a moment to compose himself and make sure he was thinking about their quest to the printer, then inserted his finger, and suddenly he felt a swooshing sensation, like falling in a dream. Just as quickly, it was over, he was back to normal and the machine was printing another report. It was similar to Magnolia's in content, but undoubtedly written in his style – he noted that there was a certain stiffness and formality in the prose, the numbering was Roman and a few footnotes had crept in.

'There!' she said, delighted. 'I can see that we'll be making a few return visits. Isn't it a lot easier than writing reports yourself?'

There was no denying it, although Greville planned to research the Reporters in more detail, so that he could make an informed decision when in full possession of the facts. Deciding to take a properly weighed up risk was one thing, but taking reckless chances with one's intellect was quite another.

They began to walk back, this time at normal speed. The trip was going to take some time – the pad informed them that the total distance was now closer to five and a half miles, and accordingly they slowed down as they reached a Displacer.

'So if we use this, we'll get to the other end of the corridor?' Greville asked the pad. 'Is that closer to the office?'

It was; they would emerge a mere five hundred metres away, but even so, there was something about the Displacers that Greville didn't trust. Indeed, they was *nothing* about them that he *did* trust. He looked to Magnolia for guidance.

'Let's walk,' she said. 'We're legitimately on company business, and that course the other day said that the Displacers aren't to be used for getting from one end of the corridor to the other. And it's great fun walking on the carpet in bare feet.'

So they walked, not particularly quickly, she swinging her shoes and telling stories about the various departments as they passed them (the actuarial department had three layers, accessed upwards by ladders and downwards by slides; the head of Research and Development [apart from losing staff to the Thousands] commuted in via Displacer from a world where dinosaurs were alive and well; one should never go to a meeting held by the Offworld Admin Reconciliation Department because their meeting terms of reference had been muddled in translation; they were meant to say that meetings should be conducted in an orderly fashion so that everyone had a turn, but somehow electricity and good conductors had entered the mix, so now everyone had to have an electric shock) and for the second time in quick succession, Greville realised that he was enjoying himself at work.

All too soon, they reached the post room. They swiped in, but Dylan must have been out on his rounds as the room was empty.

'I'll put a note in his virtual locker,' Magnolia decided, 'I don't want to leave one just lying about for anyone to read.'

She took a page from her notebook, scribbled something brief in her spidery flourish, signed it, then folded it in half and wrote Dylan's name on it. She opened a skymail cupboard that Greville recognised as hers (her post binders were an energetic pink) and put the note inside.

'That's *your* cupboard, not his,' Greville observed.

'That's okay – I wrote his name on it, so it will go to his as soon as I shut the doors,' she said, doing just that and then opening the doors to show him that the note had gone. 'That's all you have to do if you want to send something to anybody else, then it's quite secure as only they can open their own cupboard.'

They swiped out of the post room and carried on to their office, and having walked over ten miles in her company, Greville was startled to discover that they were running out of corridor before he'd run out of conversation. If he'd previously spent all morning with another auditing colleague, then by now they would be exchanging sporadic and laboured sentences which started with 'so' and ended with a lame observation about work. Or, more likely, one of them would have invented an errand that involved ducking into a random office and hiding until the other had gone away, saving the embarrassment of walking back in awkward silence.

It was a curious feeling, to begin to realise that perhaps his social skills were improving. Something was definitely happening…he seemed to be making an uncertain transition from being someone who *couldn't* to someone who perhaps *could*. It reminded him of a happy long-ago Saturday morning when he'd finally grasped that he could swim. The delineation between being a non-swimmer and a swimmer was a blurry one, and only when he'd flailed and splashed his way from one side of the shallow end to the other without touching his foot down at all, did he appreciate that he'd broken through the barrier. What was more, having *become* a swimmer, he hadn't *un*-become one; he hadn't been to the pool again for three weeks, yet as soon as he tried, he found himself water-borne again. He hoped that his newfound and unexpected ability not to be an awkward idiot for several hours at a time would prove to be as unshakeable as his ability to swim.

Chapter 20

A lava lamp had appeared on Myhill's desk on their return to the office, and the man himself was watching it with rather grudging attention. His desk was slightly neater than usual and bore surprisingly little evidence of food, although one didn't have to look very far to find that the assorted packets had just been dumped on the floor to one side. There were still a few coffee cup rings in evidence, a heavy sprinkling of crumbs and the odd smear of ketchup. A blob of the iridescent substance inside the lamp detached itself and floated gently upwards, touching the top before beginning an unhurried descent.

'AND WHY HAVE YOU ONLY LOOKED AT FOUR FILES?' demanded a very strident female voice, making Greville jump so much that he nearly shut his fingers in his drawer as he put away his pens.

'I...errrr...I...that is to say...' he began reflexively, before processing that the censorious tone could not possibly be directed towards him, as he had never been the sort of auditor who thought that four files would suffice as a representative sample.

'I...errr...I...' said Myhill, his face colouring in indignation rather than embarrassment, as if his tie had been done up too tightly (it usually hung limply at half-mast). Only then did Greville realise that the voice was emanating from the lava lamp.

'IT'S SIMPLY NOT GOOD ENOUGH!' the voice opined, and as it did so, the words formed in the air, several feet high, not so much sub-titles as super-titles.

'It's his manager,' supplied a Cuthbert, never averse to other people getting into trouble. 'She's offworld, so she can only get to Earth when the wormholes are aligned.'

'AND WHY HAVEN'T YOU INTERVIEWED THE HOLISTIC DÉJÀ VU DIRECTORATE? THAT WAS SCHEDULED QUITE CLEARLY FOR LAST MONTH IN THE AUDIT PLAN.'

'Because it doesn't *exist*,' he said, with an aplomb which Greville couldn't help but admire. 'I think it's more of a concept? It only exists if you go back to it?'

'IT'S A CONCEPT EMPLOYING ELEVEN PEOPLE! I NEVER HEARD SUCH NONSENSE!'

'It's not *there*,' Myhill insisted, casting a longing glance at his food pile. Lunch time was fast approaching, after all. 'I went to look, and it wasn't *there*. It wasn't there when I went back again, either.'

'IT WAS THERE YESTERDAY, SO TOMORROW I SUGGEST THAT YOU GO BACK TO YESTERDAY AND HAVE ANOTHER LOOK. IF YOU HURRY, YOU MIGHT EVEN GET A REPORT TO ME BY THE END OF LAST QUARTER.'

A large blob growing up from the floor of the lamp stretched upwards, thinning and thinning until it collapsed again.

'AND WHAT ABOUT THE FILE REVIEW FOR THE LOST POLICY PROCEEDS DEPARTMENT?'

'They're at the far end of the corridor,' Myhill explained, sounding almost bored, whereas Greville would have been quailing in the face of such a public grilling. '*No-one* comes back from the end of the corridor.'

'My ones just have,' said Mr Valentine, emerging from his office. 'And if *they* can do it, *anyone* can.'

Magnolia frowned a little at the implied slight, but instead of wasting her breath by saying anything, she started sorting through some papers on her desk.

'Can't you have your meeting somewhere more appropriate?' Arabella/Rose demanded, glaring at the source of the noise. 'Some of us are trying to work.'

To the uninformed, it would look as if she was 'working' on nothing more pressing than a crochet string, impeded by the cat who was batting at her creation. But her insights couldn't be forced, and they came through the most easily when her mind wasn't over-burdened.

In response, the liquid inside the lamp began to quiver until the whole thing was rocking on the desk, and with a sudden, sucking sound, Myhill was pulled inside, a miniaturised version appearing in the midst of the lava. Greville watched in horrified fascination as Myhill blew out air bubbles, flailed about and banged on the inside of the glass.

'He's drowning!' he said. 'We've got to *do* something.'

Mr Valentine took a dispassionate look.

'No he's not. He's...*acclimatising*.'

'He's *drowning*,' Greville insisted. 'We've got to save him!'

'Drowning?' said Mr Valentine doubtfully and without urgency. 'Isn't that the one where you have too much fun-liquid and fall over?'

There was no time for any more nonsense, so Greville went to unscrew the top and release the miniature Myhill.

'Stop!' said all three Cuthberts in unison. 'You'll create a breach in the fabric of space!'

Greville froze as there were simply too many things to weigh up, and as he did so, the miniature Myhill stopped flailing, took a spasmodic gulp and then another one, and then he seemed to be breathing normally again.

'There,' said Mr Valentine. 'Acclimatising.'

He was right. The miniature Myhill put his miniature hands on his miniature (but still rather corpulent) hips and turned to remonstrate with the lava-creature, wearing a familiar expression of mulish belligerence.

'Here are our reports,' Magnolia said to Mr Valentine, handing them over. He received them with suspicion, inspecting them minutely from all angles, before starting to smell them. Greville took this as his cue to go to lunch.

'You need to fill in your lie assurance form,' called Mr Valentine, nose still pressed to a report which made his voice sound squashed. 'You haven't done it yet.'

'It's *life* assurance,' said Greville, rather boldly for him, 'and I *have* done it.'

Jolly tedious (and slightly alarming) work it had been, too, as there had been pages and pages of ways in which he might meet his demise which never would have occurred to him.

'No, no, no, no, it's *lie* assurance. Assurance that you'll tell lies.'

Mr Valentine paused to watch Myhill in action, his mouth moving silently in synchronicity with the miniature Myhill's.

'*Lies*. Like *he's* doing. Or maybe it's assurance that you *won't* tell lies…?'

His pudgy, long-nailed hand disappeared under his jacket, and when it emerged, he was holding some forms instead of the reports.

'I, the undersigned, promise not to tell lies,' he read.

'What if we're lying when we sign the form?' Magnolia asked.

'Well, you can *carry on* lying, can't you? It's perfectly clear.'

'How does the form know whether we're lying when we sign it?' said Greville wanting to join in with the fun. He wasn't a natural joiner-in of fun, and felt it incumbent to put in some practise.

Mr Valentine fixed him with his bottomless gaze, which seemed to suck all light from Greville's soul.

'It will know,' he said, his voice assuming the rumbling bass that resonated with awful power in the pit of Greville's being. 'The form sees everything. Do not treat it lightly.'

Suddenly, the whole thing seemed a lot less funny. Greville, chastened, took a form from the monstrous fingers and stole a look at Magnolia. Luckily she appeared oblivious to his discomfort as she had been looking for her pen.

'I promise not to tell lies,' she said, her fingers crossed, and signed her form, giving a careless shrug before returning it.

'What's this?' said Mr Valentine suspiciously, holding up his own crossed fingers, only he'd somehow managed to cross his middle and fourth fingers.

'It makes whatever you've said into the opposite,' she told him. 'It's in the staff handbook – page 4,293.'

'H'mm.'

Mr Valentine pondered his crossed fingers, head on one side, which drew Greville's eyes to them as well, only he'd rather not have looked because the pudgy fingers had a certain strength to them, and the nails were so very sharp, more suited to disembowelling rats than handling forms. He signed his own form, fingers crossed, and handed it back. His manager added it to Magnolia's, twisted open a hole in the air and posted the forms through. Greville only got a quick glimpse, but it was enough to show the most enormous warehouse, stretching as far as the eye could see in all directions, packed full of forms. It was quite giddying, and when the hole resealed a split second later, it took him a long moment to regain his balance.

He wanted to ask Magnolia what she was doing for lunch, but was conscious of Mr Valentine's black gaze upon him, and had the oddest feeling that he should hold his peace. He looked to see what she was doing and caught the eye of Arabella/Rose instead, who gave him a slight but unmistakeable shake of the head. It was all very strange, but strange was the new normal, and he was learning very quickly that it was best to go with the flow.

'Right, I'm going to lunch,' he announced, and departed swiftly before Mr Valentine could come up with any more forms. He'd been planning on going for a run, but the ten-mile walk had dampened his enthusiasm, so he went to the canteen instead. It was odd and agreeable to do something as normal as eating his lunch with a cup of tea while reading the paper, and he was feeling relaxed on his return to the office.

The rest of the afternoon passed pleasantly enough. Mr Valentine directed them to go to an archive store that neither of them had realised even existed, and told them to look out for anyone who was doing something they shouldn't. He wouldn't give them any further information – he had acquired a book called 'Audit Principles for Principled Auditors', and he told them (reading from its pages) that the Principled Auditor went into audits with an Open Mind, laying aside Unhelpful Preconceptions.

They hadn't found anyone doing something they shouldn't, or indeed, anyone doing something they *should*, or even anyone at all, because it seemed as if no-one else knew that the archive store was there either. After an hour or so of exploring the different levels, and not coming across anything remotely dangerous, Magnolia was bored.

'Let's see what's actually *in* some of these boxes,' she said, and pulled one from the shelf. She took out a file and opened it, revealing a mass of geometric squiggles. 'I want to see if the Transform app works.'

She took out her phone, flicked open the app and ran the phone over the text, and Greville saw how it was picked up by the camera, translated and appeared on the screen.

'It's old personnel records,' she said, delighted. 'Look at this! "Objectives for the year: 'Embrace cross-divisional convergence', 'recontextualise outcome-based growth mindsets', 'disaggregate customer-driven common core standards' – this is brilliant! The Transform glasses couldn't cope with management double-speak – anything like this, they would translate as 'do something with a particular something'.

Which, it had to be said, wouldn't have been wholly inaccurate.

She fished in her pocket and brought out her own pair of Transform glasses which were as over-sized as her regular glasses. She put them on and pushed them up her nose, a familiar gesture that caused his breath to hitch in his chest.

'There! You see? "Do something with a particular something. Do something with a particular something. Do something with an outcome-based something." Useless.'

Greville *didn't* see because he wasn't wearing his own Transform glasses, and he reluctantly got them out and put them on in front of his usual glasses. The geometric characters swam into words which were mostly 'something'. She handed him the phone and he tried that instead of the glasses, and suddenly the text was moulded into proper words.

'I'm sure there's another app that changes management double-speak into proper English,' she said. 'But I don't know if it's a free one.'

She put her Transform glasses away, and it was still odd to see her finely boned face unimpaired by thick frames. Greville removed his too, not wanting to prolong the amount of time he spent looking stupid by wearing two pairs of glasses at once. He was about to say something vaguely humorous about a fine example of management-speak he'd once heard, but then Magnolia picked the box up to return it to the shelf, the end of her heavy plait brushed across the back of his hand and his mind went blank.

'We need to think of something to do to take us to five o'clock,' she said, intent on squaring up the box so that it was in line with its companions. 'What do you fancy? Hide and seek? I can't be bothered with doing much more walking.'

'We could sit and talk,' he said, regretting the words as soon as they were out. It was one thing to fall into conversation naturally and by accident while walking along a trans-dimensional corridor; it was quite another to deliberately set out to converse. It was like planning a 'big night out' – from what Greville had overheard from former colleagues, the best nights out were the unplanned ones and the planned ones were never as good. This made no sense to him at all…if the night was unplanned, then how did everyone know what time to meet and where? And as soon as those details were arranged, then surely the night was by definition planned?

Greville himself had no frame of reference – the biggest night that he himself had been on was a former colleague's retirement do. They had met at the pub where they went the most frequently for their occasional Friday pints, moved onto the pub a bit further down the road and had finished up in the pub on the corner, having a careful half in each before being picked up and driven home by the retiree's wife. And it had certainly been planned because the man's 65th birthday had hardly come as a surprise. Although of course they had played backgammon instead of dominoes as the domino set was already in use.

'Okay,' she said. 'Let's get some tea.'

She had spied a dumb waiter, and sent down a note to the canteen, and soon they had a mug of tea each and found some kick stools to sit on.

'So,' she said, before a silence could even begin to descend, 'What made you decide to get into compliance?'

Greville thought back.

'Well, I got a summer job in an office…' he began, and found himself telling her all sorts of things that he'd never really thought about before. Ordinarily, he found conversation a careful process of move and counter-mover, but with her, it seemed to flow. He even made her laugh when he described one or two happenings that would only amuse another auditor, and five o'clock rolled around far too quickly.

'What are you doing later?' he asked, aware that the simple question was now just that rather than a potent-laden utterance. She pulled a face.

'Going to the supermarket, then tackling the ironing. But it's got to be done.'

That rather precluded doing anything together, which perhaps was as well; on their return to the office, it seemed to Greville that Mr Valentine was watching both of them, missing nothing, and that the man (if you could call him that[20]) was somehow satisfied when Magnolia picked up her giant floral bag and departed without so much as a valedictory glance in Greville's direction. Perhaps there was something in the staff handbook about auditors keeping a professional distance in case the impartial objectivity of the audit process were to be compromised? He filed

---

20   And Greville tended to, because it was more manageable than 'glitter cyclone temporarily formed into a man-like shape.

the thought carefully away.

He intended to go home via the shop, and was one turn away from the village high street, thinking idly about whether he could get away with giving the dog an extended ball-throwing session or whether he would have to submit to yet more walking when a loud voice nearly made him drive into the car in front.

'Stop! Stop now! You need to park! Park here!' said the clipboard, via his phone, which was peculiar as his phone was set to fully silent. Accustomed to obeying instructions first and thinking about them later, he obediently pulled over to the kerb, parked and walked the rest of the way to the shop. It turned out that the clipboard had been prescient because the high street was very thoroughly blocked by a stand-off between a bus and a lorry, not helped by the addition of a tractor and trailer behind the lorry and an enormous cement mixer behind the bus, and a sprinkling of bad parking. The whole mess was going to take some time to sort out.

Mrs Drew ran a practised eye over his purchases and added a lightbulb, then after further consideration, replaced it with one of the same wattage but with a different fitting. She also put a prettily wrapped bar of soap next to the rest of his groceries. Greville eyed the soap suspiciously. He favoured the sort of soap that came in a dispenser – one of the things that he and Poppy had absolutely agreed upon was the importance of having soap in containers in preference to having wet, unhygienic bars of soap lying slipperily about. He wanted to say something about the soap – he was a grown man, and surely there was a line to be drawn somewhere about the things he could be persuaded to buy and those he couldn't? But even before he'd finished the thought, he knew that he'd end up paying for everything.

He managed to turn around in the road by backing into someone's drive, then went the slightly longer way home, avoiding the high street altogether. It occurred to him that a sense of unease was developing inside him, growing stronger the nearer he got to his cottage, and feeling extremely foolish, he cleared his throat and addressed himself to the clipboard app.

'Do you…errr…know if Poppy's waiting for me at home?' he asked.

'No,' said the disembodied voice.

'No, she's not there, or no, you don't know?'

'No,' the clipboard repeated.

Greville considered. It was hard not to think of the clipboard as an omniscient being, but he knew that it was really just an advanced piece of route-finding software, and he tried to phrase the question in a way that it might understand.

'If I pulled into the driveway very quickly, would there be anything for me to hit?'

'No,' said the clipboard.

Greville wasn't totally convinced that he'd received a helpful answer but to his relief, the driveway was indeed empty when he arrived home. He went into the house, where Satan was beyond delighted to see him. The dog had helped himself to a newspaper and spent the day shredding, before scraping all the bits into a pile and rolling in it.

'Shall we play with the ball?' he asked, sending him into a frenzy of scampering and leaping.

They played with the ball for long enough to make up for the lack of walk, then Satan lay on the patio to cool down while Greville started on dinner. He changed the light bulb that had blown, then contemplated the soap in its paper wrapper. Perhaps Mrs Drew thought it would be better for his skin than his usual shower gel, although he didn't have any particular skin issues. He picked it up and sniffed at it, and discovered that it smelt strongly of strawberries, which put a completely different complexion on the situation.

He turned the potatoes down as they were boiling too enthusiastically, then found a pen and wrote Magnolia's name clearly on the soap. It was still a surprise that pretending to open a cupboard actually *did* open a cupboard, and he popped the soap inside, shut the doors and then opened them again, rather thrilled to see that it had vanished.

He really was quite tired from all the walking, and after dinner he couldn't even face wallpaper stripping, so he watched television for a bit and then went to bed with a book.

Chapter 21

Magnolia was already in the office when he arrived the next morning, and she was wearing her contact lenses again. She smiled when she saw him, and came over.

'It still tasted of soap, not strawberries,' she said, giving him an impish look, then went to put her bag away and log in.

Greville tried very hard not to imagine her in the shower, and was waging a losing battle when a tornado of glitter heralded the arrival of Mr Valentine. Today he was holding a medium sized, square box that he placed on the spare desk at the front.

'I have brought baked goods,' he announced. 'You must have some.'

He removed the lid to reveal an iced sponge cake.

'Maybe later?' said Greville, who had had his breakfast of eggs on toast (slightly short on the toast as his breakfast companion had caught one of the slices fired out by the over-enthusiastic toaster, and there hadn't been time to make any more) not long ago.

'I made it with my own hands,' said Mr Valentine, inspecting them. If that was supposed to be an inducement, then it had exactly the opposite effect. As usual, his hands were far from clean, and the nails did not appear to have been scrubbed for a very long time.

'Later,' Greville said, more firmly. With any luck, Myhill would make an appearance at some stage, rendering the whole situation moot.

'It's not optional,' his manager informed him. 'The consumption of baked goods is required to…' he paused to consult his management book, which now had a second bite missing from it… '…to "foster an atmosphere of camaraderie and form the team into a cohesive unit".'

He pondering this, frowning.

'Cohesive? That's sticky, isn't it? Why would I want you to be sticky?' He looked from the cake to his hands and back to the cake again, imagining the transference of stickiness. 'In case you need to climb walls?' He walked his hands up an imaginary wall. 'But would that be sticky *enough*? If you wanted to climb walls, then wouldn't zarian gel be better than ground up grain?'

'No, that's *ad*-hesive,' Magnolia said. Her computer had decided to give her a random test relating to reflexes and fitness to work, and she was chasing the 'start' button around the screen. '*Co*-hesive is something completely different.'

'What, then?' he demanded.

'"Cohesion" means the molecular force within a body or substance acting to unite its parts,' a male Cuthbert said, arriving at the perfect time to launch a deftly thrown spanner into the works.

'Well, there you go, then,' said Mr Valentine. 'You have to consume the baked goods so that your parts don't disunite. You'd be no use to me at all if you were separated into your component fragments.'

He looked at Greville expectantly.

'You have no reason to refuse,' he encouraged. 'All the constituents were weighed to the nearest atomic unit, and I compensated for the difference in gravity. And I irradiated it at the right temperature, to the nearest joule.'

'The correct time for cake is eleven o'clock,' Magnolia said, finally managing to log on. 'It doesn't taste as nice if you don't have it at eleven.'

'Nice?' he repeated. 'What does "nice" have to do with anything? It's not *supposed* to be nice; it's supposed to stop you diffusing.'

He continued to mutter to himself under his breath, but Greville was relieved to see him put the lid back on the box. Mr Valentine consulted his book again.

'Is it a multiple of 365.2422 days since you emerged from inside another human being? Because if it is, I need to make this an incendiary cake to celebrate that…' He read a bit more, his lips moving, and then went over the same phrase a few more times as if he couldn't believe what he was reading. 'To celebrate that you have successfully stayed alive for another 365.2422 days? Is that something to celebrate? I suppose it is with you lot, as you seem to expire very easily. And even if you'd stayed alive, of course you'd probably have degraded a bit.'

'What are we doing today?' Greville asked, keen to move the conversation away from cake.

'You're doing an A and Q session with the prospective new client. The one with the silver box to solve. You provide the As and they provide the Qs. The other bidders will be there too because it's an open format, so if they provide better As than you, there's a chance that they might get the business instead.'

'What sort of things are they going to ask?' Greville enquired. He knew a lot about audit processes, but not a lot about anything else.

'I don't know *that*! *They're* asking the Qs, not me! *I* can't ask the Qs, can I, because I don't know what they want to ask.' He shook his head in woeful wonder at

Greville's lack of comprehension. 'The whole point of it is that you make up answer to whatever they want to know. It could be *anything*.'

This was hardly comforting, and Greville opened his mouth to ask for more detail, but Mr Valentine waved him off.

'No, no, no, no, you're supposed to *answer* the Qs, not ask any more. Now, run along because you're supposed to be there at 9.'

He checked his two watches, seeming to favour the one that was upside down.

'You'd better get a move on or you're going to be late, which means that you'll fail one of your objectives. The meeting is in one of the great halls.'

Once upon a time, Greville would have been paralysed by the very idea of going to a meeting for which he had not prepared, at a location which he had not checked out beforehand, on a topic on which it was likely that he had no knowledge. Now, it was almost exhilarating to be thrust into a situation where he would have to live on his wits. It saved all the tedious hours of working out answers to every conceivable question, 95% of which were never needed.

'Okay,' he said, grabbing his pad and pens. Magnolia put the jacket back on that she'd only just taken off, picked up her own things and followed him into the corridor.

'Turn right,' said the clipboard via his phone, without needing to be asked. 'Count ten doors on the right, then go back one.' It was silent for a second. 'No, count *eleven* and go back *two*.'

That room was indeed a great hall, laid out with a central lectern and four sets of tables and chairs arranged as if for a seminar. Three sets were occupied. The beetle people were already there, scuttling about and changing chairs with each other over and over again. The Gelapegos were there too, sitting gelatinously behind one of the tables, football sized eyes rolling slowly in all directions. And there at the nearest table sat Poppy and her colleague, both prim and poker faced. Myhill stood at the front behind the lectern, holding his wrist in front of his face the better to see his watch, and as they entered he looked up crossly.

'You made it,' he said, sounding disappointed. 'The deadline was nine o'clock. Now, hurry up and sit down because we need to get started.'

Greville and Magnolia sat. He tried to give Poppy a quick, professional nod as it didn't seem right to ignore her altogether, and in return she delivered an intense and mournful gaze that he struggled to interpret. He was also distracted by Myhill's appearance. For the second day in a row, the man's tie was done up properly, and today he was wearing a (slightly soiled) jacket that nearly did up and he'd plastered down his sandy hair with water, somewhat inexpertly so that the finished effect was akin to a field of standing wheat after a heavy storm. It wasn't lost on Greville that all this effort was for Poppy's benefit, and he wasn't sure why he *minded* when

Poppy should be nothing to him any more. But he *did* mind, and was annoyed with himself for it.

'Right then,' Myhill said, with a look at Poppy's legs that was meant to be sur-reptitious. 'I'm in charge. This is the last stage of the tender process. You two are ahead at the moment…'

'I thought we'd won?' Magnolia interrupted, not impressed with being faced with yet more hurdles and having observed Myhill's somewhat partisan inclinations.

'You sort-of won, but a client has the right to call 'Shenanigans!' if they think that the process hasn't been carried out fairly, and I called it,' he said, smirking in a manner which he evidently felt was alluring in Poppy's direction. 'Which means that we have to have a decider round.'

'But we won the last round,' Magnolia returned. 'That stupid box thing was an open and fair competition.'

'I cried 'Shenanigans' because I think you cheated,' said Myhill, provoked out of all semblance of diplomacy. 'So it doesn't really count. And if you interrupt me again, you'll be struck out for…for…unprofessional conduct.'

Magnolia looked as if she had a great deal more that she'd like to say, but had to restrict herself to glaring at him. Myhill managed to glare back for a few long seconds, then had to look away, trying to pretend that he was doing it through choice rather than discomfort.

'Now then, we'll start with the questions. There will be three, and the worst answer in each round earns you elimination.'

He ran his gaze slowly from group to group, savouring the temporary power that had been vested in him.

'The first question is…what's the best dinosaur? And the people answering first are going to be…' again, the slow perusal of the groups, '…*you*.' He pointed at Poppy and her colleague, attempting a rictus-like smile.

'What do you mean?' Poppy said. 'Dinosaur? How do you *mean*, dinosaur? Does it stand for something?'

Myhill shook his head in agitated disappointment.

'Okay, you two can be next,' he said, nodding in Greville's direction and taking care to avoid Magnolia's glare.

'The best dinosaur is the stegosaurus,' Magnolia said, without missing a beat. 'Because it's got a great shape, it's got those decorative things all along its back and it's vegetarian.'

'Not bad,' he said with evident reluctance. 'Not bad at all. Right, you next,' he said, pointing to the beetles. Greville eased his Translator app on so that he could hear what they were saying.

'…do you want a fight?' one of them asked his colleague, and now that Greville could hear what they were saying, he interpreted the frantic movements of their feelers as aggression when previously he'd thought that they denoted busyness.

'Do *you* want a fight?' the colleague responded.

'Why are you looking at me like that?' said a third. 'Do *you* want a fight?'

At Greville's secondary school, a somewhat idealistic head of department had decided that it would be A Good Thing if General English were taught in mixed streams so that the boys would have a chance to socialise with all the different strata. The beetles' conversation was reminiscent of that in General English, which had been something of a cultural shock to those in Greville's stream. He and his peers were more accustomed to listening to the teacher in respectful silence and asking for extra homework than to treating lessons as social occasions and throwing missiles, the least offensive of which was a paper aeroplane. The only time that Greville had made a paper aeroplane in class, it had been part of a physics lesson to do with aerodynamics which had involved a lot of weighing, measuring and calculation, and had culminated in a voluntary but well-attended after-school film about Concorde.

It eventually filtered through to the beetles that they were expected to answer the question.

'The dung beetle,' said one of them. 'Are you looking at me funny?'

His tentacles were waggling furiously.

'Errrrr…good answer,' decided Myhill.

Greville wanted to point out that actually, it *was* a good answer because on Earth it was known that dung beetles had evolved in line with dinosaurs, so it was possible that on their planet, a similar evolutionary development had taken place. But he didn't want to prejudice Myhill towards the beetles.

'You! What's the best dinosaur?' Myhill demanded of the Gelapagos, who were sitting quiescently next to each other. Their heads – or at least, the top parts of their beings which resembled an incipient upwards growth from a lava lamp – drew together, as if in conference. Greville turned his attention to the app.

'Where's the food?' one said.

'What's the best *dinosaur*?' Myhill repeated. '*Dinosaur*?'

'The Oniricons taste the best, but they're too fast,' said the other. 'The Aralbutes are easy to catch, but lumpy.'

Greville and Magnolia exchanged incredulous looks. It was mind-blowing that their world still had dinosaurs…and that they ate them.

Myhill nodded sagely. 'Good answer. Now…'

'It wasn't a good answer! It was a stupid question!' Poppy piped up. 'What's the point of all these questions?'

'To see if you can do 1,080° thinking,' Myhill said. 'We don't want to give this contract to anyone who can only think in a straight line.'

Greville thought through the maths. He'd heard of 360° thinking so 1,080° must be…spinning around on the spot. It was as good a metaphor as any for the daily reality of the work place.

'T-Rex,' said Poppy's companion, speaking with authority. 'The T-Rex, because it can tear all the other dinosaurs to shreds.'

She looked challengingly at all the other contenders.

'Good answer,' said Myhill, relieved. 'That's what we like in our contractors – a bit of aggression. Now then, you lot are out because a dung beetle isn't a dinosaur. Off you go.'

The feeler activity became more frenzied, overlaid with multiple cries of, 'It's *your* fault' and a free-for-all ensued with furiously kicking legs and much action from the ferocious-looking mouth-pieces. Eventually the melee made it to the door and disappeared into the corridor which, after all, was the correct place for a fight.

'Next question: what do you do if you come across an anomaly?' Myhill said, and it was interesting watching him trying to respond to Poppy's questions about whether he meant an accounting anomaly or a rift in the fabric of space in an odd cryptic way designed to help *her* without helping them.

'Report it to the correct authorities using the authorised procedures,' said Magnolia, stepping smartly over the ongoing verbal haziness and earning herself a dirty look from Poppy's companion, to which she was utterly impervious. Poppy came up with something similar but not as snappy, and the Gelapagos said that they would go to lunch and chew it over. When they were eliminated, Greville was anticipating a slow and glutinous departure and was preparing to step smartly out of the way so as not to become embroiled in their relentless, sticky egress, but instead they began to quiver like shaken jellies, then disappeared as if they had never been.

'Right then, it's between you and you,' Myhill said, nodding at the respective teams. 'I've got a number written on this piece of paper, and whoever is the closest, wins.'

Greville, getting into the spirit of reckless boldness, was about to guess the first number that came into his head when Magnolia elbowed him. She had the oddest expression, and Greville wondered if she was feeling faint. Her colour had drained away and she was looking strained. He noticed that Myhill appeared to be trying to mouth something to Poppy, but as he was turned away from him and as Greville wasn't any good at lip-reading, he wasn't at all sure what it was.

'Eleven billion,' said Poppy's colleague.

'Eleven *million*,' said Magnolia.

Myhill turned over his piece of paper, jubilant.

'There!' he said to Poppy, holding it up. 'You've won. Eleven billion is the right answer. I'll be in touch shortly with the full contract. I look forward to working with you.'

'No,' said Magnolia. 'That says eleven *million*. Count the zeros. Six zeros. It's nine for a billion.'

'No it isn't,' said Myhill. 'It's...' He counted zeros, frowning. 'Well, I *meant* to put eleven billion, so that's what counts.'

'Well, you *put* eleven *million*,' said Magnolia. 'So *that's* what counts.'

'No...that says *billion*,' said Myhill, and taking out a pen, added another comma and some very small zeros.

'The cameras are watching,' Magnolia said, angling her head upwards. 'They can see everything you do. They can see this. They can see you cheating. They didn't see *us* cheating on the box challenge because we *didn't* cheat.'

Myhill looked up at the ceiling, seeming to know exactly where the hidden cameras could be found. Greville wondered if similar cameras were everywhere, feeling acutely guilty at what he might have been recorded doing despite the fact that it was very unlikely that he had anything whatsoever to feel guilty about. Myhill craned his neck one way, and then the other, as if trying to calculate the angles and whether they might have missed him adding the three extra zeroes. But then he saw Magnolia's face and realised that this was one fiddle he was not going to cash in on. He sighed, and bowed to inevitability.

'Okay, you lose,' he said to Poppy and her colleague. 'So you might as well be on your way. And next time you're invited to tender, try not to mess it up. *Twice.*' He snatched up his piece of paper and started to stomp out, then came back again.

'I'll give you my business card in case you want to contact me about...anything,' he said, feeling in each pocket in turn and shedding chewing gum wrappers and screwed up napkins, finally producing a dog-eared card which had already been used for the scribbling down of other phone numbers. He handed it to Poppy who accepted it doubtfully and wrapped it in a tissue before putting it in her pocket.

He gave her a nod and a lingering stare which was probably meant to be smouldering and enigmatic, but which instead gave the impression that he'd noticed that her skirt was tucked into her underwear and was wondering whether to tell her, and backed away from her as he stared. The effect was rather spoiled when he reversed into a chair and nearly fell over. He picked himself up looking annoyed rather than embarrassed, treated her to a rakish nod and waddled out. Poppy's colleague stomped out after him. Poppy herself approached Greville, and when he took a step backwards, she took another one forwards, and now she was close enough to smell.

The familiar perfume brought a sudden wave of connection to his previous life.

'I need this contract,' she said, her voice low. 'I really need it, Greville. Please. Just admit that you cheated, then we can have it. I want to make partner, and I need this contract to clinch it.'

Magnolia was hovering, her mouth pressed into a displeased line.

'Well, I…errr…I…' said Greville, making his way towards the door. It was strange enough seeing his ex-fiancée in this work environment; it was stranger still trying to adjust to their new positioning with respect to each other. How were you supposed to behave towards your ex? Greville wasn't at all sure, having never had an ex who was the product of such a weighty relationship.

'I'm all by myself now,' she added craftily. 'I've got to pay all the bills alone, and I really need to be made partner.'

They were back in the corridor. The beetles were still fighting, contained in a segment of corridor by two force fields which had automatically sprung up to contain the fracas. The force fields also contained all sound, so it was as if someone had pressed the 'mute' button on the undignified goings-on.

'No,' said Greville. He wanted to say that he was sorry, but he couldn't quite bring himself to give voice to the lie because he *wasn't* sorry about winning the contract.

'Please?' she said, in a small and hopeless voice, the tears welling up in a way that he simply couldn't bear. This time, there was no Satan to defuse the situation.

'I'm sorry,' Greville said, and now it was no longer a lie. He really *was* sorry, although he couldn't have said what about. Upsetting her? Disappointing her? The denouement of their relationship?

'I can't live without you, you know,' she burst out, then turned blindly and blundered into the nearest room to get away from him, and before he could shout a warning, the door slammed behind her. Greville peered through the door, feeling sick at heart when he saw other rooms leading off that one, and yet others leading off them. He opened the door to plunge after her, but was pulled up short by an iron grip on his jacket sleeve which also grasped the skin beneath. He tried to wrench away, and now there was also a painful grasp on his waist which yanked him bodily back into the corridor. He tripped and sat down hard, and charged for the door again, but Magnolia stood in front of it and shoved him backwards. He went to charge one more time, but the desperate urgency seeped away, leaving him deflated.

'She's gone,' Magnolia told him, giving voice to what he already knew. 'I'm sorry. It's too late.'

He stood clenching and unclenching his fists, frantic to do something and with no viable course of action. Magnolia gave him an appraising glance to check that he wasn't going to try to push past her, and then turned just her head to look through the glass.

'I can't see her,' she said. 'She's not there. I'm sorry.'

Poppy's scent still hung in the air, providing a visceral link to his previous existence only a few short months ago, when he'd truly thought he'd loved her.

'We've got to do something,' he said. 'We've *got* to.'

He peered through the glass himself, Magnolia taking an unembarrassed, precautionary hold on his belt, and whichever way he looked, he was met with rooms leading onto other rooms, like reflections in a dressing table mirror when the side mirrors were angled in a particular way. He heard her take in a deep breath and let it out very slowly.

'Okay,' she said. 'We'll try to get her back. I kept all the stuff from…you know… my uncle. We could go over that again and see if there are any clues.'

She didn't let go of his waistband until he'd turned away and began to accompany her back to the office. He walked numbly at her side, his mind spinning. If only he'd been quicker. If only he hadn't upset her so much. If only he'd let her have the contract. He'd wanted to make a good impression to Mr Valentine, but it wasn't worth this.

Arabella/Rose looked up as they came in, giving them both an appraising glance.

'You were fast enough, then,' she said to Magnolia, a statement rather than a question.

'Yes, *she* was fast enough, but *I* wasn't,' Greville said, stung out of his usual deference. 'Why didn't you tell *me* that I had to be fast?'

'Because that's not how it works,' she returned, arching an eyebrow. 'I say what I see. I *can't* say what I *don't* see'

This did not feel like a satisfactory answer, yet Greville couldn't think of anything concrete with which to upbraid her, which was a shame as he'd never before felt brave enough to remonstrate with someone like Arabella/Rose. He sat down while Magnolia went to look in the cupboard, coming out with an archive box which she put on his desk. Mr Valentine emerged from his office, holding a fistful of cake.

'You won?' He enquired, oblivious to the strained atmosphere.

'They won,' complained Myhill, emptying loyalty cards out of his wallet to see if he'd got enough stamps for a free lunch. 'But they cheated. Again.'

'Hmmmphh,' he said, pleased. 'So now you can…'

'No – there's been an accident,' Magnolia said. 'Someone from one of the other teams went into a Thousand. We need to find them straight away.'

'The one with the connection?' he said, his brow furrowing as he looked at Greville, and he inhaled several times as if trying to catch a whiff of something. 'Yes, you're right – I can't smell it any more. So much for that.'

Myhill paused in the act of sorting his cards into piles.

'Not the one in the beige suit? Your old one?' he said, affronted, as if Poppy had gone missing deliberately to foil the less than salubrious plans that he had for her. 'Do you have to ruin *everything*? Now I'll have to start all over again. I wonder if her friend is single?'

He logged onto the database and began to check whether he could extract her details.

Magnolia seemed to realise that if they wanted their boss to allow them time to investigate, he wouldn't be impressed by sentimental appeals.

'Perhaps it might be worth something, if we managed to find some of the others?' she suggested. 'Maybe there would be a reward?'

'Well, if you can get the other ones back as well, I suppose it wouldn't do any harm. I mean, those other ones that I thought were you, but weren't. You know the ones. I'll just send the mitigations to do what I wanted you to do this afternoon, once they're back from their post-course course.'

He crammed the fistful of cake into his mouth and returned to his office, the closing of the door cutting off the enthusiastic but somewhat unrefined eating noises.

'I kept everything,' Magnolia said, opening the box and pulling out the top file. 'Here's all the skymail correspondence with the Lost and Found department. They're in charge of trying to find things that are lost, and deciding what to do with things that just turn up out of nowhere. And all the correspondence with Internal Investigations.'

'A-HA!' said Myhill from the next desk. 'There you are, you little beauty. Come to daddy. There we go. Skymail, telephone number...now, why doesn't it say if you're single?'

'Because it's a client database, not a dating webite?' Magnolia suggested.

'But it doesn't even say how old she is,' he complained. 'I don't want to waste my time on her if she's an old boot, do I?'

She noticed Greville's stricken expression – the door handle on the Thousand was probably still warm from Poppy's touch, and already Myhill had forgotten her completely – and touched his sleeve.

'Come on – let's find a room and do this somewhere more private,' she said, shooting a venomous look at Myhill which bounced off him. Indeed, he raised a chubby hand in farewell as they gathered up the box and went in search of a quiet space.

Chapter 22

They returned to the magnificent library in the end, which appeared as deserted as it had been on their previous visit, and they set the box down on the desk they'd used before. Magnolia sent for some tea, returning with two mugs.

'I *am* sorry, you know,' she said, setting them down on the inlaid marble coasters. 'About Poppy. And I'm sorry that I had to stop you going after her, but you couldn't have helped her. As soon as she let go of the handle, it was too late. You *have* to believe it. I wasn't trying to get rid of her – I was trying to stop *you* being lost as well.'

He looked at her solemnly; her face was a study in earnestness.

'Yes, I know.'

He'd felt a spike of raw anger when she'd held him back, her strength remarkable for one so slight, but out of the heat of the moment, he realised that she was right. From that first instant, Poppy had been beyond salvation.

'We'll find her,' she said. 'With both of us working on it, we'll find her, don't worry.'

She gave him a brisk pat, and went to take the lid off the box and Greville put a preventing hand on it.

'It's not just because it's her,' he said. 'It's because…because…'

The words dried up in his throat. He'd never seen anyone die – or go to their death – right in front of him before, and it had shocked him very badly. Warm, thin fingers pressed down on top of his.

'Never mind about that now. We'll get her back first, and we can worry about all the other…stuff…later. It doesn't matter at the moment.'

She withdrew her hand, allowing him to remove the lid; he lifted out the top file and opened it, and had barely done so when Roland swirled sootily into being in front of him, sword raised aloft.

'It didn't smell of vanilla!' Greville exclaimed. 'Mess, mess, mess!'

The sword swung in a murderous arc, singing through the air; there was simply no time to do anything but freeze, braced for a fatal blow that never came. When he dared to look up, the sword inexplicably was safely in its owner's scabbard.

'Sorry about that,' Roland said. 'Force of habit.'

'But it *didn't* smell of vanilla,' Greville repeated, rather lamely. 'It didn't!'

'I can't work out how to get back,' Roland said, addressing himself to Magnolia, having identified her as the brains of the outfit. 'I popped over to deal with a payroll clerk who was trying to look at expenses records that she shouldn't have access to, and now I can't remember where to go. It all looks the same around here.'

'Where are the others?' asked Greville, looking around for tell-tale inky clouds.

'They went back. I just wanted to check that she was okay because she was crying, and you can't leave womenfolk crying, can you, and when I turned around, they'd gone. I didn't see which way they went.'

'You can cross the dimensions, can't you?' Magnolia said, regarding him speculatively. Roland rolled his eyes.

'They're not dimensions, really. It's all just a massive bowl of soup when you get down to it. All this business of thirteen dimensions, or fifteen or however many they're up to now. Nonsense. It's soup. You go in whatever direction you want, and you come out where you're supposed to. Except for here. This one's a funny one, and I can't always find the thin bit.'

'When you're doing your rounds, do you ever see anyone who's been lost in a Thousand?' she persisted.

'Those ones with all the fiddly bits that won't stay still? Nope. When people go in there…' he slapped his hands together as if trying to crush an insect between his palms, the noise making them jump despite the fact that one insubstantial surface meeting another should have produced no noise at all. 'That's what happens. The End. No more. Finito.'

This was disappointing news, and his vehemence meant that there was no point in questioning him further. Instead, she pulled out her phone.

'Do you know where the thin bit is?' she asked, making Roland prick up his ears, and in response the pad app drew a languid line which pointed just to the right of the nearest book shelf. Greville looked where it was pointing, and he found that he could see it too. It reminded him of the thinnest part of a very old bedsheet which had experienced years of wear, worn to translucence yet not quite to a hole.

'Quickly,' said the pad. 'It's going.'

'See you,' said Roland, hurrying off, and when he reached the thin spot, he vanished into it as if into thick mist.

She inspected her tea which now contained flecks of soot, shrugged and drank some anyway. Greville sank down onto one of the hard, wooden chairs.

'So that's that, then.'

'So what's what?'

'You heard him. No-one survives the Thousands.' He smacked his own hands together in dismal imitation of Roland.

'No, not necessarily. In fact, not at all. He hasn't even worked here that long. There are probably all sorts of things he doesn't know much about. In fact, there's precious little he *does* know. I was only asking him on the off chance, just in case.'

'But I…'

'No,' she said briskly. 'You can't give up already.'

Greville eyed the box of files and opened his mouth to point out that she'd given up on her uncle, but it seemed unnecessary and unkind. She followed the line of his gaze.

'We did everything we could. Everything. But I've worked here longer now, and got more experience, and I can probably think of more things to try. It's too late for my uncle, but perhaps it's not too late for Poppy. Here, give me that file.'

She turned it towards her and glanced at the hieroglyphic writing.

'This is the Lost and Found file. All this paperwork…' she fanned the pages from back to front with her thumb. 'All they say is, "We haven't found anything. Please submit another 'missing item' form at the start of the next lunar semester". Look.'

The Transform app on her phone morphed the hieroglyphs into words, and they reviewed several pages which read exactly as she'd said. She put the file face down on the desk and pulled out the next one. The writing was squiggly this time, and the file was fatter.

'Internal Investigations file. They searched absolutely everywhere. All the dimensions. Forward and back in time. The phases. You can see the result of every search – concluded. That's what that red stamp says. And then this top page – it says that they've agreed with the Lost and Found team that there is no point in continuing the search because there's nowhere else to look.'

She went to put that file upside down on top of the first one.

'Hang on,' said Greville. 'Can I have a look?'

He wasn't the sort of auditor who took other people's word for things – not even the word of people who had gone over the file many thousands of times, and if that made him unattractively pedantic, then so be it. He used his own Transform app to sweep over some of the pages.

'It says, "inconclusive", not "concluded", he said, holding the phone over the red stamp.

'No it doesn't,' she said impatiently, moving next to him to peer over his shoulder. 'It says…'

She nudged his hand away and tried her own phone, with the same result.

'I don't understand it! They must have edited the file! But all the pages have an indelible date mark, and….'

Quickly, she checked date marks, examined pages for signs of tampering and tried to spot if anything else was amiss. Several pages bore her own careful page parkers, and she compared her hand-written notes safely contained in the pocket at the back against the file contents.

'It's all here. It looks exactly as I remember it. But…'

The red imprints looked genuine enough to Greville, as if they'd been put there using a real ink pad and a rubber stamp, and they looked genuine enough to Magnolia as well. Even so, she examined them from different angles and ran her finger over the dried ink. Something occurred to her.

'Have you got your Transform glasses?' she asked, and when he provided them, she put them on.

'There!' she exclaimed. 'There! It says "concluded" now!' Taking the glasses off again, she reverted to the phone app. "And now it says "inconclusive".'

Greville tried the glasses too, and it was exactly as she'd said. They did indeed render the squiggles as "concluded".

'What do you believe, over the phone or the…' he began.

'Oh, phone. Always phone. The glasses are *rubbish*. I thought that they were good once, but that was before we got the app.'

She turned to the front page. 'And this says, "Investigation pended; awaiting further advice on where to look from the Lost and Found team". *Pended*, not suspended.'

The nuance wasn't lost on Greville, who took up the first file again, opening the top page.

'And the Lost and Found team never did anything else because they were waiting for another form,' he said. 'So they were both waiting to hear from each other.'

'And *I* thought they'd both done everything they could,' Magnolia said, her voice almost a sob. 'I chased and *chased* them for all their wretched update reports every month. I thought…I thought…well, it doesn't matter now because it's too late for all that. It's what we do next that counts. I vote that we go and see the Internal Investigations department. In person.'

'Okay then, let's go.'

Greville had the most dreadful feeling of time running out, perhaps prompted by seeing Myhill's anguished flailing in the lava lamp. Of course, Greville had actually been in a Thousand, with Dylan as his guide, and (unlike the lava lamp) there was plenty of air in the Thousands. She wouldn't suffocate; she'd die of dehydration or hunger. Or maybe time worked differently in there, in which case she might already be dead, or have been dead for a hundred years. Perhaps they were already too late.

'Internal Investigations isn't in this building,' she said. 'And I've never met one of the investigators in person. If I rang them, I'd always get their voicemail. If I skymailed them, I'd get a standard acknowledgement…look, they're all filed here. They used to send their reports to that big thing in the post room, and that's the only contact I had.'

Greville addressed the pad app.

'Do you know where the Internal Investigations department is?' he asked, and in response it drew an ornate question mark which flashed a few times before un-drawing itself.

Magnolia made a face. 'That doesn't surprise me. If it wasn't for all these reports, it would be hard to believe that the department even exists.' She addressed her own app. 'Can you get us anywhere near the Internal Investigations department?'

This time, the question mark was smaller and made slow circuits of the screen, and just as they were beginning to think that it had got stuck in some sort of loop, the question mark formed itself into an arrow, which took them back into the corridor.

'It's going to be beyond the room with the Reporter, isn't it?' Greville said. He was still feeling the effects of their previous long walk, and while the prospect of a walk with Magnolia on company time would normally be appealing, today it seemed to be the most dreadful waste of time, walking all that way while maybe Poppy was hurtling towards a lonely, agonising end. But after they had passed only a few doors, the pad's arrow bent right, pointing into the sort of small room suited to small meetings. Indeed, there was a meeting going on at that very moment. The arrow flashed insistently, drawing itself bigger and bigger. Greville peered in, uncertainly. The very prospect of interrupting a meeting made him acutely uncomfortable, even if he knew the people involved (which he didn't) and had good reason for doing so (and judging by his running app, which frequently sent him up dead ends, electronic navigation devices were far from infallible). He didn't want to go blundering into the meeting only for the pad to tell him to make a u-turn and come back out. He imagined Poppy collapsing of thirst, reached for the handle and blundered in before he could think better of it.

Everyone stopped talking and looked at them.

'Sorry,' said Greville. 'Sorry. I…errr…I…'

The arrow now pointed to a second door, to the left, which led to a second, identical room.

'Wrong room,' he said, 'Sorry.'

The second meeting room was thankfully empty, and they went from there back into the corridor – if not an actual u-turn, then maybe the next best thing. Still, at least the pointless diversion hadn't wasted much time, and maybe…

'Look,' said Magnolia. 'We can see the end of the corridor from here.'

She was right – the blank wall was only about fifty metres away, and Greville sent an unspoken apology and a wave of gratitude to the pad.

'Thats okay,' it wrote generously, if slightly ungrammatically.

Soon, they were faced with an expanse of wall, which had no more openings than previously. The room to the right still opened onto the Reporter; the room to the left opened onto a Great Hall which was totally empty. Magnolia felt every inch of the wall, and Greville did the bit at the top, which she couldn't reach. There were no hidden openings, or boxes to swipe or thin patches.

'We need to go over it, under it, round it, through it or do something complicated to do with time,' Magnolia said, undaunted. 'That's all. There has *got* to be a way.'

The pad was no help; a thick black line representing the wall went right across the screen from left to right, while a row of different-sized arrows bobbed at it and then retreated, like tadpoles that were feeding.

'Perhaps it can't get a signal?' she suggested, watching the arrows' slow and repetitive dance. 'Perhaps it's being blocked somehow? Even the old version never used to get baffled, not even if it was taken through a Displacer.'

'It's hopeless,' Greville said, the words bursting out. He almost wanted to sit and cry…with guilt, with grief, with sheer frustration…but there was nothing to sit on and he felt too hollow for tears.

'No, not at all,' she said, wearing the determined expression that suited her so well. 'There's *got* to be a way round this. In this building, people can fax themselves, documents can be delivered before they've been written and you can get to the canteen through a cupboard. Do you honestly think that there's no way round a stupid *wall*?'

She thought hard, looking intently at the wall as if willing herself to the other side, and he saw the precise moment when she seized hold of an idea.

'Technology's no good here, so we go old-school. Let's go!'

She went into the Great Hall which was arranged, like so many of its fellows, as an old-fashioned school gym with wooden climbing bars on the walls. Heedless of her office clothes, she began to climb, and when she reached the top, pushed a ceiling tile up and aside.

'Ha!' she shouted down to him, her voice muffled as her head was in the space above the room. 'There's no wall up here! We can get across!'

By the time he'd climbed to join her, she had already removed a tile to expose the room on the other side and was looking down. The other room definitely wasn't in the familiar stamp of a Great Hall, although it was big enough. Perhaps it was how a Great Hall might look if transported several thousand years into the future, all iridescent white walls and mirrors with a smooth white floor.

'There are no bars,' she said. 'I think we'll have to jump.'

It was quite a long way down; comfortably an ankle-breaking height.

'I'll hang down and then let go,' she decided, but before she could make a move to do so, Greville grabbed her, determined not to lose two ladies in one day.

'No. Let's see if we can jump down into the corridor itself. The ceiling will be lower.'

They moved along, pulling up another tile, and now they were above a futuristic version of the corridor, very white, very clinical and with a lower ceiling. It smelt clinical as well…too clean and with an almost medical connotation.

'I don't like this,' she said, kneeling so that she could put her head through the hole and look further up the corridor. 'I'm not sure that we…' She caught herself. 'Never mind. We've got no choice, and we're Compliance, aren't we? Access all areas and all that.'

'I'll go first,' Greville said quickly, intent on salvaging a vestige of masculinity and acutely aware that his contribution to their success had been zero, or less than zero taking into account his negativity. 'Then I can help you down,' he added, overcompensatingly.

Her expression said very loudly that she didn't need any help and in fact resented the offer, but she kindly bit back whatever sharp words she wanted to say and instead watched as he lowered himself down. She followed after him, dangling into the corridor, and he was then faced with the conundrum of deciding where to grasp her that wouldn't hurt or annoy her, but which would help her land gently. It would really have been a lot better not to have said anything. He grabbed her ribcage, the bones defined beneath his fingers, finding her impossibly light. How could so much strength and energy be contained within a person who must surely weigh less than Greville's two largest cast-iron weights?

'We ought to work out how to get back up,' she said, gauging the height to the opening which they'd made. 'You could boost me up, but then you'd need something to climb on, and I don't see anything.'

She looked into the room which, on the other side, had held the Reporter; this room was as clinical as any dentist's office, containing a spotless white desk and a white chair of an interesting, smooth organic shape which was barely recognisable as a chair.

'I'll get that thing there,' she said, pointing to the chair, but when she tried the door, it was locked. She began looking around for other things that he could stand on.

'There's probably another way out,' Greville said, impatient to be off. 'They'll let us out another way.'

This made sense – in this environment, there were usually too many entrances and exits rather than too few – but even so she shot a concerned look up at the gap in the ceiling before reluctantly following him away.

'Where's the Internal Investigations department?' he asked his pad app, determined to maintain the initiative. The pad drew another question mark which bounced unhurriedly in a lazy zig zag. Greville's heart sank; he had been hoping that once they'd traversed the wall, it would be able to pick up a signal again.

'Where's the nearest we can get to the Internal Investigations department, please?' Magnolia asked, and the question mark became an arrow – a futuristic, cleanly drawn arrow with careful curves and a precise point, and that point indicated that they should continue up the corridor in a straight line.

They checked rooms to left and right as they went, seeing no-one. The small meeting rooms contained an immaculately white table and a suitable number of white, organic chairs. The office-sized ones contained white desks, white chairs, white computers. The floors were smoothly white. The light came from units fitted seamlessly into the walls and ceilings. All the doors were locked.

After a few minutes, the arrow swung left a few metres before they reached a corridor crossroads. This was new; their own office only had the one, straight corridor, and the occasional lateral meanders were more in the spirit of odd one-offs rather than deliberate architecture. Obediently, they turned left, and the app indicated that they should head that way for a short distance before turning right again. Greville began to relax; it was reassuring to have a confident lead to follow, and when they reached the right-hand turn, he rounded it with bold assurance. Now they could see some people…up ahead was a cluster of Gelapagos, only of course they were transparent instead of green to fit in with the sterile environment. The swivelling eyeballs were absent, too.

'We're here to talk to the Internal Investigations department,' Magnolia said, quickly opening the right app. Her words were translated as, 'Blob…blob…blob,' which may have meant something to the Gelapago look-alikes as they drew nearer with their rolling gait.

'Blob…blob…blob,' said the nearest being, which strangely was translated as exactly that.

'The app doesn't seem to be working,' said Magnolia, and had another go, speaking more slowly and clearly.

'We're from Compliance. We…'

The creatures rolled inexorably onwards, making blobbing noises as they approached.

'We're here to speak to Internal Investigations. We need to…'

There was something relentless about their globular progress which suddenly reached the tipping point between curious and dangerous.

'Run!' said Magnolia. There was no time to take her shoes off as there were straps that needed to be undone, so she ran as best as she could back the way they had come, clumsy and slipping instead of nimble and fleet of foot. Greville pulled ahead of her, hoping vainly that perhaps he might somehow be able to leap high enough to haul himself back into the roof space, then pull her up as well. The beings rolled behind them, far faster than they looked. They reached the first corner and rounded it fast…too fast as Magnolia slipped on the smooth surface and fell. She tried to scramble up and he tried to help her, and in the next instant there was an unbearable weight on top of them. Just as Greville felt that he would surely be crushed to death, he felt himself sinking into the warm gel within.

He tried to fight his way out, but his movements were slow and effortful; a pocket of air had formed around his face, for which he was grateful yet which would only last for a minute or two. The thing reversed direction and rolled away, and there was so much white all around that it was impossible to get any bearings. He caught a glimpse of Magnolia being bowled along behind, her mouth open; he couldn't tell if she was screaming or trying to breathe.

There was no time for anything except to try and stay in contact with the rapidly staling air pocket; he was being rolled at a bewildering speed. Just as he thought that he must surely suffocate, he felt himself sinking, then the thing's weight rolled away from him, leaving him dazed and breathless on the floor. The air tasted so sweet and it was such a relief to be out of that cloying prison that all he could do for several moments was lie there and enjoy breathing.

'Are you okay?' she asked, cautiously pushing herself to a sitting position and checking to see if she was injured.

'I think so,' he said. He felt as if he'd been playing a childhood game where you had to spin around and then try to walk in a straight line, but he wasn't actually hurt. He wasn't even wet, although he felt slightly sticky all over.

They were in a very white room with curved corners and edges, and the door fitted so seamlessly that it was impossible to see its outline even though they knew where to look for it. High above, there was a grill set equally seamlessly into the ceiling and even if they could have reached it, it didn't look as if it would open as it appeared to be moulded as part of the ceiling rather than added to it.

Their phones had been spat out next to them, and Magnolia picked hers up.

'Can you get us near to the Internal Investigations department, please?' she asked, in the spirit of trying every possibility, no matter how remote.

They both watched as the pad wrote 'you are here', the words appearing underneath each other in the middle of the screen. Next, it drew a series of arrows, bobbing inwards towards the words, and that was all it had to say.

Chronitus…feel sick…boring waiting for them to say the thing you've just heard them say…

Chapter 23

The floor was hard, cold, smooth and very, very white, like fresh snow with the sun on it.

'I feel sticky,' Magnolia said, patting herself experimentally. 'I could have done with some of this sticky stuff on the soles of my shoes earlier, then we wouldn't be in this mess. Or a bit of chronitus. Why would it work for something stupid like Myhill's number on his idiotic piece of paper, and not for something like this?'

'It wouldn't have helped much,' said Greville. 'Even with a few seconds' head start, we couldn't have climbed back up quickly enough.'

His eyes were repeatedly drawn to the ceiling vent – pointless really because it was comfortably out of reach and looked utterly impregnable. And the most fearsome tool with which they were armed was probably Greville's red pen, which would make no impression at all on such a sturdy structure. But the vent was the most interesting feature – indeed, the only feature – of this dazzling, smooth-sided cube, and it kept attracting his gaze.

'I hope we're not going to be stuck in here for too long,' she said. 'Because I wanted to go for a run later.'

She was leaning back, looking for all the world as if she were reclining by a pool with nothing more vexing on her mind than whether to go for a swim or get an ice cream.

'Aren't you worried in case they chop us up, or do experiments on us, or…or *eat* us?' he asked.

'What good would worrying do? There's nothing we can actually *change*, is there? Okay, let's have a good worry.' She screwed up her face and pressed her hands to her temples, a study in concentration. 'Please don't eat us…please don't eat us… please don't eat us. There. I just did my best worrying, and we're still here, and it's made no difference to what's going to happen. They'll eat us or not eat us, and we'll worry about it when it happens.'

'Are you really not worried? Not even about dying?'

'Well, I'd rather *not* die, and if they try to eat me or do experiments on me, I'll do my best to stop them, but when you sign a contract to work here, you're signing up for all this as well, aren't you?' She swung a hand to indicate their current prison. 'And it's been a real blast up until now, hasn't it? You can't expect to cherry pick all the best bits and not have to deal with the pits. So the best thing to do for now is relax and save our energy in case we need it later.'

Greville tried very hard not to look upwards again; it was a pointless reflex, and no matter how much he looked, it wouldn't do any good.

'Do you think...' he began, but now *she* was looking upwards.

'Uh-oh, we've got company,' she said, climbing to her feet. An insect had made its way through the vent and was walking across the ceiling, an impressive feat considering the smoothness of the surface, and then it made a transition to the wall.

'Let's hope it's not a biter,' Greville said, getting to his feet as well. He wondered whether they ought to squash it when it got within range. He never squashed insects; in fact, he took great pains to rescue them from the house and put them outside, but this was an alien insect and perhaps a single bite could kill. As they watched, a second insect emerged and then a third. They were six-legged, and perhaps the size of a woodlouse, and quite disconcertingly speedy. The first one was fast approaching the height at which he'd be able to reach it, as a fourth and fifth insect appeared through the vent. He took his shoe off, ready to set to work.

'Stand back,' he told her. 'I'll deal with this.'

He had already started to swing the shoe when something about the insects' waving appendages caught his attention, and he paused, flicking on the Translate app.

'...want a fight?' said the insect, via the app. 'You're in our space! You don't belong here!'

Magnolia (having completely ignored the instruction to stand back) peered closely at the pathfinding insect which by now had reached her nose height.

'It looks like one of those beetle people,' she said, the phone translating what she said into the beetles' busy chattering. All the beetles began to speak at once, and the app had trouble keeping up. The words which emerged the most frequently were, 'stupid', 'cheat' and 'the place that smells funny'.

'Why are you so small?' Magnolia asked.

'Why are *you* so big?' returned the first beetle. 'We haven't changed. You've gone really big. Enormous.'

Greville was reminded of Myhill in the lava lamp; while inside it, he had been part of his manager's world, and so looked small, while really he was the same size still. It was only the perspective that had altered.

The last few beetles caught up with the trailblazers and as they did so, a few more began to emerge through the vent. Greville wondered if they were going to be eaten after all.

'What are you doing here?' demanded a beetle, and with so many of them beginning to cluster, it was hard to tell which one had spoken.

Magnolia tried to explain about the Thousands and the Internal Investigations department. It was hard to concentrate with so many beetles to keep an eye on because the brisk, scuttling motions made it seem that they were up to something. Something that would possibly turn out not to be very nice.

'Rooms change all the time,' said a beetle. 'Sometimes you go into a room and walk along for a bit, and before you know it, it's gone completely upside down.'

'And some of us disappear forever every day,' said another. 'I don't know what's so special about *you*. There's millions and billions of you, and a few less would be neither here nor there.'

He (or it might have been a she) waved tiny antennae in a furiously aggressive manner.

'Have you heard of the Internal Investigations department?' she persisted, patiently. 'Is it near here?'

'Are you stupid?' a beetle demanded. 'It isn't near *anywhere*! It's a *concept*.'

She looked at Greville, puzzled, and the beetle misinterpreted her expression.

'Are you saying *I'm* stupid? Do you think I don't know what a concept is?'

The wave of anger spread quickly across the insects, and in no time, all the antennae were waving and the rate of scuttling increased. More of them were making their way into the room all the time. The Translator app only caught the odd word or phrase, and none of them were good. It picked up things like 'succulent', 'soft' and 'get in through the ear'.

'Can you get us out of here?' She asked. 'I've got sugar.'

The effect on the beetles was startling; the scuttling and the antennae-waving stopped, as if they were all intent on what would come next. 'Lying...she's lying...I want some...she's lying,' said the Translator.

'Can you get us out?'

The chattering intensified. 'Cut them up...smaller than that...eat the rest...'

'Can you get us out without cutting us up?'

The consensus was that they could, and that it would involve doing something with the electronic lock.

'All right,' she said. 'Get us out and then you can have the sugar.'

'But first we'll have to neutralise you.'

Neutralise...neutralise...the word reverberated around the room, taken up by all the beetles, and then they began to swarm down the wall as if by mutual agreement.

Magnolia and Greville backed away, and now the insects were crossing the floor towards them, not quite a carpet but more than a scattering. The creatures reached Magnolia's phone, surrounding it and thronging over it, spindly articulated limbs pawing at its controls.

'Do you think we should…?' Greville said, torn between not wanting to be entered via his ear and not wanting to start stamping prematurely.

'They're doing something with my phone,' she said. Indeed, the bits of the screen that could be seen between the flailing legs were flickering in different colours, far faster than any human would be able to achieve. They finished and stood back.

'You're now neutralised,' said the Translate app. The beetles noticed their lack of appropriate response. 'Neutralised! *Neutralised*! We've added you to the visitors' list so that the Cleaners won't try to neutralise you again. Because we've already done it! Are you stupid?'

Some of the little creatures had returned through the vent and it wasn't long before the door unsealed and slid open, the beetles responsible trickling in from the other side. There was a general air of expectancy with the insects sitting still with only their feelers moving. The activity increased when Magnolia produced a chocolate bar and set it carefully on the floor.

'Go away,' said the Translator. 'Before we decide that you're *not* too fatty to eat after all. Go *away*.'

She picked up her phone and they stepped out of the room, careful not to tread on any little bodies. Behind them, a fight was predictably breaking out, with creatures swarming all over the chocolate and each other, flailing away in a frenzy of limbs. The pad had redrawn its modern-looking arrow.

'What shall we do?' said Greville, watching as the arrow began to flash with increasing vigour.

'How do you mean?'

'I mean, do you want to go back, or carry on? It looks as if it might be dangerous.'

'Well, *of course* it's going to be dangerous! *Everything* here is dangerous!' She regarded him with irritation. 'Do you expect me to wimp out at the first sign of trouble?'

Greville's experience with annoyed women – and she was looking distinctly annoyed – was that any further utterance of his, no matter how well intended, only tended to inflame the situation, but there was no time for dithering about.

'No,' he said. 'But…but…'

'But what?' she demanded, already looking appreciably crosser.

'But…I couldn't bear to see you hurt.'

For a long moment, he felt the full force of her scrutiny as she weighed his words, then her expression softened.

'No-one's ever said that to me before.'

'They should have. Because you deserve to be kept safe.'

By unspoken agreement they began to follow the arrow, which led them along several stretches of dazzling white corridor and around a few corners, until they rounded one and came face to face, or face to shapeless mass, with another group of the globular creatures. Or of course, it might have been the same group as they had no discernible distinguishing marks. They froze, poised to run again, but this time the Cleaners ignored them completely, continuing their slow and aimless progress. Even so, it was nerve-wracking to squeeze past them and continue up the corridor.

'I think it's a good thing that there's some security,' said Magnolia once they were safely past. 'It means there's something worth protecting. I can't imagine what it might be though. I mean, if those things are effectively white cells which treated us as the virus and put us in a holding cell. Is this place some sort of body...are we inside a being?'

'I don't think so,' Greville said. 'It doesn't feel...organic enough. And the beetles – I don't think they're part of a bigger whole. We've seen them in our bit, haven't we? They seem to have their own civilisation.'

The pad led them along several miles of featureless corridors, past frequent clusters of Cleaners, and Magnolia took her shoes off to speed progress. Eventually the pad indicated that they had reached their destination – a white door with 'Facilities Department' on it. Magnolia knocked, and the door slid seamlessly aside.

It was a 'small meeting room' template of room, only laid out as a reception area, with a white desk bearing a white computer – one of the ones that had evolved beyond the need for a screen, so everything was projected onto the air – and sitting at the desk was a white-clad receptionist. Not a beetle, although Greville had been half expecting it. The woman appeared perfectly human – young, immaculately groomed and with a supercilious air that would not have been out one who worked in an upmarket beauty studio. Her icy blondeness and alabaster skin fit perfectly with the whiteness of her surroundings.

'We need to speak to someone in the Internal Investigations department,' Magnolia said, the Translator app rendering her words into a musical language.

'Do you have an appointment?'

'Well, no, but...'

'Sorry, meetings are by appointment only.'

'Can I make an appointment then?'

'You have to ring this number.'

The woman handed Magnolia a card which she scrutinised.

'I've phoned this number about a million times. No-one ever picks up.'

'Leave a message and someone will get back to you.'

'But they don't, though. No-one has ever got back to me. Not even once, and this is important.'

The receptionist raised an eyebrow.

'Ring the number. Someone will get back to you. Good day.'

Greville expected Magnolia to argue; they had been through too much to be fobbed off so easily, and he never expected her to give up so readily on their quest. He was surprised when she stood mutely observing the receptionist who had turned back to her typing, manicured nails creating words which appeared in the air.

'What's pi calculated to the last digit?' she asked conversationally. The receptionist looked at her, her expression mid-way between outrage and puzzlement.

'Three…point…one four one five nine two six…'

She spoke faster and faster, reeling off digit after digit, then she began to flicker in and out like a projector screen that was on the fritz. When it didn't seem as if she could speak any faster, there was a faint bang, a slight aroma of burning circuits and she winked out altogether.

'There,' Magnolia said. 'Let's see what happens now.'

'How did you know?' Greville asked. She was always one step ahead of him, and while it was embarrassing, he also couldn't stop himself from finding it inappropriately compelling. There was something about seeing that much pure intellect in action, and with so little apparent effort, that fascinated him every time he witnessed it.

'I've seen it before. Once you've seen a couple, you learn how to spot them. Didn't you notice how flawlessly beautiful she was? Built by a man, some man's idea of a perfect woman.'

'Not mine,' said Greville, before he could stop himself. He didn't want her comparing herself to an icy artificial construction and finding herself wanting. 'I prefer…'

But there was no time for him to expound any further because the inner door was sliding open and two men emerged, wearing navy cargo trousers and navy polo shirts with a logo on the pocket.

'What have you done with Laetitia?' one of them asked, walking over to the desk and doing something with the electronic box of tricks that sat under it.

'Nothing,' said Magnolia. 'She just started to malfunction. I was only asking about the Internal Investigations department.'

'What about it?' said the second man, irritably. Greville looked past him into the room beyond – a Great Hall which had the usual school gym format rather than being pristine white. While he couldn't begin to name any of the forest of electronic equipment inside, it was indisputably an IT department.

'We need to speak to someone in it,' she said. The man folded his arms.

'Well, you can't.'

'We jolly well can,' she told him, producing something that was a cross between a train pass and a police badge. 'Compliance. Access all areas.'

'Doesn't work here,' he said, unimpressed.

'Access *all* areas,' she insisted, handing it over. 'Look.'

The man looked, rather sourly, and handed it back.

'I'll show you it,' he conceded. 'But you still can't speak to anyone.'

It seemed as if Magnolia had other ideas about that, but she wisely accepted the compromise, expecting to be directed to another office. Instead, the man indicated that they should follow him into the room. He led them past banks of enormous metal cupboards, all stuffed to overflowing with complex looms of wiring and tiny flashing lights, until they reached a clearing holding half a dozen ordinary laminate-wood desks at which sat a variety of bored-looking employees who were wearing the same uniform. Two were playing a card game, only with cards that bore pictures of fantastic creatures rather than an ordinary deck. Another was talking on his mobile while sending an email. A fourth had taken apart something that might have been a hard drive or might have been something else altogether and was poking at it desultorily with a screwdriver. A fifth was reading the paper while eating a doughnut and the sixth was picking at something crusted to the inside of a mug using a biro.

There on the floor next to one of the desks was a box similar to the one that had controlled Laetitia, and attached to it with peeling clear tape was a square of paper with hieroglyphs on it. Hieroglyphs that Greville recognised even without the Transform app because he'd seen them over and over again in the files.

'Internal Investigations!' he said, pointing. She'd seen the words at the same time, and her eyes were shining with triumph.

'And that one belongs to the Lost and Found department,' she said, indicating another box with a label written in looping squiggles. 'Now, all we need to do is find who works there.' She held up her compliance badge. 'Compliance! Access all areas! Who is responsible for these?'

The Translator app transmitted her words, and in return she got uninterested looks from the card players and a shrug from the doughnut eater.

'Excuse me,' she said more loudly, 'Who…'

A phone on one of the desks rang, and after four rings, the Internal Investigations box lit up.

'You are through to the Internal Investigations department,' said the box, via the app. It went on to tell the caller that they could leave a message, or if they wanted a form, they should send a skymail to a certain address.

'Who put this thing on loudspeaker?' said the hard drive tinkerer, flicking a switch which silenced the automated voice.

'Who deals with the messages?' Magnolia demanded, and getting no response, plucked the screwdriver smartly from his fingers. He regarded her sullenly.

'No-one. It's *automated*. That's why it's called an *automated system*. Because no-one has to do anything with it. It pulls in data from across the entire system, analyses it and compiles a report.'

'And what if the results are…inconclusive?'

'It sends a report to L & F, over there,' he said, pointing to the other box. 'Then that one does a system sweep and compiles a report, and sends it back to *that* one.'

'And what happens if they both keep sending reports to each other, and nothing's getting done?' she asked, her voice low, and Greville saw that she had subconsciously altered her grip on the screwdriver and was now holding it like a martial arts practise knife.

The man made a face.

'It gets added to the 'pending' spreadsheet, until one of us has time to deal with it.'

'Show me.'

Something in her tone prompted him out of his torpor, and he bad temperedly gestured a spreadsheet into being. She leant into it, tracing downwards with a slender finger.

'There!' she exclaimed. 'That's my uncle! How *dare* you leave my uncle on a spreadsheet?'

'Because we've been busy.'

'Is Poppy on there?' Greville asked, coming over to have a look. She wasn't; nor were the two who had disappeared the week before.

'Things don't get put on there until the system has finished with them,' the man said, still sounding bored.

'And if you weren't "so busy", what would you do about the things on the spreadsheet?'

'Look into them, probably,' he said, idly flicking onto a social networking site.

'Look into *this* one. NOW.'

He opened his mouth to say something insouciant, and she was faster.

'Look into this one now or I will invoke an emergency audit, right this second, and I'll close this whole office.'

For a long second, he seemed disposed to argue with her, then he defaulted to taking the line of least resistance, opening the spreadsheet again. He clicked on a few things, pulling up a screenful of text which even without using the Transform app,

Greville recognised as being the sort of thing that a programmer would understand and that an end user would not. After hopping through a few more screens, the technician called across to the card-players.

'They're still using the Beta version.'

'Didn't we do a stable release a couple of years ago?' replied one of them.

'No – there were still a few bugs that we needed to work out, so we kept the Beta running.'

The other card-player rearranged his hand.

'Could we do a full restart and do the stable release at the same time?' he suggested.

The technician blew out his cheeks and rolled his eyes, but started typing again.

'What's going on?' Magnolia demanded, having had enough of being completely ignored.

'I'm doing a restart. You lot are still using the Beta version,' he said it as if it was somehow their fault.

'The Beta version of what?'

He didn't reply for long enough to make it evident that he thought it was a really stupid question.

'The *building*. You're using the Beta version, which isn't stable, so every now and then, you get the odd pocket…' He broke off while he negotiated something tricky. 'Like if you're using a spreadsheet, and you split a cell, sometimes it throws out all the rows…' He did something else, and a progress bar appeared, tracking steadily across the screen, then it winked out, to be replaced with another one. 'And it's like if you hide a column; it's there but you can't see it…'

A box appeared in the middle of the screen, containing a few words.

'There. That's done it.'

He reinstated the social networking site and started writing a comment under a photo of a creature that was wearing a collar that could have been a dog or equally, mighty have been a large scorpion.

'What happens now?' she persisted, whereas Greville would probably have slunk away, having correctly interpreted the technician's body language as a request for them to leave.

The man actually turned around to glare at her, which did not trouble her in the least.

'I've fixed it! So now you can go back there, and if you've got any other gripes, you'll need to fill in a form and send it to Internal Investigations.'

'And what about the people who have just disappeared?'

'They'll be back, I suppose, if the split cells have been rebooted. And if you want anything else, you'll have to fill in a form.'

He returned to the dog/scorpion, and Magnolia looked at Greville with cautious joy.

'Did you hear that?' she asked. 'She's probably going to be okay.'

Greville *had* heard, and was feeling overwhelmed with relief. Poppy might be alive! It suddenly seemed incumbent to get back as quickly as possible.

'What's the quickest way back?' he asked, and although his question was directed to Magnolia, it was the pad app that answered, drawing a confident arrow which began to flash insistently. They walked out through reception, where Laetitia was in the process of blinking back into existence, except she had been oddly aged by her malfunction. Her hair was now grey and thin, her face heavily lined and the manicured hands were liver-spotted.

The pad directed them right even though Greville was certain that they'd come from the left, and it seemed to pick up on his hesitation.

'This ways fastest,' it wrote untidily, and appearing to realise that what it had written wasn't entirely correct, it had another go. 'This is way fastest', it put, and then scrubbed that out as well. Its third attempt was 'This way', and it seemed wise to put their faith in its conviction.

It led them to a Displacer, which looked much the same as the Displacers in their part of the building, except of course that it was blazingly white and very, very new, as if the protective plastic film had only just been peeled off. Greville regarded it doubtfully.

'How come we can use one of these to get back when it didn't work the other way?'

'That's down to The Wall,' she said. 'The Displacers pick up on where you want to go, but you can't think about going from our side to here because The Wall acts as a block. But on the way back…well, it doesn't because we *know* where we want to go, don't we?'

This made about as much sense as anything else he'd heard lately.

'Is it safe, do you think?'

'For goodness sake, Greville! *You* traipse back through all the miles of corridors and climb through the ceiling again if you want to! If you're not in such a terrific hurry to get back and see your old girlfriend, that is.'

She was really cross now – cross and hurt – and there was no reply that he could think of that would help. Instead, he mutely followed her into the Displacer, aware that his silence was incriminating him as much as a poorly judged remark would have done, and the machine whirred smoothly and silently into life like a brand new (and quite expensive) washing machine doing its very first load. Greville was aware that *something* was happening, and it happened so efficiently and gently that when they came to a rest it was a surprise to discover that they were already back outside the office.

Chapter 24

Greville looked up and down the corridor, trying to decide which way to go.

'Where's Poppy?' he asked the app, and its screen remained utterly blank. There was no way of rephrasing the question to give it a navigational slant, so he headed back towards The Wall, looking into rooms as he passed them. It was notable that there were not any Thousands. Magnolia followed on behind, not sharing his urgency and not making any particular effort to keep up. The corridor was also full of people – not confused people startled to find themselves transported out of a spreadsheet, but perfectly ordinary people going about their business – which made it difficult to see at a glance if Poppy had reappeared. He kept walking, until suddenly he saw her.

'Go away,' she said. 'I can't bear to talk to you. Not when you're being so cold.'

She mopped somewhat theatrically at her eyes with a floral-printed tissue.

'How did you get here?' he asked.

She had obviously been expecting him to enmire himself in an emotionally charged conversation and was brought up short when he refused to join her in her wallowings.

'I went in *there*,' she said, pointing, 'and I obviously wasn't supposed to because I got washed back out. It was a…a tidal wave of warm air. Is that how Security works here? You're lucky I wasn't hurt, otherwise I'd be suing.'

'How long did it take, from when you stepped in til you were…washed…back?'

Poppy frowned at him, displeased that he was more concerned with the mechanics of the situation than with her emotional well-being.

'About…I don't know…five seconds? And I don't think the interval should be set that short. What if people go into a room by accident? Surely they should be given time to realise their mistake rather than…being thrown out? And surely…'

'Are you hurt?'

Again, she was non-plussed by the direction of the conversation.

'Well, not so much *physically*, I suppose, but I just feel so…so…'

'Good,' said Greville, and turned around to locate Magnolia, surprised not to find her at his elbow. Instead, she was quite a distance back, talking to someone that he didn't recognise, and when he drew closer, he could hear that she was discussing outstanding audit actions while looking rather stern.

'Well, I'm not going to ask you again, so if it isn't finished by the end of next week, I'm going to escalate it to an amber *starred* risk,' she said. She turned away, her expression if anything darkening further when she saw Greville.

'Is your girlfriend all right?' she asked.

'She's all right,' Greville said, 'but she's *not* my girlfriend. *You're...*'

He stopped, painfully aware that he'd overstepped the mark, and probably by quite a long way. Of course, in the privacy of his own mind he'd been imagining for quite some time that she *was* his girlfriend; that their paths were converging and that there was a real possibility that they might proceed (at least for a while) together. But he hadn't ascertained her feelings on the matter, and he wasn't even sure how one set about making the transition from being people who had an affinity to being part of a proper couple. With Poppy, it had just *happened*, and without him really realising it, let alone actively bringing it about.

'I'm what?' she asked, and it was more impossible than ever to read what she was thinking. She was suddenly intense, and although she didn't exactly seem angry, he had the impression that strong emotions weren't far away.

'My...errr...my...I mean, that is...'

He was in agonies. If he said it out loud and she dismissed him, it would be the end of so much. He grabbed his courage in both hands and pressed onwards.

'My girlfriend. That is, if you want to be? I mean...I mean...'

'Okay, then,' she said, and now she was smiling her quiet, secret smile. 'Seeing as you've asked me so nicely.'

He beamed back at her, elated. It was like finding out that you had somehow passed an exam when your answer to the thirty-five marker on the binomial theorem had been so muddled that you were sure you'd failed – only better. Utter relief, sprinkled with joy. He belatedly remembered what he'd been going to tell her.

'Poppy said she was only in the room for five seconds,' he said. 'And it must have been a good couple of hours, so...so...'

Her eyes widened as she realised the implications, and she let out a silent, awestruck 'ohhhh'.

'There's a time differential? You really think that there could be a time differential?' she asked.

'Based on what she said,' Greville replied carefully, never one to make rash, unqualified statements.

Magnolia leaped onwards to the practicalities.

'So say she'd been in there two hours, and it really must have been more rather than less. But let's stick with two. Two hours equates to…to seven thousand, two hundred seconds. So dividing by the five gives a ratio of…one second of real time to one thousand, four hundred and forty seconds in a Thousand. How many days are there in five years?'

'One thousand, eight hundred and twenty five, not adjusting for leap years,' Greville said promptly. Not because he was quick at mental arithmetic (or rather, not *only* because he was quick at mental arithmetic) but because the sort of things that he was accustomed to auditing quite often ran in five-year cycles, with various odds and ends needing to be evenly shared out throughout the period.

'Okay,' she said, so we divide that by one thousand, four hundred and forty, and we get…'

Greville saw where she was going with this.

'About a day and a quarter.'

'A day and a quarter!' she repeated, 'That's all? So he could still be alive!'

'If the figures are right,' Greville said, not wanting to be the one to add the prudential footnote but unable to stop himself. 'But that's a very rough calculation, and…'

'Maggie! What have you done to your hair?' said a man who was striding towards them. 'Have you been playing about in a Time Forgot? I've *warned* you that they're not toys. This place isn't safe, you know.'

Magnolia whirled around.

'Uncle?' she said, and hurled herself into his arms, thin, strong arms wrapped tightly around his back and shoulders already beginning to heave with sobs.

The man, who had the appearance of a scholar, and one who also probably liked rambling and taking notes about birds in his spare time, shot Greville a querying look as if seeking an explanation for his niece's strange behaviour, but he evidently decided to offer comfort first and get to the bottom if it all later, hugging her back as if it was a perfectly ordinary thing to do in the middle of a busy corridor.

'There, there, Maggie, it's okay,' he said. 'You shouldn't worry so. It was just a wrong turn, that's all. I was testing a theory. I missed my dinner, of course, and I had to sleep on the floor, but I've been through worse.'

'It was five years ago,' Greville offered. 'You've been gone five years. There's a time difference.'

His expression changed.

'Five years? Five *years*? I've been gone five years? But…it was only yesterday!'

He correlated Greville's explanation with Magnolia's reaction, and freed a hand to assess the length of the heavy blue black hair.

'Five *years*!'

Magnolia raised a blotchy face from his chest, leaving a damp patch on his shirt, and looked up at him.

'I thought you were dead. We *all* did.'

'Margaret too? *Margaret*? Is she all right? She hasn't died? She thinks...she thinks...'

'She's fine,' said Greville, taking charge. 'Magnolia and I saw her recently. She's perfectly fine. She just misses you a lot.'

'I've got to call her, right now. Where's a phone that works?'

'Here,' said Magnolia, passing him her handset. 'It's ringing.'

Her uncle ducked into an empty room for privacy, leaving them alone in the unusually busy corridor. Magnolia watched the steady flow of people.

'It must be the reboot,' she observed. 'You never normally see anyone out here, do you? Only in the offices. I think the Beta version kept everyone slightly out of phase to stop overlap or accident.'

She wiped her face carefully on her sleeve.

'I'm so happy. I'm so very, very happy. I want to go back with him, to my aunt's house...to *their* house, but I think I'd be in the way. She really loved him, you know. She's going to be so pleased. Her biggest fear was that he'd die first, and she'd be left, because he's a few years older than she is, but now...now I suppose that he's *younger*, so that's even better.'

The man himself strode out of the room, giving Magnolia her phone back, and he looked as if he might have been crying too.

'I'm going home,' he said. 'I'll talk to you...later.'

They watched him hurry away.

'Let's go back to the office,' Greville suggested gently. 'We need to tell Mr Valentine that we've got all the people back.'

She allowed him to take her arm and lead her in the right direction.

'How come you've got a special "compliance – access all areas" pass and I haven't?' he asked, thinking that perhaps it might be wise to nudge her towards a less emotional plane after the high drama.

'What?' she said, momentarily surprised. 'Oh, you haven't been here long enough to be eligible to apply for one. There's an induction procedure – not something I'd want to go through again. I had a headache for about a month afterwards, and not all the scars have disappeared, but nothing worth having is easy to get.'

They passed the post room, which wasn't quite in any of the locations where it usually was.

'Hang on,' she said, and swiped in, Greville following. Dylan was sitting on an upturned waste paper bin, his head in his hands, looking at his feet; as soon as they entered, he leapt up with alacrity.

'I was…just having a rest for a second,' he explained. 'I'm about to go and do the second delivery.'

'We found them,' Magnolia told him. 'All the lost people. Everyone who's ever wandered into a Thousand. They're all back.'

Dylan started to smile, then frowned instead, searching her face to see if she was telling the truth.

'You found *all* the lost people?' he repeated. 'But you can't have. Some of them have been missing for years.'

Greville could understand his scepticism. Not so long ago, Dylan would have thought it very funny to tell someone that something which really mattered to them was resolved, wait until they started to jubilate and then say, "HA – joking!", so it wasn't surprising that he expected this behaviour in other people.

'We really found them,' she said. 'It was a…a technical issue, and it's been fixed now. Everyone's all right because there was a time difference. Quite a big one.'

Temporal anomalies weren't anything out of the ordinary for a post room officer who worked in their building, and Dylan didn't query it, although he still didn't look convinced.

'Look,' she said, swiping the door open again. 'The corridor isn't out of phase any more. Everyone's visible.'

He looked, and after watching for several long moments, he began to believe her.

'So they're all safe? The ones that went the other day, and your cousin, and the post room manager, and the one before him and the one before *him*…'

'Uncle,' she corrected. 'And they're all safe. I met my uncle a few minutes ago and he's on his way home now.'

A wave of utter relief swept over his face, making him look guileless and far younger.

'Thank you,' he said very quietly, addressing himself to the floor near her feet. Just as quickly, his habitual sly expression was reinstated.

'You might have got them to leave the corridor alone,' he complained. 'All those wretched people. It's going to take me forever to get my rounds done with all that lot in the way.'

And with that, he added a wire basket of very, very tiny internal envelopes no bigger than postage stamps to his trolley and headed out into the melee. Magnolia and Greville continued onto the office, where they were met with an environment that was far from soothing. Mr Valentine had evidently just finished yelling at Irina, who was crying. Greville wouldn't have believed that Irina even *could* cry, let alone be provoked into it by a mere telling-off from a manager, only he had had several first-hand experiences of the man's bad temper, and understood how primevally terrifying it could be. At the next desk, Piers, evidently embarrassed by all the drama, was trying to do sums a little too fast on a calculator, with the result that he had to keep clearing it and starting again. Mr Valentine turned round as they came in, his face still purple and his eyes bottomless black sinkholes.

'We've found all the lost people,' Greville said, a little more loudly than he would normally have done; he felt that the magnitude of the feat deserved the extra volume. To his disappointment, the room carried on much as before. Arabella/Rose continued to crochet (perhaps already somehow aware of this development); the Cuthberts continued to type at an impossible speed (although Greville suspected that they were having to try very hard to conceal that they were impressed) and Myhill continued filling his pulled-apart sandwich with crisps. Only Mr Valentine had anything to say.

'What have you done *that* for?' he demanded, his complexion growing even more purple. 'I wanted it to take at least two weeks, or even a complete lunar cycle. How am I going to make any profit from it when you've finished already? Isn't there any chance that you could put a few of them back again, until I've agreed a consultancy fee structure?'

'No,' said Greville. 'They've all gone their separate ways. The building's been fixed so that it can't happened again, so perhaps you could charge for that?'

'Fixed? So there's no more rooms leading into other rooms? How are we going to get rid of idiots from now on? We'll have to use the disciplinary procedure, and that takes forever. It's far easier to just let nature take its course.'

He paced up and down making irritated huffing noises.

'You...two had better go home before you do any *more* damage. Go away! I don't want to see you again before tomorrow.'

They didn't need telling twice. Magnolia collected her outsize floral bag and departed very swiftly. Greville wanted to tell her that she could call him later if she would like to do so, and felt a ripple of contentment that he would now dare to phone her himself just to see how she was. He closed down his computer, evading its importunate insistence that he should clear out his Skymails, collected his things and made his way to his car. He was half-hoping to hear the Mustang's tell-tale burble, but she must have already gone.

Satan was desperately pleased to see him home so early. The day was warm, but not oppressively so, and accordingly Greville changed out of work clothes and into something that would be comfortable for dog walking, and fetched the dog's lead. They went the long way through the woods and Greville ambled at a leisurely pace while Satan crashed about tracking down and pursuing smells, and made half-hearted attempts to catch rabbits that were far too fast for him. He deferred calling Magnolia until he got home, partly to give her some space, and for it not to seem that he was harassing her and partly for the sheer pleasure of having something to look forward to. He topped up Satan's water bowl, got himself a drink of lemonade and went to sit on the patio under the umbrella. She must have been waiting for his call as she picked up straight away.

'Are you all…' he began, but didn't get any further.

'It's so brilliant!' she burst out. 'My aunt's so happy! So, so happy! I can't believe he's back!'

He had never heard her so loquacious, and it was fun to sit and listen, making the odd encouraging noise to prompt her to continue. Eventually, she ran out of steam.

'Do you want to come round?' he suggested. 'For dinner? I could cook, or we could order in.'

She thought it through.

'You know, I think I'd like that,' she said. 'I feel so…so…*so*…there's not even a word for how I feel, and it's just too much to cope with. I'm going to drive myself distracted if I stay here by myself.'

He emptied and refilled the dishwasher while he was waiting, and took the opportunity to wash out the cutlery drawer which seemed to attract a mystifying amount of crumbs. It wasn't long before he heard the now-familiar noise of the car spluttering into the drive, and he and Satan went out to meet her. She was looking happy but tired, and fell into his arms as if it was the most natural thing in the world. He held her gently as she laid her cheek against his chest, feeling her heart beating, feeling her breathe, waiting quietly for her to pull away first. Satan's wet nose pressed insistently between them, and when he realised that he was failing to get their attention, he trotted off to look for his ball.

'Would you like a drink?' he asked as they walked back to the house. 'Tea? Wine? Beer?'

'I need a beer,' she said, and accepted a bottle and a glass. He assessed the situation. Now that the adrenaline was subsiding, the emotional upheavals of the day were taking their toll on her, and she was desperately weary. She probably needed food sooner rather than later, and so he pulled out a few ingredients and started to cook. She took her glasses off so she could rub her eyes, then sat and watched, Satan's slobbery head in her lap, too tired to make much in the way of conversation, although somehow it didn't seem to matter.

They ate at the kitchen table, looking out across the garden, then he put the plates in the dishwasher (having company was no excuse for slovenliness) and they went into the living room to watch the second half of a film which involved some aliens of rather unimaginative design trying to take over the world. They didn't appear to have much of a plan, let alone a coherent strategy, and their Displacer-equivalents were positively laughable. He made a comment to Magnolia about the poorly thought through controls, and when he didn't get an answer, turned to look at her and found that she had fallen asleep.

She looked absolutely beautiful asleep – utterly relaxed in a way that he'd never seen her before, her habitual fierceness extinguished, her radiance shining through. He watched her for a long minute, then another one, taking in the dense black lashes, the alabaster complexion, the fine-boned fingers. He had a guilty feeling that he was somehow taking advantage of her by gazing so yearningly while she was oblivious to his actions, and he forced himself to look away. She was breathing more deeply now, and it seemed a shame to wake her, and he also didn't like the idea of her driving home alone in the unruly Mustang, tired to the very limit of her endurance and having drunk a beer. He stood up very carefully so as not to disturb her, and went to fetch his spare duvet and pillow. She barely even stirred as he arranged her comfortably, then he tip toed off to his own room.

It was such a momentous occasion to have her...*her* under his own roof, and Greville felt that he ought to spend the night awake and marvelling over this turn of events. But the day had been a long one for him as well, and it took only a few minutes for him to fall asleep himself.

He woke up before the alarm the next morning with a vague sense that it was an auspicious occasion, as if it were perhaps Christmas or his birthday, and then he remembered the events of the night before. Even though he couldn't see her or hear her, somehow it was as if the house was less empty. He got up and crept to the living room door, reluctant to burst in but not quite liking to knock in case she was still asleep.

'Greville? Is that you?' she called, sparing him from the agonies of dithering.

He went in, and saw that she was sitting up in the midst of the makeshift bed, blue-black hair distractingly dishevelled.

'Nothing happened,' he burst out, because suddenly it seemed very important that she should be assured of this. 'Nothing at all. You fell asleep, so I just...I just...I didn't want you to drive home when you were that tired, so I just covered you up so you wouldn't be cold. That's all.'

'For goodness' sake, Greville, I wasn't *that* drunk,' she said. 'I remember what I did.' She reached for her glasses and put them on, and now she was smiling at his earnestness. 'If anything, I owe you an apology as it was very rude of me to go to sleep after you'd kindly cooked me dinner.'

She pushed her glasses up her nose. 'Thank you for looking after me,' she added, addressing herself to the floor, perhaps uncomfortable with having shown herself to be less than invincible, and having allowed herself to fall into a position where she required help.

'Errr, do you want a cup of tea?' He asked. She was still fully dressed, but it seemed almost indecent to be gawping at her when she'd only just woken up, and he was glad to escape to the kitchen. She followed him a few minutes later, still yawning, accosted on the way by Satan who was as delighted as Greville that they still had a guest, and a lot more open about expressing his delight.

'You need some breakfast,' he said. 'You're not driving home until you've had something to eat.'

She pursed her lips, but in a pleased way.

'I've really got to get back and get organised.'

'You've got time for toast,' he said, more firmly. 'It will be done before the kettle's boiled. And it's early still.'

He made tea and toast for both of them, which she consumed with joyful relish.

'I've got to go,' she said when she'd finished her tea. 'And you're not to hug me because I need a shower. But thank you for yesterday. I don't know what I'd have done without your support. See you in work.'

She gave him a quick, impish smile, touched his arm and went out to her car, and he watched her drive away.

Chapter 25

Greville arrived in the office the following morning to discover that Mr Valentine's mood had improved very little from the day before. He was crashing about in his corner office, picking things up and putting them down, not exactly looking for something but as if he was trying to do an impression of a person who was looking for something. There was something not quite methodical about his search. He paused and looked round when he heard Greville come in, a bundle of files in his hands, and let out a displeased growl. He sniffed at the air, not seeming to like whatever whatever it was that he smelt, then put the files down and picked up some more. Inured to his strange ways, Greville logged on and obediently began to clear out his Skymails.

The Cuthberts had evidently had a falling-out as all three were sitting with eyes front and jaws fixed, the human Cuthbert (whichever he or she was) not moving a single muscle, and those who were the clones not moving a single component. Myhill was eating a relentless supply of egg muffins washed down by an enormous vat of coffee and Irina was trying to fold one of the vast paper spreadsheets and doing quite a bad job of it, tentatively assisted by Piers, who seemed to have a little more idea on how to set about the task but who was too afraid to intervene very effectively. Arabella/Rose was doing something with a cushion and some lace bobbins, or perhaps it was Rose/Arabella as she looked knowing and at ease in the manner that cats seem to manage so effortlessly.

Magnolia wasn't far behind him, and today she was wearing a cheerful pink fitted shift dress which clung to her neat figure in a rather distracting way, and matching high heeled pink shoes. She gave him a brisk, arch nod and sat down. Mr Valentine came out of his office and sniffed the air again, more fiercely this time, and whatever he divined from the exercise did nothing to improve his mood. He pointed at Greville and then Magnolia.

'You and you. Come here. Now.'

It seemed wise to obey him as he didn't look as if he was disposed to be reasonable. Greville was expecting either the second half of the telling-off from yesterday for resolving the Thousand Rooms too quickly, or to be dispatched somewhat peremptorily on audit business. Magnolia got up as well, and came over, and Myhill stopped eating momentarily to watch, always pleased to see other people getting into trouble.

'There's some nonsense between you two,' he said. I can *smell* it. A connection. *You* are doing romantics with *you*, and *you* are doing romantics with *you*. It's not on. Romantics are forbidden. It's all in the staff manual. No romantics between staff as it leads to inattention, carelessness and lack of impartiality.'

Greville's heart froze inside his chest, and he didn't know what to say. He couldn't deny it, because, of course, it was true.

'So now I'm going to put an end to it,' Mr Valentine continued. 'There are to be *no* romantics at work. It's the law. But I'm going to be reasonable and give you a choice.'

His zapper was suddenly in his hand, looking all the more frightening now that it was potentially going to be applied to a head in the very near future.

'Either one of you gets zapped in the head and sent back to the other side, or one of you gets banished to one of our other branches so that you never see each other again. If I find out that there has been any contact between you whatsoever after the banishment, then one of you will get zapped in the head.'

Greville felt sick. His first impulse had been to volunteer for the punishment to keep her safe, but that would mean that all knowledge of this strange environment would be wiped from his mind. But what sort of relationship could they have if she had to keep her career a secret from him? He couldn't see it working. And if they were both zapped, it seemed an unbelievable shame to lose such a unique career. And what if one of them were banished and they could never communicate again? It was utterly unthinkable. He stole a glance at her, and she was looking equally stunned. After the pleasant security of the previous evening, it came as the most devastating blow.

'There's one other way,' Mr Valentine continued. 'The most certain way to eradicate romanticating. It will sort out all this nonsense pretty much instantly, according to the literature, and it will never come back.

Greville's heart fell further. Perhaps it was some sort of jolt to the brain so that they wouldn't even recognise each other any more, or…'

'We do a welding, right now. That will sort it out.' His hand went under his coat and the head zapper disappeared, to be replaced with the staff handbook. 'No, no, no, not a welding…h'mm…a *wedding*. That's it. That's the kiss of death to romanticing. We do a wedding right now, otherwise…' The zapper reappeared.

Myhill was agog, not even noticing that the yolk from his egg muffin was dripping onto a page of the file he had just opened. Irina stopped folding; Piers stopped hovering ineffectively; the Cuthberts stopped glaring straight ahead. Only Arabella/ Rose continued to work calmly with her lace bobbins. Time seemed to freeze more effectively than in a Room that Time Forgot. Greville felt the most thoroughly winded that he'd ever been in his life. He couldn't speak; he couldn't even breathe. Magnolia was the first to regain her composure.

'Works for me,' she said, and now there was a bright spot of pink on each cheek. Another drop of yolk landed on Myhill's file.

'Really?' Greville breathed, hardly daring to tempt fate by asking her to repeat it. She shrugged in her offhand way, but she was almost-smiling.

'Yeah. Why not? We were going to end up here anyway.'

'Gravel?' prompted Mr Valentine. 'Wedding or zap in the head? Come on – we don't have all diurnal period. But I don't think it *can* be "wedding". That doesn't make any sense. It's not even a word. It's *welding* that means joining two things together permanently, isn't it? But I don't see how it would work because you lot just melt at high temperatures, don't you?'

'Yes,' said Greville. 'Yes, yes, of course yes.'

'Hang on,' said Myhill, 'that means that you've got to put up with *her* forever. Forever and ever and ever. *Her*. Forever.'

He glowered at Magnolia, who glowered back.

Greville fixed Myhill with a look which, to his astonishment, caused the man to look flustered and start fumbling awkwardly with his muffin.

'I was just saying,' he said, abashed.

Unlikely as it sounded, Greville discovered that he had become the sort of man who could silence another man with no more than a glance. He would have to try and recreate the expression in the mirror and see how it looked.

'Yes to welding or zap in the head?' Mr Valentine said, running out of patience.

'Yes to welding…I mean wedding,' Greville said. His boss sighed and put the zapper away.

'Okay then,' he said, reading from the staff handbook. 'It says here that you need a ring. A ring? Is that right? What's that for? Is it a punishment ring?'

'No,' said Greville. 'It's a…'

Mr Valentine frowned, puzzled.

'Well, if it's *not* a punishment ring, how are you going to make her do what you want?'

Myhill snorted his breakfast everywhere.

'It's not that sort of ring,' Greville said. 'It's a different sort. I know where to get one.'

His boss sighed and raised his eyes to the heavens.

'Well, run along then. But don't take too long about it because I've got a client unbriefing to go to.'

Greville ran, all the way to a little shop which he sometimes passed if he was out jogging at lunchtime. He looked into the window, and was delighted to see that the ring was still there.

'Can I see that purple ring in the window?' he asked the assistant, who fetched it for him. He picked it up. It was made of a grey metal that he wouldn't have liked to have named, and looked vaguely mediaeval. The ring had a horizontal groove all the way round, with an intersecting vertical groove every quarter. Tiny purple stones were set in every right angle.

'They're amethysts,' said the assistant.

'This is a wedding ring, isn't it,' said Greville, who was very far from being certain about these things. 'Have you got any engagement rings that might look… right with this one?'

'Oh yes,' said the assistant, and he brought out a tray of similar rings.

'That one,' said Greville, picking out a plain ring bearing a single, large rectangular amethyst which he thought would look well on a strong, thin finger.

'What size do you need?' the assistant asked.

'I don't know. I…I…' Greville was dismayed to be falling at such an obvious hurdle. Why hadn't he asked her? And he badly didn't want to look like an idiot by ringing her. And perhaps *she* didn't even know – he'd never seen her wearing any rings.

He did what he did best – assembled the available data and worked his way through it. He knew what size Poppy was, and he mentally compared Poppy's pink, tapered fingers with Magnolia's. Where Poppy's were dainty and rounded, Magnolia's were sinewy and lean, but he really did think that the overall size was the same. He told the assistant a size, and soon the rings were nestling in a purple velvet heart shaped box. Greville chose a ring for himself made from the same metal, only plain, and even after adding an amethyst tiara, the total for everything was rather less than a good meal for two at a reasonable restaurant.

'I'm getting married,' he said to the assistant, unable to contain himself. 'Today.'

The assistant considered. 'To the lady with the black hair? The runner? The fast runner?'

'Yeah,' said Greville, beaming.

'Well done, mate,' he said, offering a hand to shake. 'That one's a keeper.'

He ran back to the office, where Mr Valentine was waiting impatiently. Magnolia beamed as soon as she saw him.

'Right then, let's get on. I've got other more important things to do than dealing with you two.'

'Are you authorised to conduct weddings?' Greville asked.

'What? Yes, yes, yes, of *course* I am. I'm authorised to do *everything*. Now then, say after me…no, no, no, that's if you want to declare your intentions to invade a non-adjacent territory. You don't want to do that, do you? No? Well, you may want to one day.' He flicked through a few more pages. 'No, that's declaring martial law…no, that's *revoking* a state of martial law…h'mm, where is it? I thought I knew where it was.'

While he thumbed pages, Greville showed Magnolia the tiara.

'You don't have to wear it, but I just wanted you to feel like a princess on your wedding day. If you want to, of course.'

'Of course I want to,' she said, delighted, and stood for him to put it on her head.

'Right, say after me, "I…" and you say what your name is – your *real* name; I'm not having you wriggling out of it *that* easily -"declare that I will love you, honour you, protect you and save you, forever and ever, to the grave and beyond, on pain of death.'

Magnolia said it first, then Greville. The usual marriage vows of 'having and holding' seemed rather feeble next to the heroic might of 'protect and save', and 'until death us do part' was piffling and trivial when set against the utter permanence of 'to the grave and beyond'. Oddly, instead of thinking that it was an awfully long time, Greville's first thought was that it wasn't anywhere near long enough.

'Get the rings,' Mr Valentine said briskly, and Greville pulled his plain metal band out of his pocket and handed it to Magnolia. 'You…put the ring on *you*…oh, it just fits on like that? It doesn't get implanted? That doesn't seem very permanent. And say, "This ring is a symbol of my eternal love, which will burn for all time and never dim".

Then it was Greville's turn to put the ring on Magnolia. He opened the purple box, and she gasped.

'You remembered!' she breathed.

Greville wanted to say that it would simply be unthinkable to forget a single detail about what she'd ever said or done since he'd first laid eyes on her, but there wasn't time. He put the band on her finger, and when he said that it was a symbol of his eternal love which would never dim, he meant it more than he'd ever meant anything before.

Mr Valentine was leafing impatiently backwards through the staff handbook, pausing at one particular page which he smelt, tore out and ate before continuing.

'Oh. I was supposed to deliver a pre-commitment briefing to all personnel covering essential information such as the rules for the use of force, procedures governing the accountability and security of weapons and control of ammunition.'

'That sounds like *martial* law?' suggested Arabella/Rose.

'No, no, no, no, this is the bit about what happens when you *un*-weld and have to fight over who gets to keep the domicile and who retains whose allowance-thing that you're given when you're no further use at work, but where there's a stupid rule against shooting you. Why would you *pay* useless people to stay alive, getting in everyone's way, when you could just…'

He seemed to remember that he was in a hurry, consulting both watches and blowing out an angry breath.

'Martial…marital…from this book here, they're pretty much the same. Lots of rules, lots of collateral damage, lots of defending of untenable positions, and it looks to me that the only difference is the position of the 'i,' he said, with a perspicacity that was probably unintended. 'Right then, so you've got two choices. We can find a Forgot and do it all again, but this time with all the briefings, or you can just ratify the contract and read it afterwards.'

A contract appeared, written on aged parchment in faded copperplate and bound with pink ribbon, very similar to Greville's employment contract, and about as thick as it, at around four inches. It would take an awfully long time to read all that.

'Sign in heart's essence, and then you're all done.'

'They don't *have* heart essence,' said the female Cuthbert. 'Which is strange, as they're afflicted with *hearts*. Probably the most inefficient system *ever*.'

Mr Valentine rolled his eyes to the very heavens, exasperation embodied.

'Well, seeing as we don't have forty *million* solar periods for evolution to put *that* right, I suppose you'll have to sign in blood.'

He produced the now-familiar instrument which seemed to be a very slender pen, and which when uncapped proved to house a sharp lance. Magnolia turned to the back page, took the lance from him, pricked her finger without a yoctosecond's hesitation and made a bright smear above her name. Greville followed suite, feeling exhilarated that a union as momentous as theirs would not be defiled by something as pedestrian as the mere signing of a register.

'Those whom I have welded, *none* shall tear asunder!' he roared in a rumbling bass that permeated every atom of every being in the room, lending aweful, reverberating might to the culmination of the ceremony. 'YOU MUST KISS YOUR BRIDE!'

Greville did not need to be told twice, kissing her gently but firmly, hardly even aware that anyone else was even in the room. He had her *forever*, and that was all that mattered, and he knew that nothing but this would really be of consequence ever again.

'*I'm* in charge of enforcing all this, so if I find out that you haven't been sticking to the terms of the contract, I'll hunt you down and kill you,' Mr Valentine said conversationally, breaking into their bubble. 'But then, that shouldn't be too hard really because you'll be back in here every morning, won't you, so I'll just wait for you to come in and do it as you turn up. And of course, we've got those two over there to take over from you if I have to kill you, so it would all work out quite nicely.'

He tucked the staff handbook away, bringing out a clipboard bearing a substantial wodge of papers, the topmost of which was in the form of a list. Judging from the quantity of unticked boxes running down the right-hand margin, Greville felt confident to guess that they were outstanding audit actions.

'We've wasted quite enough time on all this nonsense,' Mr Valentine said. 'So now I want you two…but you're one now, aren't you…so I want you *one*…but what happens if I want you to do different things? You're both *halves* now, really, so what does that mean for payroll…? Anyway, I want you *one* to go and see why the astral projection department hasn't done their outstanding audit actions, and it's got to be today because they won't be near enough for another twenty-four thousand teraseconds. And don't think I'll be paying you overtime if you don't get back before the window closes, because I won't.'

He thrust the clipboard at Greville, spun himself into a cyclone of glitter and headed for a ventilation grille.

'Not *that* one,' said Myhill, with apathetic irritation. 'You don't work here! That's *ours*! Your rent agreement doesn't cover that one!'

Greville beamed at his bride.

'I love you,' he said.

Outside of his marriage vows, he'd never said it to her before, and now that he had, he couldn't imagine why not. It was so fundamentally true. Perhaps he hadn't even really dared to recognise that this constriction in his chest, the compulsion to protect her and be with her was love, having never felt anything so all-encompassing before, or perhaps…

'I love you too,' she said, and it was simultaneously unnerving and electrifying to be the sole focus of her intense, relentlessly analytic gaze. She was smiling very slightly in her secret way, and no-one but him would even appreciate that this was how she smiled when she was the most pleased. She caught his left hand in hers and held it up so that she could examine their rings. Instead of shining with shallow brightness, they had a soft gleam that would be deepened and not diminished by the passage of time.

'You need to get a move on or you won't reach the astral projection department in time,' said a Cuthbert, intruding on the moment.

'What's it got to do with *you*?' Greville demanded, the words out before he'd even realised he was going to say them. 'You're nothing to do with our team.'

The Cuthbert made a disparaging noise and muttered something to the female Cuthbert.

'And if you've got something to say to me, say it to my face,' Greville continued.

It was as if his body had been taken over by someone else – someone bold and reckless, who didn't really care whether he might get into an argument or not. He became aware of a general hush in the room; everyone was looking at him, not least Magnolia, who was regarding him in puzzled wonder.

His phone beeped discreetly.

'It's left, today. In fact, you have to turn left for most rooms' said the pad, sounding vaguely affronted that the rooms' locations had been fixed without its even having been told, far less consulted. 'Turn left.'

Greville collected his notepad and his red pen (from the apparent quantity of the outstanding audit actions, it was going to be a red pen sort of day) and they headed out of the office.

'He's been short with you because his brother's coming back from abroad,' Arabella/Rose said as they walked past. 'He wants to let him have the cottage, and he's embarrassed to tell you because you've done all that decorating.'

'I beg your pardon?' Greville said, startled, but not so much that he forgot his manners, and she just shrugged and continued with her lace.

He felt an incipient worry float away before it had even fully settled. Once he'd achieved the pinnacle of claiming someone utterly brilliant – in fact, someone he'd thought *unattainably* brilliant – his subconscious had briskly assembled a 'to do' list, and at the top had been the question of where they'd live. The answer was unlikely to be the little rented cottage, and (having never terminated a lease before) the somewhat over-developed part of his brain that liked to worry was already doing just that. With this concern gone, for the time being there remained only audit actions to worry about, and they weren't even a worry – more of a satisfying and inevitable triumph of checklists over poor excuses.

'Left,' reminded the pad, sounding bored. 'It's all going to be left from now on. Left, left, left.'

They turned left, Magnolia's stride curtailed by the height of the elegant heels and the very fitted shape of the dress's hem, and it was stimulating to see her sheer athleticism reined in; it was like watching the Mustang being driven slowly. He could see the speed and power bursting to get out.

'Stop staring at me,' she said brusquely. 'We've got work to do.'

She continued to step along with great poise, professionalism embodied, her notepad and pens in her hand.

'There will be time to play later,' she added, her face so utterly impassive that he wondered if he'd misheard her. But then she shot him a look of such sheer mischief that he was nearly eviscerated on the spot. 'Now, come along, Mr Hunt. Work first.'

He followed after her, trying to get his breath back, and he knew that he was the luckiest man who had ever lived, on any planet, in any universe, since the beginning of time.

The End

Tracey Valentine
27 August 2016

Printed in Great Britain
by Amazon